LAWFUL DECEPTION

Books by Pamela Samuels Young

Vernetta Henderson Series

Every Reasonable Doubt (1st in series)

In Firm Pursuit (2nd in series)

Murder on the Down Low (3rd in series)

Attorney-Client Privilege (4th in series)

Lawful Deception (5th in series)

Dre Thomas Series

Buying Time (1st in series)

Anybody's Daughter (2nd in series)

Short Stories

The Setup

Easy Money

Unlawful Greed

Non-Fiction

Kinky Coily: A Natural Hair Resource Guide

PAMELA SAMUELS YOUNG

LAWFUL
DECEPTION

GoldmanHOUSE
PUBLISHING

Lawful Deception

Goldman House Publishing

ISBN 978-0-9864361-6-1

For information about special discounts for bulk purchases, please contact the author or Goldman House Publishing.

Pamela Samuels Young
www.pamelasamuelsyoung.com

Goldman House Publishing
goldmanhousepublishing@gmail.com

Cover design by Marion Designs

Printed in U.S.A.

For my dear friends
Sara Vernetta Finney-Johnson
and Felicia D. Henderson,
your compassion, courage and strength
amaze me more and more each day.

PROLOGUE

Bliss Fenton took a sip of champagne as she glared across the room at the obnoxiously happy couple. They indeed made a striking pair. Their slim, toned bodies draped in designer wear and expensive jewelry. So trendy. So California chic.

Setting her champagne glass on the tray of a passing waiter, Bliss snaked her way through the crowd, hoping to get a better view. As she moved, her blonde curls bounced as if lifted by a cool breeze. At 5'8" and 120 pounds, her delicate frame was all slopes and curves. A body specifically designed for exhibition.

The partygoers were packed like human matchsticks inside the gaudy Hollywood Hills mansion. The home, if you could call it that, was a testament to excess. Just like the couple. Too much of everything. Too many art deco chairs, too much bronze and glass, and so much artwork the walls could barely breathe.

Only a few feet away from the couple now, Bliss found herself shoulder-to-shoulder with a too-tanned man with greasy hair. He winked at her. She sneered back at him and moved on.

A devious smile fractured Bliss' face as she returned her attention to the couple. She imagined the angst they would experience the minute they spotted her among the partygoers. Fletcher's lips would contort into an ugly grimace, but then coolly transition to a barely perceptible smirk. He was not the kind of man who was easily rankled. That was the reason he was a millionaire several times over.

Mia, however, would not be able to hide her emotions. Fletcher's prissy little black princess would toss Bliss a snarl that bellowed, *What the hell are you doing here?*

It was Mia she wanted to punish most. Bliss had pleaded with God to curse her former friend with a pain ten times more intense than her own. She wanted Mia to live it. Breathe it. Curl up in bed with it. Just as she had.

Bliss refused to blame Fletcher for the poor choices he'd made. He was a man. And men, by nature, were weak. Still, he too would pay just the same.

The call of vengeance tugged hard at Bliss' soul, urging her, daring her, to march right up to the couple and confront them. But she held back. For the moment. Patience had always been her most virtuous trait.

Fletcher hustled to the front of the room and began singing the praises of the newest songstress to be added to his stable of artists, LaReena Jarreau. Bliss remembered cuddling in bed with Fletcher and listening to him brag about creating her stage name, since Janice Harris had no pizzazz.

"The first time I heard her voice," Fletcher said, throwing his arm around the bony twenty-something dressed in hooker gear, "I knew she was going to hit the music world by storm. You have to agree that what we heard tonight was—as the youngsters say—off the chain."

Everyone applauded as the hip, dark-haired CEO of Karma Entertainment grinned, happy to be on show. The only thing Fletcher enjoyed more than being rich was having everyone know it.

Mia remained off to the side, perfecting the look of the coy, supportive fiancée. That had been Bliss' mistake. Accepting her at face value. While Mia's visual package was quite alluring—all charm and beauty—on the inside, she was pure evil. Truth be told, Mia wasn't all that different from her.

Bliss Fenton, not Mia Richardson, should have been on the arm of the music industry mogul tonight. It had never occurred to Bliss that her long-time yoga buddy could walk into a party and take her new guy's breath away. Literally.

At the time, Bliss had been dating Fletcher for a short six months. She'd invited Mia to the party at Fletcher's Beverly Hills home for the sole purpose of showing off her new man to her smart, uppity faux-friend. Bliss could still remember Mia waving as she glided into the party, the crowd parting so effortlessly it almost seemed choreographed.

Seconds before, Fletcher had been talking nonstop about his label's next release, but the sight of Mia had caused him to lose his train of thought. When Bliss had formally introduced them, the lust in Fletcher's eyes further telegraphed the gravity of her mistake.

Only days after the party, Bliss' time with Fletcher began to dwindle, explained away by late night meetings that couldn't be avoided or last-minute business trips to New York. Mia, too, had started cancelling their after-yoga coffee chats and finally stopped coming to yoga class altogether.

It was a month later, when Bliss saw Fletcher and Mia pictured together in *Billboard*, that she first learned of their betrayal. Her subsequent rage-filled calls to both of them had been ignored. And now, Mia was at Fletcher's side, while Bliss had been pushed right out of his life.

A burst of applause snapped Bliss back to the present. As Fletcher seemed to be wrapping up his speech, Bliss moved closer, stopping inches behind Mia. She leaned in, her lips almost grazing Mia's right ear.

"Congratulations on your engagement."

Mia's head whipped around, her dark brown skin now ashen gray. "You...you shouldn't be here."

Bliss spoke in a firm whisper. "Neither should you. You backstabbing bitch."

Mia took a step back. "This is not the place to make a scene."

"Okay, then," Bliss said, moving into the space Mia had abandoned. "Shall we step outside?"

A second later, Fletcher wedged himself between them. "You walk yourself out of here right now," he said through clenched teeth, "or I'll have security carry you out."

Although no voices had been raised, all heads turned in their direction.

Bliss didn't move.

Fletcher, always cognizant of appearances, wore a stiff smile as he spat into Bliss' face. "If you don't leave, I swear I'll have you arrested."

After three long beats, Bliss winked. "You'll both be hearing from me."

Bliss couldn't help smiling as she sashayed through the buzzing crowd.

Fletcher and Mia would suffer for their disloyalty. Bliss only wished she could be there to see their stunned faces when they learned what she had done and realized there was absolutely nothing they could do about it.

CHAPTER 1

I should have shown Fletcher McClain to the door 30 minutes ago, but the words seem to be stuck in my throat. I hate to admit it—even to myself—but I like having him in my space again.

"So will you take care of this for me, Vernetta?"

He's been pacing the length of my office for several minutes now. When he first stormed in and slapped the *Petition to Establish Parental Relationship* on my desk, he was so wound up I thought he might be on the verge of a stroke.

"I'm not a family law attorney, Fletcher."

Employment law and some occasional criminal work are more up my alley.

"I don't need an expert in family law," Fletcher insists. "What I need is a good negotiator. Someone who can talk some sense into this nutcase and make her go away. And I'm confident you can do the job."

The issue isn't whether I could handle his case, but whether I should. They say a lawyer who represents himself has a fool for a client. Perhaps a lawyer who goes to battle on behalf of an ex-lover is just as foolish. Especially if the old flame hasn't quite flickered out yet.

According to the petition, Fletcher's ex-girlfriend Bliss Fenton has named him as the father of her three-month-old daughter, Harmony. Fletcher, however, claims the petition is all lies. Even though he hasn't taken the court-ordered paternity test yet, he wants me to set up a meeting with Bliss and offer her some "chump change," as he puts it, to go away.

"It looks like she filed that petition herself. I need this nonsense over and done with before she gets an attorney involved."

I take another look at the petition. Bliss has indeed filed it *in pro per*, which is easy enough to do. The petition is a simple two-page form that requires checking a few boxes.

Falling into one of the chairs in front of my desk, Fletcher fixes me with a look so intense I almost shudder.

"I really need you, Vernetta."

His lips angle upward, just slightly, and I feel a warm tingle in a place where my happily married self definitely should *not* be tingling. I break his gaze and fiddle with my cuticle.

Classically handsome, Fletcher has sandy hair, strong cheekbones and wide brown eyes with lashes too long and thick for Mother Nature to have wasted on a guy. He's still the only white guy who ever stole my heart.

"Fletcher, you could find a million attorneys to handle this. Why don't you let me recommend a friend who has expertise in family law?"

"See, that's what I love about you, Vernetta. I don't know many lawyers who would turn away a paying client with my kind of dough. You're the real deal."

"Unbelievable." I stare across the desk at him, shaking my head. "You're still as cocky as you were when we were know-nothing sophomores back at USC. It's not always about money, Fletcher."

"It's always about money, my sweetness."

Damn him. Hearing his pet name for me after all these years has me tingling again.

A quiet chirp interrupts his subtle flirting. He pulls the phone from the inside pocket of his jacket. Glancing at the screen, he frowns and sets it on the corner of my desk.

"How can you be so sure it's not your kid?" I ask.

"Because we broke up almost a year before that kid was born."

"Shouldn't you wait for the results of the paternity test?"

"Don't need to. It's not my kid."

"I'm confused. If it's not your kid, once you have the results, it's over. Why pay her anything?"

"You don't know Bliss Fenton. Even after the results come back, she'll have something else up her sleeve. I need this thing buttoned up once and for all. Paying her off will accomplish that."

My gut and years of legal experience tell me there's more to the story. "You certainly seem awfully stressed over an allegation that has no merit. What's the real deal?"

Fletcher repositions himself in the chair.

"I'm getting married in three months and this whole thing has my fiancée climbing the walls. Bliss timed this to embarrass Mia right before our wedding. I need it resolved as soon as possible."

The news that Fletcher is getting married surprises me. I've followed his career for years and figured he was a confirmed bachelor.

"So what's Bliss got against Mia?"

"Well...um...they used to be friends."

I squint. "Oh, so we're dealing with a woman scorned."

It's one thing to lose your man to another woman. It's quite another to lose a charming, high roller like Fletcher McClain to someone you considered a friend.

He shrugs. "That's basically the crux of it."

"But it still doesn't make sense. Bliss wouldn't serve you with a paternity suit if there were no chance you could be the father."

"You haven't been listening. This woman is extremely conniving. She probably read that *Forbes* article and came up with this scheme to shake me down." He pauses. "Did you happen to see it?"

Fletcher landed the number three spot on *Forbes'* list of the top music industry moguls. He's the only one on the list under 40. His net worth is estimated at $450 million, just behind Clive Davis and JayZ.

"Of course I saw it. Very impressive."

He points a finger at me. "You haven't done too bad yourself, counselor. You've handled some pretty high-profile cases."

Over the years, Fletcher sent me handwritten notes, congratulating me when one of my trials hit the press. Keeping up with his achievements is the only reason I read *Billboard*.

"So how much do you plan to offer her?"

"A hundred grand should do it. I'm willing to go higher if I have to. Maybe two-fifty. And I want a written agreement with an ironclad confidentiality provision."

I'm about to say he's putting up a lot of cash to get rid of a bogus claim, but for a man with Fletcher's bank account, we're talking peanuts.

"We may have to play dirty to force her into a settlement. I want you to retain a private investigator to dig up some dirt on her in case we need it. And trust me, it's out there."

"Are you serious?"

"As a heart attack. Once you meet her, you'll understand."

"How'd you even end up with this woman?"

"It's your fault," he quips. "After you broke my heart, I was so devastated, I opened up my heart to whoever came along."

"Yeah, right." I scan the petition again. "It says here the child was born in January of this year and she's three months old." I glance skyward and do the math in my head. "Let's see...Assuming a nine-month pregnancy, that would place conception sometime in April of last year."

"Exactly. The kid can't be mine. We broke up in February, eleven months before she was born. I remember because it was two weeks before Valentine's Day."

"Maybe your timing is off."

"It's not."

"And there were no hookups after that?"

"Nope." He brushes the lapel of his Canali suit, then raises his right hand. "Scout's honor."

"I still don't understand why you don't want to wait for the test results before approaching her. You'd be in a much better negotiating position."

"I'm taking the test tomorrow, but it could be a couple of weeks before I get the results. I want this thing resolved yesterday."

His cell phone chirps again. He grunts and picks it up. "Excuse me a second."

His long fingers awkwardly tap the screen. I assume he's sending an email or text message. Another minute or so passes before he looks up, his face full of annoyance.

"Uh, that was Mia calling from the lobby." He scratches his jaw. "She's on her way up."

"Hmmm. So it's your fiancée who's running this show."

"Not really. Well, I mean—"

I'm not used to seeing the smooth-talking Fletcher McClain at a loss for words. He moves to the edge of the chair. The relaxed air we'd been basking in has been sapped from the room.

"The real deal is Mia wants me to sue Bliss for defamation. She thinks I'm meeting with you to talk about the defamation case. But I think it makes more sense to give Bliss a few dollars to disappear."

"Okay, *now* I get it."

"Let's keep that under our hat. And, um," he rubs his chin, "Mia's a bit on the jealous side. Let's not mention that we used to be an item, okay?"

Fletcher was never the type of guy who'd let his woman call the shots. This alpha dog has turned into a poodle.

"No problem. Our conversations are attorney-client privileged."

Fletcher straightens in his chair. "Oh, so I'm your client? Great!"

I raise both hands, palms out. "I haven't committed yet. But your fiancée can't—"

"Just flow with me on this, okay? I'll handle Mia. You just play along." His confident charm reminds me of the first time we met over a decade ago.

I was walking across campus when Fletcher stopped me with a corny pick-up line.

"Do you believe in love at first sight? Or should I walk by again?"

I'd never met a white guy—certainly not one as gorgeous as Fletcher McClain—who had the swagger of a brother. After a bit of prodding, I agreed to meet him for lunch.

And here he is still charming me more than a decade later.

My assistant pokes her head in the door. "I have a lady out here who says she—"

The door flies open and a woman bustles past Deena into my office.

A perfectly coiffed, black beauty marches right up to my desk and peers down at me. I have to push my chair back to get her out of my personal space.

"You better be a barracuda," she says, firing her words at me. "Because that's the kind of attorney we need to show that scandalous slut Bliss Fenton that she's playing with fire."

CHAPTER 2

Bliss swung her silver Audi into the parking lot of the Ralph's supermarket on Lincoln Boulevard, cut off the engine, then held up her hand in an appeal for silence.

"No lecture this time, okay?" Bliss turned to face her best and only friend sitting in the passenger seat.

Jessica Winthrop took in a long breath. "Only if you agree to act like a civilized human being today."

For three months now, Bliss and her ex-boyfriend, Dr. Joseph Franco, had been meeting in this public location to transfer their six-year-old son Aiden from one parent to the other. Their relationship was so antagonistic that a judge had declared their respective homes off limits.

"Aren't you tired of all the drama?" Jessica asked.

"I really wish you would criticize that asshole as much as you do me."

"He's not my friend. You are. Just let it go."

"That's easy for you to say."

Though she was nothing short of a plain Jane—long, reddish-brown hair, an unremarkable face and the physique of an undernourished pear—Jessica had snagged the kind of man Bliss had spent her whole life maneuvering to marry. Paul Winthrop was a successful venture capitalist. After marrying him, Jessica gave up her career as a bank manager.

"You two have a beautiful son together," Jessica said, glancing toward the backseat at her sleeping godson. "You need to think about Aiden's best interests."

Bliss pointed at the clock on the dashboard. "The asshole is seven minutes late."

"How about we use his name today? Just for practice."

Bliss rolled her eyes.

Jessica was the only constant in Bliss' sad life. Their friendship dated back to freshman year in high school. While every other girl at Winchester High had shunned the gorgeous blonde newcomer with the sexy name, Jessica had reached out to her, never concerned that her own light didn't shine nearly as brightly as Bliss'.

Jessica pressed her hands together in a prayer pose. "Promise me this'll be a drama-free exchange. Pretty please."

Bliss spotted Joseph pulling into the lot and slapped her hand against the dashboard. "I can't believe it! That asshole has a new car!"

Jessica cupped her forehead. "Bliss, please don't—"

"That Benz had to cost almost a hundred grand. That's probably why he was three days late with my child support last month. And why is she with him again? I'll never understand what he sees in her. She has the face of a rodent."

Jessica got out and unbuckled Aiden from his car seat. "Just behave yourself."

Once Aiden was out of the car, Bliss squatted so they were at eye level. "You be a good boy, okay? You scream for Mommy if Daddy does anything bad to you."

Jessica exhaled. "Please stop putting that nonsense in his head."

"And you make sure you don't let anybody touch you down there. You scream if they—"

"That's enough." Jessica grabbed Aiden's hand and started marching him across the parking lot. When they were a yard away, he squirmed free and jumped into his father's arms.

Dr. Joseph Franco was an orthopedic surgeon whose patients included an impressive list of professional athletes. He was a tall, gregarious man with bushy blonde hair. Today, anxiety contorted his face.

"Hey, Jessica. Thanks for being our go-between again. I'll have him back on Sunday by five. I'll call you if I'm running late."

"No you won't!" Bliss stood just a few feet away. "If you're late, I'm calling the cops."

"I'm not biting today," Joseph said, mostly to himself. He finished securing Aiden into his car seat and closed the door.

"And why is that cunt here?" Bliss shouted.

"I've asked you before to watch your language around Aiden. And if you call Lena out of her name one more time, I'll be the one calling the cops."

Jessica gripped Bliss by the forearm and started tugging her toward the car. "Okay, everybody, let's all go to our respective corners."

"By the way," Bliss yelled back at him, "since you can afford to buy a new car, Mr. Successful Orthopedic Surgeon, I'm going back to court to ask for more child support. You're obviously doing a lot better than you claimed the last time we were in court."

The threat stopped Joseph in place. He stormed up to her.

"If you need more money, get a job," he seethed. "I'm already paying you ten grand a month and I'm struggling like hell to do that."

"From the looks of your new ride, you don't seem to be struggling at all."

"Can you act like a decent human being for five seconds? Just five measly seconds."

"Just tell your attorney I'll be asking the court to amend our child support order." Bliss flashed him a smug smile.

Joseph reflexively balled his fists. "I'll kill you before I pay you another dime."

"Did you hear that, Jessica? He just threatened my life!"

Joseph shook his head and slowly backed away. "Get her away from me."

As Joseph climbed into his car and sped off, Jessica chastised Bliss with a frown.

"I should be the one in that car with him," Bliss sniffed, her voice cracking. "I'm the fabulous one."

Jessica threw an arm around her friend.

"Nothing good is going to come into your life until you change the way you treat people," Jessica said, trying to be gentle. "Kindness attracts kindness."

"I don't want to hear that crap!" Bliss snapped, pulling away from her. "When people screw over me, I screw them back. And speaking of getting screwed, Mia and Fletcher are about to get theirs."

Jessica threw up her hands. "Why are you constantly causing drama?"

Bliss laughed wickedly. "Because I'm good at it."

CHAPTER 3

I t takes me a tad under two seconds to realize that I don't like the soon-to-be Mrs. Fletcher McClain. I will never understand how the greatest guys end up with the bitchiest women.

After grudgingly shaking my hand, Mia sits down in the chair next to Fletcher and starts calling the shots.

"I'm sure Fletcher told you I'm a corporate attorney," Mia says. "I plan on being very involved in the case. How soon can we see a draft of the complaint?"

Mia does not give me time to answer her first question before firing off another one.

"And what kind of experience do you have litigating defamation cases?"

I wait for Fletcher to shut her down, but to my surprise, the big music mogul doesn't open his mouth.

"As I was just telling Fletcher," I begin, "since he's my client, it's best that I deal only with him. If you—"

"Fletcher doesn't have a problem with my being involved." She reaches over and pats his thigh. "I have a stake in this too."

"Well, I'll make sure you're involved when it's appropriate to do so."

Mia's head tilts sideways at the same time her lips flat-line. "You don't seem to understand. I'm here to help. You'll need all the fire-power you can get against Bliss. She's a very vicious woman."

And apparently so are you.

I clear my throat. "Let me discuss this with my client and—"

"We're both you're clients. I'm about to be his wife."

Fletcher finally finds his voice. "C'mon, babe." He takes Mia's hand. "We have to let Vernetta handle this her way. If she needs your help, she'll ask."

I don't like this little farce, but I continue to play along. For now.

"I'd like to refer you to a friend who has extensive experience defending high-profile child support cases."

I hit a few keys on my computer, searching for the attorney's name. "You'll need to understand your rights and obligations if it turns out the child is yours."

Mia's eyes bug out like a startled cartoon character.

"Excuse me? *If?* There's no way Fletcher is the father of Bliss' bastard baby. She's just trying to wreck my life. If you don't believe in this case, maybe you aren't the right lawyer for us."

I wait for Fletcher to calm her down, but once again, he remains mute.

Who is this man?

"Maybe you and Fletcher should discuss what you'd like to do and get back to me."

Fletcher pulls Mia close. "Honey, we've already discussed this. I want Vernetta to handle this for us. She's a brilliant lawyer and, on top of that, I trust her. She's just doing her job. Covering all the bases."

Mia starts to tear up. "Nobody understands what I'm going through. Bliss has to pay for this. You don't know how manipulative she is. This isn't the first time she's pulled something like this."

"Really? It could be helpful to the defamation case if she set up another guy." I smile over at Fletcher. I hope he appreciates the way I'm playing my role.

"This is her M-O." Mia pats away her tears with two manicured fingers. "She has a six-year-old son she's getting child support payments for. Ten thousand dollars a month. She also has a three-year-old son. No telling how much money she's getting for him."

I'm baffled that the prissy Mia would even have a friend like Bliss.

"How did you two become friends?" I ask.

She clasps her hands and sets them in her lap. "We were never close. We just started hanging out after yoga class. I still can't believe she's doing this."

Fletcher kisses Mia on the cheek. "We're going to work this all out and our wedding is going to be fabulous."

"We're getting married in the South of France," Mia brags. "In the same village where Brad and Angelina tied the knot."

Good for you.

They both get to their feet.

"Fletcher," I say, "I need a quick second with you. Alone."

Mia opens her mouth to object, but Fletcher leads her to the door. "We'll only be a minute."

Once she's gone, I stand so that I can look Fletcher in the eyes.

"I just want to be sure you're being honest with me. Is there any way that kid could be yours?"

He responds with a bad imitation of Bill Clinton. "I did not have sexual relations with that woman."

I don't crack a smile. "Please answer my question."

"I've been one-hundred percent straight with you, counselor. Bliss Fenton is simply out for revenge."

I stare at him long and hard. "Can I ask you one more thing?"

"Shoot."

"What in the hell do you see in her? She's cute and all, but she's a bit high strung."

Fletcher chuckled. "Mia came off a little hard just now, but she really has a heart of gold. You'll see that once you get to know her. Maybe you and your husband can join us for dinner sometime. As a matter of fact, I'm having a shindig at the house Thursday night. You should come."

He gives me a hug that lasts way too long and feels way too good.

"I hope your husband is as good to you as I would've been."

"He is."

"Sorry to hear that." There's a long awkward patch of silence. "You ever wonder what it would've been like if we'd made it?"

I smile, but don't otherwise respond to his question.

"Thanks for taking my case."

"You're welcome."

Just before he grabs the doorknob, I stop him.

"I have some free legal advice for you."

"Shoot."

"Get a pre-nup."

He winks. "It's already drafted."

"That's good to hear. Just make sure you get it signed."

CHAPTER 4

To Bliss' dismay, Jessica had insisted on celebrating her birthday at El Cholo Mexican restaurant in Santa Monica. Sure, the food was great, but Jessica's husband earned enough dough to jet them off to a five-star restaurant in Milan or Paris. But Jessica liked to play down their wealth.

"I'm with the Winthrop party," she announced at the hostess' stand, then turned away to conduct a visual scan of the bar.

Nothing noteworthy. Men with real cash didn't hang out at places like this, so Bliss didn't either. Tonight, though, she had to suck it up for her best bud.

A young man dressed in a Mariachi getup looked at his clipboard, then stared into her cleavage.

"They're in our private dining room in the back."

As he led the way, the grinning kid kept turning around to gawk at her. He looked so excited you'd have thought he was escorting Jennifer Lopez down the red carpet.

When she reached the room, Bliss gave Jessica a quick peck on the cheek, waved at her husband Paul and waited for introductions to the other three couples. Two of the men were Paul's business partners, the third, a golfing buddy. Bliss felt no awkwardness at being the only solo member of the group. In fact, she preferred it this way. While the women prattled on about nothing, their husbands would be staring at her tits when she reached for the salsa, checking out her ass when she walked to the ladies' room and wishing they were taking her home instead of the spongy saps sitting next to them.

Bliss handed her gift bag across the table. "Happy birthday! Enjoy thirty-five because forty will be here before you know it."

Jessica laughed. "As long as I have my honey, I count every year as a blessing." Jessica gave Paul a mushy kiss.

One of the women was talking nonstop about a new client at her PR firm. Though she hadn't been there ten minutes, Bliss had heard enough. It was time to place the focus of the conversation where it should be. On her.

"Well, I did it!" Bliss reached across the table and took a sip of Jessica's margarita, anxious for her own to arrive.

Jessica grimaced and rubbed the back of her neck, a signal to Bliss that she should not proceed down the current path.

"And just what did you do now?" Paul asked, chomping on a tortilla chip.

He was tall and slender with a head full of wavy black hair. Bliss often wondered how Jessica had landed such a catch.

Bliss paused to make sure she had everyone's attention. "I served Fletcher McClain with a paternity suit today."

She gathered from one of the men's furrowed brows that he was familiar with the name.

"The head of Karma Entertainment?" asked one of Paul's colleagues.

"That would be the one. He's my daughter's father, but refuses to claim her. A paternity test will soon put an end to that."

The man's eyes glowed. "If that's true, you and your daughter have hit the lottery. I'd bet that over her lifetime, he'll end up paying you a couple million dollars in child support."

Bliss smiled. "I'm expecting a lot more than a couple million."

One of the women folded her freckled arms. "The man should take care of his kid, but it shouldn't take millions to do that."

Bliss took no offense. "All I want is my daughter's fair share of her father's income."

"Just be careful," one of the men warned. "Rich people don't like to part with their money."

"Well, there's nothing he can do about it. The law is the law." She turned to Jessica's husband. "Hey, Paul, I need a recommendation for a good attorney. And I want a real shark."

Paul grunted. "No way. I'm staying out of it. I have business associates who run in his circle."

"I think I know just the right lawyer for you," said Paul's golfing buddy, ignoring a snide look from his wife.

"Really?" Bliss said, her interest piqued.

The man took out his phone to look up the number. "And she might just be even more ruthless than you are."

CHAPTER 5

After Fletcher's departure, I spend another thirty minutes at work, then pack up and drive home. On the way, I call my best friend Special and tell her I have some good news for her. She arrives at my Baldwin Hills home minutes after I do.

I assume the look of excitement on her face is in anticipation of what I have to share. I'm wrong.

"I'm finally meeting Darius tomorrow night!" She sounds like a sixteen year old who's just gotten invited to the prom. "This brother is *The One*. I can feel it."

"Can you please just meet the man before deciding you want to marry him?"

Special has been husband-hunting on MyHarmony.com for several months now.

"We've been emailing and texting and talking on the phone for seven long weeks. I know everything I need to know about him. We have so much in common. Two women on my job found husbands on MyHarmony. They really know how to match people up. And get this. He's an ex-Marine who worked in the counter-terrorism unit. He's now a security consultant for Fortune 500 corporations. So he can help me with my investigations. How cool is that?"

"You only know what he's told you, which may not be the truth."

"I'm an almost-full-fledged private investigator, remember? I've thoroughly checked him out. Didn't find a single red flag."

"Please, just take it slow."

"I'm trying, but it's hard. This man is so incredible. He's romantic and smart and funny and open. He's definitely husband material."

"Okay, whatever you say."

She flops into a chair at the kitchen table. "I didn't come over here for you to rain on my parade. Can you at least fake some excitement for me?"

"If you're still this excited after you've been dating him for six months, then I'll get excited."

Special waves off my skepticism. "So what's the good news you have for me?"

Now I'm the excited one. "First, I'm very proud of you for getting your part-time gig as a PI's apprentice."

Special spends her day working as a manager at Verizon, but sleuthing is her true passion. Her investigative work uncovered evidence that led to a conviction against one of my clients being overturned.

"Thank you very much, counselor. I still can't believe that heffa Girlie Cortez didn't get disbarred for what she did."

"At least her license was suspended for nine months. Anyway, my good news is that I need your skills on another case. Of course, you'll need to partner with Eli since you don't have your license yet. And this is a paying client. One with some very big dough. You can bill by the hour."

Special rubs her palms together in excitement. "Tell me more."

"My client got served with a paternity petition by his ex-girlfriend, Bliss Fenton. She claims her daughter Harmony is—"

"Hold up. Her name is Bliss and her daughter's name is Harmony? They must be black because that's straight ghetto."

I chuckle. "Nope. I checked her out online. She's blonde-haired and blue-eyed. Very pretty girl.

Looks like a model. Anyway, my client swears the kid isn't his."

"Has he taken a paternity test?"

"He's taking it tomorrow. He wants me to negotiate a settlement with the woman to go away. And he thought it would be a good idea to have a PI dig up some dirt on her just in case we need to apply a little pressure."

Special has a puzzled look on her face.

"What's the matter?"

"Your client sounds a little suspect. If the kid isn't his, why pay her anything? He should just wait for the test results."

"Even after the paternity test proves he's not the father, he still expects her to try to cause more drama. He figures she'll disappear forever if the price is right."

"How can he be so sure the kid isn't his?"

"They broke up eleven months before the child was born."

"So?"

My friend has me totally confused.

"What do you mean, so? Do the math. He couldn't be the father if he hadn't last slept with the woman in almost a year before the kid was born."

"Yes, he could."

"I'm not following."

"She could've stolen his sperm."

"Stolen his sperm. What are you talking about?"

"Instead of throwing out the condom after he got his jollies, she might've stuck it in the freezer. I saw that on *Being Mary Jane.* And when she's ready to pop out a little one, she just thaws it out, sucks it into a turkey baster and shoots it you know where. And boom! Dude is a papa. A lot of professional athletes get popped that way."

Special's implausible scenario gives me pause. Both Fletcher and Mia described Bliss as conniving. But would she really go *that* far?

"That's crazy."

"But it happens. So who's my new client?"

I lead her into the den and wait for her to sit down.

"It's Fletcher McClain."

She rears back on the couch. "That fine-ass white boy you dumped sophomore year? Isn't he head of Karma Entertainment?"

"That would be the one."

"Oh my God!"

"I need you to see what you can find out about his maybe-baby mama. Fletcher's apparently not the first man she just happened to hit with an unplanned pregnancy."

"I can't believe Fletcher's finally getting married. I figured you had scarred him for life. I bet you anything he's marrying a sista."

I nod. "Yep. I met her today."

"I knew it! That white boy definitely had the hots for black women back at USC. His fiancée is one lucky heffa." Special takes out her cell phone.

"What're you doing?"

"Going to Google Images. I want to see what she looks like."

"You don't even know her name."

"I don't need to know her name. This is the Internet age. I'm Googling *Fletcher McClain* and *fiancée*."

"Oh snap!" she says in mere seconds. "Here she is. Her name's Mia Richardson."

"I already know that."

"Wow!"

"Wow what? She's not *that* cute."

Special arched a brow. "If I didn't know better, I'd think you were a little jealous. I didn't say *wow* because she's cute, even though she is. I said *wow* because she kinda looks like you."

"No, she does not."

"Oh, yes, she does. You both have the same facial structure. Nice cheekbones and pert noses. She also looks to be about your height and even has bangs like yours. I told you that man never got over you."

"Who never got over you?" My husband steps into the room.

"This gazillionaire white guy Vernetta dated in college."

Jefferson folds his arms and rests them against his muscular chest. "Is that right? Let me see him."

Before I can stop her, Special hands Jefferson her phone.

"Wow," he says, staring at the picture for way too long.

I suck my teeth. "*Wow* what?"

"This chick standing next to him favors you. Same complexion and cheekbones and she has long bangs like you."

"That's his fiancée," Special announces.

"So he likes sistas." Jefferson gives the phone back to Special. "Vernetta, you need to ask your daddy whether he forgot to tell you about a long-lost sister."

"He never got over Vernetta dumping him," Special blabs. "So he went out and found himself a look-a-like."

"Is that right?" Jefferson, who ran his own electrical contracting company, starts unlacing his steel-toed work boots. "I never knew you dated a white boy, not to mention a wealthy one. So exactly how much money does this dude have?"

Special continues blabbing like she's a tell-all book. "According to *Forbes* magazine, he's worth four-hundred-and-fifty-million dollars. He runs Karma Entertainment."

Jefferson whistles. "So homeboy is Oprah-rich, huh?"

"Oprah's net worth is in the billions, not millions," I correct him. "Why don't we talk about something else?"

Both of them ignore me.

"I'm going to be working as an investigator on his case," Special brags. "Digging up dirt on his ex-girlfriend. Vernetta's representing him in a paternity case."

"You have a really big mouth. Maybe I need to rethink my decision about hiring you. This case is confidential."

Jefferson kicks off one of his boots and rubs his shaved head. "So dude's trying to get out of paying child support?"

"He says the kid isn't his," Special continues.

"Sounds like a poo-butt move to me. Especially since he has all that dough."

It's time to cut this conversation short. "Special, can I please talk to you in the kitchen?"

She sulks after me.

"Why'd you just blab all of that stuff to Jefferson?"

"Girl, stop trippin'. Your husband can handle it."

Special's cell phone rings. She glances at the screen and squeals. "This is Darius. I have to take it."

She rushes out of the kitchen and down the hallway. "Hey, gorgeous," she coos into the phone.

Jefferson enters the kitchen. "If the dude has that much money, he's probably paying you some big cash, huh?"

"Just my regular hourly rate."

"No discount for being your ex?"

I smile. "Sounds like you might be jealous."

"I have no reason to be jealous."

I both like and dislike his confidence on this point. "Fletcher invited us to a party at his place. You wanna go?"

Jefferson walks past me and opens the cabinet next to the refrigerator. "Sure."

"I'm surprised that you want to meet him."

He places a bag of popcorn into the microwave oven. "I couldn't care less about meeting that dude," he says with a sheepish grin. "But I'd love to get a look at your twin sister in the flesh."

CHAPTER 6

The black Lincoln Town Car slowed as it reached the DNA testing center on Wilshire Boulevard.

Fletcher peered out of the back window. The receptionist had warned him that paparazzi often staked out the place hoping to luck up on a shot of a celebrity entering the building. He didn't want to get caught up in any of that.

"Hey, Lester," he called to his driver, "we're early. I don't want to go in right away. See if you can find a place to park on the main street."

Lester circled the block and parked in front of a donut shop.

Perspiration crept down Fletcher's left armpit. No one would believe that the great Fletcher McClain was nervous. There was no way that kid was his. *So why am I stressing?*

He pulled out his iPad and responded to several emails, listened to a couple of voicemail messages, then gave Lester the signal to take him to the back of the facility. He'd made arrangements to enter the facility through a rear door.

When he made it to the reception area, a pretty black girl showed him into a private waiting room the size of a jail cell.

"I'll need a copy of your driver's license and you'll need to fill out these papers." The woman handed him a clipboard with several pages attached.

"How long will it take to get the results?"

"About two weeks."

"Is it possible to get them any sooner? I don't mind paying extra to have them expedited."

The woman shook her head. "This is not the kind of test you want to rush. We check and double-check our results. It takes time to do that."

"Understood."

He began filling out the paperwork, realizing that he hadn't had to do something like this in years. Whenever he had doctors' appointments, the forms were sent to his office ahead of time and his assistant Gabriella filled them out.

He'd been given the option of using a fake name for the information that would be sent to the lab. This protected against some Joe spotting a famous name and selling the results to TMZ. He chose the name Jake Griffin, his best buddy from high school.

As he waded through the paperwork, he paused when he got to a question asking where the results should be mailed. His home was out. Fletcher did not want to run the chance of Mia seeing the results before he did. Nor did he want Gabriella opening them. He pulled out his phone and looked up Vernetta's office address. He'd send them to her.

The woman returned to retrieve the paperwork and also took his photograph and thumbprint.

"How long is this going to take?"

"You should be out of here in about twenty minutes."

She led him into another room where a man dressed in blue scrubs took over.

"I'm Dave. I'll be drawing your specimen."

"Blood test, right?" Fletcher asked.

"Blood and saliva. I'll also swab the inside of your cheek. Won't hurt a bit."

Dave picked up a tourniquet and tied it around Fletcher's forearm, then examined the crook of his arm.

"You've got lots of nice, thick veins. Great."

"So, how accurate is this test?"

Fletcher couldn't seem to stop himself from asking questions he already knew the answer to.

"Ninety-nine-point-nine percent."

"Are there ever any errors?"

"Rarely."

"*Rarely?*" That wasn't the response Fletcher wanted to hear. "So what could cause an error?"

Dave hunched his shoulders. "The lab equipment could be contaminated or not calibrated properly. Or a specimen might be mislabeled or the results could be put into the wrong account."

"How often does that happen?"

"It's never happened here. I'm just telling you the stuff they tell us in training. Don't worry, our tests are always accurate."

"Sorry to sound so paranoid, but the woman I'm dealing with is so nuts that I wouldn't be surprised if she managed to pull some strings to fix the results and tag me with a kid that's not mine."

"Other than paying off the lab tech, that's highly unlikely," Dave said.

Highly unlikely? "Has that ever happened?"

"Not to my knowledge. Relax. You're in good hands."

Dave drew five vials of blood, then swiped the inside of Fletcher's cheek with two extra-long Q-tips and placed them inside separate plastic bags. He then placed the vials and Q-tips into separate white envelopes.

He held the envelopes out for Fletcher to review. "If all of your information is correct, I need you to sign your name right here."

Fletcher checked and double checked, then scrawled his fake name on the two envelopes.

"Is the testing done here?"

"Nope. We send them to our lab in Arcadia."

"That's a long way to travel."

"Don't worry. We have strict chain of custody procedures. Everybody who touches these specimens has to sign a statement explaining what they did with them."

"How do they conduct the test?"

"What we're doing is an autosomal D-N-A test," Dave explained. "There are several markers that—"

"Never mind." Fletcher cut him off. "Sounds complicated. I should've paid more attention in biology."

He pulled out his cell and asked Lester to bring the car around.

As he waited, he tried to suppress the anxiety throbbing in his chest. He had no reason to worry. The kid wasn't his. It was as simple as that.

CHAPTER 7

I dial Bliss' cell phone number and wait. By the third ring, I assume she isn't going to pick up. I leave a short message explaining that I represent Fletcher McClain and ask her to return my call. Ten minutes later, she does.

A call from a lawyer would make most people nervous, even if they hadn't done anything wrong. I sense only curiosity, not concern, from Bliss Fenton.

"So Fletcher hired an attorney. Very interesting."

I'm not sure what that means, so I let it go.

"Thanks for calling me back. Based on your petition, it looks like you're representing yourself. Is that correct?"

She doesn't answer right away. If Bliss has an attorney, I'll have to end the call and speak with her counsel.

"I don't have an attorney at the moment. No need to waste a bunch of money on lawyers. Once Fletcher takes the paternity test, this is a done deal. But now that Fletcher has a lawyer, I guess I should consider hiring myself a mouthpiece too."

I hope to have this matter all wrapped up long before Bliss has time to do that.

"That's up to you," I say. "However, I think we may be able to resolve this without you having to spend money on an attorney."

"So Fletcher is finally ready to admit that he's Harmony's father?"

I sidestep her question. "I'm wondering if you'd be willing to come to my office to discuss settlement."

"We don't have anything to settle. The paternity test will do that."

"As you know, Fletcher doesn't believe he's the father of your daughter."

"And as you know—or maybe you don't—your client is a big fat liar. He is most definitely Harmony's father."

The flash of anger in her voice reverberates through the phone.

"Are you saying you two didn't break up more than eleven months before your daughter was born?"

"Depends on how you define *break up*."

"And how do you define it?"

"Ms.—What did you say your name was again?"

"Henderson. Vernetta Henderson."

"Ms. Henderson, I feel like I'm on the witness stand and I don't particularly like that feeling. Why don't we skip the bull? Exactly what is Fletcher trying to pull?"

"Fletcher is hoping the two of you can reach a financial agreement that would make this matter go away."

"My daughter's not a *matter*." Her voice hardens into steel. "And she's not going away."

"Please forgive my poor choice of words. But I do have a rather generous offer that Fletcher would like to present to you. Would you be willing to come to my office so we can discuss it in person?"

The line seems to go dead, but I wait her out.

"So Fletcher plans to offer me a few bucks to disappear? Is that how he wants to make *this matter go away?*"

"I would really prefer to give you the details in person."

"I don't know what Fletcher told you, but trust me, he is definitely Harmony's father."

As confident as Fletcher is that he is not the father, Bliss sounds equally confident that he is.

"It would be great if we could talk in person," I press.

"Sure. I'd at least like to hear what he's putting on the table. I'm busy for the next couple of days. How about Friday?"

That's three days from now. I was hoping to meet with her sooner, but decide not to push it. We schedule the meeting for eleven and I hang up.

I sit there for a few minutes wondering if Fletcher has given me the full story. Then I remember Special's theory about women getting pregnant by confiscating sperm-filled condoms. If that's what Bliss did, it would explain how Fletcher could strenuously assert that he isn't the father at the same time Bliss insists that he is.

I turn to my computer, call up Google and start researching turkey baster pregnancies.

CHAPTER 8

Special checked her makeup in the rearview mirror and applied another coat of passionate plum lipstick. She was so thrilled about meeting Darius that she felt like a bubble ready to burst. If the man turned out to be half as wonderful in person as he was on the phone, he would definitely be *The One*.

She paused abruptly and gave herself a stern look in the eye.

"Just calm down," she told herself.

Vernetta was absolutely right. She needed to take it slow. Every time she got hyped about a guy, she only ended up getting her feelings hurt in weeks or months, sometimes even days.

"Slow," she mumbled. "Take it slow. I'm just meeting a new friend. Not a husband."

Stepping out of her car, Special glided toward the restaurant. She had insisted that Darius choose their meeting spot. She wanted to check out his taste early on and prayed he didn't select some tacky chain restaurant. She was pleasantly surprised when he picked Lido's in Manhattan Beach. She loved Italian food.

Standing at the hostess stand, Special scanned the room, hoping to spot him before he noticed her. She'd intentionally arrived a few minutes late. She wanted Darius already seated so he could watch her strut toward him. Her bright yellow, t-strap dress—thigh-high in the front, floor length in the back—showed off her best feature, her mile-long legs. On most dates, she'd be showing enough cleavage to make a grown man want to breastfeed. Tonight, she revealed just a sliver. No need to bombard the brother with all of her goodies at once.

The hostess seated another customer, then directed her attention to Special. "My reservation's under the name Darius Reed."

The perky brunette flashed a big grin, then whispered. "He told us all about meeting you on MyHarmony. That's how my cousin met her husband. I have my fingers crossed for you two."

Special's face glowed. The fact that Darius was blabbing their business to the hostess meant he was just as excited as she was. *Nice.*

"Follow me," the woman said. "Mr. Reed requested a secluded spot out on the patio."

When Special saw him in the flesh, the apprehension eased from her body. She'd heard horror stories about people posting pictures online that had no resemblance to how they looked today. That wasn't the case with Darius.

He's even finer than his profile picture.

Darius had mentioned that he worked out, but this man had the bulging chest of a professional body builder.

"You are one fine sista," Darius blurted out, as soon as she was within hearing range. He picked up a single, long-stemmed rose from the table and handed it to her.

Special hesitated for an awkward moment as the hostess pulled out her chair.

Why don't you get your butt up and give me a hug?

During her drive over, Special had fantasized about their first hug. He should have been the one pulling out her chair.

Strike one.

That simple mistake was enough to make her slow her roll. She did not want a man who didn't have basic home training. Her lips were about to twist into one big pout when she caught herself. She would not let that one *faux pas* ruin the entire evening. Darius would have to screw up at least two more times before she wrote him off. She would let it go. For now.

Special placed the flower to her nose and took a whiff. "Thank you very much."

"You're most welcome."

As they sat there gazing at each other with smiles so big their cheeks hurt from smiling so much, it was as if no one else existed.

Darius had thick, luscious lips flanked by deep dimples on both cheeks. His hair was closely cropped and his face cleanly shaven.

"Just give me a few more minutes." He shifted in his chair. "You're so beautiful, I just want to look at you."

She let him.

"I'm not sure we have anything left to talk about," Special quipped. "I feel like I already know everything about you."

"There's more," Darius said with a mischievous wink. "I didn't give it all up. I'm kinda cautious about opening myself up to people. There're way too many fake people in L.A."

"Wait a minute." Special's right hand flew to her hips. "So you've been holding back on me?"

Darius winked. "You'll learn everything you need to know when the time is right."

"I'm going to hold you to that."

"Tell me more about your work as a private investigator," he said.

"I'm not quite official yet. I'm working as an apprentice for a friend of mine to rack up enough on-the-job hours to take the PI exam."

She went on to tell him about her new case, neglecting, of course, to mention any names or too many specifics. "I've already started checking out the woman online."

"That's a good place to start. You should also delve into court records too. You can do that online now. And you'd be surprised how much intel neighbors are willing to divulge."

"That's great advice. I'll definitely follow up." These tips weren't anything she didn't already know, but she didn't want to bruise his ego. "So do you miss being in the military?"

"I miss the camaraderie, but I dig what I do now. Helping companies strengthen their security platforms allows me to use all the stuff I learned in the Marines on a more strategic level."

Darius rested his forearms on the table and repositioned himself in the chair for the second, or was it the third time? Special smiled. The brother was probably just flexing, trying to show off his muscles. She could see the outline of his impressive pecs through his tight-fitting Lycra shirt.

"What I do now is also a lot safer and gives me time to smell the roses," he continued. "I just closed escrow on a vacation home in Palm Springs. Paid cash for it."

He paused to dip a piece of bread into a dish of olive oil and Parmesan cheese.

If he was trying to impress her, it was working. "I love Palm Springs."

"Then we'll most definitely have to take a drive down there for the weekend."

"Just say when and I'm there."

They ordered appetizers and entrées and their conversation continued to flow.

"So did you remember to bring yours?" Darius asked.

"Yep." Special opened her purse, pulled out a copy of her MyHarmony.com questionnaire and handed it to him. Darius placed his on the table in front of her.

"This is scary," Special exclaimed as she read. "Our answers are almost exactly the same on nearly every question."

Darius smiled and nodded. "I guess they knew what they were doing when they hooked us up."

By the time dessert arrived, there were only a handful of customers left in the restaurant.

Darius glanced around. "I guess we're closing the place down tonight."

"Sure looks that way."

He reached across the table and grabbed her right hand and held it in both of his. "There's something we need to talk about. Something important."

In a snap, his somber tone had cast a dark curtain of dread over the entire evening. Special felt her stomach do a double flip.

"I should've told you this the first time we talked," Darius began. "So I'll need to ask your forgiveness for not doing that."

Special fought the urge to pull her hand away.

"If you're asking for forgiveness on the first date," she joked, hoping her nervousness didn't show, "that can't be a good sign."

The brothers in L.A. are so dang trifflin'! If this man tells me he's married, I swear to God I'm going to punch him in the face.

"Okay, let's hear it."

"I neglected—intentionally neglected—to tell you something about myself. Something important. But I needed to know that we could connect without it getting in the way."

"You're starting to scare me, Darius." His nervousness was beginning to rub off on her.

"I noticed the expression on your face when I didn't stand to greet you when you first arrived," he said.

"Actually," Special admitted, wanting him to hurry up and get to the point, "I *was* a little put off by that."

"Yeah, um…well, there's a reason I didn't get up."

Darius slowly pushed back from the table, which left her even more confused.

It wasn't until he lifted the tablecloth and Special saw the wheelchair that her heart stopped beating.

CHAPTER 9

I've been sitting in the waiting area outside Fletcher McClain's office long enough to be perturbed. I'm anxious to talk to him about my research on the turkey baster cases. Our scheduled meeting should have started twenty-six minutes ago.

His assistant, Gabriella, a gorgeous Salvadoran, apologizes for the third time for her boss' tardiness.

"He'll be on his way down from the boardroom any minute now. Why don't I have you wait in his office?"

Fletcher's office is about the size of a ritzy hotel lobby and has the same posh ambience. There's a marble desk in one corner and a living room setup in another, complete with a couch, two armchairs, and a coffee table. I take a seat on the leather couch and enjoy the view of the Hollywood Hills. Five minutes later, Fletcher flies into the room and plops into an armchair across from me. He's not wearing a jacket and his shirtsleeves are rolled up to the elbow. An earpiece protrudes from his left ear.

"Hi, Fletcher. I wanted to talk to you about—"

He holds up a finger cutting me off as he speaks into his Bluetooth earpiece. "Talk to Jackson about that, and don't sign the contract until I've had a chance to go through it one more time."

He stands up, snatches a bottle of Tums from his desk drawer and pops two pink tablets into his mouth. I'm certain the deep creases etched into his forehead weren't there when I saw him two days ago.

The phone on his desk rings, but he ignores it.

"Gabriella will get it." He returns to the armchair. "Okay, what's up? Did Bliss take my offer?"

Instead of looking at me, he's scrolling through his phone.

"Fletcher, I'm going to need your full attention."

"You got it"—he glances up at me, then back down at his phone—"for the next seventeen minutes. Sorry, but it's turning out to be a hellacious day."

"We're going to need a lot more time than that."

"Fine, but you can't have it today." He slips his phone into his shirt pocket. "The clock's ticking. So shoot, counselor."

"First, I wanted to let you know that I have an appointment with Bliss on Friday morning. Hopefully, she'll take the money and run. But I have to be honest. After talking to her, I don't think she will. She's pretty insistent that the child is yours."

He shakes his head. "Not possible."

I inhale. "I think I have an explanation for why Bliss is so confident that you're the father. It's a little far-fetched, but it's a very real possibility. I've been researching—"

"I don't mean to be rude, counselor, but I need you to cut to the chase. Time is money."

I decide not to take his curtness personally and do as instructed. "Bliss might've stolen your sperm."

"Excuse me?" Astonishment bathes his face. "How in the hell could she do that?"

"I'm assuming you used a condom when you were with her."

"Always."

"They're called turkey baster pregnancies. It's where a woman retrieves sperm from a used condom and uses a turkey baster or a syringe to inseminate herself. We need to consider the possibility that Bliss did that to you."

Fletcher takes off his earpiece and sets it on the coffee table. I definitely have his full attention now.

"So even if the child was born eleven months after you last slept with her," I continue, "it could be your kid if she saved your sperm."

He squints in confusion. "That's crazy."

Fletcher is a bright guy, but he seems to be having trouble wrapping his mind around this concept.

"Wouldn't the sperm cells dry out or something?"

"Not if the semen is frozen. That happened in several of the cases I read about. I copied a few articles for you." I place a folder on the coffee table. "You should read them when you have some time."

"If you're trying to scare the hell out of me, Vernetta, you've accomplished your goal."

"I just wanted you to be aware of this possibility."

Fletcher rubs his jaw and stares out of the window.

"No way." He whips back around to face me. "She never had access to my condoms. I either tossed them in the trash or flushed them down the toilet."

"Always?"

He hesitates. "Yeah, I'm almost certain."

"And you never let her take it off?"

He hesitates again. "Uh, a couple of times. Maybe."

He stands up and starts pacing.

"This is nuts. I only dated that psycho for six months. She's not going to disrupt my life like this. If she—" He abruptly stops talking. "Hey, if she got pregnant by stealing my friggin' sperm, that would be fraud."

"Yeah, probably. But even if you have a valid fraud case, that has no bearing on your obligation to pay child support. If the kid is biologically yours, you'll be on the hook financially for the next eighteen years. The law will focus only on the well-being of the child. It doesn't matter how she got here."

Fletcher dashes back over to his desk, grabs the Tums bottle and pops two more pills.

"And Fletcher, with your income, the child support payments are going to be pretty significant. I spoke to a family law attorney this morning. California uses a straightforward mathematical equation. After subtracting your basic living expenses, it could be somewhere around ten percent of your monthly income."

"Bullshit! I made five-hundred grand last month. Ten percent of that is fifty grand. Over eighteen years"—he must've been a whiz in math because he calculates the numbers in a flash—"that would be ten-point-eight million dollars!"

His voice goes up two octaves and his face looks as if it might crack. "Nobody needs that much money to take care of a kid."

"The law doesn't base child support on how much the kid needs, but on how much the parents earn. The child is entitled to have the same standard of living as the non-custodial parent."

"But I didn't want a kid with her and she knew that."

"Doesn't matter."

"I'm not paying her fifty grand a month!" he shouts, spittle flying from his mouth.

"It wouldn't be fifty grand. Your living expenses would have to be subtracted so—"

"If that bitch stole my sperm, I'm not paying her ass a dime."

I lower my voice in hopes of encouraging him to follow suit. I don't remember Fletcher being such a hot-head. The attraction I'd felt for him during our initial meeting evaporates.

"If the kid is yours, you won't have a choice."

His chest is heaving up and down as if he's just run up a flight of stairs at full speed. Fletcher is successful in business because he has vision. His next words convince me of that.

"If it turns out she stole my sperm and that kid is mine, it makes sense to get her to agree to a child support arrangement now, before she gets a lawyer involved."

"True."

"When you speak with her, I want you to make a two-tiered offer. A lump sum payment for her to sign a confidentiality agreement and go away never to be seen again. But if the kid is mine, I'll pay her seven grand a month in child support."

"She's unrepresented. So it's possible a court might later undo your agreement because she wasn't adequately advised of her rights."

"I'll deal with that if and when it happens. And if the kid is mine, I'm suing that cunt for fraud and asking for millions in damages. Then we can just call it a wash. If she wants to play dirty, I will too."

"Okay," I say, wondering where this case is going.

"What else can we sue her for? What about emotional distress? That should get me some major damages, right?"

"We can include it, but you probably won't recover much for it."

"Why not?"

"You'd have to prove that you actually suffered emotional harm."

For the first time since my arrival, Fletcher smiles. "Trust me, Vernetta. If I have to pay Bliss Fenton fifty grand a month, I'll be a friggin' basket case."

CHAPTER 10

Girlie Cortez scanned her cheap desk calendar and frowned. Her two o'clock appointment was yet another potential client pleading poverty.

Before her suspension from the California Bar, Girlie would've snubbed her nose at a family law case. As a litigator, she considered herself among the legal elite. One of only a few prominent Filipina attorneys in the city, she attracted major clients based on her ruthlessness in the courtroom. Girlie also had an innate sexiness about her—enhanced by her shapely body, great legs and long, silky hair—that further enhanced her appeal, at least with male clients. But now she was stuck in a solo law practice, eating only what she could kill.

Girlie had only agreed to meet with Bliss Fenton because she wanted the colleague who had referred her to keep the referrals coming. She was bound to get a big hit. Eventually. Girlie planned to listen to the woman's story, give her enough free advice to make her even more distraught about her situation, then tell her she couldn't help her without a ten-thousand-dollar retainer. There was no way she could take a child support case on contingency. It could be months or years before she got paid.

Her fall from grace had been embarrassingly public. Being forced to give up her partnership at Donaldson, Watson and Barkley was one thing. But the nine-month suspension for knowingly allowing a witness to lie under oath had almost caused her to lose her home.

But Girlie was no quitter. Yes, at the moment she was leasing a shabby office on the low-rent end of Washington Boulevard in

Pasadena, away from the hustle and bustle of downtown Los Angeles. But she was confident that she could work her way back into a lucrative law practice. It would just take time, patience and a little luck.

No longer having the luxury of an assistant to escort clients into her office, Girlie walked out to the lobby to greet Bliss Fenton herself.

The woman who stood to shake her hand was not what Girlie had been expecting. Bliss Fenton dressed as if she had more than a little dough. The suit she was wearing was an Armani. Girlie knew that because she'd seen it in the window at Saks a few weeks back and couldn't afford it. She hoped Bliss wasn't some rich penny pincher who was trying to play her.

"Why don't you begin by telling me what's going on?" Girlie said, once they were seated in her office.

"It's been quite an ordeal. Fletcher McClain is the father of my three-month-old daughter Harmony. But he claims she's not his. Then all of a sudden I get a call from his attorney asking me to come to her office to discuss settlement."

"If he's denying paternity, what's there to settle?"

"Exactly."

Bliss opened a pink folder. "Here's a copy of my petition.

Girlie looked it over. "You prepared this yourself?"

"Yep. A paralegal at the court's Self-Help Clinic helped me."

"Looks like you did everything right."

"Do you know who Fletcher McClain is?" Bliss asked.

Girlie shook her head. "Can't say that I do."

Bliss pulled more papers from her folder and handed them across the desk. Here's an article about him that ran in *Billboard* magazine last year.

As Girlie read the article, she began to see green, lots of it. "This guy is worth four hundred and fifty million dollars and he's sweating you for child support?"

Bliss nodded.

Girlie tried to keep the excitement out of her voice. The stars were finally aligning. In addition to child support, she would also go after

McClain for attorneys' fees. A man with this much dough could afford to pay her regular rate and then some.

"I really don't have the money for an attorney of your caliber," Bliss said. "If you can't take my case on contingency, perhaps you can refer me to someone else who might be able to."

No way, my dear. This one is all mine.

"Let's hold off on talking about my fees until I fully understand your case. I'd like to attend the meeting with you at his attorney's office. What's his name?"

"It's a her." Bliss removed a thin notepad from her folder. "Her name's Vernetta Henderson."

Girlie felt a jolt of adrenalin shock her like a prod from a hot poker. She glared at Bliss. "I know her. She doesn't practice family law. I wonder why she's representing him?"

Bliss hunched her shoulders.

This case was nothing short of a gift from God. Girlie was sure of it. Not only could she go after the wealthy Fletcher McClain for attorneys' fees, she'd also get to exact a little payback against Vernetta Henderson. Girlie still blamed Vernetta and her meddlesome friend for digging up the evidence that led to her suspension.

"And you're one hundred percent sure Fletcher McClain is the father of your daughter?"

"Absolutely."

Girlie didn't need to know more right now. She was just thrilled to have a case that offered the potential to replenish her dwindling bank account *and* stick it to her nemesis.

"I'd like to take you on as a client," she said. "My fees are four-fifty an hour."

Bliss gasped.

"But don't worry about that. I think we'll be able to recover my attorneys' fees from Mr. McClain. Let's see what he's offering you. I suspect it's going to be offensively low. But it's my plan to collect every dime your daughter deserves."

And every dollar I deserve too.

CHAPTER 11

Eli Jenkins snapped his meaty fingers in Special's face. "Did you hear anything I just said?"

"Sorry," she muttered with a vacant expression. "I have a lot on my mind."

"Apparently so. But this Fletcher McClain guy is paying you a nice chunk of change to dig up some dirt on this Bliss Fenton chick. So if I were you, I'd pay close attention to the knowledge I'm imparting."

Eli was the size of a bouncer, but had the heart of a teddy bear. He'd been a successful PI for a couple of decades and had worked his way into a lucrative business, sleuthing for lawyers and small companies. Special was lucky to be doing her apprenticeship under his tutelage.

"Yes, sir, bossman." Special laughed, holding up her notepad. "Let's go over it again. I think I blanked out at the part where you were explaining what to look for in the court records."

"You gotta be kidding me. That was ten minutes ago."

She raised her right hand. "I swear you have my full attention now. I spent some time last night searching for Bliss' name in the civil court records but didn't find anything. I'll hit the family law cases tonight. And I want to start my surveillance of her. Can I still use your van?"

"Sure, but you better take care of it."

Eli had a rickety van that masqueraded as Jenkins Heating and Plumbing Company. Special knew from her many late-night surveillance rides with him that most people noticed a strange car parked in front of their house, but looked right past a commercial truck or van with a company name sprawled on the side.

"I'm hoping to get some more information about her paternity case against her son's father from the court records. Then I'll see if he'll talk to me. Any ideas for my initial cover story when I approach him?"

"If she's jacking him the same way she's jacking Fletcher McClain, he'll probably have no trouble spilling his guts and trashing her. But let's take a break. I need to know what's going on with you."

Special fiddled with her ink pen.

"C'mon, girl. You can trust me. You know I've got your back. What's up?"

"Man trouble," Special admitted.

Eli smiled. "I figured as much. "Who's the problem dude this time?"

"What do you mean, *this time*? You act like I always have man trouble."

"Girl, you're a mess when it comes to men. Instead of hunting them down, you need to wait for love to find you."

"I don't have that kind of time. I prefer to be proactive."

"So what's the deal? You think the dude's steppin' out on you?"

"Nope, he's actually the perfect guy for me. We click on so many levels. He's an ex-Marine. I met him online."

"If you met him online, no telling what the real deal is. Give me his name. I'm going to investigate him myself."

"You know I've already researched that brother every which way. He's legit. That's not my problem."

"Okay. So what *is* the problem?"

Special took in some air. "He's a paraplegic."

Eli leaned back in his chair. "You didn't know about his situation before you met him?"

"Nope. We talked for almost two months before meeting in person and he never told me."

"That's a problem right there."

"I understand why he didn't tell me," Special said, feeling protective of Darius. "If he had, I wouldn't have wanted to meet him. And now that I have, I still dig him as much as before." She told him more about Darius' background. "But I just can't get over the fact that he's permanently confined to a wheelchair."

"That's understandable. I have a buddy who has a spinal cord injury. He and his wife have a pretty cool relationship. A lot of paraplegics have tremendous upper body strength. The only thing he can't do is walk."

Special doodled on her notepad. "But what about sex? I can't see giving up sex for the rest of my life."

"My friend's pecker works just fine."

"Seriously?" Special looked as amazed as a kid watching a fireworks' show. "Even though he's paralyzed?"

"Yep. Ain't that a blip?"

Special took a moment to consider what Eli had just said.

"It won't be easy dating a man who's paralyzed," he continued. "But the dude sounds like he's got it going on. That's a lot more than I can say about some of your past men."

"That's cold."

"It's the truth."

Special continued to doodle.

"Just spend some time with the dude and figure out if you can hang. Ain't like he's asking you to marry him tomorrow. You're always rushing things. Like I said, stop chasing love and let it find you."

Special nodded. "I just don't want to end up hanging out with him out of guilt. I already feel sorry for him."

"That's on you. I suspect he doesn't feel all that sorry for himself. After my buddy got shot, it was a long time before I stopped seeing him as helpless. We still get together for poker once a month. He still invites us over for the best barbecue in L.A. We even went to the movies last week. Practically everything he did before his spinal cord injury, he still does. Except now he does it from a wheelchair."

Special gave serious thought to what he was saying.

"Give the man a shot," Eli urged. "You never know what could come of it. If nothing else, he could end up being a good friend. And we could all use more of those."

CHAPTER 12

"I don't believe you." Jessica threw up her hands. "With everything that's going on, you're dating a new guy?"

Bliss twisted from side to side, admiring her new outfit in her bedroom mirror. The tight red dress seemed to caress every curve of her slim body.

"Who says it's a new guy? Anyway, just because I filed that paternity case against Fletcher doesn't mean I have to act like a nun."

"Please tell me this guy isn't married."

Bliss responded with a devious smile.

Jessica sighed. "I guess that means yes."

"If a woman can't keep her man at home, that's her fault. Not mine."

Jessica flopped onto the corner of the bed. "If a man's not happy at home he should talk to his wife rather than cheat on her."

"See, that's the problem. Talking isn't going to solve a thing. Women need to understand that God didn't make men to be monogamous. That's why the men in the Bible had so many wives. They're just not built that way. All men want to cheat. Some act on it, some don't. If a woman wants to keep her man, she needs to make sure things stay spicy in the bedroom. If the sex gets boring, he's definitely going to stray. I've had my share of married men and what they did with me, they couldn't do at home with their prudish wives."

Bliss turned away from the mirror. "Why do you look so down in the dumps?"

"I think Paul is seeing someone."

"No way." Bliss smoothed down the front of her skirt. "Not Perfect Paul. At your birthday dinner he was all over you."

"That's how he acts in public, but at home he ignores me. We rarely have sex. He's either working around the clock or out of town. There must be someone else."

"Oh, give up with the woe-is-me act. If Paul *is* screwing around, do what you need to do to fix the situation."

"If I knew for sure he was having an affair, I'd be too devastated to even want to fix it."

"See, that's why it's so easy to have an affair with a married man. Their boring, insecure wives don't know how to fight for what's theirs. First, you need to spruce yourself up. Look at how you're dressed."

Jessica glanced down at her floral sundress. "What's wrong with the way I'm dressed?"

"For one, you never show any cleavage"

"Paul doesn't like that. He says it looks slutty."

"Yeah, that's what he's telling you. I bet his mistress is showing off her boobs. And when was the last time you had sex someplace other than the bedroom?"

Jessica's cheeks colored.

"Oh my God! Don't tell me the bedroom is the only place you have sex."

Jessica lazily hunched her shoulders.

"Okay, this is an emergency situation. First, we're going shopping to get you some new clothes and then we're going to have a little primer on reigniting the fire in your marriage. Maybe I'll take you by A Touch of Romance to pick up a few sex toys to liven things up."

Before Jessica could object, Harmony cried out.

Bliss hoisted her hair into a high bun. "How does this look?"

"Excuse me, but don't you hear your daughter crying?"

"She'll be fine. Anamaria will check on her."

"Unbelievable." Jessica marched out of the room and returned cuddling Harmony to her chest.

Bliss looked at the two of them through the mirror. "You're spoiling her rotten. I don't want her expecting to be picked up every time she cries."

Aiden and Jonas ran into the room. Aiden grasping a peanut butter sandwich, Jonas holding up fingers dipped in the brown goo.

"Mommy pretty!" Jonas dashed straight toward Bliss with outstretched hands. She jumped to the right, just in time, her hand on his head, holding him at bay."

"You're going to mess up my skirt," Bliss screeched. "Get back in the kitchen. Anamaria, please come get them!"

Both boys shrank away.

"Bliss!" Jessica yelled, almost as loudly as Bliss. "You shouldn't yell at them like that."

"And they shouldn't come running at me with sticky fingers."

Jessica placed Harmony in the middle of Bliss' bed, then consoled the boys with a group hug before handing them off to the nanny.

"Instead of scolding them all the time, you need to spend some quality time with them."

"They're fine. Anamaria takes good care of them."

"That's my point. *You* should be taking good care of them."

Bliss ignored her friend's advice. "Guess who I'm meeting with on Friday?"

"I don't want to know about your married men."

"Fletcher's attorney," Bliss went on. "She wants to discuss settlement."

"Great. I'm sure whatever he offers you will be fair. You should just take it and move on."

"Not on your life. I have an attorney who's going to the meeting with me."

Jessica shook her head. "Can I ask you something?"

"Depends on what it is."

"Is Fletcher really Harmony's father?"

"I don't believe you asked me that. Of course he is."

"So you were with him after he started dating Mia."

"Depends on what you mean by *with him*."

"Bliss, c'mon."

"The full story will be told in due time." There was a twinkle in her eye. "For now, mum's the word."

Jessica fell quiet again. "How come you never talk about Jonas' father?"

"Because I just don't." Bliss' tone was overly curt. "So don't go there." Bliss fanned her hair across her shoulders. "How do I look?"

"Breathtaking as usual."

"Thank you very much."

"Bliss, please tell me you're not about to target another wealthy guy for child support."

"If you weren't my best friend, I'd resent that question." Bliss turned sideways to admire her frame in the mirror. "But this fabulous body can't handle another pregnancy. Besides, after the child support I get from Fletcher McClain, I won't ever need another dime."

CHAPTER 13

"So this is where you could've been living, huh?" Jefferson leans forward to peer through the windshield of his car.

We've just entered the grounds of Fletcher McClain's Beverly Hills home. Jefferson pulls to a stop, hops out and hands the keys to the valet. He's too enthralled with Fletcher's majestic digs to notice that I need help getting out of the car in my tight skirt and four-inch heels. Another valet opens my door and I stumble out without his assistance.

"This place would make ten of ours," he marvels. "Nobody needs this much house."

I pull out my lighted compact and check my lipstick. "Believe it or not, this is just one of his three homes."

"That's just wasteful."

I'm hesitant about delivering my next words, but plunge ahead anyway. "Hey, sweetie, Fletcher's fiancée doesn't know we dated in college. So let's not mention it, okay?"

Jefferson waits a beat before responding. "That was years ago. Why would she trip?"

"I don't know. Fletcher says she's kinda jealous. So he asked me not to bring it up."

Jefferson does a slow nod, as if he's still giving it some thought. "Okay, whatever."

A striking, fiftyish black woman dressed in a maid's garb, greets us at the door and leads us down a wide hallway. The minute we step inside, I can feel the heavy base from the music reverberating through the floor and walls.

"Dude must like having good-looking sistas around," Jefferson whispers into my ear. "Can't blame him for that."

The woman points toward the backyard. "Everyone's out on the terrace."

"*The terrace*," Jefferson mimics in a la de da voice when she walks away. "Poor folks have a patio, but rich folks have a terrace."

"If you're going to make fun of everything, we should leave now."

"Okay."

He knows darn well I don't want to leave. "C'mon, boy."

Through the windows of the sparsely decorated living room, we see multiple groups of partygoers stationed at various spots around a circular terrace. Beyond the terrace is an Olympic-size pool and a backyard almost as big as a baseball field. I expected the party to be shoulder-to-shoulder people. The crowd, however, is small and intimate. Twenty, maybe thirty people tops.

Jefferson whistles. "Just think, you could've been the one living up in this crib instead of your twin sister."

"Cut it out, Jefferson."

We'd just stepped outside when Jefferson nudged me with his elbow. "Is that Snoop over there on that lounge chair?"

I turn to take a look. "I think it is."

"Hmmm. So your boy is all up in the celebrity mix."

"He runs a record company. I would expect as much. You sound impressed."

Jefferson shoves both hands deep into his pockets. "Celebrities don't impress me. They put their pants on one leg at a time just like I do."

From the way he's staring at the people crowded around Snoop, my husband is more than impressed.

"So why'd you dump the guy?"

I've been wondering when Jefferson was going to get around to asking me about Fletcher. "It just didn't work out."

"Why?"

"I don't know. It made me uncomfortable when people stared at us whenever we went anywhere. Like we were doing something wrong.

One black guy even had the audacity to ask me why I was dating a white boy. Like dating Fletcher was somehow betraying him."

"So if it hadn't been for that, you would've stayed with him?"

"I doubt it. Our families weren't exactly thrilled. The one time I met his mother, she was polite, but about as warm as a tray of ice cubes. My dad definitely wasn't happy about my dating a white guy, and he said as much. But why are we even discussing this? We were barely twenty years old. The odds of us making it were slim to none. I married the man God intended for me to marry. And that would be you."

I give him a sloppy kiss on the lips.

"You ever regret missing out on all this dough?"

I hate it when my husband shows signs of insecurity. But I provide him the reassurances I know he needs.

"Of course not." I hurl my arm around his waist. "I have everything I need and then some."

"Well, I'll tell you this much. If I had passed up on a babe who could've had me living large like this, I'd be mad as hell."

I playfully sock him in the arm seconds before Mia floats toward us.

She's dressed in pink leggings and a flowing chiffon caftan. She smells like an ocean breeze. I immediately feel overdressed.

"First, things first, Vernetta. I owe you an apology. I was a little over the top in your office the other day. You'll have to forgive me. This whole thing with Bliss has me totally stressed out. I'm just glad you're going to help us get through it."

She embraces me in a way that almost feels genuine.

Special had done a little digging into Mia's background, more for our curiosity than anything else. She was raised in Detroit, but by middle school had been plucked from her economically depressed neighborhood by the A Better Chance program and shipped off to a boarding school on the East Coast. She'd attended college at Cornell, but hadn't landed at a top tier law school or law firm.

Mia releases me and turns to Jefferson, who stares at her like she's a ghost. For the life of me, I will never understand how anyone could see a resemblance between the two of us.

"And who is this hunk?"

"My husband, Jefferson."

He extends his hand, but Mia ignores it and gives him a big hug instead.

"I normally wouldn't say this in front of my wife," Jefferson says, feigning shyness, "but you are absolutely stunning."

"Well, thank you."

Since everybody thinks she looks like me, I guess it's a good thing that my husband finds her attractive.

Mia half turns and points. "Fletcher's over there talking to Jamie Foxx, probably trying to negotiate some deal. That man works nonstop."

Now, *I'm* impressed. Snoop is one thing, but Jamie Foxx is another.

Just as Mia walks away, Jefferson drops his nonchalant demeanor. "There's Nicki Minaj," he says pointing. "You think Fletcher can get me a picture with her? The boys at work would trip hard."

"I thought you weren't impressed by celebrities."

"That girl's celebrity status is not what I'm impressed with. Her ass belongs in a museum."

"You better be glad you have a very secure wife."

He pecks me on the cheek. "I am."

We make our way over to Fletcher. He takes a break from his conversation to introduce us to Jamie. I try not to swoon when he shakes my hand. Jefferson's eyes, meanwhile, are tracking Nicki's every move.

Fletcher is wearing jeans and a white shirt, with the tail out. Jefferson shoots me an evil eye because he'd wanted to wear jeans, but I insisted on slacks. The actor moves on, leaving us alone with Fletcher.

"I heard a lot of good things about you, bro," Fletcher says.

Jefferson's brows briefly furrow. "Same here."

"I'm really relieved that Vernetta is handling this matter for me."

Jefferson places his arm around my waist and pulls me close. "My wife is indeed the best attorney money can buy."

"True dat," Fletcher says.

I feel Jefferson tense just before he gives me a look that does not require interpretation. *Why is this white dude trying to act like a brother?*

I wish I knew. Fletcher has never talked this way around me.

"Let me give you guys a tour of the house."

We follow Fletcher through both levels of his home, which is mind-blowingly fabulous. Huge windows everywhere, brightly colored furniture and unique lighting fixtures fit for a science-fiction movie. I lose count of how many rooms there are, each one worthy of a decorator's showcase.

Jefferson keeps rolling his eyes, and the second Fletcher is out of earshot, he mumbles, "Your boy is whack. Real ballers don't have to brag about what they've got."

Someone pulls Fletcher away and we spend the next hour socializing with the other guests, while Jefferson occasionally steals glances at Nicki Minaj's backside.

"I'm going to find a bathroom," I tell Jefferson. "When I come back, Nicki Minaj better not be hitting on you."

"If she wants me, it would be rude to deny her."

I don't need to use the restroom. What I want are a couple minutes alone with Fletcher. As luck would have it, we come face-to-face in the hallway. I step in close and lower my voice.

"Have you told Mia about those turkey baster cases yet?"

"Nope. I decided not to."

"Are you serious? Why not?"

"Because there's no need to. The paternity test is going to prove that the kid isn't mine."

"But just in case you're wrong, it might be smart to prepare Mia for the possibility that Bliss set you up."

Fletcher waves me off. "You sound like you're convinced the test is going to show I'm the father. Do you know something I don't?"

"I just don't think Bliss would've filed a paternity petition against you if she knew you weren't the father. She must've set you up."

"I'm not ready to go there yet. Besides—"

When Fletcher stops mid-sentence, I glance over my shoulder.

Jefferson is staring at us, which causes me to reflexively take a backward step, out of Fletcher's personal space. Jefferson heads past us into the bathroom without uttering a word.

"Hubby didn't look too happy just now," Fletcher jokes. "I hope he doesn't get the wrong idea. Does he know about us?"

I ignore him. "I think you should talk to Mia sooner rather than later."

"Telling her about those cases would mean I think there's a possibility that kid is mine. I'm not dealing with the drama that's going to produce unless I absolutely have to."

"Okay, you're on your own." My words feel ominously heavy as they leave my lips. "I just hope you know what you're doing."

CHAPTER 14

"You should've told me."

Special sat across from Darius at a small table outside the Starbucks in the Ladera Center. Her words were delivered without anger, but she couldn't shake the sadness from her voice.

"If I had, you never would've given me a shot."

She hesitated. "You don't know that."

"Yes, I do."

It had only been a couple of days since Darius stunned her at dinner. At the end of the date, Special had asked him to give her some time to take it all in. Earlier that day, she arranged to meet him for coffee.

"I understand why you didn't tell me in the beginning," she said, "but you could've at least told me before we met so I would've been prepared."

"And then what? You show up for dinner out of guilt, then never return my calls again?"

That was exactly what she would've done, but she wasn't about to admit it.

Special stared across the small table, admiring his sexy lips. "I just never imagined myself dating a handicapped person."

Darius grimaced and his facial features tightened. "I'm not *handicapped*. I'm a guy with a spinal cord injury."

Special pressed a hand to her chest. "Oh, Darius, I'm so sorry. I didn't mean to—"

He exhaled and didn't speak for a few seconds. "No, *I'm* sorry." He reached for her hand and squeezed it. "I overreacted. I know you didn't mean any harm. It's just that I despise that word."

"So what should I say? Is it okay to refer to you as a paraplegic?"

He exhaled. "How about just referring to me as Darius? I need you to see *me*, not my wheelchair. I hate the way people have treated me since the accident. Like I should be pitied. Most people are afraid to even look at me, much less touch me. But with the exception of the ability to walk, I'm still the same dude."

How in the world can I date this man when I don't even know the right words to say to him?

"I think we have a real connection," Darius went on. "All I want you to do is give us a chance. If it doesn't work, it doesn't work."

She took a sip of her coffee and cursed her luck, or lack thereof. There was indeed something special between them. But finding out about Darius' situation had changed everything. They could never go for a hike or wrestle in bed or have wild, crazy sex. And what would her friends and family say when she introduced them to her new boyfriend? They'd think she'd lost her mind.

"I'll tell you whatever you want to know about my situation. Just ask. Most people have a lot of misconceptions about people with spinal cord injuries."

She did indeed have a million questions. "Were you injured in the Marines?"

"Nope. About six years ago I was driving home from work, minding my own business when a long-haul truck driver fell asleep at the wheel and hit me head-on. One second my life was all good. And the next..." His voice trailed off.

Despite all the activity around them, silence engulfed their table.

"I like you a lot," Special said, almost apologetically. "A whole lot."

"Same here."

"I know you must have some more questions," Darius prodded. "I'll go ahead and answer them without you having to ask. I get around fine in my wheelchair and as you saw on our first date, I drive, too. My Lexus is equipped with hand controls."

"Everything you do for yourself, I can do for myself," Darius continued. "I don't need or want a caretaker. I got a pretty big settlement from my accident, so I was able to customize my house with furniture and appliances that are easily accessible from my wheelchair. I do all my own cooking, and I don't mean to brag, but I'm pretty good at it. I'd love to have you over for dinner sometime."

This was all too much. She needed life to be simple. Dating a man in a wheelchair was not a burden she wanted to take on. But strangely enough, she was still very much attracted to the muscular man sitting across from her. What she really wanted to ask about was sex. She wondered if what Eli had said about his pecker still working was true.

"So, um, are you able to have sex?"

Darius chuckled. "Oh, so you wanna have sex with me? That's certainly a good sign."

Special couldn't help but blush. "That's not what I said."

"Fortunately for me, that body part still works like a charm."

"Really?"

"Yep. As a matter of fact, since my injury, it's not thinking about sex that gets me going. I have what you call reflexogenic erections. Now, I can just rub it and it gets hard. Wanna feel?"

"Boy, you need to behave yourself."

They both laughed for a good long while.

"But how can you have an erection if the lower half of your body is paralyzed?" she asked.

"There are degrees of spinal cord injuries. A complete spinal cord injury means the spinal cord was completely severed, which was the case with actor Christopher Reeves. I'm an L1 incomplete. My spinal cord is partially connected, which gives me limited function below the waist. And by the way, erections aside," he says with a wink, "I possess some other bedroom skills that I'm told are pretty top-notch."

Special giggled softly. "You're a mess."

She thought about how it would feel to run her hands along his brawny arms. But a second later, she tensed with uncertainty about moving forward with him.

"You're not adverse to having a friend who happens to have a spinal cord injury, are you?"

"Of course not."

"Okay then. Consider this the beginning of a new friendship. It may go someplace or it may fizzle. Let's at least give it a shot."

There was no way she could say no to that. He was right. There was nothing wrong with being friends. But it wasn't going any further than that.

Special forced a smile, raised her empty coffee cup and feebly proposed a toast. "To our new friendship."

CHAPTER 15

After my brief telephone chat with Bliss Fenton three days ago, I'm not at all optimistic that today's meeting will lead to a quick resolution of Fletcher's paternity problem. My job, however, is to represent my client to the best of my ability. When my assistant notifies me that Bliss Fenton has arrived, I decide to personally march out to the reception area to greet her.

I like to consider myself cool under fire. But there are times when no matter how hard you try, your emotions get the best of you. That's exactly what happened when I saw Girlie Cortez standing next to the striking Bliss Fenton.

My throat suddenly goes dry and I experience a few seconds of vertigo. I'm not happy to see the most unethical attorney I've ever had the displeasure of going up against. I quickly regroup and try to play off my shock.

"Nice to meet you, Ms. Fenton." I extend my hand to her, still hoping that perhaps they aren't together.

"Nice to meet you as well," Bliss says. "I hope you don't mind, but after our conversation, I decided I should probably bring an attorney with me."

It would've been nice if Bliss had let me know she'd be bringing Girlie, but I'm beginning to see that Bliss Fenton is just as conniving as Mia and Fletcher said she was.

I nod at Girlie, who's smirking like she's just caught a hostile witness in a lie. I almost said *Nice to see you again*, but that would've been a bald-faced lie. "My office is right down this hallway."

By the time we're all seated around the table in my office, I'm sufficiently composed. My adversary, on the other hand, looks like she's been through the ringer. Admittedly, she's still an attractive woman, but she's picked up a few pounds, and her face has a bloated look that tells me she's probably been using junk food as a stress reliever.

"Didn't know you were practicing again," I say.

I'm sure Girlie doesn't like my veiled reference to her suspension, but she pretends my comment is no big deal.

"You can't keep a good woman down."

But you're not a good woman.

Bliss has a puzzled look on her face and turns to Girlie. "You quit practicing law for a while?"

"Just for a short time. I was going through some personal issues."

Personal issues my ass.

"But I'm back in full swing now. Better than ever. Let's get down to business, shall we?"

I'm itching to tell Ms. Fenton that her attorney had her license suspended. But that would be petty.

"I understand that your client wants to make my client an offer," Girlie begins.

"Yes." I reach for a pen, simply to have something to hold. "As Mr. McClain has already advised Ms. Fenton, he doesn't believe he is the father of her daughter. He took the paternity test earlier this week, but it'll be about two weeks before the results are in."

"Then why are we here? Why not wait the two weeks for the results? Maybe they'll show he isn't the father. Unless," Girlie pauses to place a finger to her chin, "Mr. McClain is well aware that he's Harmony's father and wants my client to sell herself cheap."

"I assure you, that's not the case. His concern is that once the paternity test proves he isn't the father, he might be facing other allegations from Ms. Fenton. Let's just say he's willing to buy himself some peace."

"*Other allegations?*" Bliss' eyes narrow. "Exactly what are you talking about?"

"I understand you and Fletcher's fiancée have a past. He's hoping that his offer will encourage you to move on with your life. He was pretty shocked when you showed up at that party in Hollywood and accosted Mia."

Bliss angles one of her narrow shoulders. "Nobody accosted her. She's a lying—"

Girlie rests a hand on Bliss' forearm. "We're only here for one reason. To hear Mr. McClain's offer."

I'd wanted to spend some time bonding with Bliss before putting Fletcher's offer on the table. But Girlie's presence short-circuits that plan.

"My client has authorized me to make what I consider a very generous offer in light of the circumstances," I explain. "His offer is in the six figures and it would require a strict confidentiality agreement."

"How much in the six figures?" Girlie presses.

"Let me finish before discussing the precise numbers. I've recommended that Mr. Fletcher make a two-tiered offer. One offer applies if he isn't the father, and the other if it turns out he is."

Girlie folds her arms. "Just a second ago you said he wasn't the father."

"We don't think that he is. But there are all kinds of clever ways a woman can get pregnant these days without a guy's knowledge." I smile over at Bliss, who glares back at me. "So as Mr. McClain's lawyer, I felt it was my responsibility to have him consider the possibility that he could be the father even though he'd broken up with Ms. Fenton at least eleven months before Harmony was born."

"Why don't you just get to the point?" Bliss snarls. I could tell from the twitch of her nose that my comments irked her. *Good.*

I decide not to put my full settlement authority on the table. I want to have some room to move if they seem interested.

"If, as Fletcher believes, he is not the father, he would be willing to give Ms. Fenton a one-time payment of one-hundred-and twenty-five thousand dollars."

They both chuckle in unison. I ignore them and keep going, directing my words to Bliss.

"You'd be required to sign a confidentiality agreement and you must never have any further contact with Fletcher or Mia again. This would include in person, in writing, verbally or even discussing them via social media."

Bliss rolls her eyes. "This is ridiculous. They aren't that important."

"And if he is the father, he would pay you a stipend of seven-thousand dollars a month."

Girlie and Bliss turn to face each other at precisely the same moment. This time, neither woman is laughing.

"I don't know your client's annual income," Girlie says, "but according to *Forbes* magazine, Mr. McClain has a net worth of four-hundred-and-fifty-million dollars." She glances down at a yellow legal pad. "I estimate that he makes at least ten million a year, which is probably low. But if that's the case, his child support would be about ten percent of his monthly income. I calculate that to be somewhere in the neighborhood of eighty-three thousand dollars a month. So your offer is not just low, it's insulting."

I'm stunned by the counteroffer, but don't show it. "You seem to have snatched ten million dollars out of thin air."

"Okay, then. Exactly how much does Mr. McClain make a year?"

"I'm not at liberty to disclose that information."

"Well, until we have it, accepting a settlement is not something we're willing to do. So I guess we're done here."

Girlie jumps to her feet and Bliss joins her.

"You're now on notice that Ms. Fenton is represented. So any further communications with her should come through me." Girlie speaks to me like she's scolding a child.

"No problem."

After they walk out, I debate who I should call first. Special, to commiserate about this witch being back in my life. Or Fletcher, to tell him that having Girlie Cortez on this case is an even bigger problem than going toe-to-toe with Bliss Fenton.

CHAPTER 16

Special fought off the jitters as she sat in the waiting room of Total Orthopedic Solutions, where Dr. Joseph Franco was one of five specialists on staff. When she'd made her appointment, Special claimed to be a runner with a knee injury, which wasn't a total lie. She planned to let the doctor examine her knee, then tell him the real reason for her visit.

Once she was shown into the exam room, she changed her mind about slipping into the paper gown.

Eli was right. If Bliss was as conniving as everyone claimed, Dr. Franco wouldn't have a problem dishing on her. She balled up the paper gown and stuffed it into the trashcan.

A tall man wearing a white coat and a welcoming smile entered the exam room.

"Nice to meet you." He extended his hand. "I'm Dr. Franco. My nurse should've given you a gown. I'll go—"

"I don't need a gown." Special took in a long breath. "I'm not really here for medical advice."

The doctor raised a brow and set his clipboard on the counter. "Okay...So why *are* you here?"

"I work for a private investigator and I'm hoping you can provide some information related to one of my cases."

The doctor's neck began to redden. "If you expect me to disclose confidential medical information about one of my patients, that's not going to happen."

Special realized that she better start talking and talking fast.

"Your ex-girlfriend Bliss Fenton filed a fraudulent paternity petition against my client. She claims Harmony's his daughter, but he doesn't think she is. We're hoping you'll be able to share your experiences with her. It might help my client with his case."

After an uncomfortable beat, Dr. Franco checked his watch. "I have two more patients to see before lunch. Why don't you wait for me in my office."

It was another forty minutes before Dr. Franco returned and took a seat behind his desk.

"I'll tell you straight up, Bliss Fenton is not one of my favorite people. She's a selfish, greedy, vindictive woman. Frankly, I think she could be bipolar. It worries me every day that my son has to spend most of his time with her. But before I spill my guts, why don't you tell me about your client."

Without disclosing Fletcher's identity, Special explained her theory that Bliss got pregnant by stealing her wealthy client's sperm from a condom. Dr. Franco was tongue-tied by the time she finished.

"Like I said, I always thought she was a little off, but this confirms it. I recently leased a new car. Now she's trying to increase my child support payments from ten grand to fifteen grand a month. That woman is malicious to the core."

Dr. Franco told Special that he met Bliss at a San Diego hotel, where he was attending a medical conference. Only weeks later, he moved her into his Seal Beach home. In a matter of days, he found her to be insecure and clingy and wanted her gone.

"I didn't see it then, but she has some serious abandonment issues that date back to her childhood. When I told her the relationship wasn't working for me, at first she was enraged. Being rejected seemed to ignite something wicked in her. But a day later, she had calmed down and asked for my help finding a job. She wanted to work in my office, but that would have been a disaster. We agreed that she would continue to live with me until she found a job. I also agreed to pay her rent for six months once she found a place she could afford."

Special wrote as fast as she could, trying to get it all down.

"She was super sweet for the next few weeks while she claimed she was looking for a job. That was probably when she put her plan into motion. We continued to have sex, but I always used a condom, even though she was supposedly taking the pill. When she got pregnant, I just figured it was my bad luck. But now, after what you just told me, I bet she stole my sperm and inseminated herself just like she did with your client."

Special saw nothing but regret on the doctor's face.

"I feel like such an idiot. I should've seen her coming a mile away. I think she went to that medical conference looking for an easy target like me."

According to Dr. Franco, Bliss had been raised in foster homes until she was close to ten. After that, she lived with an elderly aunt and uncle, who didn't treat her very well. Though it had never been clear to him what had happened to her parents, he suspected that they had a drug problem. During the time they lived together, she never had contact with any family members. Jessica Winthrop was the only friend he knew of.

"Well, there could be one bright side for you," Special said, hoping to cheer him up. "If it turns out the kid is his, my client's going to be on the hook for child support. And whatever it is, it's going to be a pretty big number. So Bliss will probably drop her plans to go after you for more money."

Dr. Franco arched a brow, then chuckled softly.

"You obviously don't know Bliss Fenton. It's not just about the money for her. It's about how much drama and strife she can cause for the person who rejected her. So tell your client to get ready. When it comes to getting revenge, Bliss will never have enough."

CHAPTER 17

I take the cowardly way out and decide to deliver the bad news about my failed meeting with Bliss and her attorney over the phone, rather than in person. Fletcher's had me on hold now for ten minutes.

"How did it go?" As usual, his rushed tone conveys that he has more important tasks on his plate.

"Not good," I say.

"She didn't bite?"

"She didn't even lick. The worst part is that she showed up at my office with an attorney who's more devious than Bliss could ever be. Her name is Girlie Cortez."

Fletcher doesn't say anything so I keep talking.

"To give you an indication of just how sleazy she is, she was suspended by the State Bar for allowing a client to give perjured testimony. I was the opposing counsel in that case."

Still nothing from Fletcher.

"Are you there?"

"Yeah. I'm just trying to decide whether I should jump out of the window now, or later," he jokes. "Now what?"

"We'll just have to wait for the test results. Bliss seems pretty confident that the kid is yours. She may have taken the turkey baster route."

"As I've already told you, I'm not giving that bitch fifty grand a month."

I pause for three short beats. "Actually, Bliss' attorney estimates that you make ten million a year, so she wants eighty-three grand a month."

Fletcher sputters a bit before any words actually leave his mouth. "That's insane! Start preparing that lawsuit. If she stole my sperm, I'm suing her for fraud and anything else you can come up with."

"We'll need to know the test results before we can—"

"I know that," Fletcher snaps. "If it turns out that kid is mine, I want that lawsuit ready to go so you can serve her the same day we get the results. What other claims can we add besides fraud?"

The vengeance in his voice unnerves me.

"Conversion and—"

"What's conversion?"

"The civil equivalent of theft."

"Okay." He nods his consent. "What else?"

"Intentional infliction of emotional distress."

"Great. Let's do it."

"You understand that even if you prevail, Bliss won't have the money to pay the verdict."

"She has money. She's getting child support from her other kids' fathers and she also has a townhouse in Playa Vista that's probably worth close to a million bucks."

"We can put a lien on her townhouse, but child support payments are judgment proof."

"I don't care. I still want to sue her. I want to expose exactly what she is."

"Even if it means putting your business in the street. I thought you were concerned about Mia being embarrassed by all of this."

"Mia isn't the one who might have to pay that psycho. I am. Did you hire that private investigator?"

"Yes, I have someone on it."

"They dig up anything yet?"

"I doubt it. It's only been a few days."

"Well, put a rush on it."

"I just want to make sure you understand that a lawsuit like this could generate some unwanted publicity."

"I don't care. If Bliss got pregnant by stealing my sperm, I want the world to know about it."

"Her attorney doesn't play by the rules. Are you sure you want to go to war against her?"

"What other option do I have?"

"Okay. I've given you full disclosure."

"Do I sense a little fear on your part, Vernetta? Sounds like you might be a little intimidated by Bliss' attorney."

If we were meeting in person, rather than on the phone, Fletcher would be able to see that his comment makes me bristle. "Of course not."

"Great," he says. "Consider me fully informed. Just understand this. I don't plan to sit back and let Bliss get away with this. So pull out your lawyer fangs and get to work."

CHAPTER 18

F or the past few days, Special had enjoyed getting to know Darius. Their time together, however, had been limited to lunch dates.

She'd kept making excuses when Darius suggested catching a movie or a trip to the Venice Pier or even dinner. But she could tell that Darius was growing tired of her lame excuse that she was too busy to go out at night because of all the time she was spending investigating Bliss Fenton. As a result, her growing guilt was the only reason she'd relented and decided to let him take her on a real date.

They were now headed to the AMC Dine-in Theater in Marina Del Rey to catch the latest Kevin Hart movie. When Darius found out she'd never been to the theater before, Darius insisted on taking her.

Special had suggested meeting him at the theater, but Darius insisted on picking her up from her house in Leimert Park. She'd been peering through the curtains of her living room window so she'd know the exact moment that he arrived. As soon as his car pulled up to the curb, she grabbed her purse and scurried outside. She didn't want him to have to go through the hassle of getting into his wheelchair and coming around to open the car door for her.

"Hey, Darius!" She greeted him with a super cheery smile as she eased into his Lexus. Maybe if she forced herself to sound happy she might actually feel that way.

She pecked him on the cheek before buckling her seatbelt. This was Special's first time in Darius' Lexus. She tried not to stare at the hand controls he used to operate the car, but she was curious and couldn't help herself. There was a long bar, not much bigger than a bicycle pump, connected to the brake and gas pedals. The handles at the top allowed Darius to control the pedals.

She found it odd that his legs were crossed at the ankles and off to the left. He must've caught her staring, because he smiled over at her and explained.

"I cross my legs to keep them out of the way," Darius explained. "But don't worry, I have full control of the car."

Though she felt embarrassed that she'd been caught staring, his explanation did reduce a bit of her anxiety.

"I used to come to this theater all the time before they remodeled it. Now it's the only place I like to see a movie besides my den. All the seats are reserved. I already purchased our tickets online. You're going to love it."

He seemed so happy to be out on a date with her. Special still wasn't sure how far she wanted this thing with Darius to go. If she was being honest with herself, she was only on this date because she didn't want to hurt his feelings. So far, Darius hadn't made a move toward anything physical and that was just fine with her.

"Have you seen any of Kevin Hart's other movies?" Darius asked.

"Every single one of them," Special said, breaking into a smile. "But I like his TV show, *The Real Husbands of Hollywood*, the most. That boy is a stone fool."

Maybe it was all in her head, but their small talk felt stilted. Special was so uncomfortable, in fact, that she wanted to jump out of the car while it was still rolling down the street.

Darius turned off Lincoln Boulevard onto Maxella and pulled into the underground parking structure of the Marina Marketplace. It was usually hard to find parking in this complex on a Saturday night, but in no time Darius spotted a handicapped stall and eased his car into it. At least being with Darius meant access to prime parking.

She reached over to unhook her seatbelt when Darius placed his hand on her arm.

"I need you to relax. I promise you're going to have a good time tonight."

Before she could lie and say she *was* relaxed, he leaned over, lifted her chin and kissed her. When his tongue slipped between her lips, she felt her body quiver. He took his time, savoring her, then pressed his forehead to hers and held it there for several seconds.

Wowza!

That was the most sensual first kiss she'd ever experienced. The boy had skills in the lip-locking department. He pulled away sooner than she actually wanted him too.

Special flung the car door open and hopped out. As Darius prepared to extract himself from the car, Special remained standing near the passenger door pretending to look through her purse. She half watched as he reached into the backseat and pulled the base of his folded wheelchair between the seats.

After unfolding it and setting it just outside the open car door, he reached into the backseat again for one wheel and snapped it onto the chair. Then repeated the move with the other wheel. After adding a seat cushion and locking the wheels in place, he hoisted his body from the car to the chair.

He released the brakes, rolled backward and closed the car door. "Ready?" he asked, whirling around to face her.

Special walked next to him, careful to make sure she wasn't moving too fast or too slow. She'd dated a couple of men who were shorter than her, but this felt like walking alongside a child. Next time, she would wear flats.

They headed up a ramp that took them to the top level of the complex. Walking past a couple of restaurants, they reached the theater in seconds. Special had planned to open the door for him, but Darius got there first.

"After you, beautiful lady."

To Special's surprise, the lobby looked more like a nightclub than a movie theater. It had a full bar, as well as lounge chairs and cocktail tables. Special prayed Darius didn't want to hang out in the bar. She scanned the area hoping she didn't spot anyone she knew. It would be just her luck to run into one of her nosy ass co-workers. She could imagine Reetha or Kiana running back to the office and blabbing that Special was so hard up she was dating a man in a wheelchair.

Luckily, Darius never even glanced in the direction of the bar. After the attendant scanned their tickets on his phone, they headed straight for the theater. Once again, he opened the door for her before she could open it for him. She was surprised at how nimble he was in his wheelchair.

"Our seats are on the back row," he said.

Special sank into one of the big red leather chairs that reclined like her daddy's favorite resting spot. Darius pulled his wheelchair into an open space next to her that was reserved for handicapped seating. The theater had a massive screen so every seat in the house was a good one.

"These chairs are fabulous," she said, propping up her feet on the footrest.

"I knew you'd like it. They have waiters who come around to serve you and you can even order drinks."

It wasn't long before a team of waiters dressed in black poured into the theater. Special ordered the carne asada tacos and a glass of white wine. Darius had the fish and chips and a rum and Coke. Special wanted to order a Long Island Iced Tea, but after the kiss that brother had laid on her, she needed to have all of her senses intact. Just fantasizing about the next kiss made her moist.

Without warning, Darius leaned over and kissed her again.

"I don't remember giving you permission to kiss me again," she teased.

"Yes, you did."

"And when did I do that?"

"The way you kissed me in the car, I could tell you wanted me to do it again."

"You sure have a lot of confidence."

"Always have, always will."

This brother was everything he had professed to be in his MyHarmony.com profile, except that...

Stop it!

Focusing on his disability had to stop. Darius had one con and a ton of pros. It made sense to at least enjoy all the good things about him.

They were done eating by the time the movie trailers were over. With her belly full and the light buzz from the wine, Special hoped she'd be able to stay awake for the movie. Darius took her hand, which felt good in his. By the time the movie was over, she couldn't remember the last time, she'd laughed so hard.

"Kevin Hart is crazy," Special said, still cracking up.

"And crazy is making him some big time bucks."

Special was on her feet when she realized that Darius hadn't moved. As she quickly sat back down, she realized that he was waiting for the crowd to dissipate, which would make it easier to exit the theater in his wheelchair. If she was going to make this work, she had to start thinking more about him. She fished around in her purse, found her lipstick and started touching up her lips.

Darius gave her an odd look, as if she was doing something wrong.

"What's the matter?" she asked.

"I don't know why you're putting that lipstick on. I'm just going to kiss it off."

Special blushed like a schoolgirl. *I hope you do.*

CHAPTER 19

Fletcher McClain learned a long time ago that smart businessmen cut their losses early and move on. That was the only reason he was sitting at a table at Fig & Olive on Melrose, waiting for Bliss Fenton to arrive.

When his assistant Gabriella contacted Bliss to extend the lunch invitation, Fletcher had listened in on the call. Bliss had, of course, been curious about the reason for the invitation, but Fletcher never doubted that she would accept.

The sole purpose of this meeting was to do what Vernetta had failed to do: negotiate a reasonable child support arrangement with Bliss to keep the legal system out of his financial affairs. If the kid turned out to be his and the matter got before a judge, he would most certainly get screwed.

What Fletcher planned to propose was more than generous, double what Vernetta had offered her.

He had a document setting forth the terms drafted by a lawyer he played golf with who'd been sworn to secrecy.

Although he'd been lost in the anxiety of his own thoughts, Fletcher sensed the precise moment that Bliss entered the restaurant even before spotting her. He saw several men shift their gaze in her direction as if controlled by a switch. Bliss had that kind of effect.

The woman was still a beauty. He liked the way her sexiness pushed the envelope, but didn't quite open it. She was dressed today in a simple white dress with bold black lines that outlined her slender body. No excessive cleavage, just enough to spark the imagination. No skirt hiked up to crotch-level. Bliss had a flirtatious air about her that she'd probably been born with.

Despite her stunning looks, Fletcher had never considered her anything more than a good time. A woman would need to be much more than a great lay for him to consider her marriage material. Aside from her natural beauty and her superb skills in the bedroom, Bliss didn't have much else going for her. Mia might never surpass Bliss' skills in the bedroom, but on the intellectual front, it was like comparing a first grader to a Ph.D.

Fletcher stood and pulled out her chair. "How are you, Bliss?"

"A little curious."

She sat down across from him and placed her small clutch on the table.

"Your assistant was pretty tight-lipped about why you wanted to have lunch with me."

"That's my Bliss. Always one to get right to the point."

"Wow. *My Bliss.* I like the sound of that. But I suspect Mia might not."

It was not going to be easy for Fletcher to keep his cool, but there was no question that he must. He'd negotiated marathon deals with some of the biggest a-holes on the planet. If he could survive that without putting his fist through a wall, he could manage the next hour with this female psychopath. He'd begin by taking the highroad.

"I'm sorry we're in this situation. I—"

"*Situation?* Is that what you call bringing a child into the world? A *situation?*"

Fletcher refused to take the bait.

"I invited you to lunch because I'd like to put an end to this. Let's consider this a private mediation. Forget what my attorney offered you. I have a much better deal."

"Sounds like I should have brought my attorney with me."

"Not necessary. I think you're smart enough to make decisions for yourself."

"Apparently not as smart as the brilliant Mia Richardson. Is that why you chose her over me? Her amazing intellect? It couldn't have been her skills beneath the sheets. On that front, I'm pretty sure I was the best you've ever had."

Fletcher tried not to let his expression convey that she was right. The subtle rumbling in his groin only seconded her statement.

He looked around for the waiter. "Maybe we should order lunch first. They have an excellent dirty martini."

Bliss giggled. "Oh, so you plan to get me drunk before you screw me."

Fletcher's lips flattened into a tight, thin line. "Look, Bliss, I'm sorry about the way it went down between us. Sometimes things happen that are just out of our control."

"That is so true. It was certainly like that every time I gave you head. When I was on my knees taking every inch of you down my throat, everything was completely within my control, not yours."

He was getting aroused and it pissed him off.

"Are you hard yet?" Bliss eyed him over the rim of the glass. "It never took you long. If you are, we could have your driver disappear for a bit and have a quickie in the backseat. You always enjoyed it when I blew you in the car."

Fletcher averted his eyes, but what he wanted to do was slam his fist on the table. "Why don't I tell you what I'm proposing?"

He pulled an envelope from the inside pocket of his jacket.

"I don't think the kid is mine, but to buy myself some peace, I'm going to make you the following offer." He opened the envelope, took out a cashier's check and set it on the table.

"This check is made out to you for two-hundred-and-fifty-thousand dollars." He then pulled out a document. "If you sign this settlement and confidentiality agreement right now, that check is yours. We both go our separate ways. That means no more surprise visits at parties you're not invited to and no contact whatsoever with either me or Mia. Now, if by some miracle, it turns out that the kid is mine, that agreement says I'll pay you fifteen grand a month until the kid is eighteen. Of course, I'll also cover private school and college tuition, and you can keep the two-fifty."

Bliss showed no reaction.

"But you'll have to sign the agreement right now, right here, or the deal's off."

He took out a silver pen and held it out to her, but she didn't reach for it, forcing him to set it on the table.

"This makes everything fast and convenient. Neither one of us will have to hire an attorney and go through a long court fight. It's a win-win for both of us."

Bliss took a slow sip of water.

"The fact that you doubled the offer your attorney made tells me you're running scared." There was no emotion in her voice. "But I'm really disappointed that your offer doesn't mention anything about visitation rights. You want to be part of your daughter's life, don't you? Your mother would love to have a granddaughter."

Fletcher sucked in a breath and scratched his jaw. "Let's handle that after the test results are in."

Even if she was his, he wasn't sure he wanted anything to do with the child. Raising Bliss' kid would certainly be an issue for Mia.

"Would you like to see a picture of your daughter?" Bliss took a photograph from her purse and set it on the table in front of him. "Everybody always says Jonas is the spitting image of me. Well, I think Harmony looks exactly like you."

He didn't want to look at it, but the photograph seemed to draw his eyes in. The child was as beautiful as her mother. He studied her for signs of himself. She had Bliss' blue eyes and golden hair. Contrary to what Bliss had just said, he saw nothing that branded her as a McClain.

"She's a cute kid."

Bliss batted her lashes. "I'm just glad she has your nose and not mine."

Fletcher picked up the photograph and placed it back on her side of the table.

Bliss set it back in front of him. "You should have at least one picture of your daughter."

He pointed at the envelope. "That document lays out everything I just proposed. It's only four pages. I made sure my attorney didn't include a lot of confusing legal jargon. He wrote it in clear, plain language."

A flash of anger streaked across Bliss' face. "Don't insult me. I may not be a law school graduate like your little chocolate mocha, but I don't need *plain language.*"

"I didn't mean it like that. I only wanted—"

"What you want is for me to act like the bimbo that you think I am. Two-fifty? Fifteen grand a month? You must be kidding."

Fletcher wiped his palm down his face. Brokering this deal was turning out to be harder than any contract he'd negotiated all year.

"I'm curious, Bliss." He propped his elbow on the back of his chair. "Just how much child support would be enough for you?"

"My daughter is entitled to a lifestyle consistent with the income of both of her parents. And lucky for Harmony, her father happens to be filthy rich."

"Go on."

"I'm very much interested in negotiating an agreement with you, but let's make it a lump-sum payment. I don't want to have to wait for your check to arrive in the mail every month."

He liked the idea of paying Bliss off and never having to think about her again.

"And just how much of a lump sum are we talking about?"

"After reading that *Forbes* article, my attorney says you probably make at least ten-million dollars a year, and I'm entitled to ten percent to care for your daughter. That would be approximately eighty-three grand a month. But if you're willing to give me a lump sum payment, I'll give you a big discount and accept forty thousand dollars a month. I already did the math. Over eighteen years, that would be eight-point-six million and change. That's what I want. Eight-point-six million dollars."

Fletcher felt a rush of heat inflame his chest. He'd been proud of that *Forbes* article and the fact that it let the world know just how much of a baller he was. Now, he viewed it as a curse.

"Pay me a measly eight-point-six million," Bliss repeated, "and your daughter and I will be out of your life for good."

Fletcher had a habit of smiling when he was actually seething inside. It worked great during deals and it benefited him now in this crowded restaurant.

"I need you to hear me and hear me clearly."

Fletcher placed both forearms flat on the table and leaned forward until the tip of his nose almost touched hers.

"If that kid is mine, I'm going to accept my legal obligations and do right by both of you. But if you insist on being a greedy cunt about this, your precious little daughter could very well end up motherless."

Bliss' smile was twice as big as his. "So you're threatening me?"

"It's not a threat at all." He could feel her warm breath on his face. "It's a promise."

CHAPTER 20

When I see Girlie Cortez's name appear on the display of my desk phone, I know it's going to be a bad day. I wait until after the third ring before picking up.

"Hello, this is—"

She doesn't allow me to get my greeting out.

"I don't know what kind of game you and your rich client are playing, but I'm not having it." Her tone is all attitude.

I massage my eyes with my thumb and forefinger. "Good morning to you too. I have no idea what you're talking about."

"If that's the way you want to play it, fine. Just understand that if Fletcher McClain contacts my client again to discuss settlement without my authorization, I'm going to file a motion with the court and bring both of you before the judge."

I sit up. I knew nothing about Fletcher meeting with Bliss, but refrain from denying it until I've had a chance to speak with him.

"I wasn't aware that Fletcher had spoken to Bliss. And frankly, there's no reason the two of them can't discuss their case. Perhaps you need a little refresher on the law."

"He presented her with a settlement agreement and threatened her after she refused to sign it right there on the spot. Did you draft that agreement?"

"As I just told you, I have no idea what you're talking about."

"That was a yes or no question, Ms. Henderson. But don't bother responding, you've just told me the answer. Luckily, my client isn't as stupid as either of you thinks she is. First, you insult her with an offer of seven thousand dollars a month, then Mr. McClain ups it to fifteen grand. It seems to me that your client is pretty worried about the results of his paternity test."

"Time will tell," I say.

"Indeed it will. You can tell Mr. McClain to forget about that discount Bliss mentioned at lunch. We want the full eighty-three grand a month, and we're going to get it."

"You'll never see that in a million years."

Girlie chuckles. "As you say, time will tell. Just remember that—"

I know it's childish of me, but I hang up in her face. If I hadn't, I might've challenged her to meet me in the alley behind my office. I've never had another opposing counsel get to me the way Girlie Cortez does.

I dial Special's number. "You need to pray for me because I want to strangle Girlie Cortez."

"Dang, she's acting up already."

"I just hung up in her face."

Special laughs. "That heffa sure knows how to push your buttons."

I give her a quick recap of my call with Girlie.

"Girl, your boy Fletcher may be in for some big trouble. I think Bliss Fenton intentionally targets wealthy men. I talked to the father of her oldest son Aiden and he says watch out. The curious thing is, I can't find a thing about the father of her middle child, Jonas. I think that baby daddy must've paid her off in order to protect his identity. That would explain how she's living in an expensive townhouse in Playa Vista. There's no way she can cover her expenses just with what she's getting from Aiden's father."

"That information could be pretty helpful in our fraud case if it turns out that Fletcher is the father. So keep digging."

"And you take it easy," Special counsels me. "The next time you have a meeting with that wench, call me. I want to be there."

"Oh, that would go over well. I'd be the one pulling you off of her."

"Hey, whatever works."

"So how's it going with Darius?" Special had called me in tears after their first date, but I urged her to give him a shot.

She hesitates. "It's going."

"That doesn't sound too positive."

"We're getting to know each other. We went to the movies the other night."

"I'm proud of you for hanging in there with him."

"I've been doing a lot of research online about the disabled."

"Well, first you need to stop referring to him as disabled. I litigated a disability discrimination case once and it turned out to be a real education. The preferred term now is *people with access and functional needs.*"

"Girl, that's too long. I ain't saying all of that. That's why I still say Black instead of African-American."

I laugh. "If you like hanging out with him, just enjoy the time you spend together. Don't focus on the fact that he's in a wheelchair."

"That's the same thing Darius told me. He's actually a lot of fun. Sometimes I almost forget he's in the wheelchair."

"Just make sure you give enough attention to this case. With Girlie Cortez involved, we need to be prepared for all-out war. And I need as much ammunition as I can get."

CHAPTER 21

Fletcher refuses to take my call, so I send him an email explaining why he should not have any further communications with Bliss. Five minutes later, I receive a two-word response.

Got it.

I leave work early and pick up some Thai food. Jefferson and I have a date to binge-watch *Ray Donovan*. I slip into my favorite sweats and cuddle up next to him on the couch.

It's great to put my day behind me and relax. For the time being, I decide not to tell Jefferson that Girlie Cortez is my new opposing counsel. Girlie brought nothing but stress into my life during our last case. He'd probably want me to drop Fletcher as a client.

Just when I'm beginning to think I'm off the hook and Jefferson has forgotten about my little covert conversation with Fletcher at his party, he brings it up out of nowhere.

"Your boy Fletcher has some issues."

Here it comes. "Is that right?"

"Yep. He ain't the baller he pretends to be."

A siren starts wailing in my head. Fletcher McClain is not a topic I want to discuss with my hubby tonight. It's been a few days since the party. I had expected Jefferson to bring it up on the ride home. But he spent most of the drive teasing me about how much I favored Mia.

"Can we talk about something else?" I say.

Jefferson keeps going even though he knows I hate it when he talks while we're watching TV.

"Dudes who have real money don't spend all their time bragging about it. And I hate it when white guys try to act like they're black."

I don't say a word, hoping he will move on to another topic.

"So what's going on with his case?"

"Just waiting for the results of the paternity test. He should have them next week."

"Does the kid look like him?"

"I don't know. I haven't seen her. And anyway it would probably be hard to tell just by looking at her. She's only three months old."

"Has he even seen her?"

"I don't think so."

"If it were me, I'd want to at least take a look at the kid. But then again, I have strong genes. I'd know my blood right away."

"Yeah, sure you would."

We go back to watching TV and I'm hoping Jefferson withholds his next comment until the commercial break. But then I remember that we're watching Netflix. So there are no commercial breaks.

"I think the dude wants to get into your pants," he says.

"No, he doesn't. He's about to marry a very smart, attractive woman."

"A smart, attractive woman who favors you. I used to work with a white dude who had it bad for sistas. Your boy Fletcher has that same thing going on. He's even got a fine-ass black housekeeper answering his door. Is his secretary black, too?"

"Nope. She's from El Salvador."

"Figures. Does he even like white women?"

"His maybe-baby mama is white."

"That's probably why he's being so hard on her. Dude don't like white chicks."

I place a finger to my lips, a signal for Jefferson to be quiet. "We're missing the good part."

He picks up the remote and pauses the TV.

"That night when I saw you in the hallway at his place, you guys were standing close enough to kiss. What were you talking about?"

There it is.

My man is so true to his nature. It's rare for Jefferson to fly off the handle. He prefers to let things simmer. That question has obviously been simmering for a while. I'm offended that he thinks I might be messing around with a client, right in front of his nose, no less. And I want to tell him that. But I know better than to stonewall him. I've learned over the years that the best course of action is to proceed with caution. To keep this conversation from turning into a full-fledged argument, I need to answer his question calmly and without attitude.

Jefferson has turned to face me, but my eyes are glued to the frozen TV screen. If I look at him, I might just tell him to grow up.

"We were discussing the case," I say.

"Why were you standing so close to him?"

"Because I didn't want Mia to hear what we were saying."

"So what were you saying?"

I tell Jefferson about the turkey baster cases and my theory that Bliss may have gotten pregnant by inseminating herself. I explain that I was trying to convince Fletcher to prepare Mia for that possibility, just in case the paternity test tagged him as the father.

"Why are you so convinced that the girl set him up?"

"Because Fletcher swears he hasn't slept with her in over a year. It just makes sense. I don't think Bliss would go to the trouble of filing a paternity petition if the kid wasn't his. If she knew the test would prove that Fletcher wasn't the father, she'd be trying to get some quick cash to go away without waiting for the results. Since he hadn't slept with her for almost a year before the kid was born, the only way she could be his is if she stole his sperm."

"Unless your boy is lying to you about the last time he boned her."

"He has no reason to lie to me. I'm his lawyer. Clients tell their lawyers everything."

"And how many times has that *not* happened?" His voice is drenched in sarcasm.

He has a point. "More than it should have," I say with a laugh. "Can we finish watching *Ray Donovan* now? Pretty please."

I reach for the remote, but Jefferson holds it out of my reach.

"Dude's lying to you. That kid is his. He's going through this denial farce because he doesn't want your twin sister to find out he screwed his ex after he got with her."

"And you know this how?"

Jefferson hunches his shoulders. "It's just a feeling."

"Okay, great. Time will tell. Now please un-pause the TV."

"You know dude was checking out your ass every time you walked by, right?"

"A lot of guys check out my ass. I have a nice ass."

"Is that right?"

"Yep, that's how I got you, isn't it?"

He cocks his head. "True dat."

He kisses me, then slides his hand underneath my thigh and squeezes my left butt cheek.

"His girl looks a lot like you, but she ain't got nothing on you when it comes to your ass."

I kiss him back. "So who's cuter, me or her?"

"Hmmm." Jefferson rubs his chin with his free hand, then hits a button on the remote, returning sound to the room. "Let's just finish watching TV."

This time *I* grab the remote and pause the TV.

"Boy, you better answer my question."

I climb into his lap, straddling him, not at all surprised to feel his erection. He nuzzles his nose between my breasts.

"And if you don't answer it the right way," I threaten him, "you may not get a treat tonight."

Jefferson grins up at me. "You, baby," he mumbles, kissing my breasts. "Ain't nobody finer than you."

CHAPTER 22

"Will you please stop frowning? You look absolutely fabulous."
Bliss and Jessica were in a dressing room at Bloomingdale's in the Century City Mall. Bliss had outfitted her in a short, skirt and a low-cut T-strap blouse.

Jessica turned sideways in the mirror. "I'm not really sure Paul will like this. He's very conservative."

"Forget about Paul for now. What about you? Do you like it? Don't you feel sexy?"

A shy smile eased its way across Jessica's thin lips. "Kinda."

Before hitting the mall, Bliss had taken Jessica to her colorist, who brought Jessica's hair to life with some bright cinnamon highlights and large, spiral curls.

"But I do love my hair." She swung her head so that the curls danced around her face. "I've always wanted to color my hair, but Paul said he liked it the way it was."

"Trust me, if he liked it the way it was, you wouldn't be suspecting him of cheating."

At that comment, Jessica's eyes fell and her shoulders slumped, but Bliss didn't seem to notice.

"Just wait. He'll like everything about the new you. I wish I could be there when you meet him for dinner tonight. If he does have a mistress, he'll be dumping her and running back home to you."

"Thanks for the constant reminder."

Bliss gave her friend a hug. "I'm sorry. To be honest, I really don't think Paul is messing around. He loves his work too much. If anything, his job is his mistress. He doesn't seem like the cheating type."

"You're confusing me. I thought you said all men cheat."

"No. I said all men *want* to cheat. A lot of them are just too scared to do it. God didn't make men with a monogamy gene. Your hubby is just overworked. You two will be fine. Especially once he sees you in that outfit."

Bliss' phone rang. She glanced at the screen, then hit decline. "Anamaria again. I'll call her when we're done."

"It's probably something with the kids." Jessica's face was heavy with concern. "Call her back."

"I guarantee you it's not important." Bliss handed her phone to Jessica. "Anamaria's always overreacting. You call her."

Bliss tried on a short leather skirt as Jessica called her back.

As Jessica listened, her face clouded. "There's some baby aspirin in the medicine cabinet. We're leaving now." She started peeling off her clothes before even hanging up.

"It's Jonas, right?" Bliss said. "He's always faking."

"I don't believe you. Kids can't fake fevers. And anyway, it's not Jonas, it's Harmony. We're going home to check on her."

Bliss pouted. "She'll be fine. I had my mouth all set for the stuffed mushrooms at Seasons 52."

"Bliss! We need to go home."

"We will. Right after we finish eating. I'm beginning to think you're obsessed with my daughter. You better not turn out to be one of those crazies who kidnaps her friend's kid and starts pretending that she's the mother."

A look of genuine hurt spread across Jessica's face, which then blazed into anger. But instead of voicing what she felt, Jessica turned away and mumbled under her breath. "Your kids would be a lot better off living with me."

"What did you say?"

Jessica was immediately apologetic. "I'm sorry. You know how much I want kids. It just bothers me that you're not more concerned about Harmony. I shouldn't have said that."

"Apology accepted." Bliss blew her a kiss. "But we *are* having lunch. I'm driving, remember? So unless you're going to take a cab back to my place to check on Harmony, you're stuck."

Halfway through their meal, Bliss stuck her hand across the table. "Give me your earphones."

"My earphones? Why?"

"Just give them to me."

Jessica pulled them from her purse and watched as Bliss plugged them into her phone.

"I had lunch with Fletcher on Monday and something told me to tape it. So I turned on the recorder on my iPhone right before I sat down and left my purse open on the table. And I'm so glad I did."

Bliss handed the earphones back to Jessica and once she'd placed them in her ears, Bliss tapped the screen of her phone. "Listen to this."

In seconds, Jessica's face went from blank to bewildered. When she finally removed the earphones, her eyes were wide with fear. "I can't believe Fletcher threatened you like that. I'd be concerned if I were you."

Bliss swiped the worry from the air with a flicker of her fingers. "I'm not afraid of him. But just in case, I'm emailing you a copy of this recording for safekeeping."

"I can't believe you turned down fifteen thousand dollars a month. Have you lost your mind?"

"I'm entitled to a whole lot more than that and Fletcher knows it. That's why he tried to get me to sign that agreement right there on the spot. He thinks I'm stupid. Joseph does too. We have a hearing date next week to hear my request for more child support for Aiden."

"Bliss, you need to be careful. People are murdered over a lot less money than we're talking about here. And you have not one, but two men that you're putting to the test."

"Relax, my friend. I have everything under control."

Thirty minutes later, when they had entered the parking structure, Jessica spotted Mia three parking stalls away. To Jessica's dismay, the two enemies had already locked eyes.

Mia was charging toward them like an attack dog with tunnel vision.

Jessica snatched Bliss by the arm. "Let's go."

"No way. I'm staying right here." Bliss shoved her bags at Jessica and planted herself like a tree stump.

"Bliss, Harmony needs us. We have to—"

"Which baby daddy's money are you spending today?" Mia asked, getting in Bliss' face.

"Whoever's money I'm spending, it's none of your damn business."

"I guess we'll be seeing you in court soon. Make sure you save some of your child support money for the jury award we'll be getting. And just so you know, that defamation lawsuit was *my* idea."

Bliss' forehead creased. "What defamation lawsuit?"

"Don't play dumb. The one Fletcher served you with last week."

"No, sweetie, Fletcher hasn't served me with a lawsuit. And he didn't say a word about defamation when he treated me to lunch yesterday at Fig & Olive."

"You lying whore."

Bliss knew she had her. "You should keep better track of your man. Fletcher wanted to discuss child support arrangements. Offered me fifteen thousand dollars a month. I don't know what lie he's telling you, but he knows he's Harmony's father."

Mia seemed to sway unsteadily, even though she was wearing flats.

"Bliss, let's go." Jessica pulled her several feet away, but Bliss turned back to yell another taunt.

"Looks like you're going to be a step-mama."

Mia just stood there, as if she'd been slapped into silence.

"You're just plain evil!" Jessica hurled their bags into the backseat and climbed into the car. "There was absolutely no reason in the world for you to do that."

"Perhaps," Bliss said with a look of total satisfaction. "But I certainly loved every minute of it."

CHAPTER 23

Every other block or so, Special fought the urge to make an illegal U-turn and hightail it back home.

What the hell am I doing?

Although things had been great with Darius, she didn't know where she wanted to take this. Sooner or later, he would want to do more than just kiss and she wasn't sure she would ever be ready to go that far. She should just cut the strings now instead of letting guilt force her to show up for yet another date.

Before she knew it, she was turning off Sepulveda Boulevard onto 77th Avenue, then made a quick right onto Arizona street.

"Wow. This brother is livin' hella large," Special said, taking in the expansive ranch style homes in Darius' Westchester neighborhood. "I wouldn't mind living up in here."

Pulling to a stop, she checked her lipstick in the rearview mirror, climbed out of the car and straightened her skirt. It was sufficiently short and, this time, her cleavage was on full display in a midriff tank top. She might as well give the brother a treat since it had probably been years since he'd been with a woman. At least one of her caliber.

She was about to knock on the door when it opened. Darius rolled back his wheelchair to allow her inside.

He whistled. "You look amazing."

Special's eyes were glued on the L.A. skyline through the large picture window in front of her. She'd only seen views like this in Baldwin Hills and View Park. But she didn't want to seem easily impressed, so she kept it to herself.

"Thank you, sir. Nice place. And something certainly smells good."

"Just a little something I threw together."

She followed him into the dining room where the table was set with candlelights and colorful matching plates and glasses. The food sat near the end of the table in chaffing dishes.

"I made red snapper, brown rice, broccoli spears and my special German chocolate cake."

"Alright now. I love a man who can throw down in the kitchen."

"And I know I shouldn't brag, but I'm quite the cook. Have a seat while I get the wine."

"I can help you," Special said, making a move to follow him.

Darius stopped her. "Beautiful lady, I have everything under control. Please have a seat."

Special tensed as she sat down. She'd spent a couple of hours online researching the do's and don'ts of dating a paraplegic. And one of the biggest no-no's was treating them like they needed help with everything. She had to remember that.

She peered into the kitchen and saw that the counters, cabinets and even the stove, were a few inches shorter than the norm. She saw a long stick with a hook on the end of it, which she assumed he used to grab items on the upper shelves.

Darius returned with the wine bottle already uncorked. He rolled his wheelchair up to the table, then took her wineglass and filled it. At that moment, she was not on a date with a man in a wheelchair. She was sitting across from a gorgeous, sexy man who had prepared a romantic dinner for her and it felt wonderful.

Darius picked up her plate and started to fill it with food.

"Oh, Darius, I can do that. Let me—"

He hung his head and kept it there, then slowly raised it. "Special, I'd like to fix your plate and that's what I'm going to do."

"Okay, okay. Sorry."

She clasped her hands together underneath the table and again reminded herself to kick back and let him run the show.

Darius finished fixing her plate, then made one for himself.

Special took a bite of red snapper. "Oh my God! This is fabulous."

Darius smiled. "Thanks."

She squinted at him. "Did you really cook this? If I go through your trash am I going to find takeout containers from some gourmet restaurant?"

"Nope. All my doing."

They laughed and joked all through dinner. Darius was smart and funny and made her giggle like a schoolgirl. After setting the dishes in the sink, they moved into the den.

"I'm a bit of a movie buff. I have an extensive collection." Darius handed her a sheet of paper with his alphabetized movie list. "Take your pick."

Special scanned the paper. "Wow. You must have every movie ever made."

Darius smiled. "Not quite."

She started to pick a romantic comedy, but didn't want Darius to get any ideas if there were any sex scenes. So she chose an action adventure staring Bradley Cooper instead. They cuddled together on the couch underneath a blanket.

Twenty minutes later, they were making out like two horny teenagers. She wasn't sure how long they'd been at it when he gently took her hand and placed it on his groin.

"Feel that?" he said between kisses. "I told you my equipment still works. See what you made it do."

Special slid her hand away. She could handle a little necking, but she wasn't ready to have sex with the man. Not yet. Maybe not ever.

"Uh...I should help you clean up the kitchen," she mumbled.

"The kitchen can wait."

Darius was licking her neck now, and despite her mental misgivings, her body didn't want him to stop.

When his hand crawled beneath her skirt, she sprang forward, then jumped to her feet.

"Uh...why don't I clean up the kitchen for you. That's the least I can do after that great meal you prepared for me."

She was out of the room before Darius could stop her.

He joined her in the kitchen, remaining in the doorway, watching her as she rinsed the dishes in the sink.

"I have a dishwasher, you know."

"I saw it. I just felt like doing it the old-fashioned way."

The room fell quiet except for the running of the water and the tinkling of the dishes.

"I know dating a guy in my situation is a little strange for you. So I'm going to give you as much time as you need to get used to things. Okay?"

She turned around to face him. "Thanks. I really do like you a lot."

"I know you do."

"You certainly sound awful confident about that."

"I am."

He rolled his wheelchair over to her and she bent to hug him, throwing her arms around his massive chest. Everything felt so normal when she hugged him like this. She wasn't sure how long they were in that position before she felt his fingers creeping up her skirt, sensually massaging her thighs as they climbed higher and higher.

She loved the way he took his time and how his fingertips were so soft. He eased down her panties and touched her in places that made her whimper. When he leaned forward and buried his tongue between her thighs her body went limp.

"Darius, I—" Special tried, but couldn't finish the thought.

As he went to work, expertly, delicately pleasuring her, she felt shivers of gratification igniting every nerve in her body. As her moans intensified, so did the swaying of her body. But Darius held onto her—a slender thigh in each one of his massive hands—refusing to let her lean too far to the left or right, despite the involuntary spasms of pleasure overwhelming her senses.

When she finally climaxed, harder and stronger than she could ever remember, she fell forward, collapsing into the wheelchair along with him.

It was close to a minute before her eyes met his. A proud smile lit up his face.

"See," Darius said, peppering her face with kisses. "I told you I had some top-notch skills."

CHAPTER 24

When Gabriella walked into the eighth-floor conference room at Karma Entertainment and slipped Fletcher a note, anxiety pressed down on him like a heavy boulder that wouldn't budge.

Gabriella's handwritten message stated that Mia needed to speak to him immediately and that she was very upset. Mia rarely came to his office, especially not in the middle of the afternoon, so Fletcher knew it was something major. His best guess was more drama from Bliss. He told his second-in-command to carry on with the meeting as he followed Gabriella out of the room.

"How dare you lie to me!" Mia yelled, even before he stepped inside his office.

Fletcher closed the door behind him. "Honey, why are you so upset? What are you talking about?"

"I just ran into your ex-girlfriend. She claims you didn't sue her for defamation like you told me you did. And that you offered to pay her child support. Is that true?"

"Honey, please sit down and lower your voice."

"You need to tell me—"

"I said sit down!" Fletcher's voice boomed across the room. "I need you to be quiet for a second and listen to me."

Mia obeyed his command and fell into one of the chairs in front of his desk. Her mouth had been silenced, but her eyes still raged.

Fletcher took the chair next to her, repositioning it so they faced each other. He reached for Mia's hand, but she snatched it away.

"Vernetta and I have a strategy here. We—"

"You took that whore to lunch and offered her fifteen thousand dollars a month? What kind of strategy is that?"

Since the anxiety level in the room was already off the scale, Fletcher tried to take it down a notch.

"Please, sweetheart, I need you to listen to me. When I'm finished, I promise you're going to understand everything, okay?"

Blinking back tears, Mia slowly nodded. Fletcher took her hand and this time she let him.

He had to think fast. Now was probably a good time to tell Mia about the turkey baster cases, but he was still reluctant to do that. Fletcher was used to rolling the dice. It was almost as if voicing the possibility that Bliss' child might be his would make it so. In his mind, if he kept telling himself the kid wasn't his, she wouldn't be.

"I'm sorry I let you think I'd sued her for defamation. That's not off the table, but like I said, Vernetta had another strategy that I wanted to pursue first. She thinks Bliss simply wants money. So she thought I should offer her two-fifty to see if she would jump at it. And if Bliss—"

"Two-fifty?" Mia squinted. "Bliss didn't mention that."

Fletcher felt like pumping his fist. The tale he was spinning was going to work out just fine.

"Of course Bliss didn't tell you the full story. We're talking about a very vindictive woman. I offered her a two-part deal, subject to a confidentiality agreement. Two-hundred-and-fifty-thousand dollars to go away and never contact either one of us again. And if the kid somehow turned out to be mine, she'd get fifteen thousand dollars a month in child support. I only agreed to that much because Vernetta says I could be on the hook for a whole lot more."

He made a mental note to make sure Vernetta backed up his story that this was all her idea in the event Mia ever approached her to verify his lie.

"But I don't understand why you would offer to pay child support for a kid that isn't yours."

"I only offered to pay her child support *if* the kid turned out to be mine. Vernetta described it as a preemptive strike. She figured that if

Bliss was lying about me being the father, she would jump at the two-fifty and disappear."

Mia revved up again. "But she didn't jump at it. So what the hell does that mean?"

"It means Bliss has something else up her sleeve. You know better than I do that she's vindictive and mean-spirited and nobody knows what's in her messed-up little head. All I know is that kid isn't mine."

He could see Mia's mind working through the line of thinking he'd just laid out. He also noticed that she seemed to soften every time he maligned Bliss. He would need to do more of that.

"But you never slept with her after we got together. So it's impossible that baby is yours."

"C'mon, Mia. You know how devious that sick whore is. I actually had a nightmare that she paid someone at the testing facility to forge the test results. I asked the guy who took my blood and he said it could happen. I wouldn't put anything past her."

Mia just stared at him.

"You and I are getting married in the South of France and we're going to live a wonderful life together. My primary goal in life is to make you happy."

He squeezed Mia's hand and she squeezed back. He had her.

"Bliss pulled this stunt because she wants to upset you," Fletcher continued, more impassioned now. "Spending two-fifty to be over and done with her would've been well worth it. The fact that she didn't take it means she has more bullets to shoot at us and we have to be ready for the fight. She wants to destroy our relationship. But I'm not going to let that happen."

Mia smiled weakly. "I love you so much."

"If you really mean that, then you have to have confidence that I can handle this." Fletcher took Mia by the chin. "Everything's going to work out just fine. I promise."

As he kissed her, Fletcher prayed like hell that what he'd just said was true.

CHAPTER 25

As Jessica drove to Patina restaurant to meet her husband, she was even more nervous than she'd been on their first date over a decade ago. It had taken some arm-twisting to get Paul to agree to dinner on a Thursday night. He finally gave in, but insisted that he had to return to the office afterward.

Since Paul was such a time freak, Jessica expected him to already be seated when she arrived. For Paul, six o'clock meant six o'clock. Not a minute before or after. She imagined herself floating toward his table as he marveled over her fabulous makeover. But Paul was standing right there in the entryway and spotted her the second she stepped inside the restaurant.

Jessica inhaled and waited for her husband to compliment her new look. His eyes shined with surprise, then seemed to cloud with disappointment. Just as she was about to walk over to him, the hostess indicated that their table was ready. As she trailed behind him, Jessica had to be careful with every step. The strappy pink shoes Bliss convinced her to buy felt like walking on stilts.

Paul waited until the hostess disappeared before speaking. "Let me guess. This is all Bliss' doing, right?"

Jessica's eyes fell to the table as her heart tumbled to the floor. "I guess that means you don't like it."

"You're beautiful the way you are. I'd really prefer that my wife didn't expose her breasts to the world."

"My breasts aren't exposed to the world. I'm only showing a little cleavage."

"And what's with all the makeup? When did you start wearing fake eyelashes and hot-pink lipstick?"

Jessica's eyes started to water. "I thought you'd like it."

"No, *Bliss* thought I'd like it. You know me better than I know myself. I don't want you to change a thing about yourself. You're fine just the way you are."

"That's the problem. I want to be more than just *fine*."

When the first tear fell, Paul reached across the table and took her hand.

"I'm sorry, honey. But I just don't like the influence Bliss seems to have over you."

"She's my friend."

"No, honey. You're *her* friend or more accurately, her lapdog. You take care of her kids better than she does. You run her errands. You practically idolize her. Bliss has no other friends because no one is willing to put up with her nonsense. The way she gets pregnant just for the child support is obscene. I don't understand why you insist on condoning her outrageous behavior."

"This is not about Bliss. It's about you and me. We never have sex anymore. We never spend any time together. I feel like I'm losing you."

"You're not losing me." Paul squeezed her hand. "I told you, this deal has me stressed to the max. I love you."

Jessica started to whimper.

"C'mon, babe, please don't cry. We're in a public place. Tell me what it's going to take to make you stop crying."

"You already know what would make me happy." Jessica dabbed at her eyes with her napkin. "A baby. I want a baby."

Paul released her hand. "We've already discussed this, Jessica. We made a deal when we got married. No children."

"I know. But I feel differently now. You love it when Bliss' kids hang out with us for the weekend. I know you'd feel the same way about your own kids."

"Having kids over for a weekend is not the same as having them around twenty-four/seven. I don't want that responsibility. Maybe you should consider going back to work. And not in banking. Try something completely different. I think you'd make a great interior decorator."

"A job won't take the place of being a mother."

"This isn't the time or place for us to discuss this. I'm not hungry anymore. I need to get back to the office. I'll try to be home before midnight."

And just like that, Paul was gone. Jessica ordered an apple martini and wondered when and how she had lost touch with the only man she'd ever loved.

Maybe she'd be better off behaving more like Bliss and thinking only of her own wants and needs. To hell with what Paul wanted. She deserved to be a mother. Bliss wouldn't ask permission. Neither would she. She would just stop taking the pill.

Despite his assurances, Jessica wasn't convinced that Paul didn't have someone else in his life. Now, having a child was more important than ever. If Paul did end up leaving her, at least she would have his child.

CHAPTER 26

Special Sharlene Moore felt herself falling and falling fast. She could barely concentrate enough to keep up with her day job, much less her investigation of Bliss Fenton.

Staring at the flowers on her desk, Special knew she had to slow things down with Darius. But the man was pouring it on like sweet-tasting syrup. Not just flowers, but love notes secretly dropped in her purse, romantic phone messages and the best sex on the planet. If she didn't watch herself, she was going to find herself totally sprung.

Her cell phone rang and she smiled when she saw Darius' name appear on the screen.

"How's my baby?" He had the sexiest baritone.

"Great, now that I'm talking to you."

They chit-chatted about nothing, then Darius asked if she was free that evening.

Special normally didn't tolerate last-minute invitations, but with Darius, all of her long-held rules were being tossed out of the window. She enthusiastically accepted his invitation.

"And bring an overnight bag. No more excuses about spending the night. I want you in my bed tonight. All night."

As she hung up the phone, doubt crept back in. In her mind, staying all night was crossing a line, moving from lightweight dating to a full-fledged relationship. Despite the fun she was having, Special still wasn't sure where she wanted to take their relationship. She cared enough about Darius that she didn't want to hurt him. It wasn't fair to let things continue if she was ultimately going to turn tail and run.

She closed her eyes and pressed both hands to her face. *What in the world am I doing?*

Special arrived at Darius' house at six-thirty and he drove them to dinner at the Warehouse in the Marina. They returned to his place just before nine and fell asleep on the couch watching an old Bruce Willis movie.

"We better get to bed." Darius shook her awake. "I have an early meeting."

He reached out for his wheelchair and hefted himself into it. She followed him into the bedroom, every step shrouded in nervousness.

"Which side do you sleep on?" she asked.

"The right, but take your pick."

She walked into the adjoining bathroom and marveled at how large it was. There was a bench wedged next to the toilet, which she assumed Darius used to help position himself on the toilet. As she started removing her makeup, she couldn't help but snoop in the medicine cabinet. She found a number of medications, but recognized only one: Viagra.

"So that's how he gets it up. Men and their stupid peckers."

When she was done snooping, she slipped into a black lace nightie. She decided against bringing her sexiest lingerie. She couldn't risk giving the man a heart attack. Special eased open the bathroom door and was about to step back into the bedroom, when she froze.

Darius was sitting in the middle of the bed, his back against the headboard going through an odd routine of lifting his legs and allowing them to flop back onto the bed. Then he pulled them upward, bringing his knees to his forehead. She wasn't sure how long she had been watching when he spoke.

"I go through this routine morning and night," Darius explained. "Stretching out my muscles helps me stay flexible."

"Oh, uh, I…" Special was embarrassed that she'd been caught staring. She stepped into the bedroom, but didn't get into bed.

"Come here." Darius patted a spot on the bed next to him. "If we're going to be together, you have to know what my life is like."

It took a few seconds before Special joined him, sitting down near the foot of the bed, instead of where he had indicated. She remained silent, both dreading the information he was about to share, but also hungering for it.

He grabbed his right leg and stretched it upward again.

"Most people give no thought to getting dressed or undressed. It's a bit more of a challenge for me."

She watched him remove his shirt, then ease off his pants, shifting from side to side as he slid them down one leg, then the other.

Special swallowed. She didn't need to know everything all at once. She wanted to tell him that she had heard enough for now. The words, however, stayed stuck in her throat.

"Do you have any questions?" Darius asked.

"Um, how do you use the bathroom?"

"I basically had to learn to train both my bladder and bowels to void on a schedule." He smiled. "But maybe we shouldn't go there just yet. It's not a pleasant subject."

She watched him lean from side to side, lifting his bottom from the bed for a few seconds. He'd done that several times while they were watching TV."

"Why do you lean sideways like that?" she asked.

"You can feel your bottom, but I can't. I have to do this every thirty minutes or so to keep from getting pressure sores."

She realized now that during their first date, when she thought Darius had been flexing his muscles, he'd actually been going through this exercise.

"Come here."

She got up, rounded the bed and climbed in from the opposite side. The smile that tinged his lips told her he wanted to have sex. But what she'd just seen had killed any urge she might've had. Unfortunately, Darius was at full attention.

"Uh, do you have to take anything to get an erection?" She wondered if he was going to own up to the little blue pills she found in the bathroom.

"Oh, so you were snooping around in my medicine cabinet, huh?"

Special's face flushed.

Darius laughed. "I can get an erection, but Viagra helps me maintain it." He pointed at his groin. "See."

Special tried to laugh, but she really wanted to turn and run. She had no idea how it would feel to have intercourse with a man who had no sensation below the waist.

Darius obviously sensed her reluctance.

"Hey, babe, I know this is a lot to handle. But I want you to know what's up."

Reaching over, he eased his hand underneath her nightie and meandered up her thigh. She tried to fight the growing arousal, but it was no use. After slipping into a condom, he then slid down until he was lying flat on his back. He motioned for her to climb on top of him.

"I don't want to crush you."

"You're kidding, right? There's no way you could crush me. What are you, a buck twenty-five?"

Special stayed put. "So can you still have an orgasm?"

"Yeah, sometimes. But tonight, I want to concentrate on you."

Darius pulled her on top of him and kissed her. In no time, Special moved instinctively against him as he kissed her neck, rubbed her back, massaged her buttocks. At first, the stillness of his lower body unnerved her, but his hardness pressing into her, soon made her forget about anything except the rays of excitement surging through her body.

Lifting her nightie over her head, Special took the initiative to take him inside her, surprised at how anxious she was to engulf him. They moaned simultaneously and Special soon found herself lost in the sheer pleasure of the moment.

CHAPTER 27

Although Fletcher McClain usually professes to be busier than God, he arrives at my office within thirty minutes of my call telling him that his paternity test results had arrived. He wanted me to give him the news over the phone, but I insisted that we needed to either celebrate or commiserate in person.

Fletcher is standing near the window, not far from my desk. "Okay, let's get this over with."

I pick up the envelope and tear it open. "Maybe you should sit down."

"I prefer to stand."

I stare at the first page and try to make sense of what I see.

"Well? The kid's not mine, right?"

Fletcher is now standing over my shoulders, reading along with me.

There are three columns in the middle of the page. The first is a combination of letters that might as well be gibberish. The other two columns, which only have numbers, are labeled *Child* and *Alleged Father*. My eyes go to the bottom of the page and I see the words that answer our question.

The alleged father is not excluded as the biological father of the tested child. Based on testing results obtained from the analysis of the DNA loci listed, the probability of paternity is 99.9998%.

I look up at Fletcher. The color has drained from his face.

"She's your daughter," I say.

"Are you serious?"

I can see from Fletcher's expression that this is truly a surprise. He paces a few steps, then falls into one of the chairs in front of my desk.

"I thought you were off your rocker with your stolen sperm theory," he says. "But after thinking about it, I can't be completely sure that I didn't toss a condom in the trashcan or let Bliss take it off. We had a lot of lunchtime romps at the W Hotel. Once we were done, I'd usually be in a hurry to get back to the office. She would've had no trouble retrieving a condom from the trashcan without my noticing it. I bet that's exactly how she got pregnant."

I give him some time to digest this life-altering news.

"Well, the good part is you have a daughter. And I bet she's beautiful."

"Yeah, but unfortunately, I have to be tied to her psycho mother for the next eighteen years. Mia is going to freak."

I have no comforting words to say, so I say nothing.

"Thanks for not saying I told you so." I see worry lines on Fletcher's face that weren't there a few minutes ago. "Of course now I wish I'd told Mia about those turkey baster cases like you told me to. At least that would've given her some time to adjust to the news."

"Do you still want to move forward with the lawsuit? It's drafted and ready to go."

"Absolutely. Now more than ever."

"I have a process server on standby. He can have the complaint in Bliss' hands within the hour if that's what you want."

"Do it." His tone is defiant.

"Are you sure you don't want to talk to Mia first? This impacts her too. You both need to weigh all the pros and cons. This lawsuit could mean a lot of unwanted publicity. Bliss could very well go to the media."

"And what? Tell them she stole my sperm? I doubt she'll do that. There are no cons worse than her coming after me for millions of dollars."

"Are you sure Mia can handle the media attention?"

"If she can't, she'll just have to figure it out. I won't let Bliss get away with this. Make that call. Serve that cunt now."

I pick up the phone, give instructions to my assistant, and hang up.

"The process server is not far from Bliss' neighborhood," I tell Fletcher. "If she's home, she'll have the complaint within the hour."

"How soon can we take her deposition? I want to hear her explain under oath how she got pregnant."

"As soon as she files an answer to the complaint, I can serve her with a depo notice."

Fletcher rises. "You asked me if Mia's prepared for this. What I want to know is, are you prepared?"

"You hired me to litigate this case and that's what I plan to do."

"That's not good enough," Fletcher barks. "I'm not just hiring you to litigate this case. I want you to obliterate that bitch."

CHAPTER 28

Bliss spent the early part of the day shopping on Rodeo Drive in Beverly Hills. A trip to two of her favorite stores, Armani and Michael Kors, always brightened her day. She'd overdone it a bit, spending upward of three grand on a pair of shoes and three purses. But she wasn't concerned about her dwindling bank account. With the additional two grand soon to arrive from Aiden's father and the boatload of dough coming her way from Fletcher, money was the last thing she needed to worry about.

She had just put the key into her front door when a thin Asian man wearing a backpack walked up behind her.

"Ms. Fenton?"

Bliss glanced briefly over her shoulder. "Yes?"

The man shoved a large white envelope into the Michael Kors bag she was carrying. "You've been served."

"What the—"

The man was jogging down the driveway before Bliss could even get a good look at him.

"What the hell!" Bliss stumbled inside, dumping her bags at the door. She rummaged through the Michael Kors bag and pulled out the envelope. She already knew what it was. Some useless motion filed by Joseph's attorney to block her request for more child support.

When she ripped it open, the words on the first page jolted her.

Los Angeles Superior Court of the State of California. Fletcher McClain vs. Bliss Fenton.

She flipped through the thick document not quite understanding what it was. She went back to the cover page and the words in the far right column sent needles of shock straight to her forehead.

Fraud. Conversion. Intentional Infliction of Emotional Distress.

Bliss stumbled into the living room just as her nanny entered, carrying Harmony. Aiden and Jonas ran up to her, grabbing her around the thighs.

"Not now," she yelled. "Anamaria, get them out of here. Now!"

The boys shrank away as Harmony began to wail. Anamaria ushered them out of the room.

Fletcher McClain had the audacity to be suing *her*.

Bliss grabbed a glass and a bottle of vodka from the kitchen counter, then stepped out on the patio and shut the glass door. She sank down into one of the patio chairs and tried to gather her wits.

After a big sip of vodka, she read every word of the complaint. Some parts confused her, but she understood the gist of it. Fletcher McClain was accusing her of stealing his sperm and was suing her for fraud and mental anguish.

She started to laugh. A deep-in-the-belly laugh that she couldn't control. The lawsuit said nothing about defamation, which meant that Fletcher had probably received the test results proving he was Harmony's father. Rather than accept his responsibility, he chose to file this bogus lawsuit.

Mia must have put him up to this, Bliss thought. If only she knew the whole story. Bliss couldn't wait until her ex-yoga buddy found out the real deal about her seemingly faithful fiancé. Both of them were so selfish and money-hungry. Giving his daughter ten percent of his income was a pittance. But if Fletcher thought this lawsuit was going to scare her into short-changing her daughter—correction—*their* daughter, he was way wrong.

Bliss stalked back into the living room, retrieved her cell phone from her purse and dialed Jessica.

Her best friend was as shocked as Bliss had been when she learned what Fletcher had done.

"So what are you going to do?" Jessica asked.

"I'm going to fight like hell. Right after I hang up with you, I'm calling my attorney."

Initially, the vodka had infused her with a warm boost of bravado. But by the time she'd ended the call with Jessica, her confidence had evaporated. Bliss never imagined that the mighty Fletcher McClain would do something like sue her for fraud. *Could he actually get away with this?* The last page of the complaint asked for millions of dollars in damages.

Bliss scrolled through her phone looking for Girlie's number.

For the first time since filing the paternity petition, Bliss wasn't just worried, she was scared.

CHAPTER 29

Instead of going back to his office after the bomb Vernetta had dropped on him, Fletcher asked Lester to take him to his favorite Hollywood dive so he could get good and wasted. He knew that Mia was probably climbing the walls, waiting to hear the test results. But he couldn't face her. Not yet.

Taking his regular seat at the bar, he signaled the bartender for a scotch.

Had he followed Vernetta's advice and told Mia about those turkey baster cases when she first urged him to, at least Mia would be primed for this news. That would have taken most of the sting out of what he now had to do. He just never figured it would end up like this.

Picking up his phone, he saw four missed calls, two voicemail messages and three texts. All of them from Mia. Fletcher deleted the messages without bothering to listen to them. He couldn't handle Mia's whiny bullshit right now.

After a couple of hours, he lost count of how many drinks he'd downed. He stood, waited for the room to stop spinning, and made his way outside to his ever-faithful driver.

"You okay, boss?" Lester gripped his arm and helped him into the backseat.

"Nope," Fletcher slurred. "I'm actually pretty messed up."

"Why don't we hit Denny's for some coffee before I take you home?"

"Excellent idea."

It was close to midnight by the time Fletcher made it home. He remained on the porch, giving himself an impromptu pep talk. Fletcher McClain was no punk, he told himself. Fletcher McClain always faced his problems head-on. Men with big balls did that. And Fletcher McClain had balls the size of basketballs. *So bring it on.*

He stumbled through the front door in his wrinkled shirt and scotch-stained pants, his briefcase in hand, his jacket folded over his arm.

Mia, still dressed in business attire, charged up to him in the foyer. "I was a nervous wreck! Why didn't you return my calls? What happened? You should've—"

He walked right past her into the great room. "Be quiet."

"Don't tell me to be quiet!" She stayed close on his heels. "You look a mess and you smell like a liquor factory. You owe me an explanation. I need to—"

"I'm not telling you a thing until you sit down and shut up!" Fletcher yelled. "Have a seat on the couch. Now!"

She flinched and took a step back. After a short standoff, Mia did as instructed.

Fletcher opened his briefcase and pulled out the articles Vernetta had given him and handed them to her.

"Read these while I take a shower."

"Why can't you just tell me what—"

He raised his voice again. "Just do what I told you to do! I'll be right back."

When he entered the room twenty minutes later, Mia looked catatonic. Instead of joining her on the couch, Fletcher settled into an armchair across from her.

"The paternity test showed that the kid is mine. I think—and so does Vernetta—that Bliss got pregnant like the women in those articles did. She stole my sperm, probably from a discarded condom, saved it, and inseminated herself after we broke up."

Mia appeared to be holding her breath.

"Vernetta served Bliss with a lawsuit accusing her of fraud earlier today. Unfortunately, it won't have any bearing on my obligation to pay child support. It's possible that I could be on the hook for payments in the neighborhood of fifty thousand dollars a month, maybe more."

Mia gasped.

"That's about it. Okay, your turn. Go ahead and let me have it."

Fletcher wished he had poured himself another scotch before sitting down. He braced himself for a flood of tears and Mia's high-pitched rant about her ruined wedding plans and how embarrassed she would be. He was going to listen to her whine for twenty minutes max. Then he'd have Lester take him to the Four Seasons. He needed a good night's sleep.

He had nodded off when he heard Mia's voice.

"I'm so sorry this happened." Her tone was ultra soft. "This is not about you. It's about me. I'm so sorry."

Huh? Why in the hell is she apologizing to me?

Fletcher tried to sit up, but couldn't. The scotch still had full control of his senses.

"Bliss did this to get back at me. You're in this situation because you chose me and not her. If you hadn't fallen in love with me, you wouldn't be facing the possibility of having to pay that vicious little whore. I'm so sorry, sweetheart."

Mia walked around the coffee table, kneeled in front of him and threaded his fingers through hers.

"Bliss is the most conniving person I've ever met and she's not going to get away with this. We're going to fight this fight together."

Fletcher couldn't believe it. "You are friggin' amazing. You know that?"

Mia cocked her head to the side. "Yep, I most certainly am."

"We need to prepare a plan of action," Mia said with a take-charge air. "We should start by transferring funds and selling property. But we can't be blatant about it. The deals have to look legit. And then we have to find ways to move a significant portion of your money out of the country. My clients do it all the time and get away with it. So will we."

Fletcher's mouth fell open.

"I suspect we can stretch out the financial aspects of the paternity case for several months, maybe even years," she continued. "And maybe you don't work for a while to reduce your income. I can take a leave of absence from my firm and you can do the same. I'd love to spend a couple years in Paris or London or even Sydney doing absolutely nothing. By the time the court makes a final decision on child support, you won't be making anywhere near what you earn now. Bliss can't get money that you don't have."

Fletcher blinked and hoped like hell he wasn't dreaming.

"And I think we should postpone the wedding until all of this is settled. If we get married, Bliss might have the nerve to come after my income."

Fletcher kissed her, then pointed at his erection. "All those brilliant little words coming from your beautiful lips are turning me on."

Mia kissed him back.

"I'm definitely *The Man*," Fletcher murmured between kisses. "Because I was smart enough to choose you."

"Yes, you were." Mia stood up and started unbuttoning her blouse and shimmying her skirt down her narrow hips. Fletcher loved the stark contrast in their complexions. His sun-starved white against her sun-drenched chocolate.

Mia peered down at him wearing only a matching red bra and thong.

He caressed her thighs, then softly kissed them.

"I'd like to hear more of your game plan, baby," Fletcher muttered. "Because I have never been more turned on in my life."

CHAPTER 30

Girlie wasn't good at consoling drunk, distraught clients. Empathy simply wasn't in her repertoire.

When she arrived at the office that morning, she had five slurred messages from Bliss Fenton, each one demanding that she call her immediately. For the last five minutes now, she'd had been listening to Bliss yell into the phone and Girlie couldn't take much more.

"As I just said, I don't think you need to be all that worried." Girlie's patience was just about tapped out. "Give me some time to research the case law in this area. This is just a move on McClain's part to intimidate you. We're not falling for it."

Her new client still sounded like a drunken basket case. She must've drank her dinner last night *and* breakfast this morning.

"I'm really counting on you to make this thing go away," Bliss cried. "This is harassment."

Bliss had repeated the same words at least three times in the last two minutes.

"What I want you to do is get some sleep and let me worry about the case, okay?"

She herded Bliss off the phone and took some time to go through the lawsuit, which she had downloaded from the L.A. Superior Court website. Vernetta had apparently grown a pair since they last went head-to-head. This lawsuit was something Girlie would have filed. She had to give Vernetta her props.

The allegations in the complaint were complete crap. At least she hoped they were. Any victory would be strictly on paper. This wasn't about money. It was about intimidation. And Girlie Cortez did not scare easily.

The claim that Bliss had stolen Fletcher's sperm did indeed concern her. That might actually constitute fraud. It had not crossed her mind to ask Bliss for a blow-by-blow explanation of exactly how she got pregnant. She figured it happened the good old-fashioned way. She would invite Bliss down to her office in the next day or so and get the real story.

In the interim, she might as well have a little fun. Girlie picked up the phone and dialed Vernetta's office.

"Hello, counselor. I just wanted to let you know I've taken a look at that bogus lawsuit you filed."

"We'll let a jury determine how bogus it is." Vernetta chuckled derisively.

"I guess this means the paternity test proved Fletcher is Harmony's father. I'd appreciate it if you'd send me a copy of the results."

Vernetta didn't respond, but that didn't stop Girlie.

"It's a shame that a man as rich as your client has to stoop so low to get out of paying child support."

"He's not trying to get out of paying child support, he—" Vernetta stopped mid-sentence. "Why don't we just let the case play itself out in court and see what a jury decides."

"This case won't get before a jury because it's nothing but an intimidation tactic. I'll get it knocked out on motion."

"Is there a reason for this call? Otherwise I'm a little busy, while you obviously are not. Must be hard rebuilding a law practice after having your license suspended for unethical conduct."

That stung, but Girlie shook it off.

"My practice is doing just fine. And after I win this case, it'll be bigger and better."

"Like I said, is there a reason for this call? I don't have time for chit-chatting."

"I just wanted to let you know I'll be filing Bliss' answer right away. We want to move on to the discovery phase as soon as possible. It's important that the real facts come out. Not this fairytale you wrote in this complaint."

"We'd like it to move along too," Vernetta replied. "Maybe we can pick some dates for your client's deposition right now. How about a week from Monday for Ms. Fenton's deposition and two days after that for Mr. McClain's?"

"Sounds like that might work," Girlie replied, without checking her calendar. Of course she didn't have any other active cases. "But let me confirm with my client."

"You do that." Vernetta hung up.

Girlie loved it. She hadn't felt this invigorated in a long time. There was nothing like a contentious legal battle to get her juices flowing.

And this time around, the case wasn't going to end in disgrace. She was going to bring the high-and-mighty Vernetta Henderson down a peg or two. And Vernetta's wealthy client Fletcher McClain was going to take an even bigger hit.

CHAPTER 31

Special loved undercover work. It made her feel like a super hero. Sitting behind the wheel of Eli's van, she fantasized about having her own TV show. *Babe Undercover.* She'd even be willing to perform her own stunts.

The van's plumbing company logo had been removed and replaced with a Lulu's Catering Company emblem. Special had been trailing Bliss Fenton for the last half hour, from her townhouse and now onto the Santa Monica Freeway east to the Harbor Freeway north. When Bliss, transitioned to the far right lane and exited at 9th Street, Special presumed she was headed to downtown Los Angeles.

Working for Fletcher McClain was demanding more and more of her time. She didn't mind using her vacation days for surveillance work. For the few hours of work she'd be doing today, she'd earn almost twice what she made at Verizon.

Bliss entered the underground parking structure of the Westin Bonaventure Hotel on Figueroa Street and Special followed. She was about to balk at the parking fee—$3 for every fifteen minutes—then remembered that Fletcher McClain was picking up the tab. Maybe she would treat herself to lunch at his expense.

Special maneuvered until her van was behind Bliss' Audi. Different attendants walked up and handed them ticket stubs at the same time.

She stumbled out of the van, anxious to make sure she didn't lose sight of Bliss, who was already strolling through the double glass doors and into a wide hallway leading to the escalators. Bliss was wearing a bad-ass red dress with her hair pulled back into a ponytail. She looked both young and hip. Despite the woman's scandalous behavior, Special liked her flair.

Bliss took a seat at a table for two at the Lobby Court Cafe and pulled out her phone. Special sat close enough to listen.

"Hey, sweetie, I'm here."

So Bliss was moving on to trapping baby daddy number four. Special still hadn't gotten a lead on the father of Bliss' middle child, Jonas. Eli had managed to access the kid's birth certificate and to their surprise, the space where the father's name should have been was blank. Eli agreed that there was something amiss and Special was determined to find out who the guy was.

Bliss put her phone away and started thumbing through a Neiman Marcus catalogue she'd retrieved from her purse.

Life was so unfair. Special had gone back at least seven years and couldn't find a single job that Bliss had held. Yet all she did every day was eat out and shop. Eli had found out that Bliss' townhouse was paid for and that she leased a new car every year. Even with no mortgage, her lifestyle was still far in excess of ten grand a month. Her new Audi and all the shopping she did would wipe that out real quick. Special figured she had a sugar daddy or two. Maybe Mystery Baby Daddy was underwriting her lifestyle.

Bliss closed her magazine and her eyes went to the bank of elevators. An attractive man in a dark gray suit glanced in Bliss' direction. He stood near the elevator buttons, but did not push one. Instead he pulled out his phone and began pressing buttons. Seconds later, Bliss' phone chirped. Special assumed it was a text from the man at the elevator.

After briefly checking her phone, Bliss went back to her magazine. *They have this thing choreographed down to a tee.*

The man stepped onto the elevator. A couple minutes later, Bliss rose and gathered her purse.

Special would bet her last dime that Bliss was on her way to the same hotel room the guy had just headed off to. So Special jumped up and took off toward the bank of elevators, getting there just ahead of Bliss. When the elevator doors opened, Special stepped inside and so did Bliss. Special fumbled around in her purse, looking for her cell phone while Bliss hit the button for the eighteenth floor.

This wouldn't be the last time she followed Bliss, Special didn't want to make eye contact. She reminded herself to wear her auburn curly wig the next time she conducted a surveillance of Bliss.

When the elevator opened on the eighteenth floor, Bliss stepped off and again, Special followed.

Pausing near a sign that divided up the rooms on the floor, she muttered out loud as she fumbled through her purse. "Where's my key?"

She still kept an eye on Bliss to see which room she was entering. Oblivious to her presence, Bliss knocked just once on room 1802. The door opened and she slipped inside.

Special thought about waiting until one or both of them left the room, but decided against it. These days, hotels had cameras everywhere. She didn't want someone from Security asking her why she was loitering. So she returned to the lobby and waited. She found a seat that gave her a view of the bank of elevators. Her plan was to follow the guy to the parking garage and take down his license plate number so she could have one of Eli's cop friends look him up.

For the next fifty-seven minutes, Special monitored the elevators like a hungry lion looking for fresh meat. She was lucky that there was little activity, as most guests were probably attending meetings in the hotel's conference rooms. When she saw the man step off the elevator, Special stood up, ready to follow him to the garage. But he started walking away from the garage, toward the hotel's east entrance, which led out onto Flower Street. Special scurried after him. She figured Bliss was still in the room. They were being extra careful not to be seen together.

Special and the man reached the traffic light at the corner of Flower and Fifth Street at the same time. He was neither tall nor short, with dark, sensual eyes. Despite a little thinning at his crown, he was still quite good-looking. Special certainly wouldn't have kicked him out of bed.

He must've worked downtown and was no doubt headed back to the office. Based on his sharp suit, Special guessed that he might be a lawyer or maybe an investment banker. He walked with the air of a man who had big money. He also strutted like a man who'd just gotten laid.

They stepped shoulder-to-shoulder into the intersection. He veered to the left and entered the Citibank building on the northeast corner. Special stayed close, stepping onto the elevator along with the man and three other people.

When he exited on the seventh floor, Special got off too. He'd paid her no attention, and had his eyes glued to his phone the entire time she'd been following him. Special loved smartphones. They made people completely oblivious to their surroundings.

The man made a right off the elevator and charged into the lobby of Vinson & Schneider, LLP as if he owned the place.

"Hey, Marty," the receptionist called out to him. He smiled and waved as he strolled past her.

Special smiled too. *Piece of cake.* Just that quickly, she had all the information she needed.

When the receptionist turned her way, Special cut the woman off before she could speak.

"I'm looking for the Donovan law firm." She had snatched the name from the directory in the lobby downstairs. "I think I'm lost."

"Oh, that's on the fifth floor," the receptionist chirped.

Special thanked her and headed back to the bank of elevators. By the time one arrived, she had already called up the website of Vinson & Schneider, LLP. On the page that said *Our Lawyers*, she entered the first name *Marty*. The search turned up nothing.

Next she entered *Martin* and four names popped up. She clicked on the first one and looked at the photograph. Not her guy. The second Martin was also a no-go. When she hit the third Martin, there he was, the smiling face of Martin Zinzer.

Dang, I'm good!

She read through his list of accolades. Zinzer was a corporate attorney, specializing in mergers and acquisitions. Admitted to the California Bar in 1987. Listed in *Elite Leading Lawyers for M&As.* She entered his name in Google and found a puff piece in *California Lawyer* that described him as *an innovative lawyer and a dedicated family man.*

Yeah right.

Google Images showed a picture of Zinzer and his wife Chloé at a Bar association function. They had three kids and lived in South Pasadena.

Special shook her head. This guy had no idea of the kind of havoc his lunchtime romps with Bliss could produce in his life.

Dude, if you only knew, you'd stay the hell away from Bliss Fenton.

She couldn't wait to share what she had found with Eli and Vernetta. Special had no doubt that Zinzer was paying Bliss for sex. She just wondered how much he was paying her and how many men Bliss had in her stable.

CHAPTER 32

Bliss has thirty days to respond to Fletcher's fraud complaint, but I receive her answer only days later. It's no surprise to me that Bliss has denied every allegation in the complaint. What does surprise me are the two additional documents Girlie includes.

By the time I finish reading the first one, I want to strangle Girlie. We informally agreed that Bliss' deposition would be taken a week from Monday, and Fletcher's two days later. But Girlie has served me with a deposition notice scheduling Fletcher's deposition first. This is classic Girlie Cortez.

"A leopard never changes its spot," I mumble to myself.

Still, that isn't what annoys me the most. It's the Section 128.5 motion that Girlie had the nerve to send. Bliss is actually threatening to countersue Fletcher *and* me, alleging that the fraud lawsuit was filed in bad faith.

I quickly Google California Civil Procedure Code Section 128.5. I filed one of these motions years ago, but I've never been the target of one.

A trial court may order a party, the party's attorney, or both to pay the reasonable expenses, including attorney's fees, incurred by another party as a result of bad-faith actions or tactics that are frivolous or solely intended to cause unnecessary delay.

The witch is accusing us of filing the fraud case to *"harass and intimidate Ms. Fenton into abandoning her right to pursue child support on behalf of her daughter, Harmony McClain."*

Who's using intimidation tactics now?

An accompanying letter explains that the motion has not yet been filed with the court. Girlie is merely providing me with a courtesy copy. If we don't voluntarily dismiss the fraud case, she says, the motion would be filed *at the appropriate time.* In the last paragraph, almost as an afterthought, Girlie puts me on notice that she intends to ask the court for a temporary child support order of twenty thousand dollars a month.

Fletcher is going to blow a gasket.

I take a few minutes to do some deep breathing and collect myself. I've outsmarted Girlie before and I'll do it in this case as well. Trying to force Girlie to keep her word about my taking Bliss' deposition first would be a waste of time. If I took the matter before the judge, Girlie would probably lie about our oral agreement. In order to win this case, I would have to start anticipating what a shady attorney like Girlie would do and stay ten steps ahead of her.

I dial Fletcher's number.

As usual, he sounds distracted. I can hear the loud thump of hip hop music in the background.

"Girlie Cortez has scheduled your deposition for a week from Monday. We could delay it, but I think it's best to keep things moving forward. You available?"

"I thought we were taking Bliss' deposition first."

"I thought we were too, but Girlie went back on her word."

"So. Don't let her."

"It's not worth the fight, Fletcher. We didn't have a formal agreement regarding the timing of the depositions."

"Why not?"

My spine stiffens at what I interpret as his questioning of my competence. "I couldn't formally schedule Bliss' deposition until after she answered the complaint." I struggle to keep my voice calm. "We verbally agreed that Bliss would be deposed first, but I should've known Girlie wouldn't keep her word. It's not a bad thing to have your testimony on the record first. I need to set up some time to prepare you. And I'll need at least half a day."

"No can do."

"Fletcher, this is serious. You'll need to make the time."

"LaReena's new CD's about to drop. I can't—"

"If you're not going to make this case a priority, you might as well take out your checkbook right now."

That throws him into silence.

"Girlie also gave us a draft of a motion seeking sanctions against both of us claiming your lawsuit is frivolous and intended to harass her. She wants you to drop the fraud case."

"What? She's the one who's harassing me," Fletcher explodes. "What's going on here, Vernetta? Do you have control of this case?"

First Girlie, now Fletcher. I would not let either of them shake my confidence.

"Absolutely. And as long as I can get you to focus on it too, we'll be fine."

"I don't want *fine*. I want an overwhelming victory so Bliss and her attorney disappear into thin air."

"That's not going to happen. The kid is yours. You're going to pay child support. The only issue is how much." I wince before proceeding. "And one more thing. Girlie says she plans to seek twenty thousand dollars a month in temporary child support."

"Fifteen grand is my max!" Fletcher roars into the phone. "This is a matter of principle!"

I ignore his rant. "You're going to need a family law attorney to handle the child support demand. My friend Darlene Hayes represents a lot of high-net-worth clients. She's smart and very aggressive. You'll like her."

"I'll kill Bliss before I pay her twenty grand a month."

"Fletcher! Stop talking like that. I hope nobody heard you say that. Is your door closed?"

I can hear movement, then what sounds like a door slamming shut.

"I don't care who heard me. I shouldn't have to pay her a dime. She stole my friggin' sperm."

"Please calm down. I need you to contact that family law attorney I referred you to A-SAP." I pause and take in a breath. "Fletcher, are you one hundred percent sure you didn't have sex with Bliss within nine months of Harmony's birth?"

"I already answered that question." I can feel the heat from his red-hot face through the phone. "Don't ask it again."

"It's my job to ask it."

"Not after I've repeatedly told you that wasn't the case."

The tension between us is now Ferris-wheel high.

"Why don't we both just calm down," I say. "I need to prepare you for your deposition. I can work with your schedule. Early morning, late night, you name it. But we have to do this. And I want to do it here in my office so there aren't any interruptions. How about Tuesday?"

"Fine."

"What time?"

"I have a series of meetings that I can't cancel. I won't be able to get there before nine p.m."

"Great. I'll have plenty of coffee ready."

"I feel like they're winning already."

"You need to trust me. You hired me because I'm good at what I do. I have everything under control."

"Just make sure you do."

As I hang up, I question whether my confident declaration is true. Girlie Cortez has blindsided me before. I can't let her do it again.

CHAPTER 33

"So exactly how does this deposition thing work?"

Bliss was sitting at a conference table in Girlie Cortez's Pasadena office. Although Fletcher would be deposed first, Girlie didn't want to wait until the last minute to begin prepping Bliss for her deposition. Something told her that Bliss would require some extra handholding.

"It's the same as testifying under oath except that you won't be in court. You'll be at Vernetta Henderson's office. There'll be a court reporter taking down your words and a videographer recording you."

"So his attorney can ask me anything?"

"No, only things that are relevant to the case. If she starts going off on a tangent, I'll object. In most cases, you'll still have to answer the question even if I do object. But if I specifically instruct you not to answer, don't say a word."

Girlie could tell that the normally collected Bliss was nervous about her upcoming deposition.

"You'll do fine. We're taking Fletcher's deposition first. So you'll get a chance to see how everything works when I depose him here at my office."

"So I get to come?"

"Absolutely."

Bliss smiled. "That should be fun. And what happens after the depositions?"

"Let's just focus on your testimony for now. I want to practice going through a line of questioning with you. The most import-ant thing I want you to remember is that you shouldn't volunteer information. Only respond to the question asked. Make Vernetta do her work. Don't give her information she hasn't asked for."

"Okay."

"And it's important that you don't make any facial expressions, particularly if you're upset or surprised. Remember that you'll be on camera and a microphone will be clipped to your blouse. If you need to ask me something, cover your microphone with your hand so it won't be picked up on the recording. I also want you to dress conservatively. If this case gets to trial, some of your deposition testimony could be presented via video to the jury. People make assumptions based on the way people are dressed, especially women. Wear a nice suit with a high collar. No cleavage."

Bliss looked down at the low-cut sweater she was wearing. "Okay."

"So, let's begin. Please state your name for the record."

Bliss sat up straighter in her chair and folded her hands on the table in front of her. She was trying to play the role of a model witness.

"Bliss Fenton. I don't have a middle name."

"That's an example of volunteering information," Girlie said. "You didn't have to explain that you don't have a middle name. I want you to answer only the question asked. Nothing more."

"Okay, okay." Bliss tapped her forehead as if to remind herself.

"Where did you meet Mr. McClain?"

"We met at a bar not far from his office. He came up to me and offered to buy me a drink. I had no idea at the time that he was—"

Girlie made a timeout signal with her hands. "You're doing it again, providing way too much information. I asked you where you met him, not how. You should've stopped after saying that you met him at a bar."

Bliss exhaled in frustration. "I don't see why it's a big deal. She's probably going to ask me to explain the rest anyway."

"You're right, she probably will. But I want you to wait until she asks you. Don't volunteer anything. If you get into the habit of not volunteering the little things, then there's a better chance that you won't make the mistake of volunteering something major that could hurt your case."

Bliss pursed her lips. "Okay."

Girlie had to remind herself to be more patient. She was beginning to have a bad taste in her mouth about her new client. Bliss' nanny had called with a concern about one of her kids. Bliss had told her to *just deal with it* and hung up the phone. She definitely wasn't going to win any awards for Mother of the Year.

"Okay, let's try it again." Girlie scanned her notes. "Did you have breakfast this morning?"

Bliss paused for a second as if it might be a trick question. "Yeah, I had plain yogurt and a banana."

Girlie hung her head and massaged the back of her neck. "I need you to listen to my question. I didn't ask you *what* you had for breakfast. I asked you *if* you had breakfast. That was a prime example of offering up too much information. The correct answer to my question was a simple *yes.*"

"But who cares what I had for breakfast?"

Girlie could see that she was going to need way more than a single session to prepare Bliss for her deposition. The woman was a beauty but she was a bit lacking when it came to brain cells.

"You're right. Vernetta isn't going to ask you if you had breakfast. I'm just trying to help you understand the danger of volunteering too much information. Maybe we should take a break."

Bliss stood up. "Good idea. Where can I find a Diet Coke?"

Girlie gave her directions to the vending machines downstairs. When they reconvened fifteen minutes later, both were a bit more relaxed.

"Let's just cut to the crux of the case. We can return to the background facts later. Mr. McClain's complaint alleges that you stole his sperm from a condom and inseminated yourself. Is that true?"

Bliss started to squirm in her seat. "Uh, well...Not exactly."

Girlie squinted. "What do you mean, *not exactly?*"

"Well, you asked me two questions." She smiled as she took a sip of Diet Coke. "The answer to one of the questions is yes, but the answer to the other one is no."

Now Girlie was the baffled one. "Why don't we take a short break from our role-playing. Just tell me how you got pregnant."

Bliss wiped a bead of sweat from the side of the Diet Coke can with her thumb. "Okay, but what if I said I did steal his sperm from a condom?"

Girlie scratched her forehead. The last thing she needed was another lying client. "Is that the truth?"

"Um...not exactly. But what if I testified that was how I did it. Could we still win?"

"Bliss, I can't and won't allow you to lie under oath. I need to understand how you got pregnant. Vernetta will definitely ask you that question."

"Okay, okay." Bliss clutched her Diet Coke with both hands, then told Girlie the story, leaving nothing out.

When she finished, Girlie gazed across the table dumbfounded. Girlie fell back in her chair as her lips curled into a bemused smile. She had to take back what she'd been thinking about Bliss lacking in the brains department. This chick was straight-up brilliant.

"So say something." Bliss wore the most devilish expression.

"I'm...uh...I'm at a loss for words. I've never, ever heard anything like that. So you planned the whole thing?"

"Basically. So is that considered fraud?"

Actually, Girlie thought, it did sound like fraud. "I'll need to do a little more research to make that determination. Let's not worry about that for the time being."

"But you look pretty worried right now. Are we going to lose?"

Still reeling from what Bliss had just revealed, Girlie struggled to keep a straight face.

"I can't make that promise regarding the fraud case. But I can promise you that no matter how Harmony got here, Fletcher can't get out of supporting her. So you'll get your child support payments. The issue of whether a judge or jury thinks your actions constitute fraud is a different matter."

"And what if they do think it was fraud?"

"Then Fletcher could win a huge award."

"And I'd have to pay it?"

Girlie nodded.

"But what if I don't have the money to pay it? Would I have to pay him out of my child support?"

Girlie shook her head. "The great thing about child support is that the payments are protected income. You'd have to pay him out of your other sources of income, of which there are none. So even if Fletcher wins a seven-figure verdict, it effectively means nothing since you can't get blood out of a turnip."

Bliss' face glowed. She raised a hand and the two women high-fived.

"You're amazing," Bliss said.

Girlie was still marveling over her client's sheer deviousness. "No, my dear, *you're* the amazing one."

CHAPTER 34

After rushing around all day to make sure everything was just right, Special now regretted her bright idea to invite Darius over for dinner. As she stood on her front porch, peering down at him, Special fought back tears.

"I'm so sorry." She covered her mouth with both hands. "I just didn't think about how you would get up the steps."

Darius was sitting in his wheelchair on her walkway, trying to calm her down. "Babe, babe, no sweat. It's not a problem."

"Yes, it is! You can't get up the steps. I should have thought of this. I can go get my neighbor. He can lift you up the steps."

"There's no need to do that."

"But how are you going to—"

"Just stay right here." He fished his keys out of his shirt pocket. "I'll be back in a flash."

Darius swiveled his chair around and rolled back down the walkway toward his car. Special watched as he opened the trunk. He took out a flat, rectangular plastic board and was back in front of her in seconds. He unfolded the board, angled it across the steps, then smiled up at her.

"It's a portable ramp," he said, grinning. He whirled his chair around so that the back was facing the ramp. "I'll do most of the work. I just need you to help guide me."

With Special's help, he easily made it up the three steps onto the porch.

"See. I have everything under control."

She reached to open the door for him, but he grabbed the knob and opened it for her instead. "After you, pretty lady."

Special finally let herself breathe again. Catastrophe averted. She wasn't going to let that happen again. She'd thought through everything else. So hopefully there'd be no more missteps.

They enjoyed turkey lasagna with red wine and cheesecake, topping off the evening with a game of Scrabble. Throughout dinner, Darius offered Special his advice about her investigation of Bliss.

He had just set up the Scrabble board on the card table when his cell phone rang. He glanced at the display, hit a button on the side, then placed it face down on the table.

"Work," he explained. "I put it on vibrate. It can wait."

Special eyed him with suspicion, but kept her thoughts to herself.

"Getting back to your investigation," Darius continued, "it's a good bet that guy isn't the only man she's seeing. She could be part of a high-class call girl ring."

"No way," Special disagreed. "She's solo. She's way too savvy to let herself be pimped out. Her townhouse in Playa Vista is paid for. She didn't save that kind of dough from years of lunchtime quickies. She has a major benefactor who's kicking her down."

"You might be right."

"And I don't think it's the lawyer guy. He's not at a top-tier law firm. A partner at a firm his size and caliber probably makes about five hundred grand a year. He has a stay-at-home wife, two teenagers in private schools and a son at Brown. After taxes and covering his household expenses, that doesn't leave a lot of discretionary cash. I doubt he's Bliss' primary sugar daddy. Whoever that dude is, he's rolling in dough. Five hundred grand a year wouldn't do it."

Darius' face shined with pride. "I like the way your mind works. You're a natural at this."

Special beamed at the compliment.

"My gut tells me the key to how she's managing to live such a high and mighty lifestyle is the father of her middle kid," Special went on. "The fact that he's nowhere in the picture means he's probably paying her big time to keep her mouth shut. I bet he's somebody famous."

Darius' phone vibrated, shaking the table. This time, Special reached for it and flipped it over. A name flashed across the screen, but all Special could make out was *Wilson* before Darius snatched it from her hand. She couldn't tell if that was a first or last name.

"Hey!" This time Darius turned off the phone and placed it in his shirt pocket.

Special laughed it off. "Why're you so nervous about me answering your phone? What've you got to hide?"

"Nothing. It's just work. But they're going to have to wait until tomorrow because tonight is all about you."

Work my ass.

Something in Special's gut began to gnaw at her. And her gut was rarely wrong. When a man refused to answer his phone in your presence, that was a sign—not just a sign, but a neon billboard—signaling that something was up. And the something usually wasn't good.

"Hey, pretty lady. Are you still here in the room with me or someplace else?"

Special inhaled. Vernetta had warned her to take it slow. She had wanted to hold off on the question she was about to ask until she was sure what she wanted from Darius. But this wasn't a normal relationship. She was considering committing herself to a man who would spend the rest of his life in a wheelchair. If she truly planned to go down that bumpy road, everything had to be on the up and up.

"Are you seeing anyone besides me?" she blurted out.

"Whoa. Where did that come from?"

"No place in particular." She studied his face for signs of deception like a cop examining a prime suspect. "So are you?"

"Are *you* seeing anyone?" Darius fired back.

"I asked you first."

"I don't have anyone special in my life at the moment. After meeting you, I even took down my profile on MyHarmony. Right now, I'm all about you."

His reassuring words caused the tight sensation in her stomach to ease a bit. She'd find out later who Wilson was.

"And you?" Darius asked again.

"Nope," Special said. "Nobody in my life and nobody even on the horizon. I'm really, really digging on you right now."

Darius smiled. "Say that again."

Special rounded the card table and bent to kiss him. "I'm really, really digging on you."

"And you're doing an excellent job at it."

Darius pushed his chair back and Special climbed into his lap. She unbuttoned his shirt and began massaging his pecs and peppering his neck with soft kisses. She had read that men with spinal cord injuries like Darius' had a heightened sense of touch in their upper body because of the loss of sensation in their lower half.

Judging from Darius' loud moans, that was most definitely the case.

CHAPTER 35

Fletcher's deposition prep should've taken place a week ago, but he repeatedly blew me off. Now that we're almost down to the wire, I have no choice but to camp outside his office.

It's close to ten o'clock at night, when he finally waves me inside.

"I've had my deposition taken before," he protests. "It's not a big deal."

"Yes, it is a big deal. It's late. So let's get to it."

We move to the corner of his office with Fletcher taking the couch directly across from the armchair where I'm seated.

"Most attorneys will begin by asking you background information, but that's not Girlie's style. She's likely to go for the jugular in an effort to unnerve you. So I'm going to run through this the way I think she will."

"Okay, shoot."

"When was the last time you had sex with Bliss Fenton?"

Fletcher frowns. "Wait. She's not going to expect me to remember the exact date, is she?"

"If you can remember, yes."

"Well, I can't."

"Okay. Then say that."

Fletcher returns to his role-playing position. He slouches low on the couch. "I don't recall the exact date."

"I'd prefer it if you said *I don't remember* rather than *I don't recall*. It sounds less like you're trying to avoid the question. And please don't sit like that at the deposition. You look way too relaxed."

He sits more erect. "Got it, counselor. I don't remember the exact date."

"Do you remember what month it was?"

"Yep."

"Don't be flippant, Fletcher. Say *yes* rather than *yep*."

He winks. "Got it, counselor. Yes."

"And you answered that question perfectly by just saying *yes* and not volunteering more information. Let Girlie pull it from you."

He grins, warming to my compliment.

"And what month was it?"

"February of last year."

"And how do you remember that it was February of last year?"

"Because we broke up two weeks before Valentine's Day."

"Where did you last have sex with my client?"

Fletcher starts to answer, then flubs his words. "Um...my place... Probably?"

This time, I step out of my legal-eagle role. "*Probably?* You remember when you had sex for the last time, but you don't remember where?"

Fletcher flashes his killer smile. "Bliss was a bit of a freak. We had sex in lots of out-of-the-ordinary places."

"Fletcher, I need you to be serious."

"I am being serious." He grabs a bottle of alkaline water from the end table, screws off the cap and chugs half the bottle.

"So where did you last have sex?" I ask again.

"My place."

"And do you mean your home in Beverly Hills?"

He nods. "Yes."

"Who initiated the date?"

Fletcher grins. "It wasn't a date."

"If it wasn't a date, then what was it?"

"A hookup. A booty call. Take your pick."

I slap my legal pad on the coffee table and place both hands on my knees. "That's not going to work, Fletcher. You're being too flippant. Your deposition is going to be recorded. And if it's played at trial, neither the judge nor the jury is going to like you. And that will hurt your case."

"*Like me?* They don't need to like me. Bliss stole my sperm. What about what they think of her?"

"It's not my job to worry about what they think of her. You're my only concern. Let's try it again. Who initiated the date?"

"Bliss did. She called and asked if she could come over to my place."

"And you agreed?"

"Yeah." He holds up a palm, stopping me before I can correct him. "I mean, yes."

"Who initiated the sex?"

He pauses. "I don't remember."

I step out of my role again. "Did you really forget or are you trying to avoid admitting that you initiated it?"

He smiles and cocks his head. "Okay, I initiated it."

"And how did you—"

"Vernetta, I don't have the energy for this tonight. I'm sure I'll be able to handle her attorney's questions just fine."

I fold my arms across my chest.

Fletcher chuckles. "I used to love it when you pouted."

"You're scaring me, you know that? I need you to take this seriously."

"It's been a long day. We're both tired. Just give me your list of questions. I'll study them and we can go over them the morning of the deposition. That's the way my attorney did it in our copyright infringement case."

"This isn't a copyright case."

"I know that. And I also know how to answer questions at a deposition."

I stare at him long and hard. "If this case goes south because you blow the depo, don't blame me."

"It's not going south. It doesn't matter when or where we had sex. All that matters is that Bliss stole my sperm and we're going to prove it. It's as simple as that."

* * *

It's almost midnight by the time I get home. Jefferson is waiting up for me and he doesn't look happy. His arms are locked across his chest and his cheeks are in the pouting position.

"I called you a couple of times. Why didn't you answer?"

"Sorry. My phone was out of juice."

"You have a charger in your car."

After the night I had with Fletcher, I don't want to talk to anybody, including my husband. "I didn't plug it in, okay?"

"No, it's not okay. I was worried about you."

"I'm sorry. I was trying to prep Fletcher for his deposition and it was like pulling teeth."

"So you've been with Fletcher all this time?"

"No. Not all this time. Only since about ten o'clock."

"Since when do you meet with your clients at ten o'clock at night?"

I must really be tired. What am I thinking telling Jefferson I'd been with Fletcher? I should've lied and said I was working on a brief.

"We scheduled the meeting late because that was the only time he was available."

"Maybe he wanted it that late because he had other things on his mind. You didn't happen to prep him over drinks, did you?"

"C'mon, Jefferson. I've had a long day. I don't have time for this tonight. You've never been insecure.

Stop acting like you are now."

"This has nothing to do with my being insecure. If I'd ignored your calls all evening and walked in here at this time of night, all hell would break loose."

He's right, but I'm feeling too ornery to admit it. "I just told you where I was. I'm tired and I'm going to bed."

"So it's like that?"

"Like what?"

"You're going to disrespect me by walking in here after midnight and then act like it's no big deal."

I sulk over and peck him on the forehead. "For one, it's not after midnight. It's only eleven-fifty-one. And two, I'm dog tired. Can we finish this discussion tomorrow?"

"Nope. I want to finish it now."

"I'm sorry. I just don't have the energy for a fight tonight."

I hurry out of the room and down the hallway. A minute or so later I hear the front door slam and Jefferson's truck pulling out of the driveway.

CHAPTER 36

Bliss and Jessica sat inside Bliss' Audi in the Ralph's parking lot listening to the radio. Bliss checked her watch, but didn't comment on Joseph's tardiness. Since she was anxious to gloat, she'd gladly wait all day for him to arrive.

"I know this is a waste of energy, but you need to behave today," Jessica warned. "At least for Aiden's sake."

"I'm going to be as sweet as apple pie." Bliss was all but beaming. "I forgot to tell you that I got Aiden's child support increased. I asked for fifteen grand, but that stingy judge only gave me twelve. An extra two grand a month is better than nothing."

Jessica rubbed her forehead. "Unbelievable."

"I filled out the papers myself and had someone at the court's Self-Help Clinic look them over. Didn't even use an attorney. Maybe I should consider going to law school. Anyway, let's celebrate by driving to Palm Springs this weekend. I could use a good massage."

Jessica didn't say a word as Bliss rattled on.

"I forgot to ask how Paul liked the outfit I picked out."

"He didn't." Jessica stared out of the window.

"What? He's crazy. I should call him up right now."

"You better not. Just stay out of it."

"You're such a doormat where he's concerned."

"That's funny. That's exactly what Paul thinks about our relationship. He says I'm your lapdog, which I guess is basically the same thing."

Bliss waited a beat. "He actually said that to you?"

She nodded.

"Well, he's wrong. You're the sister I never had. He's just trying to hurt you. Ignore him."

Jessica turned away just as Dr. Franco pulled into the parking lot.

Bliss gripped the steering wheel with both hands. "And you don't need to say it again. I'm going to behave." She swung open the door and rested her body against the rear of the car.

Joseph opened the back door of his Mercedes and began unbuckling Aiden from his car seat. He had a smug look on his face as he marched his son toward Bliss and Jessica.

"Why is he looking so happy?" Bliss muttered.

Jessica stood nearby. "Just don't start anything."

Aiden waved as they got closer. Joseph let go of his hand and Aiden ran straight to Jessica.

It took Bliss a few seconds to drop her outstretched arms.

"That's just classic," Joseph said.

Embarrassed, Bliss gently untangled her son from Jessica's embrace and held him close.

"Did you miss Mommy?"

Joseph was already walking back to his car. "Hey," Bliss called after him. "Did you get the court order?"

He slowly turned around. "Yeah, I got it. And it's fine. Whatever you want is fine. Frankly, I should thank you."

His words stunned her. Bliss had been hoping for a fight. Not this kinder, gentler crap.

"Thank you for what?"

"I finally understand that you'll never change, so I've stopped expecting you to. Lena and I had a long talk. She encouraged me to just let it go. Anything you decide to do is just going to roll off my back. As a matter of fact, it was one of the reasons I finally asked Lena to marry me. So, thank you."

He turned his attention to Jessica. "I'd love it if you and Paul would come to the wedding. We're going to do it in Jamaica around Christmas time."

"I figured you wouldn't want to be there." He winked at Bliss and continued toward his car.

Bliss seemed to be having trouble coming up with a sufficiently nasty retort. And then it came to her.

"Maybe I just might show up," she yelled. "Crash your wedding and cause a little havoc."

Dr. Franco froze mid-stride, then looked back over his shoulder. Bliss could see he was struggling to control his rage, so she pushed even harder.

"We'll see if you let that just roll off your back."

As suddenly as his anger appeared, it vanished almost as quickly. He responded in a gentle voice delivered with a smile.

"You know, Bliss, I believe in karma. You're going to get everything you deserve. And I predict it's going to happen sooner rather than later."

"Is that a threat, doctor?"

He paused, then smiled even wider. "Not at all. I don't make threats. Threats don't change things. Actions do."

CHAPTER 37

Girlie Cortez commences her deposition of my client with an affectionate smile. I've warned Fletcher not to take her at face value. Girlie's smile is likely to hide something deadly.

"Please state your name for the record."

"Fletcher Douglas McClain."

We're gathered in a cramped conference room in Girlie's crappy office building. Fletcher and I met at six that morning and spent close to three hours preparing him for his testimony. To my surprise, he turned out to be a model witness during our abbreviated prep session, listening intently to my instructions and answering my questions accordingly. Right now, he conveys the air of a man who's relaxed and confident.

Bliss has her arms folded and is avoiding eye contact with Fletcher. There's enough animosity flowing between them to ignite a whole arsenal of explosives without a match.

"Have you had your deposition taken before, Mr. McClain?"

"Yes, I have."

"How many times?"

"Just once."

"And what kind of case was it?"

Fletcher looks over at me as if I need to object. But I nod, urging him to respond. Girlie's question isn't out of line just yet.

"Copyright infringement."

"Were you a plaintiff or defendant?"

"Neither."

"Tell me about the facts of that case."

"Objection. That case isn't relevant here," I say. "I instruct the witness not to answer."

Girlie shoots me a perturbed look. "Excuse me? You're instructing him not to answer on a relevancy objection?"

I enjoy landing the first dig. "The facts of that case have nothing to do with this one. Let's move on."

She releases a long breath, which tells me she's not going to waste time pushing the issue.

"Mr. McClain, how much did you earn from your position as CEO of Karma Entertainment last year?"

That question wipes the confidence right off Fletcher's face. As predicted, she begins with an area intended to unnerve him.

"Objection. This isn't a paternity case, counselor. His income has no relevance here."

"I disagree. Mr. McClain's income has a direct bearing on the fraud cause of action. It's our contention that he only filed it as a form of harassment, to keep my client from going after his precious millions. So you can answer the question."

Even if she could prove it, it wouldn't be a defense to fraud. I could push it further, but it wouldn't be worth the fight. Fletcher's eyes dart in my direction. I give a slight nod, directing him to answer.

"I don't recall...I mean...I don't remember the exact figure."

"That's fine. I wouldn't expect a guy who makes as much as you do to remember his salary down to the penny. Just give me your best estimate."

He pauses. "Around eight million."

"If you include stock options, wasn't it more like ten million?"

Fletcher's hands curl into two white-knuckled balls.

"Perhaps."

"Perhaps or yes?" Girlie presses him.

"I said perhaps. I'd need to see my tax return to be sure."

"No problem. We'll be requesting a copy very shortly." She pauses to riffle through the stack of documents on the table in front of her. "And you own a couple of vacation homes, correct?"

This time Fletcher looks at me as if my silence constitutes mal-practice. "Yes."

She hands a piece of paper to me, Fletcher and the court reporter and asks that it be marked as Exhibit One.

"Is that a photograph of your vacation home in Aspen?"

Fletcher's jaw clinches and he sniffs. "Yeah."

"What's the current value of the home?"

Girlie has done her homework. I decide to object, even though if I were in her shoes, I'd be asking the very same questions.

"Objection, relevancy. Like his income, the value of Mr. Fletcher's vacation home has no bearing on this case nor is it likely to lead to the discovery of admissible evidence. It appears that that your questions are aimed at the paternity case, which is a completely separate matter."

She pretends as if I'm not there. "Please answer the question, Mr. McClain."

Fletcher glances my way again.

"You can answer," I say under my breath.

He grunts. "I haven't checked the real estate listings lately."

"Why don't you give me a ballpark number?"

"A couple million, give or take."

She hands him another sheet of paper. "Is this your home in Martha's Vineyard?"

"Yes, it is."

"And how much is it worth?"

"About three million."

Girlie spends the next twenty minutes or so documenting that my client is a very wealthy man, then makes an abrupt left turn to the crux of her case.

"When was the last time you had sexual relations with my client?"

Fletcher sits more erect in his chair. "February of last year. A week before Valentine's Day."

A week? During our prep session, he'd said it was two weeks before Valentine's Day. That minor discrepancy raises my antennae. *Did he forget or is he intentionally lying. And if so, why?*

"Are you sure about that timeframe, Mr. McClain?"

"Absolutely."

"So is it your testimony that you did not have a sexual encounter with Bliss Fenton on April twenty-seventh of last year?"

Now my radar is on full alert.

Fletcher pauses for much longer than he should have. "Not that I can recall."

Girlie cocks her head to the side, causing her silky hair to fall across her right shoulder. "So is it your testimony that it's possible you did have sexual relations with Ms. Fenton on April twenty-seventh, but you can't recall for sure?"

Fletcher presses his right fist into the opposite palm. "I didn't have sex with her after we broke up in February."

Bliss interrupts Girlie's flow by whispering into her ear.

Fletcher is looking more and more distressed. I place my hand on his forearm. He instantly understands my subtle signal and his fingers unfurl.

The fact that Girlie asked him about a specific date concerns me. But then again, Girlie would do something like make up a date solely to get under Fletcher's skin. Anyway, it would be Fletcher's word against Bliss'.

"Mr. McClain, did you always reach an orgasm when you had sex with Ms. Fenton?"

Fletcher locks his arms across his chest. "Yes."

"Every time?"

"Yeah. That was the point."

"Did you use a condom when you had sexual relations with Ms. Fenton?"

"Always."

"And after you reached an orgasm, what did you expect would happen with your semen?"

"What do you mean *what did I think would happen?*"

"Objection vague and ambiguous," I interject. "Maybe you could rephrase the question, counselor."

"Just answer my question to the best of your ability, Mr. McClain."

"I didn't expect her to steal it and inseminate herself," Fletcher says. "That's for sure."

"But what did you think would happen to it?"

"I expected that the condom and my semen would be disposed of."

"How?"

"Either flushed down the toilet or placed in the trash and left there." He's glaring at Bliss who's now glaring right back.

"Do you have any evidence that Ms. Fenton—as you claim in your complaint—stole your semen?"

"Yep. That kid is all the evidence I need."

"Any other evidence?"

He takes a moment to think. "No."

"So you never saw Ms. Fenton take one of your used condoms?"

Fletcher grimaces, clearly not wanting to concede this point. "No. That's not something I tend to look for after getting off."

"Did you ever ask Ms. Fenton if she took your semen?"

"Why would I? Only a psycho would do that."

Girlie turns to me. "Counselor, would you please direct your witness to answer the question?"

Before I can say a word, Fletcher responds. "No. I never asked her or any other woman if they stole my sperm."

"You've alleged a claim for intentional infliction of emotional distress. Please describe what kind of mental anguish you've suffered."

I've prepared Fletcher for this one as best as I could. His claim for emotional distress is admittedly weak.

"Well," he begins, "knowing that a psycho I didn't want to be with had intentionally brought a child into the world without my consent has caused me lots of sleepless nights. As a result of the lack of sleep, sometimes I can't concentrate in meetings and I'm also losing weight."

I hand Fletcher a note telling him to stop referring to Bliss as a psycho. He merely rolls his eyes.

"How many days of work have you missed because of your lack of sleep?"

Fletcher bites his lip. "None."

"Have you missed any days because you can't concentrate?"

"No."

"And how much weight have you lost?"

"I'm not sure."

"Can you give me an estimate?"

"At least ten pounds."

"Over what period of time?"

"Since I received your client's paternity petition."

"How much do you weigh now?"

"One ninety-five."

"And how much did you weigh the day before you received the petition?"

"I don't remember."

"Do you have any photographs of yourself that might show that you lost weight during this period?"

"I'm not sure."

Girlie turns to me. "Counselor, I'd appreciate it if you could have your client produce photographs of himself before and after he received my client's paternity petition."

"I'll have him look," I say, though I already know Fletcher doesn't have any.

"Have you been under the care of a psychologist or psychiatrist to help you deal with your mental anguish?"

"No, I haven't."

"Are you taking any medication for your mental anguish?"

"No."

"When you had sex with my client on April twenty-seventh, who initiated it?"

"I didn't—"

Fletcher starts to respond at the same time I step in to object.

"Objection, asserts facts not in evidence. Mr. McClain testified that he didn't have sex with Ms. Fenton on that date."

"Oh, I'm sorry." There's not an ounce of sincerity in her voice. "I'll rephrase. The last time you had sex with my client, who initiated it?"

"I don't remember."

Fletcher told me he initiated it. *Did he suddenly forget?* Once we received the deposition transcript, he'd have a chance to correct any errors in his testimony, but I'd prefer to get it right the first time.

"Did Ms. Fenton ever force you to have sex with her?"

He pauses. "No."

Girlie looks down at her notes, then up at Fletcher. "I have no further questions, Mr. McClain. Thank you for your time."

I'm stunned that Girlie has ended the deposition so quickly.

She catches my eye. "Can we stipulate that—"

"Excuse me, but I have a few questions for the witness." I turn sideways to face him. "Mr. McClain, did you and Ms. Fenton ever discuss having a long-term relationship?"

"Yes, multiple times."

"Tell me about those discussions."

"She kept whining about wanting a commitment. I told her that wasn't going to happen. She was a lot of fun, but she wasn't the type of girl you marry."

His last statement is an adlib that hits its mark. Bliss' cheeks flush bright red and her nose twitches.

"Did you ever discuss having a child with her?"

"Yes, I specifically told her I did not want a kid."

"And what did she say when you told her that?"

"She said fine. That she already had two kids and didn't want another one."

"Did she tell you she was taking the pill?"

"Yes, she did. And I still wore a condom to make extra sure that she didn't get pregnant."

"Did you ever give Ms. Fenton permission to take your sperm from a used condom?"

"No, I did not."

I smile over at Girlie. "I have no further questions."

Ten minutes later, we're walking out of the conference room. Fletcher holds his tongue until we're almost at his car.

"That didn't feel right in there. What do that psycho and her conniving lawyer have up their sleeves?"

"You tell me."

"Why was she asking me what I intended to do with my sperm?"

"She's probably going to argue that if you intended your sperm to be thrown away, it didn't matter that Bliss took it."

"That's bullshit."

"I agree, but it could knock out the conversion claim."

Now it's my turn to ask a few questions.

"Girlie mentioned a specific date in April. What was that about?"

Fletcher refuses to meet my eyes and starts scrolling through his phone. "Beats me."

"Fletcher, I don't like surprises. If you've been withholding something, now's the time to level with me. I can't properly represent you if I don't have all of the facts."

"I didn't have sex with her after we broke up in February, okay? She stole my sperm and inseminated herself just so she could extort me and cause all of this drama."

I look him in the eye, hoping for some telltale sign of whether he's telling me the truth.

He raises his right hand. "Scout's honor."

There isn't a lawyer alive who hasn't run across a client who wasn't completely forthcoming. My experience and instincts are sounding multiple alarms, warning me that my rich, arrogant client is hiding something.

My husband is absolutely right about Fletcher Douglas McClain. Not only is he lying to me, he probably just lied under oath.

CHAPTER **38**

Special debated with herself for a good hour about how to best approach Martin Zinzer. She could bum rush him leaving his office. Or better yet, catch him returning from his next lunchtime tryst with Bliss. She finally decided on an email as her initial outreach. Less confrontational, but more ominous than an ambush in broad daylight.

She found Zinzer's email address on his law firm's website.

Dear Mr. Zinzer,

My name is Special Moore and I'm employed by a private investigations firm working on behalf of a client who's currently in litigation against Bliss Fenton. A copy of my client's fraud complaint against Ms. Fenton is attached. Please note that I have redacted my client's name from the complaint to conceal his identity.

I'd like to speak with you regarding your relationship with Ms. Fenton. If you're willing to answer a few questions, I will agree to keep what I already know about your relationship with Ms. Fenton private.

Special left her telephone number and asked Zinzer to either call or email her with a time and place that he would be available to meet with her. Interviewing him on the telephone wouldn't do. She needed to look into the man's eyes to get a true sense of what was really going on.

Based on what she could find about him on the Internet, Special pegged Zinzer as a classic type A: driven, focused and anal. He likely rose each morning by four or five, ran a few miles or hit the gym, and arrived at work no later than seven. So she sent her email at 6:45 a.m.

She assumed that Zinzer's reply, when it came, would not be via email. A man like Zinzer might even be too paranoid to call her from his own phone and would buy a throwaway. If he needed to later deny having spoken with her, he would not want a paper trail.

When Special received a call from a blocked number at 7:32 a.m., she knew she'd pegged her target correctly.

"What's this about?" Zinzer didn't bother to offer any kind of greeting or confirm that he was indeed talking to the right person.

"I'm assuming you read the complaint."

His silence acknowledged that he had.

"I'd like to meet with you in person."

"For what?"

"I'd like to know what kind of arrangement you have with Bliss Fenton?"

"You must be mistaken. I don't have any kind of arrangement with her."

His snippy retort told Special he was not a man used to being questioned about anything, much less his personal life. But Zinzer was at Special's mercy. Not the other way around.

"You met Ms. Fenton at the Bonaventure Hotel around lunchtime a week ago today. I need to understand the nature of your relationship to assist my client with his litigation. If you deliver, his attorney won't need to subpoena you to testify at trial. We just need enough information to spring on her during her deposition."

Special wanted to pat herself on the back for her professionalism. She almost sounded like a lawyer herself. But if she had to, she would and could go hood on him.

Look, I know you've been screwing Bliss on a regular basis. I just wanna know for how long and how much it's costing you. So I suggest you cut the act and talk to me. Otherwise, I might decide to tell your wife and law partners about your little lunchtime hokey pokey.

Silence. Special figured he was weighing his options. Unfortunately, he didn't have any.

"That's fine, Mr. Zinzer. We'll do it by the book. You should expect to receive a deposition subpoena in the next couple of days."

Special hung up the phone and started counting out loud. "One thousand one, one thousand two, one thousand three..."

When her phone rang, she did a quick fist pump. *Dang, I'm good.*

Zinzer agreed to meet her at Demitasse Brew Bar in Little Tokyo, which was downtown, but a good distance from his office. He recklessly screwed Bliss at a hotel just across the street, but took added precautions to make sure none of his colleagues caught him chatting it up with her.

Special had to fake a migraine to get off work early. Just after three that afternoon, she drove through the epicenter of what used to be L.A.'s Skid Row. Now the homeless had been pushed further east and the area resembled a neighborhood that hadn't quite decided whether it wanted to be retro or trendy.

Special was already waiting for Zinzer when he arrived. She'd expected anger, but his face bore nothing but resignation.

"Is the stuff in that complaint true?" he asked, even before taking a seat.

"Yep."

"That's crazy. I can't believe Bliss did that."

"I hope you've been disposing of your own condoms. We believe Bliss froze my client's sperm and waited a year later, when he was happily engaged to another woman, to spring her pregnancy on him."

The glassy look in his eyes told me he had not.

"Bliss has two other kids. My client is her third victim. You could well be number four."

His rubbed his forehead. "I need some coffee." He stood up and went to the counter. Rather than returning to our table, he waited at the counter while his latte was being prepared.

"If I talk to you, how can I be sure I won't be called to testify at trial?" he asked, when he returned.

Special wanted to lie, but this wasn't a situation where she needed to. "You can't be. But you need to know that a man like my client doesn't want a trial. He's the CEO of a major corporation. He doesn't want the publicity any more than you do. So far this case hasn't been picked up by the media. We just need enough information to use against Bliss during her deposition so the case settles and there is no trial."

Zinzer took a sip of coffee and stared over Special's shoulder out of the window. She suspected he was imagining the worst case scenario. That is, how his involvement in this case could wreck his family life, and maybe even his legal career.

"As I said, the last thing my client wants is a trial." Special knew she needed to hammer this point home to get Zinzer to talk. "But my client has a net worth of almost half a billion dollars. He offered her fifteen grand a month in child support. But her attorney wants over eighty grand a month. And it's not out of the question that a court would give it to her."

"That's crazy!"

"I'm glad you agree."

Special could tell Zinzer still had misgivings about divulging the details of his relationship with Bliss. She had to keep the pressure on.

"I don't have a lot of time. If you want to help us, great. But if not..." She allowed her words to trail off, but she knew that in Zinzer's mind, the trail led to disaster.

He tossed back the rest of his coffee as if it was a shot of tequila, then crumbled the empty paper cup with one hand.

"Okay." He sucked in a big breath. "What do you want to know?"

CHAPTER 39

"I wish you could've been a fly on the wall," Bliss squealed. "My attorney stuck it to Fletcher yesterday. I know he wanted to dive across the table and strangle both of us. I loved every minute of it."

Bliss, along with her brood, had dropped by Jessica's Bel Air home to give her a recap of Fletcher's deposition. Bliss' excitement, however, didn't rub off on her best friend.

Jessica frowned as she cuddled Harmony close to her chest. "I hope this is worth all the energy you're expending."

"Of course it is. I'm going to be a millionaire after the money I get from Fletcher for the next eighteen years."

Bliss paused. Aiden and Jonas were chasing each other through the house.

"Will you two please be quiet!" she yelled.

The boys stopped their antics for all of ten seconds before starting up again.

"They're fine." Jessica was always glad to have them around and actually enjoyed the ruckus. "You shouldn't yell at them like that. You have no idea how blessed you are. I'd love to have a couple of rambunctious boys tearing through my house every day."

"I already told you. That's totally within your control. If you want kids, then have them."

Jessica exhaled, then kissed Harmony on the nose. "So when are they taking your deposition?"

"Tomorrow."

"Are you nervous?"

"Nope. Mine is going to be even more fun than Fletcher's."

"I will never understand you."

Bliss waved off Jessica's downer attitude. "Let's change the subject. I know Paul didn't like the clothes I picked out. But why aren't you wearing the makeup?"

"He hated that too, especially the fake eyelashes."

"That's insane. That pink lipstick looked really hot on you. I bet his mistress wears—" Bliss caught herself, but it was too late.

Gravity seemed to tug Jessica's chin downward. "So you do think he's cheating."

Bliss reached over and squeezed Jessica's shoulder. "I don't know for sure, and neither do you. But I've laid in bed next to lots of men who were on the phone telling their wives they were working late on some"—Bliss held up her hands and made imaginary quotation marks in the air—"big case. Actually, screwing me was the big case."

Jessica brushed her cheek against Harmony's.

"But even if he is," Bliss said, trying to offer comfort, "Paul isn't going anywhere. That's what most women who sleep with married men don't understand. No matter how unhappy they are in their marriage, few men are willing to leave. I learned that early in life. So for me, sleeping with a married man is all about getting paid."

They heard the front door open and seconds later, Paul stepped into the great room. He walked in and pecked Jessica on the lips, then tickled Harmony on the chin.

"Hello, Bliss."

"Hey, Paul." Bliss looked him up and down as if she was searching for some sign of his infidelity.

Jessica shoved Harmony back into Bliss' arms and stood up. She was obviously fearful that Bliss might have the nerve to come out and ask Paul if he'd been cheating. Jessica walked up to him and placed a hand on his arm.

"I made lasagna." Her voice sounded small, like a child desperate for praise.

"Can't stay, sweetheart. Just came home for a document I forgot this morning."

Jonas and Aiden barreled into the room, each grabbing a leg. "Uncle Paul!"

He embraced both of them in a one-arm hug. When he finally untangled himself, there was a small smudge on his upper thigh where Jonas had left a spot of jelly.

Paul stiffened, then glared at Jessica as if to say, *See. This is exactly why I don't want kids.*

Jessica bent to examine the stain. "I can get that out. Just let me—"

Paul held out his palm. "Don't worry about it," he said good-naturedly. "It'll only take me a second to change."

He hurried down the hallway, returning minutes later in a new pair of slacks and holding a manila envelope. "Don't wait up. I'll be late."

He was out of the door before Jessica had time to ask how late.

Jessica flopped onto the couch next to Bliss. Her eyes glistened with the beginning of tears. "We're so disconnected. I just don't know what to do."

"For one, you need to stop being a so wimpy. *I made lasagna.*" Bliss mocked her in a singsong voice. "The next time he comes home, you shouldn't be here. Hell, spend the night at a hotel without telling him. Let him wonder what *you're* doing for a change instead of the other way around."

"I don't want to play games."

"Well, you better start. Because if he is screwing around, you can bet his little paramour is playing all kinds of games to see if she can make him her husband instead of yours. Take it from me, a good-looking guy like Paul has women throwing themselves at him all the time."

"I just love him so much," Jessica whimpered. "I don't know what I would do if I lost him."

"You're not going to lose him," Bliss said with a crafty smile. "But if you do, we're going to take him for everything he's got."

"I don't care about his money. I want my husband back."

"That's because right now you have all the money you could ever spend. But once you don't have any, I guarantee you'll care then."

Jessica wiped away a tear.

"But you'll be fine because you'll get half the community property, plus alimony," Bliss continued. "But if I were you, to add some additional funds to the kitty, I'd get to work on getting pregnant A-S-A-P."

CHAPTER 40

From the moment I woke up that morning, I had a bad feeling deep in the pit of my stomach. And now, as I'm about to commence the deposition of Bliss Fenton, the apprehension only intensifies.

The deposition is taking place in my office. Fletcher and I enter the conference room and sit down across from Girlie Cortez and her smug client. They look like giddy teenagers.

Why in the hell are you two smiling like Cheshire cats?

Someone watching the scene would have thought Fletcher was the one about to be put under oath.

As he sits down next to me, he fires daggers across the table at both Girlie and Bliss.

I nod at the videographer. "I'm ready to begin."

As the videographer announces the case name, the date and time, Fletcher grabs my legal pad and scribbles on it.

Stick it to 'em!

I half smile and immediately scratch out his message with my pen.

I run through the preliminaries—name, background, work history. As to the latter, Bliss has no work experience other than a couple of jobs in her twenties. She's definitely a kept woman. Rather than dive right into her relationship with Fletcher, I ask about her other children's fathers.

"Was your oldest son Aiden the result of a planned pregnancy?"

"No."

"And who is his father?"

"Dr. Joseph Franco."

"And was Dr. Franco happy to learn that you were pregnant with Aiden?"

"No."

"Did he want to have a child with you?"

"No."

"Did he tell you prior to your pregnancy that he didn't want to have a child with you?"

"Yes."

Bliss is all smiles, which irks me.

"And how did you conceive Aiden?"

"We had sex and I got pregnant."

"Did your pregnancy involve stealing his semen?"

"Nope. We did it the old-fashioned way."

"And what do you mean by *the old-fashioned way*?"

"What I mean is," she says with a huff, "the male part is inserted into the female part."

Girlie covers her mouth to stifle a giggle.

I feel like slapping her.

"Did he wear a condom?" I ask.

"Nope."

"Were you taking the pill?"

"For most of the relationship I was."

"When did you stop?"

"When he told me he wanted to break up with me."

I hear Fletcher mutter, "Jesus Christ!"

"Does Dr. Franco pay child support for Aiden?"

"Yep. Ten thousand—excuse me—I just got a raise. Twelve thousand dollars a month."

Girlie pauses and whispers something to her client. Probably that she's volunteering too much information.

"And what about your son Jonas?" I ask. "Who is his father?"

The smirk tumbles from Bliss' face and plops onto the table. "That's...that's none of your business."

She turns to Girlie, who belatedly jumps to her rescue.

"My client won't be answering any questions about the identity of Jonas' father. That information is confidential and is not relevant to this case."

"It most certainly is relevant," I counter.

"Doesn't matter," Girlie replies. "My client won't be answering any questions about Jonas' father."

I ignore her. "Is his father someone famous?"

"I instruct my client not to answer," Girlie says. "Move on, counselor."

Bliss is boldly sneering at me now.

"Evidence of Ms. Fenton's past deceit is relevant to our fraud claim," I say. "So I'm leaving the deposition open pending the filing of a motion to compel Ms. Fenton to disclose the identity of Jonas' father."

Bliss grips the edge of the table with both hands. "You can't do that."

I stare dead at her. "I can and I will."

"I don't care. I'm not going to—"

Girlie holds up a hand and takes a second to calm her client. "Don't worry about it. She can file a motion, but she has to win it." She turns back to me. "Ask your next question, counselor."

"Do you currently receive child support for Jonas?"

Bliss hesitates, then answers. "No."

"Did you ever receive any financial support from Jonas' father?"

Bliss whirls her head in Girlie's direction and her attorney responds on cue. "As I previously stated, my client will not be responding to any questions regarding Jonas' father."

"Is your townhouse in Playa Vista paid for?"

"Yes it is."

"Did Jonas' father buy it for you?"

I don't need Bliss to respond to my question to know that is exactly the case. The fact that she looks as white as a sheet tells me everything I needed to know.

Fletcher has a cheesy grin on his face. He acts as if he's watching a boxing match and his money is on the fighter landing all the punches.

I wait for Bliss to respond.

"I already told you, I'm not going to discuss him."

Girlie taps her index finger on the table. "Counselor, you're badgering the witness. Either move on or we're leaving."

I'm not going to get anywhere pushing the issue further. I would just have to file a motion to compel them to produce information about Jonas' father.

"Did you steal the semen of Jonas' father?"

"No."

"How did you get pregnant with Jonas?"

"We had intercourse. Same as with Aiden." Bliss is back to smiling again.

"Was it your intent to get pregnant by Jonas' father?"

"We were having unprotected sex, but I wasn't really trying to get pregnant. It just happened."

"Did you tell Jonas' father that you were on the pill?"

"Yes."

"And were you really on the pill at that time?"

"Nope."

"Did you get pregnant with Aiden and Jonas because you wanted the child support payments?"

"No. I'm glad I have my sons."

Her smile is annoying me. Time to wipe it off for good.

"What about Martin Zinzer? Is it your plan to get pregnant by him too?"

That question sends Bliss into a catatonic silence. Girlie's baffled face tells me she's never heard the name Martin Zinzer.

"Ms. Fenton, would you like me to repeat my question?"

Bliss speaks haltingly. "How do you know—"

"I'm the one asking the questions, Ms. Fenton. You can answer."

"I...I need to speak to my attorney."

"Okay," Girlie says. "Let's take a break."

I ignore their requests. "You're free to take a break as soon as you answer my question." I want to hear Bliss' response before Girlie has a chance to coach her.

Girlie pushes back from the table. "If she wants to speak to me, she can. Let's go off the record."

"No, we're not going off the record."

The court reporter continues typing. She can't stop until we both agree to go off the record.

"It's improper for you to take a break with a question pending," I say. "After Ms. Fenton answers my question, then you can take your break."

"No, I don't plan to get pregnant by Mr. Zinzer." Bliss spits her answer at me before Girlie can advise her further.

We finally go off the record and the two of them hurry out of the conference room.

"I'm loving this!" Fletcher whispers to me. "You're like a pit bull."

Bliss and Girlie return ten minutes later. Bliss' little chat with her counsel apparently did nothing to soothe her. She still looks frazzled.

"So, Ms. Fenton, do you supplement your income by trading sex for cash?"

"No I do not!"

"So if I subpoenaed Mr. Zinzer, he would tell me he doesn't pay you one thousand dollars each time he meets you at the Bonaventure for sex?"

Bliss swallows. "I take the Fifth."

I laugh. "This isn't a criminal proceeding, Ms. Fenton. You can't assert the Fifth."

"Oh, yes, she can," Girlie says. "The Fifth Amendment protection against self-incrimination goes to the question asked, not the proceeding."

"Okay," I say. "So, Ms. Fenton, is it your testimony that your lunch meetings with Mr. Zinzer involved criminal activity, that is prostitution?"

Bliss snorts in contempt. "I said I take the Fifth."

Girlie looks just as uncomfortable as her client. "Ms. Henderson, you're badgering the witness."

"Are there other men besides Mr. Zinzer who pay you for sex?"

"I take the Fifth."

Fletcher rocks in his chair, enjoying the show. I fear he might break into applause at any second.

"Ms. Fenton, do you report the money you receive for sexual favors to the I.R.S.?"

"I take the Fifth."

"I'd like to schedule Mr. Zinzer's deposition for a week from today."

I slide a deposition subpoena across the table that I have no intention of serving. Zinzer's already told Special everything I need to know.

Bliss presses both hands to her cheeks. "Oh my God! Can she really—"

"Don't say another word," Girlie cautions her client.

My mission is more than accomplished. Bliss looks so rattled I feel like passing her a sedative. I pause to scan my notes. Now it's time to turn to the meat of my case.

"How did you get pregnant with your daughter Harmony?"

Bliss shifts in her seat and props her forearms on the table. "With Fletcher's sperm."

"Exactly how with Fletcher's sperm?"

"His sperm fertilized my egg."

Bliss is deliberately sidestepping my question.

"Did you do it the old-fashioned way as you just described with Aiden and Jonas' fathers?"

She hesitates. "Nope."

Fletcher is leaning forward as if he's having trouble hearing. He obviously doesn't want to miss a word.

"Did you steal Mr. McClain's sperm from a condom?"

"Nope."

"Then how did you obtain it to—as you just stated—fertilize your egg?"

"It was a gift."

Fletcher looks as confused as I feel.

"Excuse me? What do you mean *it was a gift*?"

"I mean he willingly gave it to me."

"And when did he give you this gift?"

"On April twenty-seventh of last year, nine months before I had Harmony."

Fletcher slowly eases back in his chair.

"And how did he give you this gift?"

"What do you mean by *how?*"

Bliss' feigned ignorance is pissing me off. "Was it gift wrapped?"

"Nope."

"Okay, then, how did you get his sperm?"

"I obtained custody of it when he gave it to me."

Obtained custody of it? Girlie had definitely coached her to say that.

"Ms. Fenton, I'm not clear how you *obtained custody of it*. Can you explain?"

She takes a moment to grin across the table at Fletcher. "I obtained custody of it when I gave him a blow job."

Fletcher sneers at her. "What the—"

I shoot Fletcher a hard look intending to silence him.

"Are you saying you had oral sex with Mr. McClain on April twenty-seventh, two months after you broke up?"

"Sure did."

Right now I need a paper bag to breathe into because I'm about to start hyperventilating. I do everything in my power to keep my face neutral.

"And where did you supposedly have oral sex with Mr. McClain?"

"In the backseat of his Lincoln Town Car in the parking lot at Karma Entertainment. His driver Lester can testify to that."

I steal a quick glance at Fletcher, who appears to be shrinking right before my eyes. His reaction to Bliss' testimony tells me she is speaking the truth and nothing but.

"So you're saying that you obtained Mr. McClain's semen during oral sex on April twenty-seventh of last year?"

"Asked and answered," Girlie interjects.

But Bliss is eager to answer *this* question. "Sure did."

"And after you obtained Mr. McClain's semen during oral sex, what did you do with it?"

"I spit it into a cervical cap."

Fletcher pounds the table with his fist. "You friggin' psycho!"

"Counselor," Girlie exclaims, "if you can't control Mr. McClain's harassing and intimidating conduct, we're going to have to suspend the deposition. I won't allow my client to be harassed and intimidated like this."

Normally, I would've taken a disruptive client out in the hallway for a short lecture. But we're at a crucial point in the deposition so I don't want to take a break. I glare over at Fletcher and simultaneously kick him in the shin. No audible scolding is necessary. I do, however, need to make amends for his behavior on the record.

"Understandably, Ms. Fenton's testimony is quite shocking for my client." I try to sound genuinely contrite. "I apologize for his outburst. It won't happen again."

Bliss leers at Fletcher. She's obviously proud of herself.

"You just testified that you had oral sex with Mr. McClain on April twenty-seventh and spit his semen into a cervical cap. Is that correct?"

"Yes."

"Can you explain what a cervical cap is?"

"It's a device women can use for artificial insemination. It looks like a small plastic cup. Sort of like a diaphragm, but smaller."

"Okay, so what did you do after spitting Mr. McClain's sperm into the cervical cap?"

"I inserted it into my vagina."

"Right there in the car?"

"Yep."

"And where was Mr. McClain while you were doing that?"

She hunches her shoulders. "Sitting right there. He was busy zipping up his pants. He wasn't paying any attention to what I was doing. I wasn't wearing any panties so it was easy. It only took a few seconds to insert it. He probably thought I was cleaning up down there."

"And after you inserted the cervical cap, then what did you do?"

"I got out of the car and Fletcher and Lester drove off."

"Did you ever retain Mr. McClain's semen using this method on any other occasion?"

"Nope."

"What did you do with Mr. McClain's semen on other occasions when you gave him a blow—I mean— when you had oral sex?"

Bliss smiles big. "I swallowed it."

I take a second to glance over my notes. I'm not looking for anything in particular. I just need a minute to settle my nerves. I want to slug Fletcher *and* his baby mama.

"And when did you find out you were pregnant?"

"About eight weeks later."

"Have you ever used the technique you just described to get pregnant with any other guy?"

"Nope. Just Fletcher."

"And how did you learn about this technique?"

"On the Internet. They also include instructions along with the cervical cap. It's for women who want to do artificial insemination at home. It's easier than using a syringe."

My head is spinning over how nonchalantly Bliss has just recounted her outrageous behavior.

"Did you tell Mr. McClain that you were on the pill and didn't want any more children?"

"Yes."

"Yet you intentionally conceived a child without his knowledge?"

"Sure did."

"When did you stop taking the pill?"

"When he broke up with me."

"How did you end up in Mr. McClain's car on April twenty-seventh?"

"I showed up at his office and asked to speak to him."

"And what did you want to speak to him about?"

"About us getting back together."

"And what did Mr. McClain do?"

"He had his assistant tell me to leave."

"Did you leave?"

"Yeah, but I waited outside until he left the building. When I saw him walking toward his car, I begged him to talk to me. He told Lester to wait outside while we got into the backseat."

"And once you were in the car, what happened?"

"I told him how much I loved him and missed him and wanted him back."

"And what did Mr. McClain say?"

"He said he was sorry, but he was in love with Mia."

"And then what happened?"

"I asked him if I could give him head one last time for the road." She grins. "He always said I gave the best blow jobs ever. Then, he unzipped his pants and I went to work."

"When you showed up at Mr. McClain's office, was it your intention to get pregnant and conceive a child?"

"Yep."

"A child you knew Mr. McClain did not want?"

Girlie jumps in before Bliss can respond. "Objection asked and answered."

"You can answer my question," I say.

This time, instead of addressing her response to me, Bliss locks eyes with Fletcher.

"Yeah, I knew he didn't want a kid. But *I* did. If he didn't want to be a father, he should've kept his pants zipped."

CHAPTER 41

As we leave the conference room and walk the short distance to my office, I don't say one word to Fletcher. I'm disgusted with Bliss Fenton, but I'm enraged at my lying client.

I barely wait for Fletcher to close the door to my office before lighting into him.

"You lied to me."

"Excuse me? Shouldn't we be discussing what Bliss just admitted in there?"

"You swore to me that you hadn't had sex with her in almost a year."

"I didn't swear." He said with a grin. "I said Scout's honor. That's different."

"You think this is funny?"

"A lot of people don't consider a blow job to be sex." His lips arch into a crooked smile. "Bill Clinton didn't."

I throw up my hands. "Do you understand the implications of this?"

"Yep. I'm about to win my fraud case. What she did was even more outrageous than stealing a used condom. Her actions were intentional and malicious. All we need is a few men and a bunch of married women on the jury. The verdict should be at least ten million dollars. Then we can call it a wash."

"I've repeatedly told you the fraud case is by no means a slam dunk. It may not even get to a jury. And even if you win, all of her income is judgment proof."

"I don't care. I'll take her townhouse, her clothes and whatever else she has. And I should definitely win the emotional distress claim."

"Are you hard of hearing? You have no evidence that you've suffered any emotional distress."

"So what do I need to do? Start going to a shrink and pretending to be crazy? I can do even better than that. I have a staff meeting tomorrow morning. Right in the middle of the meeting I'm going to break down and cry."

"This isn't funny, Fletcher. When Mia finds out about your little backseat rendezvous with Bliss, she's going to kill you."

That seems to sober him up.

He rubs his chin. "Yeah, that could be a problem. A big one. We have to figure out how we're going to keep Mia from finding out."

"*We?* That's not my job."

He takes out his phone and punches a few buttons. "Hey, Gabriella, please send three dozen yellow roses to Mia's office. Pronto. The card should read: *To the love of my life. Just because.*"

"So that's it? You send her roses and that solves everything?"

"Nope. But it's a start."

"She's going to leave you," I say.

He chuckles. "Mia's not going anywhere. For one, I'm rich. She loves the lifestyle and, like most women, she'll take whatever I dish out so she can continue enjoying the luxuries that I provide. And two, she hates Bliss Fenton with a passion. She'd slit her own wrists before letting Bliss come between us."

"You're way too cocky."

"No, I'm just being real. Women don't leave rich, powerful men. Even when the whole world knows about their man's sexual indiscretions, they stay. Hillary didn't leave Bill. Camille is standing by Cosby and Kobe Bryant appeased his wife with a four million dollar diamond ring. I don't care how smart the woman is or whether she has her own money. The majority of women don't leave."

My temple starts to throb as if a major migraine is coming on. "Your arrogance is unbelievable."

"Now you," he continues, pointing a finger my way, "you'd leave. You'd even leave a man like me. You like standing on your own two feet. That's what attracted me to you. A man for you is a desire, not a necessity. I saw that in you even at nineteen and it was quite a turn on. There aren't a lot of women out there like you."

"You're wrong about Mia," I insist.

"No, I'm not. Now, she'll definitely give me hell. She'll whine and throw it in my face. And I'll let her do that for a month or two. And when I've had enough, I'll tell her that if she brings it up again, I'm out. And I guarantee you, she'll never mention it again."

"You arrogant son of a bitch."

His voice hardens. "I'm still a paying client. So treat me like one."

I slap my legal pad on my desk. "Maybe you should find yourself a new lawyer."

Fletcher holds up both hands in surrender. "C'mon, Vernetta, let's both chill. I don't want a new lawyer. I want you. I don't understand why you're not more psyched about Bliss' testimony. If that isn't fraud, I don't know what is."

"It isn't that simple Fletcher."

"She set me up. What's more fraudulent than that?"

"You lied to me and you lied under oath when you said you hadn't had sex with her after February."

"It was just a friggin' blow job."

"No, it was not *just* a blow job. It was a blow job that produced a child that's going to cost you millions of dollars in child support."

Fletcher grins. "I will say this, though. Bliss may be evil as hell, but the girl blows out of this world. I've never experienced anything like it before or since."

"Fine." I fall into the chair behind my desk. "If you're okay with what your little blow job is going to cost you, so am I. Bliss wants more than eighty-thousand dollars a month, remember?"

"She's not getting that much of my money. I'll take her out first."

"I told you before, please don't talk crazy like that in my presence."

"I'm not talking crazy. I'm rich. I have people who can do all kinds of things and it will never lead back to me."

"I'm going to pretend you didn't just say that."

"You don't have to. This discussion is attorney-client privileged. You can't divulge anything we discuss anyway."

"I can if it involves the commission of a future crime."

"I'm not worried. You'd never sell me out."

"If Bliss ends up dead, you'll be the number one suspect."

"Won't matter. I'm a bright guy. I'll be halfway around the world when it happens."

"When what happens?"

"When somebody blows her pretty little brains out." Fletcher winks. "Hypothetically speaking, that is."

CHAPTER 42

"I'm not saying it's a problem," Darius explained. "I'm just saying next time, I'd prefer to get a call first."

Special was standing in Darius' living room in the midst of what was turning out to be their first fight. She'd just dropped by his place unannounced and was stunned by the reception she received.

"I'm not used to dating a man who requires me to call before dropping by. Exactly what do you have to hide?"

"I don't have anything to hide. It's just a matter of common courtesy. Next time, just call first. Now let's talk about something else."

Special refused to let it go. "I don't see why it's a problem."

"So you'd have no problem if I dropped by your place without calling first?"

"Not at all."

"Well, I'm sorry. I feel differently."

Darius turned away from her and rolled his wheelchair toward the kitchen.

"Don't walk away from me." *Oops!* She probably shouldn't have said that. "Um, you know what I mean."

Darius spun back around. "Special, I really like you and enjoy hanging out with you, but I don't need this kind of drama in my life. I didn't think you were the insecure type."

"I ain't insecure." Her hands were planted on her hips and her head tilted to the side. "I just have some basic expectations when I'm dating somebody."

"And so do I. You respect my rules and I'll respect yours."

Special wasn't even sure she wanted to be with this man and here she was acting like a jealous, stalker girlfriend.

"Who's Wilson?" she blurted out.

"What?"

"When you were at my house the other night, you got a call, from someone named Wilson."

"So you're checking my phone now?"

"I wasn't checking your phone. You turned it over to look at it and I saw the name Wilson. Is that a man or a woman?"

"Like I said, I don't need this kind of drama."

"Who is Wilson?" she demanded.

Darius threw up his hand. "A co-worker."

"Male or female?"

"Female."

"Do your female co-workers usually call you at night?"

"If there's a reason to, yeah." He opened the refrigerator, grabbed a beer and popped it open. "I'm done with the fifty questions. If this is what you're about, we should cut this thing short right now."

Special couldn't believe this man was trying to give her the ax. Did he know how many men on MyHarmony.com would give their left testicle to be with her?

"I'm serious. I dig you, but I don't do drama."

Darius continued into the kitchen and Special followed.

"To hell with you then," she blubbered, as she started to tear up. She should just leave, but her feet stayed planted in place.

"Don't cry. I hate crying. Please don't cry."

Darius reached out and pulled her into his lap.

"My co-worker was calling me so late because she couldn't make a meeting the next morning and wanted me to cover for her. That's it. And if you saw her, you wouldn't be worried at all. She's over fifty and could pass for my mother. I'm not seeing anyone else. I don't want to be with anyone else. It's all about you. Okay?"

Special sniffled into his shoulder. "Are you telling me the truth?"

"Yes, but you're going to have to trust me."

Special kissed him and enjoyed the feeling of being in his arms. She hoped this man wasn't playing any games because she was actually falling for him.

CHAPTER 43

I'm still steaming by the time I get home. I should've known Fletcher hadn't told me the entire story.

"What's wrong with you?"

My husband can read me like I have words stamped across my forehead. I'm about to lie and say I'm fine, but I need to vent. We still hadn't discussed his walking out the other night. We just pretended as if it hadn't happened. I know I owe him an apology. I need to address that issue first.

"I'm sorry I didn't let you know I'd be home late the other night."

Jefferson scratches his jaw. "Okay."

That's what I like most about my husband. He never holds a grudge. He'd just said everything was okay and he meant it. I flop down next to him on the couch.

"What's going on with you? You look hella stressed."

I kick off my pumps and Jefferson pulls my feet into his lap and starts massaging them.

"I took Bliss Fenton's deposition today. You were right. Fletcher was lying to me. He was with Bliss after he started dating Mia."

Jefferson doesn't say I-told-you-so, but there is a self-satisfied look on his face.

"And I didn't mention it before, but Bliss is represented by Girlie Cortez."

"Oh, poor baby. You're going another round with her? I guess you have a reason to be stressed."

"That's an understatement. You'll never guess in a million years how Bliss got pregnant."

"I'm listening," Jefferson says, as he flexes my right foot.

When I finish explaining, his hands stop moving. "That's crazy. She actually admitted doing that?"

"In fact, she acted quite proud of herself."

"I'm on Fletcher's team now. He shouldn't have to pay child support when a chick does some underhanded crap like that."

"That's not how it works. The law only cares about the best interests of the child. It doesn't matter how she got here. Fletcher's going to have to pay child support, regardless."

"Well, the law is wrong. I'd fight that scandalous trick all the way to the U.S. Supreme Court. At least he's going to win his lawsuit. Because what she did is definitely fraud."

I exhale. "It depends how you define *win*. No matter how big the jury's verdict is, it's unlikely that Fletcher will ever collect a dime from her."

I explain that child support payments are judgment proof. "She has no other income, so there's nothing he could go after. Though he could go after her townhouse."

"Then he should. A woman can't pull a stunt like that and get away with it."

"Apparently she can and did."

Jefferson continues to shake his head in amazement. "That chick needs to be careful. I know a dude who was ready to kill his baby mama over an eight-hundred-dollar-a-month child support payment."

"Boy, don't talk like that! People get all caught up because they have to give money to their ex. But it's not about the ex. It's about caring for the child."

"I understand that. But I'm just saying homegirl needs to understand that some dudes wouldn't bother with the legal system. They would just take her out."

I don't tell Jefferson that Fletcher has already threatened to do just that. Instead, I close my eyes, enjoy my foot massage and pray that this case doesn't go any further south than it already has.

CHAPTER 44

Jessica examined herself in the bathroom mirror. She wasn't stunning like Bliss, but she was attractive enough in her own right. She had nice eyes and great hair. And she'd made it her mission in life to cater to her husband. According to *Cosmo* that was the key to a successful marriage.

So why is my husband cheating on me?

It bothered her that she was beginning to think more and more like Bliss. Maybe she should just get pregnant. Despite his disdain for children, Paul couldn't help but love his own son or daughter.

Without giving it further thought, Jessica opened the medicine cabinet, took out her birth control pills and popped open the case. She turned the dial and one by one dumped the pills into her hand and then dropped them into the toilet.

Feeling suddenly empowered, she left the bathroom and headed toward the kitchen. As she passed Paul's office, something stopped her. She retraced her steps and stood in the doorway of his office.

She'd spent months decorating the room with dark, rich mahogany. The heavy curtains and crown molding gave the room a majestic feeling.

Jessica stepped inside and sat down at Paul's desk. The chair felt large and uncomfortable. Paul used to come home early and work from home. Even when he hibernated in his office, at least he was there with her. Back then, he just wanted to be near her, even if he had work to do.

When had that stopped?

She wondered what kind of woman Paul was seeing. Was she younger? Blonde? Was she like Bliss? No, Paul didn't like brash women. He preferred meek women he could control, like her. She was probably some airhead receptionist at his firm.

She picked up the phone and dialed his office.

"Hey, I just wanted to say hi. When are you coming home?"

"Since when do you use the phone in my office?" His voice was all irritation.

"I don't know. I...I was just looking at the decor. Maybe it's time for a makeover."

"The office is fine the way it is."

Jessica glanced around. Paul was such a neat freak. There's wasn't a piece of paper in sight.

"I'm sorry, honey. I'm in the middle of something." She could hear the click-clacking of his keyboard. "What do you need?"

"I was just wondering when you were coming home," she asked again.

"Not sure, this deal is really a bear. I'll call you when I'm headed out. Sorry, but I really gotta go. Love you."

A second later, he was gone. Jessica felt so stupid. She'd allowed Paul to become her entire world. But the reverse wasn't true. She didn't agree with the way Bliss used men, but she knew her friend was right. Paul took her for granted. She needed to do something about that.

As she stood to leave, there was something about Paul's reaction to her being in his office that set off a silent alarm. She sat back down and pulled out the middle desk drawer. Two pencils, three pens and a few paperclips all neatly placed. She tried to open the top file drawer to her right. Locked. As were the other three drawers.

Looking around, she finally found the switch to turn on his desktop computer. She wasn't sure what she was looking for. She'd seen enough true crime TV shows to know that cheating men often made the mistake of charging gifts and trips for their mistresses on their credit cards. She'd already perused their joint American Express bill and found nothing out of the ordinary. She didn't have access to any of his business card accounts. Maybe she'd find something on his computer.

Once the computer came on, she realized that the primary folder where Paul's documents were stored was password protected. She tried a number of combinations. Her birthday. Paul's birthday. Their anniversary. Nothing. Some little inkling quietly urged her to keep trying. That's when she remembered reading an article about software programs that could crack a person's passwords.

After mulling it over just a few minutes more, she walked into the bedroom and retrieved her iPhone. She typed *computer monitoring software* into Google.com. There were tons of hits, but what caught her eye was an ad for Webwatcher.com, which billed itself as a parental and employee monitoring software.

She clicked on the web link and read the explanation of how the software worked. Downloading it onto a computer would log every keystroke typed on the keyboard. That keystroke information would be sent to a secure website that could be accessed at any time, even from a mobile phone. She'd not only be able to figure out Paul's password, she'd also be able to monitor every word he typed. The software was completely undetectable and only cost a hundred bucks.

Jessica left the room again, this time to grab her credit card. From Paul's computer, she purchased the software and ten minutes later, had downloaded it. She thought about buying a GPS tracker to place in his car as well, but decided to wait on that. The first step was confirming whether Paul really was having an affair.

And if that was indeed the case, Jessica had absolutely no clue what she was going to do about it.

CHAPTER 45

"**G**irlfriend, what happened to you?" Special's face scrunches up like she's swallowed something foul. "You look whipped."

I join her at a table at The Brownstone Bistro on Pico. "And just think," I say, "I feel twice as bad as I look."

We're here because I need to download with my best friend-slash-investigator. More importantly, I need to pig out on some comfort food, regardless of the pounds it will add to my hips. I order my favorite dishes: gumbo, jerk chicken wings and lobster mac and cheese.

"You will not guess in a million years how Bliss Fenton got pregnant," I say.

Special shrugs. "She stole Fletcher's condom, right?"

"Nope."

Her eyes narrow in bewilderment. "Then how did she do it?"

"Hold on a second. I need a drink." I flag our waiter and order a Cadillac margarita.

"Okay, listen to this."

I recount how, when and where Bliss conceived her daughter.

"Get outta here!" She slaps the table with her open palm. "No way. That 'ho is super scandalous. Girl, I've never heard no craziness like that. And she admitted it?"

"She didn't just admit it, she basically bragged about it. And Girlie sat there like a deaf-mute just letting Bliss run her mouth. They wanted us to know exactly how she did it. Step by step."

"That's mad crazy. That girl got some sista in her. You sure she's not black?"

I laugh. "Not that I know of."

"Okay, you know Girlie don't play fair," Special warns, pointing a finger at me. "That means she's got a surprise or two lined up for you."

"That's exactly what I'm afraid of."

"But this definitely sounds like fraud, which means Fletcher should win his case against her."

"I hope so. I'm still researching and I haven't found a single case on point. Fletcher thinks this is a slam dunk. But I'm not so sure."

My phone rings. It's my assistant. "Hey."

As I listen I feel a throbbing at my temples. I hang up the phone and massage the back of my neck.

"What's the matter?" Special's face mirrors the distress on mine.

"Girlie just served us with some documents. My assistant is emailing them to me now."

Five minutes later, I scroll through my emails and open the first document. It's hard to read on the small screen of my iPhone, but I see enough to understand the gist of it.

"That witch!"

"What? What did Girlie do now?" Special asks.

"That witch just filed a motion for summary judgment asking the court to dismiss Fletcher's lawsuit. She also wants an examination of his assets by a forensic accountant." I pause. "And she's retracting her temporary child support demand and asking the family law court for a permanent order of eighty-three grand a month."

CHAPTER 46

I t's nice to see Fletcher serious for a change. Bliss' summary judgment motion is one thing, but the petition seeking eighty-three grand a month in child support gets his full attention.

"This has to be a scare tactic by her attorney," Fletcher says, staring out of his office window. "No judge in his right mind would award Bliss that kind of money, right?"

"Probably." Fletcher seems to crave my reassurances right now. "I suspect she asked for twice what she thought the court might be willing to award."

"Half of that is still ridiculous. And this motion is nuts too. Bliss has the nerve to steal my sperm, yet she's claiming my case has no merit and *I'm* just trying to harass *her*. This is crazy. Please tell me the court's not going to grant this piece-of-crap?"

"Let me get to work on the opposition to the summary judgment motion. I'll have a much better idea of where we stand after I check out the cases Girlie cited in her brief."

Fletcher nods.

"Girlie also served Darlene with the child support demand and request for a forensics exam since she's counsel of record in the family law case. I'm sure Girlie only sent me copies of those documents to piss me off. Darlene will be calling you this afternoon. She thinks it's a good time to move forward with a motion to compel Bliss to disclose the identity of Jonas' father, and I agree. You'll have a better chance of winning that motion in the family law case."

Fletcher is staring out of the window. I wonder if he's heard anything I just said.

"That forensics exam can't happen," he says.

"Why?"

"I'm in the middle of a major deal where I'm putting up most of the financing. If the other side gets wind of this paternity case, it could blow it for me. Do whatever you have to do to block it. At least for a couple of months."

"I'll see what I can do. But if the forensics exam doesn't happen in the fraud case, the family court's certainly going to allow it."

"That's not good enough," Fletcher said. "I don't want her looking into my finances. So fix it."

* * *

Fletcher wasn't the kind of man who would accept being uncomfortable in his own space, and for that reason he didn't want to go home. As he headed up the walkway, he braced himself for another run-in with Mia. He'd told her the deposition had gone okay, but she'd been asking for a copy of his deposition transcript as well as Bliss'. There was no way he could let that happen. If Mia found out about his backseat blow job, she'd stroke out.

He headed straight for the bedroom and undressed, putting on a pair of sweatpants and a T-shirt. He could hear Mia in the kitchen. She rarely cooked, but he smelled what he thought might be spaghetti sauce. Mia made amazing spaghetti sauce using fresh tomatoes. If Mia was cooking, he was really in for it. She was setting him up for a major push.

When he entered the kitchen, Mia was standing at the sink. He kissed her on the back of the neck.

"Hey, beautiful. Do I smell my favorite?"

"Sure do."

"How'd you have time for that?"

"I made time."

He took a seat at the kitchen table and watched Mia drain the spa-ghetti in a colander. He figured she'd wait until after dinner to start pressuring him again about the deposition transcripts. He was wrong.

"How important is trust to you in a relationship?" she asked, turn-ing to face him.

WTF?

He was not in the mood to deal with this right now. Why don't women understand when to leave well enough alone?

He stood up. "Not tonight, Mia. I had a long day."

She walked over to him, hands on hips. He liked her feistiness. It was almost a turn on.

"Fletcher, I need to know what's going on in your case. This impacts me too. I'm about to be your wife."

"I've already given you an update."

"I'm a lawyer. I don't understand why I can't review the deposition transcripts."

"Because you're not a lawyer on *this* case. Vernetta is doing a fine job. I need you to stay out of it."

"I wouldn't be so concerned if you hadn't lied to me about not filing the defamation lawsuit."

"I didn't lie to you."

"Let's not play semantics, Fletcher. A material omission is the same as a lie. You let me think you'd already served Bliss. It was very embarrassing to find out from her that you not only hadn't filed the complaint, but you also tried to settle with her."

He brushed past her. "I'm not rehashing this again, Mia."

"You can't treat me like some kind of bimbo. Is this how you treated Bliss?"

He stopped and counted to five before turning around. "I didn't have to treat Bliss like this.

She knew her place."

"Her place!" The veins in Mia's neck expanded into taut wires. "So you expect me to know my place. Is that what you're saying?"

"What I'm saying is that you need to leave me the hell alone regard-ing the lawsuit. I'm handling it."

"I don't like the way you've been treating me. Maybe this wedding isn't a good idea."

"You're right. Maybe it isn't."

The alarm in Mia's eyes made him smile inside. Calling off the wedding was the last thing Mia wanted. He had no doubt that Mia loved him. But she also loved his money and his social status. And for that reason, she might rock the boat, but she wasn't about to let it capsize.

Mia stomped back over to the sink and slammed the colander down on the counter, causing spaghetti to spill onto the floor.

"I've repeatedly told you Vernetta and I have the case under control. We don't want or need your involvement. If you bring it up one more time, then I *will* call off the wedding."

Fletcher left her standing there with her mouth in the position he liked most. Closed.

Strutting into his study with a smug smile resting on his lips, Fletcher felt like grabbing his balls in victory. Like he'd told Vernetta, women don't leave powerful men.

And he definitely held all the power.

CHAPTER 47

Special hated the thought of wasting another evening following Bliss Fenton around and ending up with nothing to show for it.

Since Martin Zinzer spilled his guts, Special was dying to catch Bliss with another unsuspecting sap. But so far each surveillance failed to catch her in the act. All the woman did was shop at expensive stores and eat at fancy restaurants.

Special's time would've been put to better use following Darius. There were a couple of times when she wanted to, but had wisely talked herself out of it. As much as she enjoyed spending time with him, she still could not quell her suspicion that he might not be on the up and up. She couldn't forget the way he'd freaked out when she picked up his cell phone the other night. Men only did that when they had something to hide.

So what is Darius hiding?

It was after nine o'clock and she was about to head home when a thought hit her. She was almost a full-fledged private investigator. And when an investigator wanted to know something, they investigated. Without giving herself time to have a change of heart, Special made a U-turn and drove in the direction of Torrance, where Darius claimed he was working late on an important project.

Just like a man, after he got her all into him, he started changing the program. She hadn't received flowers in two weeks and he'd stopped calling her every day just to hear her voice. What bothered her most was when he claimed to be working late the last two times she'd offered to come over.

Special hopped on the 405 Freeway and headed south. Darius claimed he was working on a project at the Toyota facility on Western. The dude sure worked a lot of late nights. She exited the freeway at Western, headed east, then made a right at the light. As she searched for an entrance into the facility, she wondered if she'd even be able to get inside to search for Darius' car in the parking lot. The thrill of seeing if she could was what made investigative work so much fun.

She turned onto Toyota Way and rolled her car to a stop at a small guard booth. She smiled up at a tiny Latina who approached her car. The woman had to be pushing fifty and couldn't have weighed more than a hundred pounds. They hired just about anybody to do security these days.

"May I help you?" the woman asked, peering into her car.

"I'm here to pick up my sister. She's having car trouble. She works in that building over there." Special pointed at a building behind a fountain. This was a sprawling complex and Special had no idea which building Darius might be working in.

The woman hesitated.

Special held up her cell phone. "Do you need me to call her?"

The woman paused a second longer, then waved her through. "That's okay. Go ahead."

See, that's why crazy people can come over here and blow us up. Everybody is too dang trusting.

As she drove toward the building she had just pointed at, Special prayed the woman wasn't watching her. As luck would have it, as soon as she rounded the corner of the building relief flooded her. She saw Darius' Lexus with the arrogant BALLER vanity license plate parked a few feet away.

Okay, girl, you can stop trippin'. The boy is working just like he said he was.

Special made a U-turn and was about to head home when Darius and an Asian woman came out of the building, talking and laughing. The woman, who wasn't much taller than Darius from his seated position, placed a hand on his shoulder, indicating to Special that they were more than co-workers.

A streak of jealousy sliced into her chest. *Working my ass.*

The woman followed Darius to his car as they continued their conversation.

When Darius opened the passenger door, Special thought her heart might explode.

"She better not be going home with his ass!"

Holding her breath, Special finally let it out when she realized the woman wasn't getting into Darius' car. Instead, he picked up a large envelope from the passenger seat and handed it to her.

The woman took the envelope and headed for her car, which was parked three spaces over.

"Okay, I'm definitely trippin'." Special's pulse began to return to a normal pace.

How in the hell had she become so distrustful of men? She knew exactly how, dating a series of guys who turned out to be nothing but liars. She wondered if she'd ever be able to settle in with a man and know that he was hers for the keeping. Although she was slowly talking herself down from the cliff where Darius was concerned, the doubt suddenly returned, propelling her right back to the edge.

What if homegirl was headed to Darius' house or Darius was headed to her place?

Special knew she should go home, but her car had a mind of its own and started following Darius as he drove out of the parking lot. His co-worker seemed to be trailing close behind him, which revved Special up even more. She couldn't risk letting him see her, so she fell back once they made it onto the freeway. After a mile or so, she lost both of them.

Interpreting that as a sign, she decided to just take her suspicious behind home. She stopped by Kentucky Fried Chicken and picked up a two-piece and some potato wedges. She reached into the bag and started munching on the fries before she was even out of the drive-thru lane.

Instead of getting off the 405 freeway at Manchester and heading up LaBrea to Leimert Park, Special stayed on the 405 until she got to Howard Hughes Way. By her estimation, if Darius was going home, he should be there by now.

When she turned onto his street, a little voice in her head gently urged her to turn around and go home. But another louder, stronger voice encouraged her to stay the course. As she got closer, she tried to prepare herself. The Asian chick's car would probably be parked in his driveway. If it was, so be it. At least she'd know the real deal about Darius before she really got totally sprung.

When Darius' driveway came into view, Special's heart did a quick flip-flop.

She'd been disappointed that she hadn't been able to catch Bliss doing any dirt, but she was thrilled to death to find Darius home alone.

CHAPTER 48

As I make my way through the metal detectors at the Los Angeles Superior Courthouse on Hill Street, I feel the dread of *deja vu*. The last time I argued a motion against Girlie Cortez, she pulled a fast one that resulted in a devastating loss for me. I wonder what dirty tricks Girlie has in her arsenal today. Since we have a female judge, I assume Girlie hasn't slept with her. Or at least I hope she hasn't.

I scan the piece of paper taped to the courtroom door. We're the third case on the docket. Walking inside, I give my business card to the court clerk. I'm concerned when the clerk tells me the judge hasn't issued a tentative ruling. Judge Alice Perry had always issued tentative decisions in my prior cases. She'd then allow the counsel to argue their points, and nine times out of ten, stuck to her original ruling.

Even though my research failed to turn up any cases that were directly on point, I'm happy with the opposition brief I submitted. I made some strong arguments and I think the odds are in my favor that the judge will reject Girlie's attempt to dismiss Fletcher's case. It's my hope that she will also be so outraged by Bliss' conduct, that there will be little room for argument.

Girlie saunters in a few minutes later in a navy skirt that's too short and a blouse that's too tight. She nods my way and I grimace back. The first two matters before the judge are status conferences, which seem to drag on.

The court clerk finally calls *McClain v. Fenton*. We make our way inside the well of the courtroom and stand behind our respective counsel tables.

"This is a rather novel area of law," Judge Perry begins. "I can't say I've ever come across a case with facts similar to these." She taps her pen on the thick stack of papers in front of her. "Neither of you were able to identify a case on all-fours, and my clerk couldn't find one either. I didn't prepare a tentative because I wanted to hear more argument on a couple of areas before reaching a decision."

I won't know whether that's good or bad for Fletcher until she discloses what areas trouble her.

"Ms. Cortez, you contend in your opening brief that your client's actions did not constitute fraud. Based on her deposition testimony, however, Ms. Fenton's conduct was both intentional and contrary to the wishes of Mr. McClain. Why shouldn't she be held liable for fraud?"

Girlie smiles up at the judge. "Your Honor, Mr. McClain has not and cannot prove the legal elements of fraud. There were no misrepresentations by Ms. Fenton regarding what would be done with Mr. McClain's semen. Simply because he assumed it would be disposed of and my client didn't do that, doesn't render her conduct fraudulent."

The judge nods, as if she agrees, which seems to encourage Girlie.

"In addition, my client didn't trick Mr. McClain into providing his semen," she continues. "He willingly gave it to her. In fact, I assert that it was a gift and Ms. Fenton was free to do with it as she pleased."

The judge takes off her glasses and stares over at me, a trace of a smile on her lips.

"Counselor, Ms. Cortez makes a good point. Ms. Fenton did not act deceitfully in the manner in which she obtained Mr. McClain's sperm or in what she did with it after obtaining it. She actually inseminated herself in his presence. How do you respond?"

The judge's line of questioning does not bode well for Fletcher.

"First, Your Honor, I disagree that there were no misrepresentations on the part of Ms. Fenton. She told my client she was on the pill and that she didn't want any more children. Although he was present when she inseminated herself, Mr. McClain was completely unaware of what she was doing. No reasonable person would expect that semen retrieved during oral sex would be retained and used for insemination purposes. That fact alone makes her conduct not only fraudulent, but outrageous, especially since she was well aware that Mr. McClain did not want to conceive a child with her."

Again, the judge nods as she speaks. "Ms. Cortez contends that your client gave Ms. Fenton a gift? Isn't that the case?"

"No. That was not his intent. Mr. McClain did not expect Ms. Fenton to keep his semen and use it in the manner in which—"

Judge Perry cuts me off. "But your client testified at his deposition that he expected his semen would be thrown in the trash."

"Yes, Your Honor, but—"

"And since he willingly engaged in a consensual sexual act with Ms. Fenton, doesn't that make it a gift?"

I hesitate. "Not in my opinion. A gift is something presented with the intention that it would be kept and treasured. It wasn't Mr. McClain's intention to give Ms. Fenton his semen to keep for her personal use."

The judge narrows her eyes. She's having fun with this. "He didn't expect her to give it back, did he?"

Of course, I can't say what I'm thinking. *No, Your Honor, he expected her to swallow it like she had every other friggin' time.*

"No," I say. "He expected her to dispose of it as she had in the past. Had he known her intended use, he most definitely would've asked her to give it back."

There are a few snickers in the gallery behind us, and I can see the judge is holding in a laugh herself. "Let's move on to the conversion cause of action," she says.

Girlie starts talking even before the judge gives her permission to speak. "Your Honor, as to the conversion claim, this case is no different from the decisions involving doctors sued for using their patients' cells for medical research without their permission. I direct your attention to *Moore versus the University of California*, cited on page six of my brief. In that case, the California Supreme Court dismissed the plaintiff's conversion claim for the same reasons this case should be dismissed. The patient didn't have property rights in his cells after they were removed from his body. Hence, Mr. McClain has no property rights in his semen."

That case is a problem for me. In *Moore*, a patient sued a doctor who removed his cells during treatment for leukemia and sold them for medical research, earning hundreds of thousands of dollars. Convincing a judge to ignore state Supreme Court precedent is like asking a raindrop to reverse course. Nonetheless, I give it my best shot.

"I'd like to point out, Your Honor, that the court in *Moore* rejected the conversion claim, in large part, for public policy reasons. It feared having a chilling effect on medical research. I'd argue that this court should hold Ms. Fenton liable for conversion because her conduct is *contrary* to public policy. Otherwise, we'd be condoning the granting of an economic benefit to women who trick unsuspecting men into producing children without their consent. That can't be the kind of public policy we want to encourage as a society."

The judge takes a long moment before speaking again. I hope she's giving serious consideration to my argument. She's ready to move on and turns back to Girlie.

"Ms. Cortez, as to the intentional infliction of emotional distress claim, you argued in your papers that Ms. Fenton's conduct was not outrageous or intended to cause Mr. McClain distress. Can you really say that with a straight face?"

Girlie sputters for a second, but then recovers. "What might be outrageous to one person, could be perfectly acceptable to another. This is one of those situations."

I jump in to ride the judge's point home. "Your Honor, to the contrary, I contend that Ms. Fenton's conduct was both extreme and outrageous. The fact that there are no other cases on point indicates how rare this type of behavior is."

Instead of jumping on my bandwagon, Judge Perry turns on me. At least it feels that way.

"Assuming that's correct, counselor, you presented no evidence that Mr. McClain has suffered any emotional distress."

"That's because we're still very early in this case. No psychological exams have been conducted. My client hasn't had a sufficient opportunity to offer evidence regarding how difficult this had been for him and the impact it's having on his personal life. He has a fiancée. So, of course, this has been a trying time for their relationship."

Girlie faces me instead of the judge. "My client didn't force herself on Mr. McClain. He willingly engaged in a sexual encounter with her. So that's what he'll have to explain to his fiancée."

This time Judge Perry can't hold back a smile.

"Okay, counsel, I think I've heard enough," the judge says. "I'm ready to rule. On the intentional infliction of emotional distress claim, I'm going to deny the motion for summary adjudication. I believe Ms. Fenton's conduct was indeed extreme and outrageous as a matter of law and was intended to cause Mr. McClain severe emotional distress since she knew he did not want to conceive a child with her." She pauses and points her ink pen in my direction. "But if this case gets before a jury, Ms. Henderson, your client will have to do more than claim he suffered mental anguish. He'll have to produce evidence of it."

I let out a breath. *One down and two to go.*

"A cause of action for conversion," Judge Perry continues, "requires a showing of an unauthorized act that deprives a person of his property on a permanent basis or for a set period of time. Mr. McClain argues that Ms. Fenton obtained his property, that is, his semen, without his permission. Ms. Fenton counters that the semen was a gift, given to her voluntarily. I agree with Ms. Fenton's position. The plaintiff willingly gave his semen to the defendant during oral sex. As such, it was a gift. In addition, Mr. McClain had no property rights in his semen once it left his body. On the conversion claim, I'm going to grant summary adjudication in favor of Ms. Fenton and dismiss that cause of action."

Girlie smiles. We're even now. But the fraud claim is the only one that matters.

"As for the fraud claim, I find that there were no misrepresenta-tions on the part of Ms. Fenton regarding what she intended to do with Mr. McClain's semen on that particular day. As such, there can be no finding of fraud. Her earlier representations that she was on the pill and didn't want any more children are not relevant to her conduct on the day in question. As such, I'm granting summary adjudication as to the fraud cause of action and dismissing it as well."

Judge Perry is already closing her file. I'm aching to push the judge to revisit her decision on the fraud cause of action, but that would likely earn me her wrath. So be it.

"Your Honor, I'd like to briefly revisit your decision on the fraud claim. If you consider that—"

"We're done here, counselor," the judge bristles. "Take it up with the court of appeal. Next case."

Girlie glances over at me, gloating. She's just gutted my case. The emotional distress claim is worthless. This is a total victory for Bliss Fenton.

I gather my papers as angst rocks my entire body. This isn't my first lost, and it won't be my last. That's not what's troubling me at the moment. My biggest fear right now is having to deliver this devastating news to Fletcher McClain.

CHAPTER 49

Fletcher listens quietly as I recap the judge's ruling. His face shows no visible emotion. When I'm finished, he sits there, as if I'm not even in the room.

I let the silence linger, giving him the time he needs for it to sink in.

"This is unbelievable." His voice is full of bewilderment. "Would it be worth it to appeal?"

"Maybe. Frankly, I think the judge was flat out wrong on the fraud claim. But some judges refuse to make a decision unless there's a case precisely on point. I think the court of appeal might be more likely to find fraud on the facts of this case."

"Sounds like you do think we should appeal."

"Not really. And not because we couldn't get the ruling over-turned, but because even if we won, it would only be a paper victory. The only way you're going to get any money out of Bliss is if she gets a job. And we both know that's not going to happen. So it wouldn't make sense to move forward with the emotional distress claim, even if you could prove damages."

Fletcher rubs his chin. "So this is the end of the road?"

"Only regarding the civil case. You can and should continue to fight Bliss in family court. What she's asking for is excessive. Darlene will certainly give Girlie a run for her money. I've been researching large child support awards. There've been some big ones, but not eighty-thousand dollars big."

"How big is big?"

"From what I can remember, Eddie Murphy paid fifty-one thousand dollars a month for the kid he had with Spice Girl Mel B. 50 Cent got hit for twenty-five thousand dollars a month and Charlie Sheen paid fifty-five thousand dollars a month, but that was for two kids."

"Vernetta, if you're trying to make me feel better, it's not working."

I half chuckle. "I'm sorry. But I must say, I'm surprised at how calmly you're taking this."

"Don't let the cool exterior fool you. I'm actually raging inside. Has your investigator been able to find out anything about the father of Bliss' youngest son?" he asks.

"Nope. His identity is the best kept secret in town."

"You still think it's somebody famous?"

"Maybe. Whoever he is, he definitely wants to keep his identity a secret and I suspect he paid Bliss enough to keep her mouth shut."

"Well, have your investigator keep digging. We need to focus now on halting that forensics exam."

"You need to work with Darlene on that," I say.

Fletcher nods.

"Is there something going on?" I ask. "You seem pretty unnerved about that exam."

"I just don't want to blow this deal we're working on," he says, brushing me off. "Anyway, thanks for referring me to your buddy. I really like her. Ms. Darlene Hayes is pretty ballsy. As a matter of fact, we already discussed a countermove in the event my fraud case got dismissed. I guess it's time to put our plan into action."

"A countermove? I'm not sure I want to know what you have in mind, but why don't you enlighten me anyway."

His face brightens as he lays out the plot they've cooked up. "You like it?" he asks when he's done.

My cheeks burn as I stare back at him. "If you really want to know, I think it's completely unethical since you're only doing it for financial reasons, not the best interests of your daughter."

"You're such a goody two-shoes."

"No, I just think right is right and wrong is wrong."

"Sweetheart, when there's as much money at stake as I have on the line, anything I do to protect myself is right."

"The saddest part about what you just said is that you actually believe it. You think anything goes."

"Yes, I do. Especially when all other options have been exhausted. I need to teach Bliss a lesson. Our little plan will flip the script, as the youngsters say."

He reaches for his cell phone.

"In fact, I'm going to have my new legal eagle get the ball rolling right about now."

CHAPTER 50

Bliss stared into her own smiling face in the bathroom mirror. "Girl, you are absolutely fabulous!"

She had Fletcher McClain on the ropes and victory was within her reach. Now that the stupid fraud case was history, she'd have her eighty-three grand a month in no time. She couldn't remember the last time she'd felt so euphoric.

It also felt great to have a kid-free townhouse. Anamaria had taken all three of them to the park, allowing Bliss to schedule a lunch date with Jessica.

It was becoming pretty annoying having to listen to Jessica whine about Paul screwing around. The man was showing all the signs, but unless Jessica was willing to do something about it, Bliss didn't want to keep rehashing the subject.

The doorbell rang and she called out to Jessica from the bathroom where she was putting on a second coat of mascara. "It's open. Come on in."

To celebrate the dismissal of Fletcher's fraud case, Bliss was treating Jessica to lunch at the Four Seasons in Beverly Hills.

When she didn't hear the door open, Bliss called out again.

"I said, come in. The door's unlocked."

The door finally opened and Bliss heard a voice that was not Jessica's.

"I have a delivery for Ms. Fenton," someone called out in a tentative male voice.

Bliss hurried into the living room, her face plagued with worry. She wouldn't put it past Fletcher to serve her with yet another bogus lawsuit. When she eased the door all the way open and saw a delivery-man holding a gold box of red roses, she relaxed. She knew right away who they were from. Marty Zinzer. He'd come to his senses.

The man handed her the box. "These are for you."

"Oh my God, they're beautiful."

As the man was turning to leave, Jessica walked through the door. "Who sent you flowers?"

"A secret admirer," Bliss cooed.

She opened the box, but there was no card, just a large manila envelope. She tore it open, frowning as she tried to make sense of what she was reading. With every sentence, her pulse shot up a notch.

"What's the matter?" Jessica asked. "You're turning white."

"I don't believe this!" Bliss hurled the papers and the flowers across the room.

Jessica placed a hand on Bliss' forearm. "Calm down. What is it?"

"That asshole's filing for sole custody of Harmony. Fletcher has the nerve to call me an unfit parent."

Jessica retrieved the document from the floor and started reading it for herself, while Bliss flopped down on the living room couch.

"I don't believe it. He's such a jerk. He'll do anything to get out of paying child support for Harmony.

He doesn't want her. He wouldn't even take her picture when I tried to give him one."

Jessica finished reading the document and set it on the coffee table. " I'm sure Fletcher doesn't really want custody of Harmony. He's probably just trying to force you to lower your child support demand."

"Well, I'm not doing it. It's not like he can't afford it."

"Bliss, you can put a stop to all of this right now. Why don't you sit down with Fletcher, without attorneys present, and see what you can work out?"

"I'm not working out a thing. Girlie Cortez is going to get me everything I deserve."

"And what if you lose custody of Harmony?"

"I won't." Bliss walked into the kitchen and returned with her cell phone.

"Who're you calling?"

"Girlie Cortez. My shark of an attorney is going to nip this in the bud in no time."

CHAPTER 51

Finally, Special was ready to concede that her fears about Darius cheating on her were all in her head. He was lucky to have a woman like her. There was no way a guy as smart as Darius would mess up the good thing he had with her.

Picking up her phone from the dashboard, she checked for an incoming text. She'd just finished getting her nails done at the Howard Hughes Promenade and was hoping that Darius had responded to her earlier message saying she was in the neighborhood. He had not. She made a right onto Sepulveda and headed home.

Special still didn't like the fact that Darius insisted that she call before coming over. If he was truly her man, she should be able to drop by any time she wanted.

That little voice of insecurity that seemed to be lodged in her psyche caused her to swerve into the Mobile gas station. She exited the opposite driveway and headed back up Sepulveda toward Darius' place. She planned to do a quick drive-by to see if his car was in the driveway.

When Special's car crawled past Darius' house, she was surprised to see two cars parked in the driveway. The baby Benz parked behind Darius' Lexus looked like a woman's car. The license plate—MISSMAC—confirmed that it was.

"Oh, hell naw!"

No wonder Darius hadn't responded to her text. He was too busy hanging out with MISSMAC. With a name like that, the heffa was probably a stripper. Special parked across the driveway, blocking the woman's car and charged up the walkway. She reached the porch in seconds and was about to bang on the door but thought better of it. She leaned in close, listening for voices, but only heard the mellow crooning of John Legend.

After glancing around to make sure no one was watching her, Special tip-toed across the grass and scampered down the driveway toward the back of the house.

Darius' bedroom looked out onto the backyard and he always kept his curtains open. If he was in there cheating on her, she was about to catch his ass in the act, up close and personal.

As she rounded the corner leading into the backyard, she paused, as Eli's words came back to her. *Stop chasing love and let it find you.*

Eli was right. *So what if Darius was seeing someone?* They'd only been dating for a few weeks. She wasn't sure she even wanted to commit to him in the first place. This was crazy. She should turn around right now and go home.

Special was about to do just that, when she heard what sounded like moaning. Pleasurable moaning.

She picked up her pace, ran up to the window of Darius' master bedroom and peered inside. Even though the porch light was on, she couldn't see a thing. The room was completely dark.

Her mind was playing tricks on her. She had better get a grip. She was about to go home, when once again, she heard something. And this time she was certain. It was indeed moaning, a woman's moaning. She moved to the right and peered into the window of the adjacent room, which Darius used as a guest bedroom and makeshift den.

This time, she had a clear view, thanks to a small lamp sitting on an end table. A naked woman was sitting on the couch propped up high on pillows, her legs spread wide. Darius' head was buried between her thighs.

What the—

Rage took over before common sense could take hold. Special banged on the window with both fists.

"Hey! What the hell are you doing? You lying asshole!"

She could see Darius turn around and glance over his shoulder, his eyes wide with disbelief.

"Who is that?" the woman asked as she hopped off the pillows and started scrambling for her clothes.

"It's his girlfriend," Special shouted. "Let me in!"

"I'll be damned!" Darius backed up his wheelchair and charged over to the window. "You need to leave!"

"And you need to let me in so you can tell me to my face why you lied to me."

"You didn't tell me you had a girlfriend!" The woman snatched her bra from the floor.

"If you don't leave now, I'm calling the police," Darius yelled. "You're trespassing."

Special was so mad, she feared her head might explode. She looked around for something to hurl through the window and snatched up a rake lying near a fire pit. It took four swings before the glass shattered.

Darius rolled his chair away from the window just as Special snatched off one of her red-soled Christian Louboutin pumps and hurled it through the broken glass. She was aiming for Darius' head, but the shoe hit the side of his wheelchair and fell to the floor.

The woman had run out of the room and Darius was now at the window, trying to draw the curtains.

"Are you crazy!" he yelled at her.

"No, you're the crazy one!" Special shouted back. She stuck her hand through the window and snatched the curtains so hard, the entire curtain rod fell to the floor.

"You're going to tell me to my face why you cheated on me. You asshole!"

At the sound of a car starting, Special ran toward the driveway, which wasn't easy to do in one shoe. MISSMAC was already in her car, but Special had her blocked in, or at least she thought she did. The woman edged the car forward, then backed up and swerved to the right. She sped across Darius' grass, onto the sidewalk and off the curb. The car was out of sight in seconds.

Special limped up to the front door, banging on it with both fists. She was yelling and sobbing now.

"Open this door!"

A woman in the house across the street turned on the porch light and stepped outside. "Is everything okay over there?"

The neighbor's inquiry was like a hard slap that instantly brought Special back to her senses.

I must be losing my mind.

If someone called the police and she was arrested for assault and breaking and entering, her foolishness would end her budding investigative career before it could officially get started.

She waved across the street in a loud, cheerful voice. "No, everything's just fine."

Special bent down, slipped off her lone shoe and scurried barefoot to her car. She took off down the street even faster than MISSMAC.

CHAPTER 52

"Please. Just calm down." Girlie patted Bliss on the shoulder. "There's no way Fletcher's going to get custody of Harmony."

The morning after receiving Fletcher's surprise package, Bliss rushed down to Girlie's office waving the custody petition like it was a sword. Bliss had tried to get an appointment the same day, but Girlie refused to answer her hysterical calls.

Now Bliss was sitting in Girlie's office in sweats and a T-shirt with no makeup. Her appearance alone signaled that she was ready to go off the deep end.

"That paper says I'm an unfit parent," Bliss whined, wringing her hands. "Fletcher knows about Marty Zinzer. He's calling me a prostitute!"

"He's just trying to intimidate you," Girlie explained. "He wants to avoid paying you your fair share of child support. But that's not going to happen. You have to trust me."

"I really need that money." Tears pooled in Bliss' eyes. "You can't let him get custody of Harmony."

Girlie was trying her darnedest to like her devious client, but that was a tall task. Losing out on Fletcher McClain's cash was far more important to Bliss than losing custody of her daughter.

"I've been thinking about the best way to deal with Fletcher's custody petition," Girlie told her. "He doesn't want full custody of Harmony. He just wants you to run scared and lower your child support demand. Then he'll drop the custody petition. But that's not what you're going to do. I have another plan and I think you're going to like it."

Bliss dabbed her eyes with a tissue and looked curiously at her attorney.

"I want you to listen to everything I have to say before you respond."

Bliss nodded.

"Since your ex-boyfriend wants to play dirty, we have to play even dirtier. What I'm about to propose is only temporary. After we do this, I suspect he'll drop his custody petition in a New York minute."

"Exactly what do you have in mind?"

Girlie smiled. "Actually, I think what I came up with is rather brilliant and I think you'll agree. But I need you to hear me out before you react."

Girlie laid out her plan to paint Fletcher into a corner, pointing out the pros as well as the few cons.

"And think about how Mia is going to react? She'll be beside herself."

At first, Bliss appeared shocked. But in a matter of seconds, her eyes brightened and Girlie could tell she was on board.

"You know what? I don't just like it. I love it." Bliss practically squealed with excitement.

Girlie wiggled her perfectly arched brows. "I thought you would."

Bliss pulled out a small mirror and started applying lipstick to her bare lips. "So when do we do it?"

"There's no time like the present," Girlie said. "I recommend that you do it tonight. You'll want to catch them completely off guard."

"God, I can't wait to see Mia's face."

Girlie laughed. "I wish I could be there to see both of their faces."

"Maybe I'll snap a picture for you."

Girlie leaned back in her chair, as exhilarated as her client. "That would be priceless."

The two women bumped fists.

"Girlfriend," Bliss said with sisterly admiration, "we're quite the little team. When this case is over, we need to check out our family trees because you might just be my sister from another mother."

CHAPTER 53

"**H**ow can you do this?" Jessica cried. "It's crazy."

"Can you please stop being so melodramatic for just two seconds?" Bliss complained. "I told you, it's only temporary. This is like a chess match. Fletcher made a move, now I'm making a countermove."

Jessica rolled to a stop at a traffic light and looked over at her friend. She'd only agreed to accompany Bliss on this crazy excursion so she'd have time to talk her out of it. But her pleas weren't having any effect.

"I can't believe you're actually going through with this. Neither you nor your attorney has Harmony's best interests in mind. This is going to be very traumatic for her."

"She'll be fine. She's a baby. She won't remember a thing."

Jessica glanced in the rearview mirror at Harmony who was asleep in her car carrier. She had to find a way to talk some sense into Bliss. She made a left onto Loma Vista Drive. They were just a few houses away now. Jessica couldn't believe that Bliss' attorney had actually come up with this stunt. She had to talk some sense into her friend.

"You can't possibly think this is right. How could you use your child as a pawn like this?"

"Stop making it a bigger deal than it is. I'm doing this for Harmony. To help her get what she deserves."

"No, Bliss, you're doing it for yourself. To get what *you* think you deserve."

"Why don't we just stop talking about it? We're almost there. Make a left at the next corner."

Jessica wanted to throw Bliss out of the car and take off with Harmony. Here she was dying to be a mother and Bliss was treating her daughter like an unwanted pet. It wasn't right.

Bliss pointed up the street. "The house is right over there. Thank God the gate's open."

Pulling into the driveway, Jessica held her breath as Bliss jumped out and opened the back car door. After unbuckling Harmony from her car carrier, Bliss marched up to the front door. Bliss jabbed the doorbell and waited.

Jessica got out of the car but didn't approach. She prayed no one would be home. What she wanted to do was snatch Harmony from Bliss' arms and take off. Before she could gather her nerves, the front door opened.

Bliss stood face-to-face with Mia.

"I'm here to see Fletcher," Bliss demanded.

"He's busy."

"I'll wait."

Mia sneered at her. "He'll be busy all night."

"Then I'll just have to wait here all night."

As Mia started to close the door, Bliss stuck her foot across the threshold.

"Move your foot or I'll break it," Mia threatened.

"Go ahead and try."

Jessica walked up behind Bliss. "Please, Bliss. Don't do this. Let's just leave."

Harmony started to whimper just as they heard Fletcher charging down the hallway.

"What's going on?" He saw Bliss and his jaws tightened.

The second he stepped in front of Mia, Bliss shoved Harmony into his arms.

"You want full custody?" Bliss spat. "You've got it. C'mon, Jessica, let's go."

"What the hell!" Fletcher awkwardly held Harmony away from his body as if she were contagious. The child began to wail at the top of her lungs.

"You can't leave her here!" Mia yelled. "Come get your child!"

But Bliss had already climbed back into Jessica's car and was clicking her seatbelt into place.

"Hurry up!" she called out to Jessica. "Let's go!"

Jessica remained standing near Fletcher's doorstep, tears streaming down her face.

"I said let's go!" Bliss yelled through the window.

Somehow, Jessica found her way back to the car and stumbled inside. She wasn't sure she was emotionally stable enough to drive, but started the car up nonetheless.

As they pulled away from Fletcher's house, Bliss clapped her hands and started to cackle.

"Did you see their faces? Oh my God! I wish I had taken a picture. What do you bet Fletcher will be knocking on my door tomorrow morning, begging me to take her back? It might even happen tonight. And that will be the end of Fletcher's little custody stunt."

Jessica charged across Sunset Boulevard and made a hard right at the first street, stopping in front of a parking structure at the edge of the UCLA campus. She reached across Bliss and threw open the passenger door.

"Get out!"

"What?"

"I can't believe what you just did!" Jessica shouted. "Get out of my car! You're an evil, selfish witch. Paul is right. I've been nothing but your doormat. And now I'm done. Get out!"

"You can't leave me here. How am I going to get home?"

"Call Uber."

When Bliss didn't move, Jessica threw the car in park, jumped out and ran around to the passenger side.

"Either get out or I'll drag you out," she demanded.

Their commotion had attracted the attention of a man who had just walked out of the parking structure wearing a backpack. "Is everything okay, ladies?"

Jessica didn't budge. "It will be when she gets out of my car."

When Bliss still didn't move, Jessica leaned inside to unhook Bliss' seatbelt, then grabbed her by the arm and jerked her out of the car. Bliss lost her footing and stumbled to the pavement.

"Have you lost your mind?" Bliss yelled up at her.

"No, but you apparently have!"

Jessica strolled around to the driver's side and hopped back into her car. She saw Bliss' purse lying on the floor and started to keep going. But even as disgusted as she was with Bliss, she didn't want to leave her totally stranded.

Rolling down the window, Jessica hurled Bliss' purse to the pavement, just missing her head.

CHAPTER 54

I wake up to the sound of my cell phone blaring like a smoke alarm. The clock on my nightstand flashes 11:17 p.m. I want to ignore it and go back to sleep, but a call this late is cause for concern.

I reach for my cell and I'm surprised to see Fletcher's name on the screen.

I sit up in bed, trying not to wake Jefferson. "Hello," I whisper.

Fletcher speaks so fast, his words sound like gibberish.

"I can't understand anything you just said, Fletcher. Please start over and speak slowly."

When I finally make sense of what he's saying, I have to stifle a laugh.

"And just what do you expect me to do? You got what you wanted. Full custody of your daughter."

"I never wanted custody of her. I don't know how to take care of a kid!"

"You have Mia to help you."

"She's mad as hell and locked herself in one of the guest bedrooms. This kid is screaming at the top of her lungs and I have no idea what to do about it."

"And neither do I. Call your mother or Gabriella. I'm sure they can help you out. Better yet, call your family law attorney. After all, this was Darlene's bright idea. Let her deal with it."

"What am I going to do with her in the morning? I have a record company to run."

"You should've thought of that before you put your little plan into motion. This is not a problem I can help you with. I'm going back to sleep."

I hang up the phone.

"What's going on?" Jefferson is barely awake.

"Bliss just dumped her child on Fletcher's doorstep and left." I can't help but laugh. "And he's freaking out. Mia wants nothing to do with the kid."

"Those are some weird ass people."

I lie back down, resting my head on Jefferson's shoulder.

"So what's he gonna do?"

"If I were a betting woman, I'd say he'll be returning Harmony to her mother bright and early tomorrow morning."

"Why'd he file for custody if he didn't want her?"

"So he could get her to reduce her child support demand. He expected Bliss to fight his custody petition, not hand over her daughter the way she did."

"It wasn't right what that chick did to him, but your rich ex-boyfriend should stop playing games and just take care of his kid. With all the dough he's got, I don't see why he's sweating her."

"He tried. He offered her fifteen grand a month."

"And she turned it down?"

"Yep. She wants eighty-three grand a month."

"Maybe he needs to send her greedy ass a message from the streets."

"Jefferson, cut it out."

"I'm serious. If that girl turned down fifteen grand a month, she's a straight up gold digger. You reap what you sow."

That's definitely the truth.

"I suspect Girlie Cortez crafted this little scheme. And actually, it was pretty brilliant. They're playing Fletcher like a piano."

"All of 'em are crazy," Jefferson says groggily, as I snuggle closer to him. "That kid would be better off in foster care."

CHAPTER 55

Mia had always prided herself on having everything under control. But Bliss and her bastard baby had turned her world upside down and sideways. Mia hadn't figured out yet how she was going to resolve this little catastrophe, but she had no doubt that she would.

She missed sleeping next to Fletcher last night and regretted acting so childish after that poor excuse for a mother dumped her baby on their doorstep.

Who does that?

That alone was proof that Bliss was nothing short of nuts. Maybe she'd suggest that Fletcher have Bliss tested. Mia wouldn't be at all surprised to learn the woman was bi-polar. For now, though, Mia had a much bigger problem. If the information about Bliss selling her body for sex was true—and Mia had no reason to believe it wasn't—Fletcher would easily win full custody of his daughter. But Mia had no intention of raising Bliss' child or anybody else's. She wasn't even certain she even wanted kids of her own.

Mia hadn't expected Fletcher to bond with the child so quickly. She could hear him now, cooing over her. She made her way to the kitchen where she found him holding Harmony in one hand, as he checked the temperature of the bottle he was warming with the other.

"Wow. Look at you. You're turning out to be quite the little papa."

"I had no choice." His voice left the rest of the sentence unspoken. *Since you refused to help out.*

"Gabriella brought a bunch of stuff over and gave me a crash course on taking care of a three month old. I also called my mother. By the way, she's flying in this weekend to help us out for a month or so."

That news sent a shock of dread straight down Mia's spine.

Being under the same roof as Gilda McClain was almost as bad as having this pint-size intruder in her house. The high-and-mighty Gilda treated her son like God and pretended as if Mia didn't exist.

Fletcher insisted that it was all in her head, but Mia knew better. Fletcher wasn't the first white guy she'd dated. She knew when a mother preferred that her son have a woman of a lighter hue.

Mia had asked Gilda for a list of people she wanted to invite to the wedding, stressing that Fletcher was picking up all the expenses. Gilda promised to get her a list, but that was weeks ago. Who turns down a trip to France? Anyone who didn't want her snooty friends to know she was about to welcome an African-American daughter-in-law into the family.

Mia checked the clock on the microwave. It was after eight. Fletcher should have been headed to the office by now.

"Why are you still here?"

"Working from home today." He looked down at Harmony. "Hey, sweetie, you happy Daddy's staying home today?"

The baby seemed to coo her excitement.

Fletcher grinned. "Sounds like Harmony's pretty happy about that."

If Mia was absolutely forced to raise this child, the first thing she planned to do was talk Fletcher into changing her name. Anyone who saw the name Harmony on a school application would assume she was a black kid from South Central.

Mia inhaled. She loved Fletcher and couldn't imagine not having him in her life. So she would do what she had to do. No matter how much it pained her.

"Let me hold her." She eased the child from Fletcher's arms into hers.

Harmony squirmed, then smiled up at her.

"She's such a friendly baby." Fletcher's face glowed with pride. "She likes you."

Yeah, whatever.

Mia wasn't quite sure she could pull this off. But there was a lot at stake if she didn't. She had to focus on the real prize. The life of luxury she would live as Mrs. Fletcher McClain.

The doorbell rang and Fletcher set the bottle he was holding on the kitchen counter. "I'll get it."

"Who are you expecting this early?"

Fletcher ignored Mia's question as he headed toward the front door. He returned seconds later with a woman who was a dead give-away for Kim Kardashian, ass and all.

"Hey, Mia, meet Carina, our new live-in nanny. She's an exchange student from Romania. Fortunately for us, she takes most of her classes online, so she'll be available to care for Harmony as much as we need her."

The news shook Mia so hard she almost dropped the baby.

"Nice to meet you." Carina's accent was barely understandable.

Mia appraised the woman as she shook her hand. Carina had apparently failed the dress code class during nanny school. She was showing way too much cleavage. Mia pegged her to be around thirty, a little old for a nanny career.

"Honey," Mia said, with as much sweetness as she could muster, "you hired a nanny without consulting me first?"

"This was an emergency situation and you weren't speaking to me, remember? No worries though. Carina came highly recommended by the wife of one of my golfing buddies. The family she had previously worked for moved to New York." He motioned Carina over. "Come meet Harmony."

"She's beautiful." Carina took Harmony into her arms.

"That's because she's my daughter," Fletcher boasted.

Mia thought she might just throw up.

"I'm giving Carina the guest room on the west end of the house." He turned to the nanny. "That way you'll have more privacy."

First Bliss' baby, then Fletcher's mother, now this Carina chick. There was no way Mia could afford to have a woman this attractive under her roof 24/7. She wasn't stupid, Carina would soon look around at all they had and start imagining herself as Fletcher's wife. Mia had to resort to fight-or-flight mode and she was more than willing to fight for what was hers.

Getting Carina out of her house was the first task she needed to tackle. To do so, Mia was about to transform herself into the perfect stepmother, thereby eliminating the need to have Carina around. It would probably mean going to a part-time schedule at her law firm. At least until she could find a nanny who looked like a grandmother instead of a video vixen. Mia didn't care all that much about her job anyway. She'd plan to quit practicing all together as soon as she married Fletcher.

The second task on her to-do list would require a bit more ingenuity. Bliss needed to pay for disrupting their lives. And Mia intended to make sure that she did.

CHAPTER 56

Even as a kid, Special had never been one to easily throw in the towel. The best investigators mapped out their plan, then watched and waited. Persistence was the name of this game. That's why she refused to give up on learning the identity of Bliss' Mystery Baby Daddy.

It was just after seven and based on the way Bliss was dressed, it was likely that she was headed off to meet another target. Bliss rarely dressed this scandalous. But tonight she was wearing black leggings and a midriff top that left little to the imagination. Her hair looked freshly done and she'd spent over two hours in the nail salon.

Special assumed Bliss was not off to meet Martin Zinzer. For one, the prominent lawyer had a wife and family, which likely made it difficult for evening romps. But more importantly, Special was pretty certain that their little talk had scared him straight. He'd probably swear off out-of-wedlock sex for life. When Special informed him that Bliss had extorted one, perhaps two, wealthy men for child support, he'd almost swallowed his tongue. If Bliss had gone after Zinzer, his idyllic life would have been shattered. Hopefully, he'd learned his lesson.

After the nail salon, Special followed Bliss to a vitamin shop, then to a shopping complex off Sepulveda and Rosecrans, where Bliss entered Salt Creek Grille in Manhattan Beach. Special took a seat in an adjacent booth, pulled out her iPad and pretended to be reading the *L.A. Times*.

A short time later, a good-looking man in his forties entered the restaurant and sat down across from Bliss. The girl only dealt with fine-ass men.

The man did not look happy to see her. In fact, he looked pretty irate.

"I don't have a lot of time. What do you want?"

"Wow, I don't even get a greeting. We used to be so close."

"What do you want?"

"I need more money."

The man's nostrils flared. "I've given you more than enough to take care of that kid. And now you have the audacity to ask for more?"

"Jonas is a growing boy. I underestimated how much money I'd need to raise him."

OMG! So this is the mysterious father of baby Jonas. Special studied his face. He definitely wasn't famous. He looked like a regular guy who had expensive taste in suits.

"I don't have it."

"Bull."

"Exactly how much are you looking for?"

Special shook her head. *Big mistake, dude. Just tell her you don't have it and leave.*

"Five hundred grand."

"Are you insane? I bought you that townhouse and gave you a million dollars."

Special couldn't believe it. Maybe she should consider this line of work. This heffa got a free townhouse, a million dollars, was getting twelve grand a month from Dr. Franco and was still trying to jack Fletcher McClain and this dude? This girl belonged on both *American Greed* and *The Jerry Springer Show.*

The man just stared at her, his dark eyes spewing hatred. "Like I said, I'm done. I'm not paying you another dime."

"Then I guess I'll have to have a little conversation with your wife about her long-lost stepson."

"I don't care. Do it. I'm sick of you."

Bliss' face contorted.

"And after I tell your wife, I'll go after you in court. Jonas is entitled to far more than you've given me. I don't understand why you're being so stingy." She slid a piece of paper across the table. "Here's my bank account information. Wire the money to me or I'm going to make a call. And stop it with the phony protests. We both know you're not hurting for money."

"Over my dead body," he hissed. "Or better yet, over yours." The man stood up and stalked toward the door.

Special was having such a good time looking at Bliss' broken face that she temporarily stopped thinking like an investigator. The man was climbing behind the wheel of his car when she came back to her senses and race-walked out of the restaurant. She needed to get the man's license plate number. Eli had a cop friend who could run the plates for her. She was dying to know who he was.

By the time she reached the front of the restaurant, the black Jaguar was pulling into the street, too far away to read his license plate number.

"Shoot!"

As she was about to walk back into the restaurant, Bliss brushed by, not even noticing her. She climbed into her Audi and sped off.

Special wondered if Bliss really would be brazen enough to tell the man's wife that she had a three-year-old stepson she knew nothing about.

"Girlfriend," Special mumbled to herself, "you're playing with fire and eventually you're going to get burned."

CHAPTER 57

The computer screen glared like a hot, dangerous fire. And for the most part, that's exactly what it was. Jessica was about to open a door of no return. Despite the risks, despite her fears, she sucked in a long, deep breath and started typing.

The software she'd installed on Paul's computer had performed precisely as promised. She logged into her Webwatcher account with her iPhone and obtained the password to the folder where Paul kept his documents. For the last thirty minutes or so, she'd been painstakingly opening sub-folders and documents. So far, she'd only found documents related to his business dealings. It only made sense that he would password protect those documents. After another few minutes, she was beginning to feel like an idiot. Her husband was not fooling around. Bliss was absolutely right. Paul's only mistress was his work.

There was only one folder left to review. She was about to shut off the computer, but decided she might as well finish her snooping. At first, the folder labeled *Archives* seemed to show nothing of interest to her. But then she caught sight of several American Express card statements. The account number was neither their personal account nor Paul's business account.

Jessica held her breath. This was it. She'd seen this scene played out in movies a dozen times. The credit card statements would reveal trips to hotels she had never visited, expensive dinners she never enjoyed and gifts of flowers and jewelry that had not been purchased for her. She slowly perused the statements, but found nothing of the sort. She found no charges for flowers or gifts, but she did see charges to several restaurants. She was certain that on some of the dates listed, Paul had taken her to those places.

"This is ridiculous. Paul isn't cheating on me."

She'd let Bliss cause her to distrust her husband. She was glad Bliss was out of her life, but she desperately missed the kids, especially Harmony. Just thinking about how Bliss was using her beautiful baby as a pawn made Jessica seethe with anger. She wondered if she would ever be able to forgive her.

As she was about to close the *Archives* folder, something caught her attention. She opened the sole unread document and started reading through it. Once, twice, a third time, as if expecting the words to somehow change.

She wanted to scream, yell or bang her fists on the desk. But all she could do was stare blankly at the screen. Too numb to even react.

The reason her husband was away from home for such long hours wasn't because he was having an affair. She hadn't found a shred of evidence proving that Paul wasn't exactly where he professed to be over the past few weeks: at his office working on a deal. Unfortunately, what Jessica did find deflated her heart like a punctured balloon.

Jessica wasn't sure how long she'd sat there, quietly weeping, before finally turning off the computer. She had no idea what she should do.

"What are you doing in my office?"

Paul's voice startled her.

"Just sitting here," Jessica lied. "I miss you."

She was not prepared to confront her husband about her discovery. Not now. Maybe never. Perhaps if she ignored this reality, it would not exist.

"You didn't come home last night," she said.

"I know. I'm sorry. We've been negotiating this big merger. It didn't close until about an hour ago." He came closer and stared into her sad eyes. "You've been crying?"

"I had a fight with Bliss. A big one."

Paul's eyes widened like he'd been jabbed with a stun gun.

"A fight about what?"

Jessica exhaled. They had much more important things to discuss. But she had no energy—mental or physical—to deal with it at the moment. "I don't want to talk about it right now."

Paul started backing out of the room.

"I forgot something I left at the office," he said, and seconds later, Jessica heard his car pulling out of the driveway.

CHAPTER 58

Bliss relaxed on her patio, sipping champagne from a martini glass, enjoying the cool evening breeze. Aiden was with Dr. Franco, who also let Jonas tag along so the boys could keep each other company. Harmony, of course, was in the capable hands of her reluctant papa.

Bliss had dropped by earlier that day to check on Harmony—only after confirming that neither Fletcher nor Mia was home. She was thrilled to learn that Fletcher had hired a nanny. When she saw the beautiful Carina, Bliss could only laugh. Mia was about to get her comeuppance. If Fletcher wasn't already screwing the help, it wouldn't be long.

At first, Bliss had been worried that Girlie's plan to dump Harmony on Fletcher would backfire. But Girlie assured her that Fletcher might win shared custody of Harmony, but it was unlikely that he would win full custody. So what if she only got forty grand a month? She could live off of that much money just fine and she'd only have Harmony half the time.

Now she was just waiting for Jonas' father to come around. The asshole didn't think she would tell his wife about Jonas, but he underestimated her. The man made enough money to throw away and he was sweating her over five hundred grand?

She still couldn't believe Marty Zinzer had spilled his guts about their relationship. He was still refusing to take her calls. If he'd kept his trap shut, Fletcher would have no evidence against her in their custody battle. Men were so weak.

It surprised Bliss how much she missed Jessica. She would've loved to catch a movie and dinner tonight. But Jessica had yet to call her to apologize, which was so unlike her. When Jessica did show up, Bliss was going to make her grovel before accepting her apology. Then she would put Jessica's mind at ease by explaining that Harmony was doing just fine.

An idea came to Bliss that caused a sinister smile to crease her lips. She wasn't done with Fletcher and Mia just yet. She ran inside, grabbed her iPad and returned to the patio. Once her windfall from Fletcher started pouring in, Bliss knew exactly where she wanted to buy her new home. Beverly Hills. Since she was about to become a multi-millionaire, she needed to start living like one. She typed in Zillow.com and perused the homes currently up for sale.

If she was lucky, there might be something available close to Fletcher, maybe even on their same street. If she was going to share custody of Harmony, it made sense to have her daughter nearby. That way, Harmony could also spend time with her brothers. Bliss snickered. Mia would be ready to pull out every strand of her expensive weave.

She went inside for a champagne refill before returning to her website search. The houses in Fletcher's neighborhood were in the two-to-four-million-dollar range. No big deal with the cash she had coming.

The doorbell interrupted her house hunting. She wasn't expecting anyone. Plodding barefoot into the living room, she was about to open the door, but decided to check the peephole first. She didn't want some process server surprising her with another legal document.

At first she couldn't make out the person standing on the other side of the door. She hit the wall switch, turning on the porch light and looked again. When she realized who was standing on her doorstep, she snatched the door open.

"What are *you* doing here?"

Her uninvited guest stepped across the threshold without responding.

"I didn't invite you in."

Before Bliss could say another word, the intruder raised a gun, aiming it at chest level.

Bliss instinctively covered her chest with both arms and backed away. "Are you crazy? Put that thing away. This isn't funny."

With each backward step Bliss made, the intruder took a step forward, the gun still pointed at her.

"Just calm down and put that thing down. Please! Don't do this!"

Without ever speaking a word, the intruder pulled the trigger and fired.

CHAPTER 59

"**D**efinitely personal," Detective Dean Mankowski said aloud as he crouched over the beautiful Bliss Fenton.

His eyes moved from the glamour shot of Bliss on the mantelpiece to the bloody body sprawled before him. The woman's entire chest was covered in blood, but her face had not been marred. From the head up, it was probably the best-looking corpse he'd ever seen.

His partner, Detective Thomas, peered down from a standing position, agreeing with his initial assessment. "Yep, I'd say she knew the shooter. No forced entry and no apparent robbery. Looks like the perp fired five shots to make his point."

The coroner had estimated the time of death at some time between eight and ten p.m. last night. Bliss' housekeeper had discovered her body just after nine this morning.

Mankowski began to rise, his bones creaking as his left hip popped. He was well into his forties but his body seemed to be rushing him into senior citizen hood. He had a full head of dark blonde hair that added to his masculine allure. "Let's bet? Whoever did this used to screw her? I'll put up twenty."

"We're not betting anything," Thomas said, scanning the room to make sure they hadn't been overheard. A lean African-American who looked more like an insurance salesman than a cop, his easy-going personality was a good fit for the sometimes grouchy Mankowski. "Shouldn't you be trying to play it by the book these days?"

"You're such a pussy now. That time away from me really messed you up."

Thomas smiled. "You're just lucky to have me back. Now fly right."

He was thankful to be at the scene of his first homicide after close to a year of desk duty. He'd almost lost his job after being busted for sleeping with an attorney who, unbeknownst to him, was intricately involved in a murder case he was working.

Mankowski wasn't the kind of guy who could be led around by his dick. But he'd never come up against a woman with the skills of a Girlie Cortez. It still rankled him that he'd allowed her to use him the way she had. He stared down at Bliss Fenton again. This gorgeous chick had probably used some schmuck too.

A crime scene tech walked up to them. "Detectives, there's a woman outside who wants to speak with you. Claims she's a friend of the vic."

Mankowski and Thomas made their way outside, where a petite mousy-looking woman stood on the far side of the police tape. She started yelling out to them even as they headed her way.

"Is she okay? Please tell me what happened!"

The detectives introduced themselves, sidestepping the woman's question. "What's your name?" Mankowski asked.

"Jessica Winthrop. Bliss is my best friend. Please tell me she's okay."

"I'm sorry." Thomas was always the one who delivered the bad news. "Your friend didn't make it."

Jessica dumped her head into her hands and started to wail. "The children! Oh my God, the children. They don't have a mother! I have to find the boys. Where are they?"

"There were no kids inside, ma'am," Thomas said.

"Then they're probably with the nanny," Jessica cried. "Oh my God! You can't let them see their mother like that."

Thomas put a hand on Jessica's shoulder. "Relax. This is a crime scene now. They won't be allowed back inside."

The detectives led Jessica over to their car.

"What happened to her?" Jessica asked again. "On the news they said there'd been a shooting, but that was it. Please tell me what happened."

"This is an active murder investigation," Mankowski said, "so we can't say any more than that right now. What can you tell us about Ms. Fenton. Who would want to harm her?"

Jessica pressed her hands to her cheeks. "I warned Bliss all the time that something like this could happen. But she wouldn't listen."

Mankowski's ears perked up. "That what could happen?"

"That someone would want to hurt her because of the way she treated people."

"And how did she treat people?" Mankowski asked.

"Like their feelings didn't matter. Bliss only cared about Bliss."

They were drawing the attention of a growing crowd of looky-loos. One guy was videotaping Bliss' townhouse with his phone and two more news crews had just arrived.

Mankowski learned early in his career never to take anyone for granted. Murderers were known to return to the scene of the crime to gloat over their kill. "Is that how she treated you?"

Jessica's back straightened indignantly. "What are you insinuating, detective? I was Bliss' best friend. We had a fight a few days ago, but I still loved her."

Mankowski cut his eyes in Thomas' direction.

"So what did you two fight about?"

"It's a long, crazy story." Jessica wiped her eyes with the back of her right hand and struggled to compose herself. "Bliss always went after what she wanted, no matter who got hurt in the process."

Mankowski appraised the small woman in front of him. Bliss Fenton and Jessica Winthrop seemed an odd pair for best friends. But then he reconsidered that assessment. He'd dated a lot of stunning women, and none of them had friends who looked as good. Pretty women liked to surround themselves with less attractive competition. Standing next to Jessica, Bliss would shine like the floodlights at Dodger stadium.

"So what was the fight about?" Mankowski asked again.

"Bliss was in a custody dispute with her daughter's father. I didn't like how she was handling it."

Jessica went on to tell the detectives how Bliss had dumped her daughter on Fletcher McClain's doorstep and how Jessica had kicked her out of her car.

Mankowski wanted to pat the woman on the back. He liked her spunk.

"Do you have any idea who might've wanted to kill Bliss?" Thomas asked.

Jessica didn't hesitate. "I'd start with the fathers of her children."

"How many fathers are we talking about?"

"Two. I mean three, but no one knows who the third father is?"

"I thought you said you were her best friend?"

"I am. Or...I was." Jessica was about to lose it again. "But Bliss never talked about Jonas' father. Not even to me. Fletcher is Harmony's father, and Dr. Joseph Franco is Aiden's father. Both of them had a contentious relationship with Bliss."

"What kind of work did Ms. Fenton do?"

"She didn't work. She supported herself from child support payments. Her kids' fathers were very well off. In fact, Fletcher McClain sued her for fraud to avoid paying child support, but his case got dismissed just a few days ago. That's why he filed to get full custody of Harmony."

Mankowski scratched his head. "He sued her for fraud?"

"Fletcher basically claimed she got pregnant by tricking him. Bliss was asking for more than eighty grand a month in child support for her daughter."

Thomas whistled.

"That's a lot of money for one kid," Mankowski said.

"Fletcher offered her fifteen thousand dollars a month, but Bliss insisted she was entitled to ten percent of his income."

Thomas and Mankowski eyed each other. Eighty grand a month was a whole lot of motive. "What does this McClain guy do?"

"He runs Karma Entertainment."

Jessica started to speak, then looked down at the ground as if she was reluctant to proceed. After a long beat, she did.

"If you're looking for Bliss' killer, you should start with Fletcher McClain."

CHAPTER 60

Fletcher was nothing short of amazed that in only a matter of days, he'd fallen so hard for the tiny little human asleep in her crib. He hated to brag, but his kid was darn good-looking.

Harmony's eyes fluttered open and she smiled up at him. Seconds later, however, Harmony was wailing at the top of her lungs.

Fletcher dashed to the doorway. "Carina, the baby needs you."

The nanny rushed in and grabbed the crying child. "Good morning, precious. I bet you're hungry."

She turned to Fletcher. "Hold her while I go make a bottle."

As he took Harmony in his arms, Fletcher couldn't help checking out Carina's round, firm ass as she floated out of the room. The girl wasn't just a looker. She was smart, well read and had an exuberant energy about her. It was going to be hard not screwing her.

He knew Mia didn't want a woman as hot as Carina joining their household. That was the only reason she now claimed she was thinking about going part-time to help out with Harmony. Fletcher didn't buy it. He'd never forgive Mia for pouting and sleeping in the guest room after Harmony's arrival. But as it turned out, he was glad Mia was behaving like a spoiled child. If she'd helped him pick their nanny, the woman would've been a troll.

As he cradled Harmony's small body, he felt an odd mix of emotions. It still felt foreign to hold a baby, his baby. But at the same time, he seemed drawn to her.

He looked up to see Mia standing in the doorway wearing the same frown that had been plastered across her face since Harmony's arrival. He understood how mad she was at Bliss, but it wasn't Harmony's fault.

Fletcher inhaled the baby's sweet scent. "She's so beautiful," he said, a sense of awe in his voice.

Mia stepped further into the room, but not close enough to get a peek at Harmony. "I need to understand what's going on here."

"What's going on is that this is my kid."

"You said asking for full custody was just a stunt to get Bliss to back off her excessive child support demand. But you're walking around here like you're running for Father of the Year."

"Now that I've had a chance to spend some time with her, I actually think I do want full custody."

Mia stifled a gasp. "This is something we need to discuss. I never thought—"

"You told me you wanted children," he reminded her.

"I do. But I want our children. Not—"

It was too late for Mia to take her words back. Fletcher shot her a hard glare, hoping to communicate that he was appalled that she could not accept his daughter. But he wasn't surprised. He'd overheard Mia talking to her mother, complaining that she would not raise Bliss' baby. Well, Harmony wasn't just Bliss' kid. She was his flesh and blood too. And he was falling in love with the kid. The custody petition had been all about his money, but now it was all about his heart.

Carina retrieved Harmony and began feeding her.

Fletcher left the room and Mia followed him into the kitchen.

"Fletcher, we need to talk."

"Okay, so talk."

"I need to get to work and so do you," she said. "Let's have dinner at Mastro's tonight. We can—"

"Not tonight. I had to work pretty late last night. Tonight I want to get home in time to see Harmony before she goes to sleep."

"Is it your kid or your kid's nanny you want to see?"

"Oh, Mia, give it up. I don't have time for your childish insecurities."

Fletcher flicked on the TV in the kitchen and grabbed a box of shredded wheat from the cabinet. He started pouring almond milk into a bowl, when something on the TV screen grabbed his attention, causing him to douse the counter, not the bowl, with milk.

A reporter was doing a live shot from Playa Vista. Fletcher instantly recognized Bliss' townhouse. He grabbed the remote and turned up the volume. He listened as the reporter recounted what was going on.

Bliss had been murdered. Dead from multiple gunshot wounds.

A jumble of thoughts floated around in his head, then landed with a gentle thud. He glanced over at Mia, who looked like she might faint. Fletcher wanted to faint too—over his good fortune.

Now, he wouldn't have to pay her a dime and, on top of that, he had his beautiful daughter all to himself.

CHAPTER 61

Jessica Winthrop willingly accompanied the detectives downtown to police headquarters. By the time she'd finished answering all of their questions about Bliss Fenton, Mankowski found himself speechless. He'd thought Girlie Cortez was a piece of work, but this chick had her beat by a country mile.

Thomas just kept blinking his eyes and repeating everything Jessica said.

"Let me get this straight. She was already getting twelve grand a month from one guy, who knows what from the other kid's father and she still wanted eighty-three grand a month from this record company guy?"

Jessica pursed her lips. "Bliss wasn't a bad person," she said, trying to soften the picture she'd painted of her best friend. "She'd been hurt a lot and when a man rejected her, going after his money was how she struck back."

Thomas reeled back in his chair. "Eighty-three grand a month was a lot of striking back."

Mankowski almost wished he could've met the woman. She must've been one hell of a lay. "I can't believe the woman just gave the kid to him." He couldn't help but laugh. "I bet that surprised the hell out of him."

"I begged Bliss not to do it. That's why we argued and I kicked her out of my car." Jessica played with her cuticle and seemed to be on the verge of tears. "I was just so angry that she was using Harmony as a pawn like that. Bliss expected Fletcher to bring her back the next day.

I don't know if he did or not, because we haven't spoken. And now, we won't get a chance to."

Jessica wiped her eyes with the back of her hand.

Mankowski didn't want the woman to start wailing again, so he kept the questions coming.

"Let's talk about the fathers of the two boys. What about—" he paused to look down at his notes, "Aiden's father?"

"He's an orthopedic surgeon. A few weeks ago, Bliss got his child support payments increased by two grand a month. Dr. Franco was pretty upset about that."

"How upset?" Thomas asked. "Did he ever threaten to harm her?"

Jessica started fidgeting with her purse and suddenly seemed reluctant to continue spilling the beans. "Well. . ."

"You need to be straight with us," Thomas said gently.

"They had some pretty angry arguments. And yes, he did threaten her, but I don't think he meant it."

"And what about Jonas' father?"

"Like I said before, Bliss refused to talk about him. But I always assumed she was getting money from him too."

"Any idea how much?"

"Nope."

"I bet he was another high roller," Mankowski scoffed.

"Probably," Jessica said. "Bliss only dated wealthy men. She referred to Dr. Franco as slumming."

This time, Mankowski shook his head. "Was she dating anyone now?"

"Yeah, but I don't know who. She bought a new outfit for a date a few weeks ago, but wouldn't tell me who the guy was. I think he may have been married."

"Anybody else, who might've had a motive to kill her?" Mankowski asked, even though the two suspects they had were more than enough for the moment.

Again, Jessica seemed uneasy about proceeding. "Well, I mean, maybe..."

"C'mon, Ms. Winthrop. If there's someone else Ms. Fenton had a problem with, we need to know."

"I guess I should also tell you about Fletcher McClain's fiancée, Mia Richardson. They used to be yoga buddies. Bliss was dating Fletcher when he dumped her and started seeing Mia. Bliss waited until after Harmony was born to tell Fletcher he was her father. And Bliss didn't exactly get pregnant by traditional means."

Mankowski's forehead crinkled. "Traditional means? What are you saying?"

Jessica recounted the allegation in Fletcher's complaint that Bliss had stolen his sperm from a used condom. When she was done, both men were dumbfounded.

"Bliss never told me one way or the other if the allegation was true," she continued, "but since she didn't deny it, I assumed it was."

Mankowski had been thinking about a vasectomy. The final decision had just been made. He was doing it.

Thomas scribbled Mia Richardson's name on his pad. "Sounds like you were right to warn Bliss about the way she treated people."

"If only she had listened," Jessica said, her tone somber.

Mankowski gazed over at his partner with a half smile. Solving this whodunit was going to be big fun.

Jessica averted her eyes again. "There's something else."

"Okay," Mankowski said. "We're listening."

Jessica hesitated. "I have some important evidence to give you."

"Evidence? What kind of evidence?"

Jessica opened her purse. "Evidence that might help prove who killed Bliss."

CHAPTER 62

"I still can't believe Darius' lying ass had the nerve to be cheating on me." Special stabs her soda with a straw.

It's rare that we make time for lunch these days, but Special had insisted. The only reason I relented was because I was addicted to the spinach artichoke dip at the California Pizza Kitchen.

"Being in a wheelchair doesn't make him incapable of cheating. He's still a man. Just make sure you don't go back to his house again. I can't believe what you did."

"If I'd been in my right mind, I would've keyed his car."

I point a stern index finger in her direction. "You're lucky he didn't call the police on your crazy behind. I'm telling you right now, if you get arrested, I'm not coming to your rescue."

Special laughs for the first time. "Girl, please. There's no way you'd leave me hanging. You'd be at the jail demanding my release before I could say *I'm calling my lawyer.*"

I roll my eyes and laugh along with her because she's absolutely right. "I'm tired of hearing you whine about Darius. Let's talk about something else."

"I need another case to help me forget about being punked by that fool. I was having big fun following Bliss Fenton around. You got another juicy case like that one?"

"I can put you in contact with Fletcher's family law attorney. Turns out she's just as conniving as Girlie Cortez."

I tell Special about Fletcher's custody petition and how Bliss landed a preemptive strike by dumping Harmony on his doorstep.

"That girl is her own brand of scandalous. How's Fletcher doing with the kid?"

"He freaked out at first. Called me in the middle of the night like it was my problem to solve. But he hired a full-time nanny to take care of her. I think he might have a good case for full custody thanks to the information you dug up about Bliss and Martin Zinzer. Maybe Fletcher's family law attorney can hire you to dig up some more dirt on her."

"Hell, I might do some more digging around on my own dime. I'm dying to find out who the father of her oldest kid is? I bet you it's somebody really, really famous. Like a politician."

My phone rings. I check the screen, grunt, then place it back on the table.

Special raises a brow. "Whoever that was, you sure don't look too happy to hear from 'em."

"It's Fletcher. I don't have time for his madness right now. Whatever he wants can wait."

"I can't believe you really cut him loose."

"The case is over and it isn't worth appealing. I'm still angry that he lied to me."

"Like you said, men will be men." Special stirs her strawberry lemonade. "I can't believe Darius—"

"Special, I'm tired of you harping about Darius. I do not want to hear that man's name again. He's not the first guy who cheated on you, and sad to say, he may not be the last. Get over it."

"I can't. I ignored the fact that he's in a wheelchair and he had the nerve to step out on me."

"That's the problem. You acted like you were doing him a favor by dating him. The man is smart, attractive, he's got a few bucks and he's great in bed. Men like that have lots of options."

"The women in L.A. are so desperate."

"So what does that say about you?"

She put a hand on her hip. "Nothing. I was being nice and he took advantage of me."

"You two didn't even have a committed relationship."

"So. That doesn't mean he can lie to me. He should've been kissing the ground I walked on. He's been ringing my phone off the hook, leaving me messages claiming he's sorry and wants to explain."

"You should hear him out. He could be a good contact for you regarding your investigative work."

"I don't need his help, but I do want my red-bottom shoe back. He's holding it hostage until I agree to see him. I can't believe I threw my expensive-ass shoe through his window."

"I can't believe every single thing you did that night," I say with a laugh.

My phone chirps, signaling a text message. "Fletcher again," I say. As I read his text, my eyes expand in alarm.

Special notices my angst. "What's the matter now?"

I read the message two more times, just to make sure my eyes aren't failing me.

"Bliss Fenton's been murdered," I tell Special. "The police are at Fletcher's office trying to question him."

"O-M-G! That boy would definitely be suspect number one. You think he did it?"

I refuse to answer Special's question because I don't want to even consider that possibility. My hands shake as I call him back.

Fletcher had threatened that he would kill Bliss before paying her a dime. *Had he done just that?*

"Don't say a word to the police," I direct him, without even saying hello. "Tell them you need to consult with your lawyer, then escort them out of your office."

I'm feeling more than conflicted. If Fletcher ends up charged with murder, I don't have the energy right now for another high-profile murder case. But I feel obligated to come to his aid, at least until he can retain another attorney.

His voice is low and muffled, like he's covering the phone with his hand. "They might think I'm guilty if I don't talk to 'em," he whispers.

Are you?

"Let 'em think what they want." I say, as I down the rest of my Diet Coke and grab my purse. "Just get rid of them, then meet me at my office."

CHAPTER 63

After leaving the police station, Jessica drove straight to Seal Beach to see Dr. Franco. She'd learned from Bliss' nanny that both boys had spent the past few days with him. She was surprised that Dr. Franco hadn't called her. Maybe he wasn't aware yet that Bliss was dead. That meant she would have to deliver the sad news. But that wasn't the main reason for her visit.

Bliss had named Jessica the guardian for all three of her children. She knew there was no way Dr. Franco would hand over Aiden, but Jonas was now hers.

When Jessica told him that Bliss had been murdered, Dr. Franco just sat there, immobile, staring at the floor.

"I can't believe it," he mumbled. "After everything she took me through, I actually feel sorry for her. She was a very troubled woman."

Jessica nodded in agreement. She needed to get to the point of this visit and decided to just blurt it out. "The reason I'm here is that Bliss named me the legal guardian for all three of her children."

Jessica figured she might as well test the waters. If she had a shot at also getting custody of Aiden too, she'd know within the next few seconds.

Dr. Franco's eyes registered astonishment. "Nobody's raising my son but me."

Jessica nodded. "Of course. But I'd like to take custody of Jonas. I'm assuming you don't have a problem with that."

Lena returned to the room, carrying three cups of coffee. She'd left earlier, Jessica assumed, to give them some time alone.

Dr. Franco glanced up at Lena. "Bliss appointed Jessica as Jonas' legal guardian. She wants to take him."

Lena looked hesitantly back at him, which worried Jessica. *Did they intend to keep both boys?*

Jessica was the only one to reach for one of the steaming mugs Lena had placed on the coffee table. Lena remained standing, Dr. Franco remained stunned.

"Honey," Lena placed her hand on his shoulder, "can I speak to you in private for a moment?"

The two of them left the room, but returned almost as quickly.

Lena was the first to speak, her voice tight as if she were straining to be civil. "Losing a mother at such a young age is a very tragic loss. It doesn't make sense for the boys to now lose each other. We've talked about it and we think it's best if we raise both of them."

Jessica felt the room tilt. She took her time, mentally rehearsing her words before speaking them. She would dismiss their ridiculous idea without directly responding to it.

"I agree that the boys are going to need each other more than ever before. That's why we're going to have to work together to make sure they remain close."

Dr. Franco looked over at Lena. It was clear that she was calling the shots. "Look, Lena can't have kids. We want to raise both boys."

"I'm his legal guardian," Jessica repeated, as if no further response was necessary.

Lena locked her arms across her chest, her face awash in anger. "They're brothers and they should be raised together."

Jessica stood firm. "That's not going to happen."

Lena seemed to want to challenge her further, but instead, just let out a long breath. "We need to break the news to the boys. And we should do it when they're together."

"That's fine. Let's do it now," Jessica said.

Lena's lips twisted like two taut wires. "Now really isn't a good time."

Jessica glanced at her watch. It was just after 3 p.m. She could still hear the ping of some video game the boys were playing.

"Okay, then. I'll take Jonas home now and bring him back tomorrow and we'll do it together."

Jessica needed to get Jonas out of their clutches as soon as possible. From the looks on their faces, they intended to fight her on this. But she wasn't leaving without him.

Dr. Franco finally spoke. "Look, Jessica. We shouldn't make this decision right now. Bliss hasn't even been gone for a day. Why don't you go home and—"

"I'm his legal guardian and I'm not leaving here without him." She almost felt sorry for them. They apparently loved Jonas as much as she did.

Lena stomped down the hallway as a look of resignation spread across the doctor's face.

He stood. "I'll go get him."

Seconds later, the boys stampeded into the room.

"Auntie Jessica!" they both yelled, jumping into her lap.

Fighting back tears, she pulled them close enough to smother.

"Jonas is coming home with me tonight," she told them.

"I wanna come too," Aiden said with a pout.

Dr. Franco ruffled his son's hair. "Next time."

It was so telling that neither boy had asked about their mother.

Taking Jonas' hand, Jessica led him out of the house. When they reached the porch, Dr. Franco stepped outside, closing the door behind him.

Once Jonas was anchored into his car seat, Jessica closed the door and was about to walk around to the driver's side. Dr. Franco stopped her.

"Uh ... I ... well ..." The doctor seemed to be at a loss for words.

She was confused about what else he had to say and why he seemed so tongue-tied.

"Is something wrong?" Jessica asked.

"The police are going to want to talk to me. You know better than anyone else, there was no love lost between me and Bliss. I'm probably going to be high on their suspects' list."

"I can guarantee you," Jessica said, "that list is going to be pretty long. Bliss wronged a lot of people. You shouldn't be too concerned."

From the worry lines still etched across his forehead, her comment didn't seem to offer much comfort.

"Jessica, I'd appreciate it if you didn't tell the police about my verbal sparring matches with Bliss. I said a lot of things I really didn't mean."

"The police already interviewed me."

Dr. Franco rubbed the back of his neck. "So what did you tell them? You didn't say I threatened her, did you?"

"I'm sorry," was all Jessica could say. "I didn't want to lie to the police."

As a wave of worry cast a shadow across the doctor's face, Jessica decided to throw him a bone. "If it helps, when the police asked me who I thought killed Bliss, I told them I thought Fletcher McClain may have done it."

That comment did seem to appease him a bit. "You think so?"

Jessica nodded. "As much as you hated Bliss, Fletcher despised her ten times more."

CHAPTER 64

"This might turn out to be an easy one to wrap up," Mankowski announced. "All we have to do is figure out which baby daddy hated her the most."

Thomas stroked his angular chin. "That might be easier said than done."

They were standing outside Fletcher McClain's fancy highfalutin' office at Karma Entertainment, taking in the view of the Hollywood Hills.

When they'd shown up and asked if the record exec would be willing to answer a few questions about Bliss Fenton's murder, Fletcher turned whiter than white and said he needed to make a call first.

"He's not going to talk to us," Thomas predicted. "He's in his office right now getting instructions to lawyer up."

"Maybe. But rich guys like this dude think they're smarter than everybody else. He'll talk to us anyway, then slip up and say something incriminating."

"Let's hope."

Ten minutes later, Fletcher invited them into his office. "I'm willing to cooperate in your investigation," he said. "But I just consulted with a lawyer friend of mine. She wants to be present when we speak. So once she's available, you guys can come back and ask me all the questions you want."

"If we can't talk to you now, we won't be coming back."

Mankowski let Fletcher enjoy a few seconds of relief, then added, "If you don't talk to us now, the next time we speak will be at the police station. And it's not half as nice as this swanky place."

Fletcher stuck out his chest and he seemed to stand a little taller. "So be it."

Mankowski hated rich guys.

"Will you be represented by the same lawyer who lost that fraud case you filed against Ms. Fenton to get out of paying child support?"

Mankowski could see that Fletcher was a little shocked that they'd done their homework.

"I didn't file that lawsuit to get out of paying child support. I filed it because what Bliss did to me was outrageous."

"Sounds like it wasn't what she did to you, but more like what you did to her."

Fletcher's left hand balled into a fist. Mankowski liked the fact that he was getting to the guy.

"Bliss committed fraud," Fletcher pointed out.

"Not according to the court."

Fletcher lifted his chin just slightly. "As I said, when my attorney Vernetta Henderson is available, we'll call you to make an appointment."

This time Mankowski was the shocked one. He eyed Thomas, then turned back to Fletcher. "You're represented by Vernetta Henderson?"

"Yeah. You know her?"

"I do. She's a pretty sharp cookie. I guess a guy like you would only hire the best."

"We went to college together. We go way back."

"I'm glad she's your lawyer. You're going to need a pretty good one."

This time, Fletcher didn't bite. He stared back into Mankowski's hard eyes, trying to appear as if he wasn't intimidated. But a bead of sweat trickled down the side of his face, giving him away.

Fletcher made a show of glancing at his Rolex. "Both Vernetta and I have pretty tight schedules. I'm not sure when we'll be able to get down to the station."

Mankowski wanted to slug the prick. Instead, he pulled a card from the inside pocket of his jacket and handed it to him. "I'd suggest you make it sooner rather than later."

CHAPTER 65

Jessica felt drained from everything that had happened that day, but staring down at a sleeping Jonas brought her peace.

Talking to the police for hours had been difficult. Jessica had patiently answered their questions, when she'd actually wanted to crawl into a corner and sob. Despite all the chaos Bliss had created, she still loved her friend, flaws and all.

How crazy is that?

Thank God she had pressured Bliss to name her as the guardian of each of her children a month or so after Harmony was born. At first, Bliss had resisted, insisting that nothing was going to happen to her. But Jessica didn't give up the fight, and now she was glad she hadn't.

Jessica planned to contact Fletcher tomorrow. He'd probably be anxious to hand over Harmony. For now, she was just glad Jonas was all hers.

She heard the front door open and braced herself for a conversation she knew would be difficult. But she didn't care. This time, she was going to get her way.

"Jessica! Where are you?"

Continuing to lovingly stare at Jonas, Jessica didn't answer. She still had so many things to work out.

What she'd found on Paul's computer had tilted her world sideways. Jessica had already made up her mind that she was not going to leave. Nor would she even confront Paul about what she knew. Pretending is what she'd done her whole life. It wouldn't be hard to simply go on pretending.

Besides, she had no stomach for a divorce battle. Her only goal in life now was to be the kind of mother Bliss' children deserved. Children were better off being raised in a two-parent home and that's what she intended to provide for both Jonas and Harmony.

"Honey, are you okay?"

When Paul stepped into the room, Jessica ran to him and he embraced her with a gentleness she had not felt in months. "I just heard about Bliss."

Jessica examined his face, as if searching for signs of guilt, then melted into his chest and cried.

Suddenly, Paul noticed the sleeping child. He stared over at Jonas, then down at Jessica. He seemed to know her intentions.

She pulled away from him. "We're raising him. I know you don't like children, but you'll come to love him."

Paul's chest filled with air. "It's been an emotional day for you. We can discuss this another time."

"Nothing's going to change. I also intend to get custody of Harmony. They should be raised together."

"Look, Jessica, I didn't sign up for this. We need to discuss—"

She stared him dead in the eye. "And there are some things I didn't sign up for either."

By the way his eyes avoided hers, Jessica knew he understood the full scope of what she was conveying. And like her, Paul appeared willing to act as if his misdeed had never occurred. To let it float out to sea undisturbed.

"If Fletcher McClain wants to raise his daughter, no court's going to give you custody."

"I'm going to be Harmony's mother."

Paul's face clouded with apprehension, as if he was concerned about her mental stability.

He hugged her again and kissed the top of her head. "There's no need to talk about this now."

"And there's also no need to talk about it later because I'm not going to change my mind. I plan to fight Fletcher for custody of Harmony too. He didn't want her from the moment she was born. I can't stand by and let her be raised by a woman who hated her mother. Mia will make that child's life hell."

"Honey, I think you may be in shock. Why don't you lie down for a while?"

Paul tried to lead her out of the room, but she pulled away. "I want to be here when he wakes up."

Sitting down on the end of the bed, she stared at the sleeping boy. He looked so small in the huge bed. Paul threw up his hands and left the room.

Jessica smiled at the child, her child. The child she had longed for and now finally had. She had no idea why people insisted on having their own children when there were so many kids who needed good homes. She would have been perfectly happy adopting, and now she could.

After what she'd handed over to the police, Jessica was certain that any day now, Fletcher McClain would be arrested for Bliss' murder.

Then, not just Jonas, but Harmony would be all hers too.

CHAPTER 66

Special found a parking spot half a block from Bliss' Playa Vista townhouse. The place was still roped off by crime scene tape, but there were no cop cars in sight. She watched a scruffy-looking guy with a camera taking photos of the place from every possible angle.

She was about to exit the car when her phone rang. She pulled it from her purse.

Darius again. She started to stuff it back in her purse, but thought about what Vernetta had said. Maybe he would be good to have around when she needed help with her investigations. She should hear what he had to say. Just for laughs.

"Hey, babe," Darius said when she answered.

Special grimaced. "Oh, so it's like that? I'm your babe, huh?"

"We need to talk."

"About what?"

"About our little misunderstanding."

"Is that what you're calling it?"

"Let's not do this on the phone. Meet me for dinner tonight."

"I'm busy."

"Okay, tomorrow night then."

Special wanted to scream. Truth be told, she did want to see him again and she hated herself for that. "I'll think about it," she mumbled, then hung up.

Resting her head against the headrest, she closed her eyes and reminded herself that in a few weeks Darius would be a memory just like all the other jerks she'd encountered. Special didn't know how many more failed relationships she could handle. Hell, maybe Bliss Fenton had it right. Screw them, before they screw you. Or in Bliss' case, after they screw you. She glanced at the expensive townhouses that lined the street. She would love to be living large like this.

For now, she needed something to keep her mind off of Darius. And solving Bliss' murder was going to do just that.

She grabbed her phone and climbed out of the car.

"What happened?" she asked, walking up to the photographer. Playing dumb was the best way to get information.

"A woman was murdered inside that townhouse last night. Shot five times."

"Wow, the police usually don't release that kind of information. How'd you learn that?"

"I overheard two cops talking," the guy said, as if he'd gotten the scoop of the year.

Special frowned. L.A.'s finest. That was nothing short of amateur hour.

The guy took a few more pictures and left.

Special lifted the crime scene tape, then crept over to the patio. The glass door was locked, but she peered inside and could see all the way into the living room. She gasped at the large bloodstain, which must've been the spot where Bliss had been shot. She jotted down some notes.

Gunned down near the doorway. Shot five times.

So many shots meant it was personal. And personal meant the killer was probably someone who knew her. It was not looking good for Fletcher McClain. She tugged on the door again, not that she expected it to suddenly spring open. And, of course, it didn't. She headed back to the sidewalk and did a double take when she saw two men walking toward her.

Judging from the startled looks on their faces, they were just as surprised to see her.

"What the hell are you doing here?" Mankowski barked. "This is a crime scene. Don't you see that tape? You're trespassing."

"Good afternoon to you too, detective."

"I said what are you doing here?" he repeated.

"Working a case."

"What case and who's the client?"

"I'm sorry, but that's confidential information. You should be nice to me. I might solve this case for you too."

Mankowski's nose twitched. He had no rebuttal for that. Special had indeed provided information that cracked another murder case they were trying to solve. It was the same case that led to Girlie Cortez's suspension from the Bar and Mankowski's desk duty.

"I suggest you get on the other side of that tape. Right now."

"Calm down, cowboy. We're both on the same team."

"No, we're not."

"I want to know who killed Bliss Fenton as much as you do. So what information can you share? What time did the shooting happen?"

"You need to leave."

She ignored his directive and kept talking. "Have you pulled the video from the traffic cameras at the intersection of Jefferson and Playa Vista Drive? That's the closest intersection. Whoever killed Bliss probably drove through there."

"We know that," Mankowski growled. "Now run along and play *CSI* someplace else."

Special got such a kick out of razzing them.

"You should be nicer to me. You might need my help again."

"If I remember correctly, you're not a licensed investigator," Mankowski sputtered. "You could get arrested for perpetrating."

"I'm not licensed *yet*. But I'm a fully authorized investigator-in-training. I'm apprenticing with Girlie Cortez's former investigator. You remember her, don't you? Your ex-girlfriend."

Mankowski's face flushed with color.

"Aw man, you're blushing like a teenager," Special teased. "You still have the hots for her even after she punked you, huh?"

"Who's your client?" Mankowski demanded again.

"Like I just said, that's confidential. Looks like you and Girlie will have a chance to reconnect."

"Just what do you mean by that?"

"You don't know?" Special asked.

"Know what?"

"Girlie Cortez represented Bliss in a fraud case her baby's daddy filed against her. You do know about the fraud case and the uber-rich Fletcher McClain, don't you?"

Thomas shoved his hands in his pockets, while Mankowski's face went from bright red to pale white.

"Yep," Special continued, "if you wanna know about Bliss Fenton and her dirty deeds, Girlie Cortez will have all the news that's fit to print."

CHAPTER 67

By the time I make it back to my office, Fletcher is there waiting for me. We spend the first twenty minutes in a heated argument.

"I don't care what Mia says. She's not a criminal attorney," I tell him. "You'll cause yourself more harm than good by talking to the police."

Fletcher throws up his hands. "But I have nothing to hide. They're going to think I killed Bliss if I refuse to talk to them."

"And they're still going to think you killed her even if you *do* talk to them. The police are not interested in your side of the story. If they were, they could simply have you write down a statement. What they want is a confession or for you to say something incriminating. That's why they call it an interrogation and not a conversation."

I've often had a similar debate with clients who insist on testifying at trial, who give too much credence to their perceived powers of persuasion. They're confident that they can convince the jury of their innocence, even when all the evidence points toward their guilt. Once they take the stand and the prosecutor butchers them like a pig, the damage is done and I can't undo it.

Fletcher runs a hand through his hair. "It's my decision and I think it's best for me to talk to them. I can handle those two cops."

His confident declaration is almost laughable. Fletcher is essentially a hustler at heart. He's pulled off business deals others thought were impossible. As a result, because of his history of success in the business world, he thinks he can talk himself out of hell.

I turn to my computer and start typing.

"What are you doing?" Fletcher asks.

"Preparing a short statement for you to sign. I want it in writing that you insisted on talking to the police against my advice and counsel."

Fletcher shrugs. "Whatever."

"And just to be clear, I'll represent you during the interview, but after that, I'm done. You'll need to find yourself a new attorney."

He smiles smugly. "After the interview, I won't need a new attorney because they'll see I didn't do it and move on to another suspect."

I do my best to prepare my naïve client for what's to come. I try to cover everything the police might possibly ask him regarding Bliss' murder. Throughout our practice session, Fletcher repeatedly professes his innocence. Almost to the point where he erases my doubts about his involvement.

Three hours later, we're sitting in an interrogation room at police headquarters waiting for the fun to begin. The room still reeks from the last interrogation. At least one of the former occupants was long overdue for a bath.

I was quite surprised when Fletcher told me that the two detectives who tried to question him said they knew me. This was turning out to be old home week. Mankowski and Thomas were the same detectives involved in my last case against Girlie Cortez.

The door eases open and in walks the massive Mankowski, followed by his sidekick Thomas.

"So we meet again," I say, pretending as if I'm happy to see them.

Mankowski extends one of his huge hands. "Glad to see you're in such good spirits."

I shake his hand, then do the same to Thomas. They don't bother to greet Fletcher again, but merely nod his way.

"Let's get started," I say. "My client wants to help in any way he can."

I recognize that in the police's eyes, Bliss' paternity case and Fletcher's failed fraud lawsuit gave him a boatload of motive for wanting Bliss dead. Cops often zone in on a suspect with tunnel vision, refusing to see other possible scenarios. My job here is three-fold. One, to make sure my client doesn't say anything to incriminate himself. Two, to find out what evidence the cops might have. And three, to help send the detectives down another path to solving their case.

Thomas remains standing near the door, while Mankowski takes a seat across from us at a small metal table. I suspect their respective positions during interrogations have been predetermined from years of working together. One cop focuses on the questioning, while the other hovers above, analyzing the suspect's body language, looking for signs of fabrication.

"We'll need to know your whereabouts between eight and ten o'clock last Tuesday night?"

Fletcher has his arms crossed and he's slouching in his chair like one of his hip-hop artists.

"At a listening session at my office. Listened to the entire CD for one of our new artists. At least six other people were there who can verify that."

"We'll need their names."

"No problem." Fletcher takes out his phone. "I can send you a text right now."

"It can wait." Mankowski moves closer to the table. "How are things going with you and your daughter?"

Fletcher's eyes narrow. I can tell he finds the question a bit strange and so do I. But he plays along.

"Excellent. We're bonding just fine."

"Really? We heard you weren't too happy about Bliss dumping Harmony on your doorstep."

"Well, I uh..." Fletcher seems uncertain about how to respond, but opts for honesty. "True. I was a little stunned at first. But I'm glad she's with me now."

"Yeah, okay." Mankowski flips a page on his small notepad. "Tell me about your relationship with Ms. Fenton."

It's my turn to jump in. "That's a very broad question, detective. How about narrowing it a bit?"

"This isn't a deposition, counselor."

"It sure isn't," I agree with a friendly smile. "If it were, we'd be here pursuant to a subpoena. But Mr. McClain is here voluntarily. So it would be great if you could be a little more specific with your questions."

Mankowski grunts. "We understand that you had a pretty contentious relationship with Ms. Fenton."

"That's true. She stole my sperm and inseminated herself when she knew I wasn't interested in having a kid with her. That would bother any guy."

There's a knock at the door and a rotund woman waves Thomas into the hallway. Before Mankowski can ask another question, Thomas is back, whispering into Mankowski's ear. They trade a smirk that tells me Mankowski is happy about whatever he'd just been told.

"I'm going to have to step out for a while." Thomas delivers the news as if we're going to miss him. "Another matter requires my attention."

Once the door closes, Mankowski turns back to us. "I'll just cut to the chase. Did you kill your ex-girlfriend?"

"No."

"It's our understanding that you threatened to do just that."

"Well, your understanding is wrong."

"So you're saying you never threatened to kill Ms. Fenton or even expressed the desire to see her dead?"

Fletcher pauses, then looks over at me. I want to tell him not to do that because it makes him look evasive. But I'm more concerned right now about the lie he just told. On at least two occasions he'd made it very clear that he would kill Bliss before paying her the money she was seeking. But our communications are attorney-client privileged. I pray he hasn't expressed those same sentiments to anyone else.

"Now, don't get me wrong," Fletcher continues. "What she did made me mad as hell. But I didn't want to see her dead."

A slight grin touches Mankowski's lips. "So if someone told me that you threatened to kill Ms. Fenton, they would be lying?"

"Yep."

My sensors are on maximum alert now. My experience tells me that Mankowski isn't just on a fishing expedition. He's methodically painting Fletcher into a corner. Did someone overhear Fletcher say he wanted Bliss dead? Maybe Fletcher expressed his frustration to Gabriella and the police knew about it. No. Gabriella would never sell out Fletcher to the police.

"So if someone told me that you threatened to kill Bliss Fenton, they'd be lying?"

Fletcher cocks his head. "I already answered that question."

I swallow hard. This feels like a setup. Mankowski is proceeding the same way I meticulously pose my questions in a deposition. When you have a smoking gun in your pocket, you give the witness every opportunity to tell the truth. Then you pull a surprise attack and confront him with irrefutable evidence that proves he's a big fat liar.

When Mankowski reaches for his phone and starts tapping the screen, my stomach clenches. I fear that Fletcher has just dug himself into a hole I might not be able to pull him out of.

"Why don't you listen to this?" he says. "Maybe it might refresh your memory."

He taps the screen and the first thing I hear is a man's voice. There's a low murmur of other voices and the tinkling of what sounds like silverware in the background. There's no question that the man speaking is Fletcher. His voice is low and full of venom.

"I need you to hear me and hear me clearly. If that kid is mine, I'm going to accept my legal obligations and do right by the both of you. But if you insist on being a greedy cunt about this, your precious little daughter could very well end up motherless."

"So you're threatening me?"

A jolt of silence rocks the tiny interrogation room. Fletcher is now wide-eyed when he finally faces me. His eyes are now full of fear and regret, regret for not following my advice. Mankowski sits back in his

chair, his right ankle resting on his left knee. As the recording continues, he looks more smug than I've ever seen him.

"It's not a threat at all. It's a promise."

Mankowski taps the screen of his phone, cutting off the recording.

Fletcher looks mortified. "How...how did you...Where'd you get that?"

"Bliss left it for us. She had her phone on record while you two were having lunch. We have your entire conversation on tape. Would you like to change your previous response about never having threatened Ms. Fenton?"

My hand seizes Fletcher's forearm and squeezes hard enough to leave fingerprints. "We're done here."

I stand up and Fletcher follows my lead.

His cheeks are flaming red like a spoiled toddler's. "I didn't kill that b—" He stops himself a second too late.

"Oh, so she's a bitch now? That's good to know."

"Not another word!" I shout at Fletcher.

With my hand pressed like the barrel of a gun against Fletcher's back, I push him out of the door.

CHAPTER 68

Detective Thomas was getting a kick out of the beautiful but snooty Mia Richardson. She was a little thin for his taste, but otherwise quite a looker. Fletcher McClain had picked himself some pretty, though flawed women.

He'd left a message with Mia's assistant that morning explaining that he wanted to speak with her about the murder of Bliss Fenton. From the chilly reception he'd received, Thomas figured they'd have to ambush Mia at her office, the way they'd tried to do with Fletcher. But it was just his luck that the proud little lady stalked right into the police station ready and willing to talk.

Thomas was thrilled that he would be able to talk to her before she had an opportunity to speak to Fletcher about his interview. Even better, the self-assured Mia Richardson didn't feel she needed an attorney for their little chat. She gave off the impression that she was way smarter than him. She *was* an attorney after all.

"Thanks so much for coming in," he began, trying to put her at ease.

She was dressed in a bright pink knit suit. It looked liked one of those St. John things that his wife swooned over. The detective couldn't believe how much they cost. He had a fundamental problem with paying extra money for something simply because it had somebody's name on it. He respected her for not coming in with her cleavage showing, what little she had. A lot of women tried to side track them that way.

"I'll get right to the point. We understand that you and Ms. Fenton weren't exactly on great terms."

"And who told you that?"

"So it's true?"

She huffed. "I have to assume you did your homework, so you must know how Bliss stole my fiancé's sperm."

The detective nodded, though he disagreed that any theft was involved.

"She set him up as part of a stunt to embarrass me and to get her hands on my fiancé's money. She resented the fact that he dumped her for me. You have to know what kind of person she is. Most women have kids because they love children. Bliss just wanted the child support. For her, motherhood meant job security."

"So it's true then?" he asked.

"What's true?"

"That you and Ms. Fenton weren't on great terms."

"Yes. That would be true. But that doesn't mean I had anything to do with her death."

"So what were you doing last Tuesday night between the hours of eight and ten p.m.?"

"I don't know. I was probably home reading."

"And where is home?"

"My fiancé and I live in Beverly Hills."

Mia had yet to refer to Fletcher by his name. She harped on the word fiancé as if it was a badge of honor.

"What were you reading?" he asked.

"Probably a contract related to one of my cases."

"Which one?"

"I don't remember?"

"You don't remember which case? That was only a couple of days ago."

Mia was on the edge of getting defensive. "I have a lot of cases."

Thomas paused for a few seconds. He wanted to keep her calm because that would keep her talking. The woman definitely despised

Bliss Fenton. But he couldn't get a clear read on whether she might've been Bliss' killer.

"Is there anyone else who can verify that you were at home?"

"Probably our nanny."

"*Probably?*"

"I don't remember seeing her after I got home from work."

It bothered Thomas that Mia had yet to express an ounce of sympathy over the death of her former friend. This pretty lady was as cold as an icicle.

"Look, detective, I have a busy law practice. I don't have all day to chit-chat with you. So I'll put everything on the table. I pretty much despised Bliss Fenton, but I didn't kill her. I'm not the type."

"So there's a type?"

Mia shot a condescending glare across the table. "I was referring to the kind of person who resorts to violence in order to solve a problem. That's not me."

"Do you have any idea who may've wanted to harm Ms. Fenton?"

Mia spread her hands, palms up. "Take your pick. That woman spent her life screwing over people. I'd start with the fathers of her two boys."

"Okay, that's a good segue. Let's move on to the fathers. How about your fiancé? Do you think Fletcher McClain had anything to do with Bliss' murder?"

From the stunned expression on Mia's face, she seemed shocked that Fletcher would even be on their radar.

She stiffened like a toy soldier. "Absolutely not. Fletcher chose to fight that woman in court. He wouldn't kill her. Even though he sh—" She abruptly stopped talking and smiled demurely.

Detective Thomas smiled back as he completed Mia's unfinished sentence in his head. *Even though he should have.* He wished Mankowski was here. His partner would've had fun pushing Mia's buttons.

"Maybe Fletcher lost it. I see that happen to upstanding citizens all the time. Bliss was going after him for a whole lot of money and it was very likely the court was going to order him to pay her a substantial sum every month."

"Fletcher wouldn't hurt a fly."

Thomas admired the girl's grit. Even though Fletcher had been unfaithful, Mia wasn't about to flip on her rich boyfriend.

"Maybe he hired somebody to do it?"

"That's nonsense."

"Do you recall what time he got home Tuesday night?"

"I'm not sure."

"I took a peek at Fletcher's place on Google Earth," he said. "It looks large enough to get lost in. Maybe he was out taking care of Bliss while you were home reading your contract."

"Yes, *our* place is pretty large, almost seven thousand square feet." She delivered this fact with the utmost pride. "But that didn't happen."

"How's it going raising Harmony?"

Mia gave a loud sigh. "I'm sure you can understand how difficult it must be for me to accept my fiancé's—" she instantly corrected herself—"Bliss' daughter with open arms."

Thomas frowned. The kid would have a rough life with Mia Richardson as her stepmother.

"He's her only parent now, so you're going to have to accept her."

"True. Which cuts against me being a suspect in Bliss' murder."

"How's that?"

"My killing Bliss Fenton would've left Fletcher the child's sole parent. I'm pretty smart. I would've thought that through. There's no way I would've intentionally inserted that child into our lives."

"Sounds like you're not too happy about the prospect of raising Bliss Fenton's kid."

Mia took a moment before speaking again, no doubt weighing the pros and cons of providing an honest answer.

"You're right, detective. I'm not happy about it one bit. But I didn't kill Bliss."

CHAPTER 69

I wait until we're well outside the police station and within sight of Fletcher's Town car before letting him have it.

"*Now* do you understand why I didn't want you to talk to the cops?"

His eyes fall and he hangs his head.

"My God, Fletcher! Do you know what a jury's going to think after hearing that recording? What were you thinking when—"

He raises his hand cutting me off and continues walking in long strides. "I don't want to hear it right now."

I have to jog to keep up with him. "Well, you're going to hear it whether you want to or not."

"I don't care what I said on that recording. I didn't kill her. Though I wish I had."

I spin around, paranoid that we might've been overheard. That's when I saw her. "Is that Mia?"

Fletcher glances back over his shoulder, his forehead creasing with concern. He takes off toward her.

"What are you doing here?" He takes Mia by both arms.

Mia shrugs nonchalantly. "They wanted me to answer a few questions. Just a formality. They're probably interviewing everyone who knew Bliss."

I'm stunned. "And you did that without having a criminal attorney with you? You're a lawyer. You should know better."

Mia waves her long fingers in the air as if my words are annoying puffs of smoke. "I didn't kill Bliss, so there's no reason for me to have legal representation. Innocent people generally don't go to jail."

For a second, I forgot how to breathe. "You can't possibly believe that."

"Actually, I do."

I stare at her in shell-shocked amazement.

"Babe," Fletcher says, his hands caressing both of Mia's shoulders, "you should've called me. Vernetta would've gone with you."

Like hell I would've.

"What's done is done," she says with a hitch of her shoulder. "It's no big deal. If it were, I'd be behind bars right now. So they questioned you too?"

Fletcher cupped the back of his head. "Yeah. And it was pretty brutal."

"They were only trying to rankle you, sweetie. I'm sure you did fine. Frankly, as we discussed, you should've consulted me before coming down here." She looks me up and down. "I don't think it was a great idea that you went in there with an attorney. That alone probably made you look guilty."

I try, but I can't hold my tongue. "You obviously know very little about the criminal justice system."

Mia's ears seem to prickle. "I know enough."

"No you don't. If you did, you wouldn't have made the comment you just made. When a cop interrogates somebody, he isn't trying to make a friend. He's trying to zero in on a suspect. So it's best to have counsel present."

She jams both fists against her non-existent hips, then makes the mistake of taking a giant step into my personal space. "Not if you haven't done anything wrong. I'm sorry, but I don't happen to possess the anti-cop attitudes that most blacks have."

I jam a finger in her face. "You can act all bougie if you want, but that expensive suit won't erase the fact that you grew up in the heart of Detroit. Just remember your words when you have a son—a black son—and the cops stop him for driving while black. Or God forbid, shoot him for simply walking down the street."

"My son will be just fine because I'll teach him to do what the police tell him to do. If your bru-thas"—she says her words as if she's spitting them at me—"behaved like law-abiding citizens, there wouldn't be any cop shootings. When a cop tells you to stop and put your hands up, that's what you're supposed to do."

I no longer trust my eyes because all I see is fire-engine red. "You can't possibly believe what you just said."

"I do. And I no longer have time for this ridiculous conversation."

I want to yank out every strand of her weave. "You ignorant—"

Fletcher jams himself between us. "Hey, hey, hey! We're outside a friggin' police station for Christ's sakes! Cut it out. Both of you."

"And this is who you want representing you?" Mia yells at me over Fletcher's shoulder. "But then again, you are from Compton."

Fletcher grabs my arm and drags me a few yards away, which upsets me even more. He should be trying to talk some sense into his simpleton of a fiancée, not pulling me away.

I break away from Fletcher's grasp just as a uniformed cop heads our way.

"Is everything okay over there?"

Lester, Fletcher's driver, has joined our little circle. My chest is heaving like I'd just run a hard sprint. Mia's lips are pursed so tight it looks like she's puckering up for a kiss.

"Everything's just fine, officer." Fletcher flashes his Hollywood smile. "We were just heading to our cars. Lester, why don't you take Vernetta home? I'll ride home with Mia."

"C'mon, honey." Mia takes Fletcher by the arm and wrinkles her nose at me.

Fletcher's eyes are more than apologetic. "I'll call you," he says, then walks off hand-in-hand with Mia.

CHAPTER 70

Against her better judgment, Special finally relented and decided to have dinner with Darius.

His persistence was rather impressive. He'd sent flowers twice that week and bombarded her with a bunch of apologetic cards, texts and phone calls. But the primary reason Special relented was to retrieve the mate to her Christian Louboutin pump. Never again would she use her six hundred dollar shoes as a weapon.

Darius had wanted to pick her up for their date, but she'd insisted on meeting him at the restaurant. Special chose one of her favorite places, Roy's Hawaiian fusion restaurant in Anaheim. She might as well get one last good meal out of this.

"Hey, babe, please forgive me." Darius was holding her hand and staring at her with puppy dog eyes. "That chick meant nothing to me."

Special eased her hand away. "If you say so."

"C'mon, babe. I dig you a lot and I really want things to work out for us." He exhaled like he'd had a long day. "I'm going to be honest with you. I've had some issues since my injury. Sometimes I feel a little insecure about myself as a man."

Yeah, right.

"So when a woman comes at me, it's hard to say no. These women out here are so aggressive. She just showed up at my door and forced her way in."

"I guess she also forced your head between her legs too, huh?"

Darius refused to make eye contact for more than a couple of seconds. "I know I was wrong, babe. Please forgive me. I've been thinking about getting some counseling. Maybe we can go together."

You are so full of it. Once a dog always a dog.

Special almost started to laugh. He was such a lousy actor. But the brother did have some off-the-chain skills in bed. It had been over a year since her breakup with Clayton and there was no one else on the horizon. Maybe she should keep Darius around for drought-relief.

But as soon as a decent brother looked twice at her, she was going to drop him like three-week-old leftovers.

"I'm hungry. Let's order some appetizers?" Special signaled for their waiter, who hurried over.

"We'd like to start with the beef short ribs and the vegetable spring rolls." She basically knew the menu by heart.

"Any drinks?" the bearded redhead asked.

"The Hawaiian martini would be great."

He turned to Darius. "And you?"

"Rum and coke."

The waiter was about to leave, but Special waved him back. She'd already decided on her main course. She didn't want to prolong the evening any longer than necessary. Her shoe was already stuffed in her purse. She planned to eat and leave. Listening to Darius' lies was already getting on her nerves.

"We're ready to order our entrees. I'll have the 'Ai Kai—" Special tried to pronounce the dish's Hawaiian name, but gave up and pointed to it on the menu. "The rib eye and the Maine lobster."

Darius chose the Jawaiian Jerk Spiced Pork Chop. The waiter was about to walk away, but again, Special stopped him.

"I know it takes extra time to prepare the chocolate soufflé," she told the waiter, "so we want to put in an order for that now."

"Excellent choice," he said.

Once the waiter disappeared, Darius put on a sad puppy dog face. "Tell me what I can do to get you back?"

Special had given some thought to playing him for his cash, but she was no Bliss Fenton. And she was tired of all of his begging.

"Why don't we talk about something else? Let me tell you about that case I was investigating. It's been crazy wild."

When she finished her recap, Darius was shaking his head. "So who do you think killed her?"

"Definitely one of the baby daddies. There's a third one that I doubt the police know anything about. My money is on him."

As the waiter set their drinks and appetizers on the table, Special started telling Darius about Bliss' conversation with Jonas' father at Salt Creek Grille.

"That dude was definitely hot enough to kill. I just wish there was some way for me to figure out who he is."

Darius stuffed a spring roll into his mouth and continued talking while he chewed. "I'm sure the restaurant has surveillance cameras that show him entering and exiting the restaurant. Ask them for a copy. Then show it to one of the woman's friends. Somebody close to her probably knows him."

Duh?

Special obviously had a long way to go before she developed into a top-notch private investigator. She'd just advised those detectives to check the traffic cameras near Bliss' townhouse, yet it had never crossed her mind that the restaurant might have cameras. Maybe she *should* keep Darius around for a while.

They talked easily now, both of them much more relaxed, almost as if there had never been any strife between them. Special had downed two martinis by the time they were halfway thru the main course and she was feeling pretty mellow.

Darius excused himself to go to the men's room. Special tensed as she watched him maneuver his wheelchair in the narrow aisle between the tables. One of the waiters tried to assist him, but Darius waved him away. He hated it when people treated him like an invalid. Special didn't relax until he'd made it around the last tight corner.

That was when she realized that Darius had left his phone on the table. Special grabbed it and swiped her finger from left to right. Of course Mr. Security Expert would have his phone password protected.

No problema!

She pulled out her own phone and looked up Darius' password, which she had stored under his name in her *Contacts* app. She'd studied his fingers as he punched in his password. It had only taken her three times to figure it out.

Special punched in his password—8923—and quickly scrolled through his emails, then his text messages. It was a good sign that she found nothing incriminating. She specifically searched for the name *Wilson* and saw a text that was an obvious reference to work.

Maybe Darius was telling the truth. If he were still seeing MISSMAC, there would've been emails or text messages proving it. But then again, he could have erased them.

Special was about to return the phone to Darius' side of the table when she decided to scroll back to the day she'd busted him. As she read though a texted conversation, her face grew blazingly hot.

MISSMAC: WTF??? Who was that???
Darius: Old GF, chick has issues
MISSMAC: U told me not seeg any1
Darius: Im not. Its all bout U. Not my fault crazy
B cant let go
MISSMAC: I undstan. I cant let go either. LOL!
K we hookup 2nite?
Darius: Sure. Cum now. LOL!
MISSMAC: OMW! ☺

That lying dog!

Special's right knee started moving up and down like she was bouncing a baby on her knee. *Crazy B? So that's what he thinks of me?*

When she spotted Darius' wheelchair rounding the corner she slid the phone back across the table.

"I'm so glad you're going to forgive me. Let's—" Concern glazed his face. "You okay?"

She forced her lips into a rigid smile. "I'm fine. Why wouldn't I be?"

"You don't look fine. But don't worry. Whatever it is, I guarantee you Darius will make everything all right. Let's go back to my place tonight. I have a little make-up present for you."

He stuck out his tongue and wagged it at her.

Special winced. *No telling where that nasty thing's been.*

She took another bite of her steak, which now felt like a flavorless lump of clay. Special *so* wanted to tell his ass off. She also felt a strong impulse to stab him in the hand with her steak knife. But she had to get her emotions under control. She'd wait until they got to the parking lot to confront his lying ass. She didn't want any witnesses to what was about to go down.

Darius was jabbering away, oblivious to her simmering rage. Five minutes later, she could no longer hold it in.

Special leaned in over the table. He grinned and leaned in too, probably assuming he was about to get a kiss.

"Why do men lie so much?" she asked in a facetiously cheerful voice.

Darius jerked back. "What? Where did that come from? I thought we were cool. I told you what went down."

"Oh, you did, huh?"

"C'mon, babe. Let's not go there again. That chick doesn't mean a thing to me. I haven't seen her since."

"Liar!" Special spat at him. "I read your text messages with MISSMAC while you were in the restroom. So I'm a crazy bitch, huh?"

She picked up her steak knife and propped her elbow on the table. Holding the knife in the pre-stabbing position, she pointed the blade squarely at Darius' left eye. "You want me to show you how crazy I am?"

Darius' eyes expanded. Gripping the edge of the table, he pushed his wheelchair back from the table a few more inches.

"You don't want to do anything crazy in here." He anxiously looked around the restaurant. No one was paying them any attention. Probably because Special had such a big smile on her face.

"Let me explain," he said in a stutter. "I only told her that because—"

"Shut up!" The pacing of her words slowed and her voice dropped so low it sounded like she was speaking through a voice-changing machine. "Lie to me one more time and I swear to God I'll stab you right here in the middle of this crowded restaurant and happily go to jail for it."

"You don't mean that." Darius refused to take his eyes off of the knife. He seemed to be mentally strategizing a countermove in case she actually tried to stab him. "Just put that knife away and calm down."

Special jutted the knife forward just an inch and Darius flinched so violently he rocked the table.

"C'mon, Special. This isn't funny. Put it down."

She snarled across the table at him for what felt like minutes, but was probably mere seconds. She finally laid the knife across her plate, grabbed her purse and stood up.

The relief on Darius' face set her off again. So she took a couple steps away from the table, then whirled back around.

Darius ducked sideways and threw up both hands to cover his face as if expecting a blow.

Special bent down until they were eye level, their noses nearly touching.

"If you ever call me again, I swear I'll hunt you down, chop off your pecker and mail it to MISSMAC."

As she sashayed out of the restaurant, Special's only regret was not asking for her chocolate soufflé to go.

CHAPTER 71

Detective Thomas had just finished giving his partner a recap of his interview with Mia Richardson. It was after six, yet they were now on their way to Interrogation Room 2 for their third interview of the day.

"Ms. Richardson definitely wasn't a fan of Bliss Fenton, but I'm not feeling her as the perp," Thomas said.

"That's because you think she's cute. I saw how you were checking out her ass when she pranced out of here."

Thomas almost blushed. "Yeah, right."

He led the way into the room, extending his hand to Dr. Franco.

The good doctor wore a stiff frown. He seemed to resent being there.

"I had to cancel a half day's worth of patients to get down here. So I hope it's not going to take too long."

Mankowski felt like punching something. *Another rich, arrogant prick.* But neither Dr. Franco or McClain were smart enough to avoid letting Bliss Fenton get over on them. He wished he could remind them of that.

Mankowski took the lead. "We understand that you and Bliss Fenton have a son together. Aiden."

"Yes, we do. He's with me now."

"So you plan to raise him?"

"Of course. Why wouldn't I?"

Thomas tried to reduce some of the obvious tension in the room. "This is all just a formality we need to go through to complete our investigation. Can you tell me where you were this past Tuesday night between eight and ten?"

"At home with my fiancée Lena."

"Where's home?"

"Seal Beach."

"We'll need your fiancée to confirm that."

"That won't be a problem."

Mankowski didn't like babying potential killers. "We understand that you had a pretty antagonistic relationship with Bliss Fenton."

Dr. Franco shifted positions in the metal chair. "That would be the understatement of the year."

"Why don't you tell me a little bit about your relationship."

"We didn't exactly have one. I saw her twice a week for the few minutes it took for me to pick up my son and drop him back off."

"You guys weren't able to have a civil co-parenting relationship?"

Dr. Franco leered at Mankowski as if he were a nutcase. "Detectives, I can't be the first person you've talked to about Bliss. So you must know a lot about her. That said, Gandhi couldn't have had a civil co-parenting relationship with Bliss."

Mankowski smiled, then turned serious. "What we want to know about is *your* relationship with her. We don't care how she treated everybody else."

"I didn't kill Bliss," he blurted out.

"No one said you did. You feeling a little guilty?"

"I don't have time for these TV cop games. I told you where I was when she was murdered. I live at least an hour away from Bliss, longer with traffic."

"Can anybody else besides your fiancée corroborate that you were at home?" Mankowski asked.

"It was just the two of us there."

"And what were you doing?"

"Just relaxing."

"Did you watch any TV?

"No." Dr. Fenton inhaled. "I don't watch TV. Probably listening to music."

Mankowski kept the pressure on, firing off his questions in rapid succession. "What was Lena doing?"

"Cooking dinner."

"For the full two hours?"

"Of course not. She made dinner, we ate and I went to bed. I'm an early riser."

"How early?"

"Four a.m. I work out from four-thirty to five-thirty at the L.A. Fitness on Valley View."

"What did you eat for dinner?"

The doctor paused. "Let me think. I...I don't remember."

"That was only the night before last. You can't remember what you ate for dinner?"

Dr. Fenton squirmed in his seat again. "I think we had steak, but I'm not sure. I'll need to check with Lena."

"Don't worry. We'll do that." Mankowski tried to stare him down. "Did you ever threaten to kill Bliss?"

Dr. Franco's eyes met Mankowski's for a second or two, then fell away. He took his time before responding. "Look, Bliss was not an easy woman to get along with."

"So is that a yes?"

"If I ever said anything out of line to her, it was only in response to her intentionally pushing my buttons."

"*If?* So you don't remember threatening her?"

Dr. Franco took in a lung full of air and slowly let it out. "When Bliss told me she was coming after me for more child support, I guess I lost it. I was already paying her ten grand a month and I couldn't believe she wanted more."

"I don't think you've answered my question yet."

He folded his hands and set them on the table, probably to help keep them still. "Yeah, I might've used some threatening words once or twice, but only out of frustration. I didn't mean it. I wouldn't hurt my son's mother."

"Any idea who you think might've wanted to kill Bliss?"

"Man, Bliss was no joke. She had a way of pissing off everybody she met. You should have a very long list of possible suspects."

CHAPTER 72

As Jessica stood outside Fletcher's front door the following morning, her legs were so wobbly, she wasn't sure they'd be able to hold her up. It was crucial that she remained calm and handled this conversation exactly the way she'd rehearsed it.

She wanted to talk to Fletcher alone. So after confirming her visit, she'd made a late appointment with Mia, representing herself as a new corporate client. Mia was probably sitting at her desk right now, wondering why she was a no-show.

Jessica was stunned to see a casually dressed Fletcher enter the room carrying Harmony. Unlike the night when Bliss had shoved Harmony into his arms, he appeared quite comfortable holding her.

"Guess who's here, sweetie?" Fletcher said. "Auntie Jessica."

Her heart did a back flip when Harmony cooed and smiled up at her.

"Wanna hold her?"

"Sure."

She cradled the baby to her chest, basking in her warm softness. Jessica kissed her forehead as tears welled in her eyes.

After a couple of minutes, Fletcher called out. "Hey, Carina, can you come get the baby?"

A curvy brunette bounced into the room and whisked Harmony away much too soon.

"Who's that?"

"Our nanny. And she's fabulous."

That was not a good sign. She had expected Fletcher to be so stressed out from taking care of Harmony that he'd be anxious to give her up. But since he had a nanny doing all the heavy lifting, there was nothing to be stressed out about.

Fletcher led Jessica upstairs, where they sat on the balcony enjoying the expansive grounds below.

"There're a couple things I wanted to speak with you about. First, I wanted to let you know that I'm planning a memorial service for Bliss and—"

He flashed her a timeout sign. "I'm sorry, but I don't need the specifics. I won't be attending. Hopefully, you understand. Bliss put me through a lot. I don't have a lot of warm feelings toward her."

"Okay." Jessica twirled her wedding ring back and forth. "Well, the second thing is—"

"Hold on," Fletcher said, cutting in. "I think I know what you're going to say next and let me alleviate your concerns. I definitely want you to be part of Harmony's life. As far as I'm concerned, you're her aunt. You were the only person I know of who had a pleasant relationship with Bliss. I don't know how you did it." He grinned. "Yes, I do. You managed it because you're a saint."

Jessica smiled. She wondered if the detectives had questioned Fletcher yet. Probably not. He wouldn't be calling her a saint if he knew she'd given that recording to the police.

"As a matter of fact, if you'd like her to spend some time at your place, that would be fine. I want her to stay in contact with her brothers too."

Jessica swallowed hard, trying to gather the courage to proceed. She decided to just spit it out.

"Bliss named me as Jonas' guardian. Harmony's too."

Fletcher's forehead creased in confusion.

"You're a busy CEO," Jessica continued, her words tumbling out in a rush. "Mia works long hours just like you do. It's not right for Harmony to be raised by a nanny. I can be a real mother to her."

"Hold on a minute, Jessica. Harmony's my daughter. You can see her as much as you want. I'm even willing to set up a regular visitation arrangement. But she's my kid and I'm going to raise her."

Jessica tried to put on a good face, but her lips refused to smile.

"C'mon, Jessica, don't worry." Fletcher reached over and squeezed her shoulder. "You're going to be a big part of Harmony's life. I promise."

Jessica had not really expected Fletcher McClain to just hand over his daughter. But in time, he might have a change of heart. One day the nanny wouldn't show up on time and Fletcher would be in a panic when *he* had to take on the duties of parenthood. And there was no way the self-centered Mia would want to raise Bliss' child. Harmony's presence had probably already created a serious wedge in their relationship.

Fletcher checked his watch. "Hey, I hate to be rude, but I have a conference call in a second and it's going to last a while."

"No problem," Jessica said, getting to her feet. "The bathroom's down the hallway on the right, correct?"

Jessica had spent a lot of time at Fletcher's home when he'd been dating Bliss. So she knew the layout of the house pretty well.

"You got it. And why don't you go back downstairs and spend some time with Harmony."

"Thanks, Fletcher. I'll do that. And next time I'll bring Jonas."

As Jessica made her way back inside, she struggled to control her emotions. Harmony belonged with her. Not in this cold, lifeless mansion being raised by a stranger.

God willing, she was *going* to be Harmony's mother. She would just have to be patient.

CHAPTER 73

"You okay with this?" Thomas asked. "I told you I can interview her by myself. You don't need to be here."

"Why're you treating me like a little pussy," Mankowski nearly growled at his partner. "I'm fine."

Actually, he was anxious to get another look at Girlie Cortez. Just the thought brought back images of her toned, naked body crawling across his bed. No woman had done such things to him before or since. But in the end, she'd played him like a used banjo, almost costing him his career.

He turned to see Girlie stalking toward him. But what he saw was a different Girlie. Her hair was pulled back into a bun, not seductively spread across her shoulders. She'd even gained a few pounds and looked a little haggard. Having to switch from the swanky digs of her old law firm, to this dump, was probably partly to blame. He was glad to see he wasn't the only one whose career had taken a spiral. Surprisingly, she wasn't showing a lick of cleavage. That disappointed him.

Girlie extended her hand. "So nice to see you again."

"Indeed," Thomas said.

Mankowski merely nodded.

Girlie pretended to pout. "You aren't mad at me, are you, detective?"

Thomas interceded before Mankowski could respond. "It would be great if we could talk in your office."

They followed her down a dark hallway. She'd obviously taken a long fall, much longer than Mankowski's. Compared to her old law firm, this place was like a Skid Row storefront.

"So I understand that you're here to discuss my former client. I was so sorry to hear about her death. How can I help?"

Thomas pitched the first question. "We'd like to know what you know about the relationship between Bliss Fenton and Fletcher McClain."

"What relationship? There was none. They hated each other. So you think he killed her?"

"Maybe," Thomas replied. "That's what we're trying to figure out."

"I only know what Bliss told me. I never witnessed any interaction between the two of them besides their depositions. I will tell you, though, at one point, I thought Mr. McClain was going to dive across the table and wring her neck. It was quite entertaining to see his reaction when he found out how Bliss got pregnant. Do you know that story?"

Thomas nodded. "Her friend Jessica filled us in."

Mankowski was looking out of the window. He needed to do that to keep from getting aroused.

Damn her.

Girlie apparently didn't like the fact that he wasn't paying her much attention.

"Detective Mankowski, don't you have any questions you'd like to ask?"

He locked eyes with her for the first time. "Did Ms. Fenton ever tell you Fletcher threatened to kill her?"

"Actually, yes. She even had it on—"

"We have the recording of their lunch meeting at Fig & Olive," Mankowski interrupted. "Any time other than that?"

Girlie turned her attention back to Thomas.

"Not that I'm aware of. Now her other baby daddy, Dr. Franco? Bliss told me that he'd threatened her more than once. He didn't like it when she went after him for more child support."

Thomas looked over at Mankowski as he jotted down some notes. Mankowski was leaning away from Dr. Franco as their guy, but Thomas still wanted him in the mix.

"Do you know who the father of her middle child is?" Thomas asked.

"Nope. She refused to reveal his identity, even when I told her our conversations were protected by the attorney-client privilege."

"Do you know if she had a contentious relationship with him?"

"Don't know a thing about him. She simply refused to talk about him."

Thomas twirled his pen. "Any thoughts on who might've killed her?"

"Yep."

They waited, but Girlie didn't expound. She was being the perfect deposition witness, only responding to the question asked.

"Care to tell us who you think that might be?" Thomas pushed.

"Her former friend Mia Richardson."

"Fletcher McClain's fiancée?"

"That would be the one."

"Why her?"

"Bliss and her baby rocked Mia's perfect little world. Because of Harmony, Bliss would be in their lives for at least the next eighteen years. I'm sure Mia hated the thought of that. Not to mention how Bliss got pregnant. Were you aware that—"

"Yeah, we know," Mankowski said, cutting her off again. "Jessica told us how Bliss stole his condom."

Girlie smiled seductively. "You've been misinformed, detectives. That's what Fletcher McClain alleged in his complaint. But that's not what happened."

Mankowski sat up. "What do you mean?"

Girlie took her time doling out the true facts surrounding the conception of baby Harmony. When she was done, both officers appeared ready to tumble out of their chairs. Girlie waited patiently for more questions, but it was as if their vocal chords had shut down.

"Look, detectives, you might say I know a little bit about scheming women. Some might even say, I am one." She flashed Thomas a flirtatious smile. All three of them, however, knew her smile was meant for Mankowski.

"Bliss Fenton and Mia Richardson were cut from the same cloth," Girlie continued. "I've never met the woman, but from everything

Bliss told me, I got the sense that both of them were born with the instinct to go into attack mode when put on the defensive. Sure, Fletcher McClain and Dr. Franco hated Bliss for coming after their money. But Mia hated Bliss for going after her man *and* his money, which was soon to become her money. Never underestimate how far a woman will go to snuff out the competition."

Girlie let her theory soak in for a moment or so.

"So in my humble opinion, if you're looking for Bliss' killer, Mia Richardson should go to the head of your potential suspects' list."

CHAPTER 74

Fletcher begs, pleads and twists my arm to get on my calendar. After my face-off with his pretentious fiancée outside the police station yesterday, I made it clear that he was on his own. I don't have the stomach for another big murder trial, especially one where my client consistently lies through his teeth. But here he is sitting in my office, acting like I'm the only decent attorney on the planet.

"I'm confused, Fletcher. Why do you even need a lawyer? You haven't been arrested or charged."

"C'mon, Vernetta. You know how this is going to play out. The circumstantial evidence makes me the most obvious suspect. The paternity case, the lawsuit, the money that was at stake."

"And that recording," I add.

Fletcher presses the heel of his hand to his forehead and wipes away a layer of sweat. It's sixty-five degrees in my office, so why is he sweating?

Am I looking at Bliss Fenton's killer?

The average criminal attorney would kill for a case like this. Rich, handsome, high-profile client suspected of murdering his beautiful, money-grubbing ex-girlfriend. The fact that a man like Fletcher McClain had retained me would propel me to the top of the list of go-to lawyers for the rich and famous. The media attention would be nonstop and the corresponding free publicity would result in a ton of new clients knocking on my door. But I'd almost rather defend a murderer who admitted it, than one who insisted on lying about his guilt. At least I'd know who I was dealing with.

"I know how this looks, but I didn't kill Bliss." Fletcher's eyes are pleading with me as much as his voice.

"If you didn't kill her, then you have nothing to worry about. Innocent people don't go to jail. Isn't that what your wife-to-be said?"

"Mia wasn't thinking clearly. She was out of line and I'm sorry about what went down."

"And I'm sorry that's the woman you're about to marry."

"I want to put you on retainer. They're going to arrest me for Bliss' murder. I know it. I want to be prepared. More prepared than the prosecution is."

"But you have a solid alibi, Fletcher. You were at that listening party."

"They probably think I hired somebody to do it."

"May I remind you that you did say that was what you planned to do?"

"C'mon, Vernetta, I was upset. I was just blowing off steam. I didn't' kill Bliss."

"I don't have the energy for a murder trial, Fletcher." I open my desk drawer and pull out a small notepad and scribble a name and telephone number on it. I hand it to him.

He glances at the paper, then back at me. "Who's Colin Bowman?"

"One of the few criminal attorneys I know who's better than me. If I were facing a murder charge, he's the guy I'd call. He lives in the Bay Area, practices out of Oakland. I'm sure he'll agree to temporarily relocate for the trial, if there is one. Tell him I sent you. We were law school classmates. If he can't get you off, nobody can."

"I don't want him. I want you." He flings the paper onto my desk.

"I said I don't want to do it and I'm not going to. Call Colin."

"Stop being so difficult. Name your price. I'll pay it."

"See that's what you and your little fiancée don't understand. Everybody isn't as money hungry as you two are. It's not about the money."

Fletcher's nostrils flare. The grown man who always gets what he wants is regressing into the little boy who can't handle not getting what he demands.

"Okay, then. What is it about?"

"It's about you repeatedly lying to me and even lying under oath during your deposition. If I represented you at trial, how am I going to know when you're telling the truth?"

"So I got a blow job from that psycho and didn't tell you. Big deal."

I can't help but chuckle. In Fletcher's mind, this all comes down to a mindless blow job. But it's so much bigger than that.

"Stop acting so high and mighty. This is business and I'm offering you a business proposition."

"And I don't want it."

He still acts as if he hasn't heard me. This is why Fletcher is such a successful dealmaker. He's good at wearing people down.

"There's something I need to tell you. Another reason why they're likely to think I killed Bliss."

The way I see it, the desperation in his voice only underscores his guilt. I raise both hands. "I don't want to know. I'm not your lawyer anymore."

Fletcher proceeds anyway.

"I didn't want that forensic accountant looking into my finances because he'd probably find some"—he twists a gaudy pinky ring on his left hand—"improprieties regarding the company."

I nod, showing no surprise. "Oh, so you're stealing money from Karma Entertainment. More evidence on the motive side. Great."

"It wasn't stealing. I've paid everything back. But a forensics examination might uncover some unauthorized loans. If the police find out about that, I'm further sunk."

"Yep, I'd certainly say so. Guess you should've done some better planning."

"I didn't kill that bitch!"

I shake my head. "If you and your new attorney decide that you should testify at trial, it would be a good idea if you didn't refer to the deceased as *that bitch*."

Fletcher hangs his head and I fear he might start crying. "C'mon, Vernetta, I really need you."

It hits me that Fletcher has rarely been told no. That's why it's so hard for him to accept it from me now.

"Fletcher, I'm tired of repeating myself." I hand him the paper with Colin's number on it and make a show of enunciating my next words. "I will not represent you. And there's nothing you can say or do that will change my mind."

CHAPTER 75

The two detectives stared at the photographs pinned to the cork-board across from their desks. They were discussing the pros and cons of their top three suspects in Bliss Fenton's murder: Fletcher McClain, Dr. Joseph Franco and Mia Richardson.

"Fletcher McClain is too obvious," Thomas insisted. "And he has a solid alibi."

Mankowski shook his head. "Screw his alibi. He hired somebody to do it. If you were about to lose eighty grand a month for the next eighteen years, wouldn't you?"

Thomas chuckled. "That's a lot of dough, but if that was only ten percent of what he made, it wasn't like he was going to end up a pauper. That's why I don't get rich people. I don't see why he was even sweating her about it."

"Yeah, you definitely don't understand rich people," Mankowski said. "The more they have, the more they want."

"My money is on Franco," Thomas countered. "Jessica told us how upset he was about having to pay her another two grand a month."

"That's not a lot of money for a man with three medical offices," Mankowski pointed out.

"Maybe it's not just the money, but the stress of all the drama since his kid was born," Thomas pressed. "He just couldn't take it anymore and snapped."

"Naw. I'm not buying the good doctor as the suspect just yet. If he's having some serious money problems, then I might have a change of heart. Let's make sure we look into Fletcher McClain's finances while we're at it."

"It's not just two grand. It's twenty-four thousand dollars a year until the kid hits eighteen. People kill over a whole lot less."

Mankowski could not dispute that. He pointed at the board.

"And then we have the beautiful, but frosty Mia Richardson. She reminds me of a classic sociopath. They're so put together that it's impossible to wrap your mind around the fact that they could actually kill someone. Ted Bundy, Richard Ramirez, Jeffrey Dahmer were all good-looking guys that people didn't suspect were killers."

Thomas rubbed his chin. "I guess Ms. Richardson is a possible. It did bother me that she didn't show an ounce of sympathy for her dead friend."

"That I understand. Bliss was trying to jack her man for a whole lot of cash. Although Ms. Richardson claims she was home reading a book, she might have been in Playa Vista shooting the woman who was turning her picture-perfect life upside down. For that chick, it seems like image is everything."

"Maybe," Thomas said.

"I want to add some more pressure. Make sure I'm present at the next interview."

A uniformed officer walked in and handed Thomas a flash drive. "We didn't find any home cameras on the block that might've picked up the vic's townhouse, but here's the video from the traffic camera at Jefferson and Playa Vista Drive."

"Looks like you're going to be up awful late tonight," Mankowski joked.

"I'm not doing it. I have an intern who's helping me out."

"There're at least three ways into that neighborhood," Mankowski said.

"Yeah, but this is the intersection closest to her place. I requested footage for two hours before and two hours after the estimated time of death."

Thomas riffled through the various stacks of paper on his desk. "I have the license plate numbers for the cars driven by our three suspects. If we don't catch one of them driving through this intersection, then we can take a look at the others."

Thomas finally found what he was looking for. "Dr. Franco drove a Benz, Mia Richardson a BMW and Fletcher owned a Range Rover and a Porsche but was usually driven around by a driver who—"

"Wait a minute," Mankowski interrupted with a snap of his fingers. "Maybe Fletcher's driver knows something." He flipped through his notes. "His name is Lester Watkins."

Mankowski typed Lester's name into the criminal records database. "Bingo! Armed robbery and assault. Seven years in Corcoran. He was released in 2001. Maybe he's the guy Fletcher hired to do the dirty deed. Let's go check him out."

"He's been clean a long time," Thomas said, as he typed on his computer keyboard. "If a con's going back to his old ways, it usually happens right away. But I agree he's worth a look."

"What are you doing?" Mankowski asked.

"Emailing these license plate numbers to the intern so he can start checking them against the video."

"Well, hurry up." Mankowski was already grabbing his jacket from the back of his chair. "I'm anxious to have a little chat with Lester Watkins."

CHAPTER 76

Girlie Cortez was more than thrilled to have Jessica Winthrop sitting in her office. She was just baffled as to why the woman wanted time on her calendar.

Since Jessica was the executor of Bliss' estate, Girlie planned to find the right entry point to bring up all the legal work she'd done on her dead friend's behalf. Although Girlie had taken Bliss' case on contingency, she was entitled to reimbursement for the money she spent on depositions and court filings. But she was hoping to recover some additional funds since she'd never see the windfall in legal fees she'd been expecting from Fletcher McClain. Bliss' murder was the last thing Girlie had expected. Though it shouldn't have been a surprise in light of how far Bliss pushed the envelope.

Jessica had spent the last five minutes making small talk. Yes, it was a shame Bliss was gone. Yes, it was going to be rough for her children. True, most people didn't understand Bliss.

Okay, now what?

"I guess I'll just get to the point." Jessica fiddled with her purse. "To my surprise, Fletcher wants to keep Harmony. But Bliss named me Harmony's legal guardian. I want to raise her and I want you to represent me in a custody battle against him."

Girlie sat at full attention now. Fletcher was the kid's father. No matter what Bliss' wishes were, it was highly unlikely that a court would grant Jessica custody of Harmony. She was just about to tell Jessica she was wasting her time, when the woman pulled out her checkbook.

"I know this is going to be an uphill battle, but I want to give it my all and I want you to do the same. Bliss says you know how to play dirty. You have my permission to do that. How much is your retainer for a case like this?"

Girlie had never had a case like this before and none of the clients she'd been representing lately could even afford a retainer.

"Thirty grand," she lied.

Jessica quickly scribbled across the check, tore it off and handed it across the desk.

For a second, and just a second, Girlie felt an ethical obligation to advise the woman that the odds of getting custody of Harmony were slim to none. But when she thought about how much this check would help with all of the debt she'd acquired during her suspension, her pang of conscience instantly vanished.

"I know you were representing Bliss on contingency," Jessica said. "I'm the executor of her estate. Just let me know what she owed you and I'll make sure your bill gets paid."

Girlie thanked God for her good fortune.

"Let me tell you the things that should weigh in my favor during the custody battle," Jessica continued. "Fletcher denied Harmony was his from the moment Bliss told him about her. He made it clear that he wanted nothing to do with her. I was closer to Harmony than her own mother. Bliss didn't have much of a motherly instinct. Also, I'm raising Jonas, Bliss' middle child. I know the court looks at the best interests of the child. It would be in Harmony's best interests to be raised with her brother."

Girlie wanted to tell Jessica that none of that mattered. But she had thirty thousand reasons to keep her mouth shut. So she did.

"It's going to be a tough fight. But I'll do my best," Girlie vowed.

"I know you will. I wanted custody of Aiden as well, but Dr. Franco refused. Of course, if he's accused of killing Bliss, that could change."

"Do you think he did it?"

"Not really. I think Fletcher McClain's a more likely suspect."

"If he's charged, that would certainly make it easier for you to win custody of Harmony."

Jessica pursed her lips and nodded in agreement.

"Ms. Winthrop, I'll represent you to the best of my ability. What I need you to think about over the next few days is any negative information you have about Mr. McClain. If we're going to win this, we have to prove Harmony would be better off with you."

Jessica's face deflated. "But what if I can't find anything?"

"You let me figure that out. At my old law firm, we retained some of the best private investigators in the city. The investigator will need to bill you separately. Is that okay?"

Girlie didn't want to have to give back one penny of her hefty retainer. If she thought about the case in the shower, she planned to bill Jessica for it. She'd run through the thirty grand and have her hand out for more money in no time.

"That's fine. Spend whatever you need."

It had been a while since Girlie had a client with this kind of cash flow and it felt great. She didn't quite know how she was going to do it, but even if she had to make up some dirt on Fletcher McClain, she was going to do everything in her power to get this woman custody of Bliss' baby.

CHAPTER 77

"This waiting is driving me crazy," Special whines. "I know Mystery Baby Daddy is the killer. And I bet those cops don't even have him on their radar."

Special is sitting in my office complaining because the complex where Salt Creek Grille is located has yet to turn over the parking lot video.

"Your request has to go through their corporate office," I explain. "It just takes time."

"Forgive me, but you don't seem at all concerned that your client might be charged with murder."

"That's because I don't have a client. I'm out of it. If you find some information that proves that guy who argued with Bliss killed her, I'll turn it over to the cops. Other than that, I've washed my hands of it."

"Fletcher must've really pissed you off. What did he do now?"

"It was more Mia than him."

I tell Special how Mia and I went head-to-head.

"Is she on drugs? Somebody needs to give that girl a reality check. I bet if they arrest her ass, she'll get with the program real quick. What did Fletcher have to say?"

"Nothing at the time. But later on he came by here trying to apologize for her and begging me to represent him again."

"He sounds worried. You think he killed her?"

"I have to admit that it has crossed my mind. Fletcher was livid about the possibility of having to pay Bliss so much money. He told me that if he did decide to kill her, he'd find someone to do it and they'd never be able to trace it back to him."

"He actually said that?"

I nod. "And his alibi is airtight. He was at a listening party for one of his artists. At least six people can attest to that. His hands might be clean, but who knows about his bank book."

Special is reeling from what I've just told her. "Well, before you convict the guy, let me find Mystery Baby Daddy and see if he has an alibi. That dude was most definitely hot enough to kill when he walked out of that restaurant."

"We'll see," I say.

"But if Mystery Baby Daddy is clean, my money's on Mia," Special declares.

"I've thought about that," I say. "She has some issues, but I just don't see her as a killer."

"Why? Because she's a prim and proper lawyer?"

"No, I just think she's all mouth and no substance. The kind of person who talks a big game, but would never follow through."

Special isn't buying it. "I don't know. Bliss tricked her man into having his baby, then went after his cash. That would make me hella hot."

"Don't forget that Mia started it when she stole Fletcher from Bliss," I remind her.

"Hold up," Special says. "Now you're really confusing me. Sounds like you *do* want Mia to go down for Bliss' murder."

"No, that's not what I'm saying. Everybody focuses on how evil Bliss was, but Mia did some dirt too. And what goes around usually comes around."

Special purses her lips and folds her arms. "You're just mad because Ms. Prim and Proper got all up in your face."

"That certainly didn't help. I'm just glad I'm out of it."

"So if Fletcher gets charged, you're not going to defend him?"

"Absolutely not."

"Okay, we'll see," Special says with a smirk. "Despite everything you just said, if Fletcher comes calling, I suspect you'll still go running to his rescue."

CHAPTER 78

When Mia Richardson showed up at Girlie's office the day after Jessica's visit, Girlie assumed someone was playing a trick on her. But when Mia slapped a fifty-thousand-dollar cashier's check on her desk and asked to retain her, Girlie realized it wasn't a trick. It was a dream come true.

"Ms. Richardson, are you sure—"

"Please call me Mia."

"Okay, Mia, are you sure you want to do this?" Girlie asked. "If Fletcher found out, he might not be too happy about it."

The woman smiled, all sweetness and honey. "If you don't tell him and I don't tell him, he won't find out."

Girlie had yet to pick up the check sitting on the edge of her desk. It had taken her only minutes to come to the conclusion that she did not like Mia Richardson. The woman probably knew Girlie was hard up for cash. And since she was a lawyer, she also knew what she was asking Girlie to do was highly unethical.

"Ms.—I mean—Mia, I've been retained by Jessica Winthrop. It would be a conflict of interest for me to do what you're asking."

"Like I said, I'm not here to retain you, Girlie. I'm here to incentivize you."

Girlie hadn't given the woman permission to call her by her first name and didn't like the fact that she simply took that liberty. She should tell her to get out now. But, man, could she use another fifty grand on top of the thirty grand she'd collected from Jessica.

"Just so I understand, exactly what is it you want me to do?"

"I want you to make sure Jessica Winthrop wins custody of Harmony."

Girlie chuckled. "No one can guarantee the outcome of a court case. You're an attorney, you know that."

"Well, I guess I'm not asking for a guarantee. I'm just offering you some added incentive to do your best."

Girlie frowned. "I always do my best."

"I'm sorry. That didn't come out right. Maybe I should just put my cards on the table. Fletcher and I are getting married soon. We don't need a baby in our lives to complicate things. The child should be with Jessica. She's the best person to raise her. And, moreover, it's what Bliss would've wanted."

Girlie noticed that Mia hadn't once called Harmony by her name. Talk about an evil stepmother. Hell, screw the money. Girlie wanted to win just to keep the kid away from this snooty witch.

"Mia, I'm sorry, but I'm going to have to think about this. I need to make sure I'm not breaching any ethical obligations by accepting payment from you."

"But no one has to know that I've made that payment. That cashier's check came from a checking account that won't be very easy to trace." She winked. "I won't tell if you won't."

Fletcher McClain certainly liked venomous women. Hell, Mia better be glad Girlie's head was in a different place. She might've moved in on Fletcher herself.

"On second thought," Girlie said, "I don't have to think about it."

Mia brightened, but her smile quickly faded when Girlie pushed the check back toward her.

"It wouldn't be ethical for me to accept that payment. Not without disclosing it to my client."

There was no need for Girlie to take this risk. Jessica had more than enough money to compensate her. Getting embroiled with this woman would unnecessarily complicate things. Then Girlie remembered what she'd told the detectives about who she thought had killed Bliss. She needed to get this killer out of her office.

Mia looked thoroughly disappointed. She retrieved the check, tore it into pieces and stuffed it back into her purse. She placed a business card where the check had been. "There's one more thing. I was wondering if I could get a copy of Bliss and Fletcher's deposition transcripts from your case."

Girlie squinted. "Why do you want to see their depositions?"

"To be honest with you, Fletcher has really kept me in the dark about exactly how his daughter was conceived. He told me that Bliss admitted during her deposition that she stole his sperm from a condom when they were dating and froze it. I just want to read her testimony for myself."

Girlie took in a breath. *Honey, if you only knew.*

"I'm not sure I should—"

"C'mon, Girlie," Mia prodded. "Those depositions aren't confidential."

The devil in Girlie wanted to blab to Miss Prissy that her rich boyfriend had lied through his teeth. She could almost hear Bliss whispering into her ear, goading her to do just that. But Girlie didn't want to get pulled into this mess.

"I'm sorry," she said. "I'd rather not. Why don't you ask Vernetta Henderson for a copy of them?"

"I don't think she would give them to me either." Mia's lips clamped shut and her nose twitched. She looked as if she was trying to restrain a temper tantrum. She abruptly stood up. "If you need my help in *any* way with Jessica's case, please give me a call."

Girlie wasn't quite sure she was interpreting the woman's statement correctly.

"Are you saying you'd be willing to provide information that might help Jessica in her custody case against Fletcher?"

Mia barely let Girlie finish her question. "That's exactly what I'm saying."

This woman had absolutely no scruples. Mia was headed out of the door before Girlie had a change of heart. "Hold on a minute."

Mia turned around.

"If you want to read the deposition testimony concerning how Bliss conceived Harmony," Girlie said, "you can go online and get a copy of the summary judgment motion I filed with the Superior Court." She paused to write down the case number. "I submitted portions of both of their deposition transcripts along with my motion."

Mia smiled warmly as she took the piece of paper. "Thank you so much. I'll definitely do that."

Girlie simply nodded. *You certainly won't be thanking me after you read it.*

Once Mia was gone, Girlie sat back in her chair and thought about Bliss. She glanced skyward and high-fived the air.

"That one was for you, girlfriend."

CHAPTER 79

The detectives found Fletcher McClain's driver washing his boss' Lincoln Town Car in the underground parking facility at Karma Entertainment.

Thomas pulled their sedan right behind it, blocking it in.

Lester charged over to them. "Move that car outta—"

They weren't wearing uniforms, but with Lester's extensive history with the legal system, he could probably smell a cop.

His rage melted into charm. "How can I help you officers?"

"Are you Lester Watkins?" Mankowski asked.

"Yes, I am. And you are?"

"I'm Detective Mankowski and this is my partner Detective Thomas."

"Mind if I get your cards," Lester asked, as if he might want to keep in touch.

Lester glanced around the garage. He was probably hoping someone walked by or maybe he was checking for surveillance cameras. The man wanted witnesses to whatever was about to go down.

It pissed Mankowski off that everybody thought all cops did these days was beat the crap out of black guys just for sport. So he took on a decidedly nice guy approach.

"We're investigating the murder of Bliss Fenton and we just want to ask you a few questions."

Mankowski was certain he saw the guy flinch. That was not a good sign.

"Where were you between the hours of eight and ten this past Tuesday night?" Thomas asked.

Lester lost his cool demeanor.

"You think I had something to do with that woman's murder. Oh, hell naw!" His hands cradled his head. "Man, you got it wrong. I'm straight up. I been a hundred percent straight up since I left Corcoran. I didn't have nothing to do with that."

"Okay, so where were you?"

Lester's thought process seemed to be bungled. "Hell, I don't know? I can hardly remember what I did this morning."

"So you don't have an alibi?"

"Alibi? I don't need an alibi. I didn't do nothin'. Man, I'm fifty-three years old and I got a nice, mellow gig. I told you, I'm straight up. You got it wrong."

"So your boss didn't pay you to knock off his ex-girlfriend?" Thomas asked, intentionally messing with him.

"What? Mr. McClain. Hell no. Y'all got it wrong. Way wrong."

Mankowski took a step closer to the car. "We're going to need you to give some thought to where you were when Bliss Fenton was killed."

Lester was breathing heavy and Mankowski thought he might go into cardiac arrest.

"Uh...what night was it again?"

"Last Tuesday night."

"Tuesday nights is when Mr. McClain has his listening parties. He lets me sit in." He stopped to think, then his eyes lit up. "Last Tuesday I was with Mr. McClain. Listening to that new girl LaReena. Mr. McClain and a bunch of other people was there too. Just ask him."

"McClain told us he was there, but he didn't mention anything about you?" Mankowski lied. "They never got the list from McClain because he stormed out of the interrogation room before providing it."

"I was there. I swear I was there."

"The whole time? You didn't even leave to go to the men's room?"

Lester looked like he wanted to lie, but smartly weighed the risk that a lie might cost him.

"I'm sure I went to take a leak at some point. But when it was over, I took Mr. McClain home and went to my old lady's house. You can ask everybody at that listening party. You can even call my old lady."

"We think maybe Mr. McClain paid you to kill Bliss Fenton," Mankowski prodded.

"Man, I ain't no killer! Check my rap sheet, man, I don't kill."

"Oh," Mankowski said. "You just assault people. A kinder, gentler criminal."

"That's it. I ain't talking no more." He went back to polishing the car.

The two detectives looked at each other. Lester was too jittery to be a hired killer. If he'd done it, he would've already told on himself.

Thomas' phone buzzed and he pulled it from his shirt pocket.

"Yes!"

"What now?" Mankowski asked.

Thomas had already taken off for their car. "The intern got a hit on one of the license plates."

"Which one?"

"He didn't say."

"I bet you it was Dr. Franco," Thomas declared with an I-told-you-so sense of glee. "The guy lived miles away in Orange County. If he was passing through that intersection around the time of Bliss' death, he's our man."

CHAPTER 80

"C'mon, dude. Can't you help a sista out?" Special had tried everything else and was now resorting to her homegirl act.

"Ma'am, I called our corporate offices and they said we can't release the video without a subpoena. I wish I could, but I can't."

The rent-a-cop who managed the shopping complex, porky Latino with a thin patchy facial hair, looked genuinely sorry.

"That video could be the key to a murder investigation," Special pleaded.

"Then have the cops subpoena it," he reasoned.

Special didn't want to do that because she wanted to be the one to solve Bliss Fenton's murder and she was certain that Mystery Daddy could be the key. The stupid cops were running around focusing on the obvious suspects. They probably weren't even trying to find Bliss' other baby daddy because they weren't as smart as she was. Special planned to deliver him up on a silver platter. But this fake cop was standing in the way of her glory.

"Okay, how much?" Special asked.

"How much what?"

"How much will it cost me to get a copy of the video?"

"I can't do that. I'll get fired."

Special eyed his badge. "C'mon, Carlos, can't you just show it to me?" She opened her wallet. She only had forty-four bucks. Not a lot of money to bribe somebody with. She flashed the bills in his face. "This is all I have."

Carlos did not look impressed.

"I'll pay you two hundred dollars if you show me the video. Not copy it. Just show it to me. They only told you not to give me a copy. They didn't say anything about showing it to me. I'll go to the ATM right now and get your money."

Special could see he was softening. He peered over his shoulder.

"You have to come back after six o'clock, when the other guard gets off," he whispered. "You can meet me in the security office. But if you see anybody else around, I'm gonna act like I don't know you. Come in through the alley." He wrote down his cell number. "Call me when you get here and I'll open the door."

"Thanks, Carlos. I owe you big time."

"Just make sure you have my money. I could get fired for doing this."

Since she had a few hours to kill until she could see the video, Special decided to pay Jessica Winthrop a visit. She figured Jessica might know Mystery Baby Daddy's identity since she was Bliss' best friend. Jessica had probably met some of the men Bliss dated over the years.

The one and only time Special had visited the posh city of Bel Air was when she'd attended a luncheon at the Bel Air Hotel a few years ago. A haven for the rich and famous, Bel Air's residents included Kim Kardashian and Kanye West, Nicolas Cage and Madonna.

"I'm definitely doing something wrong," Special mused as she drove through the exclusive neighborhood where the median home price was over two million dollars. "I need to snag me a dude who can have me living high on the hog like this."

Jessica's house was a modern architectural mix of glass and stone surrounded by a ton of foliage, obviously to keep out the looky-loos. After a hike up a long driveway, Special rang the doorbell and waited.

When a woman who matched the picture of Jessica Winthrop that Special had found on the internet opened the door, Special immediately commenced her spiel.

Once she'd explained who she was and what she wanted, Jessica's expression went from nonchalant to defensive.

"Tell me again who you're investigating Bliss' murder for? You just said you're not a cop?"

"I'm working on behalf of Fletcher McClain," she said, which wasn't a total lie since he used to be a client. "I've been hired to find out the father of Bliss' middle child, Jonas."

Almost on cue, a little boy ran up and clutched Jessica around the thigh. He had bright blonde hair and ultra fair skin.

Special stared down at the child. "Is that him?"

Jessica protectively hid the boy behind her without affirming or denying whether he was indeed Jonas.

"So Fletcher's trying to pin Bliss' murder on Jonas' father to get himself off the hook?"

"We just think he's someone the police should talk to. I was hoping you'd be able to tell me a little bit about him. You were Bliss' best friend after all."

"Bliss never told me or anybody else who he is."

This woman wasn't about to help her. Special just wished she could get inside and talk to her in a less confrontational state.

"If Fletcher killed Bliss," Jessica said, "I hope he gets the death penalty."

Before Special could say another word, Jessica slammed the door in her face.

Special blew out a frustrated breath. "Now that certainly went well."

But she wasn't fazed. In fact, Special was bubbling with excitement. Before the night was up, she'd not only have video of the man who fathered little Jonas, but possibly Bliss Fenton's killer.

CHAPTER 81

Detective Mankowski listened to the voicemail for the second time, still unable to believe it. This chick had big balls. But he'd learned his lesson. He wouldn't touch her with a fifty-foot telephone pole.

"Hi, Detective, this is me, Girlie Cortez. Give me a call when you have a chance. You and I have something important to discuss."

There was no way he would let himself get pulled into her sticky web again. What in the hell did she have to discuss with him anyway? She probably wanted to invite him over so she could spread her legs again. But Mankowski wasn't the kind of guy to get taken by the same woman twice.

"You look irritated," Thomas said. "Who was that?"

"Nobody important. So what's the status of those warrants?"

"We're getting pushback from the D.A.'s office. But I got the lieutenant working on it."

"That's crap. We've got more than probable cause."

They were finally ready to make an arrest in the murder of Bliss Fenton. One of their three prime suspects had indeed driven through the intersection leading into Bliss' neighborhood around the time frame of her murder.

"We have enough for the search warrant," Thomas said. "But the deputy D.A. thinks the evidence is a little slim for an arrest warrant. So we better hope something turns up during the search to make an arrest."

A sly grin slid across Mankowski's face. Don't worry. I'm pretty sure we'll be making an arrest tonight even without an arrest warrant. We'll just have to push enough buttons to make it happen. When can we pick up the search warrant?"

"With any luck, within the hour."

Thomas' desk phone rang. He picked it up and gave Mankowski a strange look.

"It's for you. Line two."

"Who is it?"

"You'll see."

Mankowski punched a button on his phone and snatched the receiver. "Mankowski here."

"Hey, detective," Girlie purred. "You wouldn't be avoiding me, would you?"

Mankowski ignored his partner's disapproving glare.

"What do you want?" He forced his voice to sound gruff.

"That's no way to talk to someone who used to be as close to you as I was."

"What do you want?" he repeated.

"Okay, fine," Girlie grumbled. "I was calling to share a little information with you. Something that might be pertinent to your investigation."

"I'm listening."

"Remember, I told you I thought Mia Richardson was your killer?"

"Yeah."

"Well, she met with me today regarding a legal matter."

What trouble was Girlie Cortez trying to get him into now? he thought.

"Isn't it an ethical violation for you to be talking to me about attorney-client stuff?"

"Mia didn't retain me, but our conversation only confirmed for me that she definitely wanted Bliss out of the way."

Girlie recounted her meeting with Mia. By the time she was done, Mankowski needed a blood pressure check. He hit the speakerphone button and waved Thomas closer to the phone.

"What's up?" Thomas perched himself on the edge of his partner's desk.

"Girlie, I need you to repeat everything you just told me so my partner can hear it," Mankowski said. "And don't skip a word."

CHAPTER 82

It's been months since Jefferson and I have had a real date night. Even longer since we'd ventured out on a weeknight. We'd just danced four straight songs without a break.

"You still got it, girl," Jefferson teases as we slide back into our booth.

We love the food at Kobe's Steakhouse in Seal Beach as much as we love the Derek Bordeaux Band and its old school jams.

"You didn't do too bad yourself for an old man."

I reach for a piece of shrimp tempura and dunk it into a bowl of ginger soy sauce.

"I'm surprised they haven't arrested your boy yet," Jefferson says.

"I do not want to talk about Fletcher McClain tonight," I say in a stern voice.

Jefferson acts as if he's hard of hearing. "You know he killed that girl, right?"

"He's got an airtight alibi."

"Yeah, I bet. I'm just glad you dumped his ass. I don't know if I could handle you being tied up in another big murder case."

"Me neither. I turned down this one, but there's going to be another case."

"I know and when it happens, I'll handle it. But you go into a zone when you're in trial. It's like I don't even have a wife."

I stopped chewing. "I didn't know you felt that way."

"I didn't know either. It's cool being out with you tonight." He leans across the table and kisses me on the lips.

When you're married, it's easy to fall into a routine, often forgetting to give your partner the attention he needs. The spark goes and comes, but it's definitely back tonight for us.

"Wanna have sex in the backseat of the car?" Jefferson asks.

I laugh. "No. But I'm up for some skinny dipping action in the hot tub."

Jefferson's hand shoots up. "Waiter, check, please! We gotta go home. Now!"

I start cracking up. "We're not going anywhere until I finish my food."

"I bet your boy Fletcher was shocked when you turned down his case."

"Yep. He's used to getting whatever he wants and he was surprised that the money didn't matter to me."

Jefferson raises his glass in a makeshift toast. "That's my girl. I love a woman who calls her own shots."

I tell Jefferson about my confrontation with Mia and her comment about cop beatings and innocent people not going to jail.

"She actually said that?"

"Yep. But worse than that, I think she really believes it."

"She better be careful. She had a motive too. The cops just might arrest her ass for killing that girl."

That thought made me smile. "I suspect an arrest would change her mind about the criminal justice system real quick."

CHAPTER 83

Mia gritted her teeth and tried her best to keep a smile on her face, but Fletcher's mother was getting on her last nerve. It had only been three days, but there was no way she'd be able to last an entire month living under the same roof with Gilda McClain.

Her future mother-in-law was sitting on the couch in the great room, cooing over Harmony. Fletcher's mother was a bone-thin sixty-year-old who did yoga every day, wore too much makeup and spent too much of her son's money.

"Oh, you're finally home. Are you cooking tonight, dear?"

Those were the kind of subtle digs that drove Mia nuts. Gilda knew she had no plans to cook dinner. She'd just gotten home from work and it was almost eight o'clock for goodness' sake.

"I'm sorry, Gilda. This real estate merger I'm working on is keeping me crazy busy. And Fletcher's hours are so unpredictable. We usually order out."

Gilda's nose twitched. "My boy needs a home-cooked meal every once in a while. I'll cook tomorrow."

You do that.

Mia had finally downloaded Girlie's summary judgment motion from the court file, but hadn't found time to read the excerpts from Fletcher and Bliss' depositions yet. It was almost as if a little voice in her head was gently urging her to forget about it. No matter what happened between Bliss and Fletcher in the past, it no longer mattered since Bliss couldn't cause any more drama in their lives.

Mia was about to barricade herself in the bedroom for the rest of the evening when she heard Fletcher coming through the door.

"How are my three favorite girls?" he called out. He glided into the room carrying the most beautiful yellow roses she'd ever seen. Mia's bad attitude instantly evaporated. It was about time Fletcher started paying attention to her again.

"Oh, Fletcher they're—"

"Mother, these are for you." He set the vase on the coffee table, then bent down to kiss his mother on the cheek and the baby on the forehead. He plopped down on the couch next to them. "Let me hold her."

Mia felt like she was on a different planet as she watched the threesome, all connected by blood. Fletcher acted as if she wasn't even in the room.

Carina, a.k.a. Miss Sunshine, popped into the room. "Hey everybody."

She was wearing flip flops, jeans and a tank top with no bra. Mia was going to have to have a talk with the girl about proper attire.

She eased Harmony from Fletcher's arms into hers. "I think it's time for a feeding."

Mia hated her annoying singsong voice. Somebody needed to teach that girl how to talk in a normal cadence.

Carina left the room with Harmony, singing softly to her.

"Hey, remember me." Mia waved across the room at Fletcher.

"I'm sorry, babe. I'm just so enthralled with Harmony. I never thought I'd feel this way about a kid. She's so beautiful."

He walked over and gave her a hug fit for a mannequin. Fletcher had been a little distant after her confrontation with Vernetta outside the police station the other day. They argued on the way home and Mia had been quite stunned when Fletcher took Vernetta's side.

Mia saw the writing on the wall, but she'd never been one to let someone else craft her story. If she was going to get her relationship with Fletcher back on track, she needed to get all of these people out of their house so they could refocus on each other. And she knew she'd never be Fletcher's number one focus as long as Bliss' baby was in their lives. She prayed that Girlie Cortez was somehow able to help Jessica gain custody of Harmony.

A loud banging on the door cut through the room.

"What the—" Fletcher charged toward the front of the house.

"L.A.P.D.! Open up!"

Mia took off down the hall after him. Fletcher opened the door to an arsenal of cops. Five uniformed officers stood in front of them. Others were walking around to the back of the house.

"What's going on?" he demanded.

Mankowski stepped forward. "We have a warrant to search your home."

"Search for what? I told you I didn't kill that bi—"

"If I were you, I'd watch my language. We've got cameras rolling."

Mia noticed a cop off to the side pointing a camera in their direction.

"Calm down, baby," Mia whispered in Fletcher's ear. "They want you to blow up so they can use it against you. Don't give them what they want."

Mia stepped in front of him. "I'm his attorney. I'd like to see your warrant, please."

Thomas handed it to her with a smile.

She scanned the document, but since she'd never seen one before and knew nothing about criminal law, she had no idea whether it was valid or not.

"Please step aside," a big cop ordered.

When they didn't move, the man bowled past them, clearing the way for the other cops to rush in. Gilda, Carina and Harmony were ushered outside with Mia and Fletcher.

Fletcher turned to Mia. "I want you to take all of them to the Four Seasons until I can figure this thing out." He pulled his cell phone from his pocket. "I'm calling Vernetta."

"Nobody's going anywhere, Mankowski said. "Especially not you."

Fletcher wasn't sure which one of them he was talking to, but before he could clarify, Mia got in Mankowski's face.

"Unless you have an arrest warrant, we can go anywhere we want." She knew that much from watching *Law & Order.*

"Lady, I'm instructing you to step back out of our way so that we can properly execute our search warrant."

Mia stayed put, both hands defiantly on her hips. "You don't have a right to—"

Mankowski turned to Thomas who gave a slight nod.

"You're under arrest." Mankowski flagged one of the officers who pulled out his handcuffs. He grabbed Mia's arm and whirled her around.

Mia's scream sounded more like a howl. "I'm a lawyer. You can't treat me like this! I will sue every one of you!"

She was struggling so violently, the officer was having a hard time cuffing her.

Fletcher was so enraged he could hardly talk. "Why are you doing this? What are you arresting her for?"

"California Penal Code one-forty-eight, obstructing an officer in the performance of his duties," Mankowski explained.

"You can't do that! This is police brutality!" Fletcher puffed out his chest and balled up his fists as if he was about to strike a blow.

Thomas stepped between Fletcher and his partner. "Would you like to join your fiancée? Because we can definitely make that happen."

Fletcher took a step back, but kept his eyes on Mankowski. "I'll sue you for everything you got," Fletcher spat.

"Go for it, buddy. I don't have much, but it's yours for the taking."

"Oh, my goodness!" Gilda was hugging herself and rocking back and forth like an addict.

Carina was off to the side sobbing in unison with Harmony.

The officer started tugging a handcuffed Mia toward a patrol car. She resisted him at every step, jerking her body in the opposite direction.

"Help me, Fletcher!" Mia wailed. "Don't let them take me to jail!"

Fletcher looked like a helpless little boy. By the time he took out his cell phone, tears were rolling down his cheeks.

Chapter 84

Just as we pull onto our street Jefferson grimaces and pounds the steering wheel with the heel of his hand. Dang!"

"What's the matter?" I glance up the street and spot what just set Jefferson off. Special's car is parked in front of our house.

"I'm not having it tonight. We have a date with a hot tub. So send her ass home."

I can't help but laugh. "Special would be so hurt if she heard what you just said. You better be glad I'm not going to tell her."

"I don't care if she knows. I'll tell her myself."

By the time Jefferson swings his car into the driveway, Special is already out of her car and running up to us.

"I saw it," she yells. "I saw the video."

"We don't care who you saw," Jefferson says, his tone gruff. "You gotta go. We're about to get our freak on."

"Hush, boy. Y'all can do that any time. This is important." Special's lips start flapping faster than the blades of a fan. "I bribed the security guard to show me the video of the man going in and out of the restaurant. I got a real good look at him too. But better yet, I got this." She waves a piece of paper in the air.

I climb out of the car. "What's that?"

"We don't care what it is," Jefferson barks. "Show it to her in the morning. Good night, Special."

"It's the license plate number of Mystery Baby Daddy and probably Bliss' killer too!"

"Good work," I tell my friend, knowing she's craving a pat on the back. "But like my husband just said, we have some business to take care of. This is our first date night in ages."

Jefferson stands at the front door, sticking his key into the lock. "So good night, Special," he repeats over his shoulder. "See you later. Preferably in a month or so."

"Dang, brother man, why're you so crotchety tonight? Girl, you gotta give him some more often."

"Let's talk about it tomorrow," I say. "There's nothing we can do with that information tonight."

"I called it into Eli. He's going to see if one of his cop contacts will look it up for him."

"I think you should stay out of it and hand it over to Mankowski and Thomas. I don't even think they have that guy on their radar. Based on the conversation you overheard in that restaurant, they definitely should."

Special scrunched up her face. "And let them get all the glory for solving the case? No way. I'm going to solve this puppy myself."

"We don't care." Jefferson steps inside and after I follow, he places one hand on the edge of the door and the other on the doorframe, blocking Special's entrance. "Good night, Special."

She ducks underneath Jefferson's arms and squeezes inside. Before he can grab her, my phone rings.

Jefferson throws up his hands. "Don't answer it."

"C'mon, babe. I have to check." I reach inside my purse. "It might be important."

When I glance at the phone, Fletcher's name flashes across the screen. I'm about to stick the phone right back into my purse, but a weird feeling prevents me from doing that. I tap a button turning on the phone.

As I listen, my emotions heighten with his every word. With Jefferson and Special staring me down, however, I struggle to keep my face expressionless.

"I'm sorry, Fletcher, but I can't get involved. I doubt she'd want me to represent her anyway. You have Colin's number. Call him." I hang up.

Special nearly jumps out of her shoes with curiosity. "What happened?"

"They arrested Mia."

"What? I told you that heffa killed her!" Special starts jumping up and down.

"They arrested her for obstruction of justice, not Bliss' murder. And, excuse me, but haven't you been saying all along that Mystery Baby Daddy killed Bliss?"

"Well, maybe," Special says sheepishly.

Jefferson is still standing at the door, holding it wide open. "I don't care who killed her. Good night, Special."

She's about to sulk out, when my phone rings again.

Jefferson's eyes plead with me. "Babe, please don't answer that."

"It's Colin. I have to take it."

I'm relieved to hear that Fletcher has reached out to him so fast. But as Colin explains, he wouldn't be able to fly down from Oakland until morning. He wants me to cover for him until then. Based on what Fletcher told him, Colin thinks I can probably get Mia out of jail tonight.

"I prefer not to get involved," I tell him.

And besides I'd love for Mia to spend a night in jail so she can see how the other half lives.

Now, Colin is pleading with me and his pleas are far more effective than Fletcher's. Or Jefferson's for that matter.

My husband knows from my pained expression that there isn't going to be any hot tub action tonight.

"It's okay, babe." Jefferson walks over, kisses me on the lips and squeezes me hard. "Do what you gotta do."

I hug him back, then turn to Special. "I need to see if I can get Mia out tonight. You wanna ride with me?"

CHAPTER 85

I don't recognize the handcuffed woman who shuffles into the interrogation room at police headquarters. Mia's weave sits askew and it looks as if she's run through a wind tunnel. But it isn't her hair, her smeared makeup or the three buttons missing from her blouse that disturbs me most. It's her eyes. Mia's eyes are dead.

As she slumps into a seat across from me, I look up at Mankowski and Thomas. "I'd appreciate it if you could take the handcuffs off. Then I'd like a few minutes alone with my client."

"Is she going to talk to us?" Mankowski asks.

"I'll make that determination after I speak with her." They're actually doing me a favor by letting me see her so quickly.

Mankowski grunts, takes off the handcuffs and leaves the room.

I move my chair to the other side of the table, close to Mia's. I don't trust that the cops aren't listening to our conversation.

"I need you to listen to me," I whisper into her ear. "When those cops come back in here, I need you to follow my instructions to the letter. Arresting you on an obstruction of justice charge is crap. They've targeted you as Bliss' killer, but they don't have enough evidence to arrest you. I think they baited you into going off so they could take you in."

The realization that she'd been set up suddenly dawns on Mia, because her dead eyes suddenly blink back to life.

"But I told you, I didn't kill Bliss!"

"Please lower your voice."

I very much want to remind my temporary client that she has nothing to worry about since innocent people don't go to jail. But doing that would be both petty and unprofessional. But it sure would feel good.

"I know you didn't kill her," I say, though I don't know any such thing. "I think I can get you out of here tonight, but I'm going to need you to do exactly what I tell you to do."

"Okay, but please just get me out of here! I can't spend another minute in that holding tank! I just can't! It stinks in there and those other women were so ghetto."

My instantaneous frown prompts Mia to try to clean up her comment.

"But there was an older woman in there who was nice to me." Mia toys with a loose thread on her faded smock. "She could tell I didn't belong there. She kept this big gangbanger-looking girl from messing with me."

Lord, help me. I can't wait to hand over this snooty child to Colin. Once he gets to town and takes over, I'm changing my phone number.

"What I want to do right now is use this interrogation for information-gathering. Like I said, I don't think they have probable cause to arrest you for Bliss' murder. Otherwise, they would've gotten an arrest warrant. People mouth off to cops all the time. It's totally within their discretion whether to make an arrest. They were hoping you got in their face."

"So they entrapped me?"

Yes, fool. They must've started handing out law degrees to just anybody.

"Entrapment's a little more involved. But basically, they played you. Since you spoke to them before without representation," I explain, "I suspect they figured you'd do it again. They wanted to interrogate you without counsel present in the hope of getting you to confess to Bliss' murder."

Mia just blinks over at me, stunned at the realization of how the criminal justice system works in practice rather than theory.

"You didn't say anything in the squad car, right?"

"No," she squeaks.

"Okay. So when they come back in here, I'm going to do most of the talking. You should only respond to a question when, and only when, I tell you to. Our goal here is to get information, not give it. You understand?"

Mia nods, but it isn't clear to me that she understands everything I'm saying. She seems to float in and out of the room.

The door opens and Mankowski sticks his head inside. "How much longer are you going to need?"

"Your timing's perfect." I make my tone as conciliatory as possible. "We're ready now."

Thomas sits down at the table across from us while Mankowski remains standing. I figure Thomas is taking the lead since he built a rapport with Mia when he questioned her before.

"Ms. Richardson," Thomas begins, "we want to ask you one more time where you were this past Tuesday evening, between the hours of eight and ten."

"Whoa, cowboy." I hold up a hand. "You arrested my client for obstruction of justice. Sounds like you want to question her about Bliss Fenton's murder. That's not what we're here for."

I want to force them to put their cards on the table.

Thomas looks up at Mankowski. It's apparent that he's the more experienced cop.

Mankowski grabs the remaining empty chair. He straddles it, with his hands griping the back of the chair.

He gives me an *aw shucks*, grin. "Okay, counselor, I should've known, you were too smart for us."

His compliment is total bull. I entwine my fingers, prop my elbows on the table and lean in. If I hadn't been wearing a dress, I would've mirrored Mankowski's pose and straddled my chair too.

"If that's the case, detective, then why don't you stop playing games and just tell us what you've got? Since you chose not to bait Fletcher into an obstruction of justice charge, it sounds like Mia's your number one suspect. But you obviously don't have enough evidence to arrest her. I guess I can also assume you didn't find anything during the search either or you would've formally arrested her for murder. So, detectives, exactly what do you have?"

The big bad Mankowski doesn't like me calling him out. But this is the fun part of criminal practice. Lawyers get off on moments like this.

The two cops make eye contact again. They seem to be able to communicate without saying a word.

Thomas retakes the lead. "Okay, here's what we got. A week or so before Bliss Fenton's death, your client threatened her in the parking structure of the Century City Mall. We have an eyewitness to that confrontation."

Mia straightens up like a steel pole. Before she breaks her promise to keep her mouth shut, I place a firm hand on her arm, shutting her down.

"A lot of people threatened Bliss Fenton," I say. "What else you got?"

"Jessica Winthrop retained Girlie Cortez to sue Fletcher McClain for custody of Bliss' daughter. Your client offered Ms. Cortez a fif-ty-thousand-dollar incentive to make sure Jessica, and not her hus-band-to-be, obtained custody of the kid."

When I briefly glance her way, Mia lowers her head.

The allegation throws me, but I don't miss a beat. "That obviously happened after Bliss was dead. Doesn't sound like evidence of murder to me."

"No, but it does go to motive." Mankowski is no longer grinning. "I think the prosecutor's opening argument would go a little bit like this. First, your client gets Bliss out of her life by shooting her down in her own home. Then she tries to make Bliss' kid disappear too."

Mia gasps, causing me to squeeze her arm harder. This girl could've never practiced criminal law. She can't even put on a game face when her own freedom is on the line.

"You need more than motive to prove a murder case, detective. You need evidence. And so far I haven't heard any. What else you got?"

Thomas looks over at his partner. This time Mankowski nods. I have a bad feeling that whatever they hit us with next could be a prob-lem. Thomas reaches inside his jacket and pulls out an envelope.

"We've also got this." Thomas slaps a photograph on the table.

I pick it up. It shows an intersection and captures four cars going through it. It must have been a digital photo because it's very clear. I can see that the street is Jefferson Boulevard.

Mia leans in over my shoulder. It takes her a moment to recognize what she's looking at. After studying it for five seconds, she starts to shake.

"What's this?" I ask.

"That's your client's BMW going through the intersection of Jefferson and Playa Vista Drive right around the time Bliss was murdered. But she told us a couple days ago that she was home reading that night."

"I didn't kill her!" Mia shouts. "I was getting my hair done that day at the House of Carlton on Lincoln. I—"

My eyes lock on Mia's. "Please don't speak until I ask you to."

"They're crazy if they think I—"

I clutch Mia's arm in a vice grip. "I've got this," I say, through clenched teeth. "Please don't say another word."

She covers her face with both hands and starts blubbering.

I turn back to the detectives, whose faces sport matching grins.

"As you just heard, my client was driving through that intersection because she was on the way to get her hair done. I'm sure her stylist can confirm that."

For Mia's sake, I pray that's true. That is something the cops can easily check out. If Mia is lying, that won't bode well for her. Regardless of whether she got her hair done, it doesn't look good that she was in the area around the time Bliss was killed.

Mankowski spreads his hands, palms up. "Doesn't mean she still didn't have time to shoot Bliss before or after she got her hair done. Hell, she probably planned it all out that way."

I know that a good prosecutor could string together this evidence and at least get past a preliminary trial. And if the case gets to a jury and Mia displays even an ounce of her snooty personality, the jury won't like her one bit. She'll be stripping off her designer duds and going straight to jail. Even if she didn't kill Bliss, Mia might soon find out that innocent people do indeed get railroaded.

My job, however, regardless of whether the evidence is weak or strong, is to vigorously defend my client, not throw in the towel when the chips are down.

"Sorry, guys. I'm just not hearing enough evidence to even keep me up at night. If you do find a deputy D.A. dumb enough to charge Ms. Richardson with murder based on this flimsy evidence, it'll never get to a jury because I'll knock it out at the prelim."

I widen my smile.

"So how about dropping the bogus obstruction of justice charge and letting Ms. Richardson go home where she belongs?"

CHAPTER 86

When I return to the lobby and spot Fletcher, I almost don't recognize him either. He looks as unkempt and defeated as Mia.

"Is that your boy, Fletcher?" Special whispers. "He looks tore up."

Fletcher rushes over to us, almost crashing into me. "Where's Mia? Can you get her out? She can't spend the night in jail. She won't make it."

"They're processing her out right now. But I suspect they're going to take their sweet time. So it could be a couple of hours."

"Oh, Vernetta, thank you. Thank you so much."

"Colin is arriving at LAX at seven tomorrow morning. Mia's free for now, but I'm not sure how long it's going to stay that way."

Fletcher gives me a weird look. "I need to talk to you." He eyes Special. "Alone."

"I'm her private investigator," Special boasts. "The attorney-client privilege extends to me."

"Special, I need you to give us a minute," I say.

She rolls her eyes and flops into a nearby chair.

"Let's step outside," Fletcher says. "I can't risk anyone hearing this."

For some strange reason, I'm nervous about what he's about to tell me. We're almost at the street before he stops.

"Do we still have an attorney-client privilege relationship?" Fletcher asks.

"Yes, that's ongoing. I can't reveal anything you've told me in confidence even though I'm no longer representing you. But as we

discussed, I'm no longer your attorney. I've already walked danger-
ously close to the conflict-of-interest line by representing Mia on the
obstruction of justice charge just now. So whatever you have to say, tell
it to your new attorney."

"Well, just for the purpose of this conversation, I need you to represent me again."

"Fletcher, I don't feel like playing any games. I can't—"

He grabs my arm so hard pain shoots up to my shoulder.

"Please, Vernetta. I'm not playing games. I will only talk to you if I
know for sure that you won't disclose what I say to anyone."

Tears well in his eyes.

"Fletcher, there are conflict of interest rules I have to abide by. I
can't—"

His eyes ignite with anger. "Why do you always have to play by
the goddamn rules? To hell with conflict of interest. We're friends. I
need to talk to you as a friend and I don't need to hear any of that legal
mumbo jumbo. I need to know that what I'm about to tell you won't
go anywhere else."

I rub my throbbing temple. "Okay, fine. Assuming I don't have to
lie about it under oath."

He scans the immediate area, then faces me again. "I found the
gun."

"The gun? What gun?"

"The gun Mia used to kill Bliss."

I take a step back. "Fletcher, what the hell are you saying?"

He speaks haltingly now, as if he's having trouble breathing. "It
was hidden in the back of my closet on the top shelf. I don't own a gun
and Mia is afraid of them. Or at least I thought she was."

Now I'm the one looking around. "So Mia told you she killed
Bliss?"

"Of course not."

"So what did she say when you told her you found the gun?"

"I haven't told her about it."

"Why not?"

"I don't know. I didn't know what to do."

"How do you know it's the gun that killed Bliss?"

"It has to be."

"You can't know that for sure until ballistics tests are done. And frankly, I don't recommend turning it over to the police. When did you find it?"

"Yesterday morning. And Mia is lucky I did. When those cops searched the house last night, they definitely would've found it. I just don't understand why she hid it in *my* closet, or anywhere in the house period. It doesn't make sense. Maybe she wanted me to find it."

Fletcher's right. That doesn't make sense. I'm convinced that he really doesn't know the woman he's about to marry. It would break his heart if he knew Mia was trying to separate him from his daughter. I don't want to be around when somebody breaks that news to him. He sure can pick 'em. There couldn't be two more scandalous women on the planet than Bliss Fenton and Mia Richardson.

"So where is the gun now?" I ask.

"It's—"

"Wait." I put a hand up. "I don't need to know."

I won't be representing Fletcher or Mia after tonight. I need to stay out of it.

"Fletcher, you need to get your own attorney," I advise him. "And it can't be me. If anyone finds out you have that gun, you could end up facing an obstruction of justice charge and a whole lot more. I'll talk to Colin and we'll come up with someone who can represent you. And don't mention that gun to anyone besides your counsel. Not even Mia because you'll probably be called to testify against her."

Fletcher massages the back of his neck. "This is all too much."

I lead him back inside and confirm that they're still processing Mia out.

As Special and I walk back to my car, she's peppering me with a zillion questions. She's like a Chihuahua, yapping at my feet. But I'm in my own head. Her words might as well be white noise.

Despite my discounting the evidence the two detectives had presented, with the addition of the murder weapon—assuming the gun Fletcher just told me about is indeed the murder weapon—Mia is looking pretty darn guilty. It didn't make sense, though, for her to hide the gun in Fletcher's closet.

Special places a hand on my arm. "Girl, are you even listening to me?"

The more I think about it, however, the more everything begins to come into focus. I understand now, why Mia hid the gun in Fletcher's closet and not her own.

"Mia killed Bliss," I blurt out.

Special practically stumbles over her own feet. "What? You think so? Did she admit it? We really won't know that for sure until we find Mystery Baby Daddy."

I shake my head, but don't say more.

Mia and Bliss are two of a kind, except that I now believe that Mia is even more vengeful than Bliss. Mia didn't just focus her anger on Bliss. She also aimed it squarely at her future husband.

To Fletcher's knowledge, Mia never found out about his backseat blow job. He'd simply told her that we lost the motion on a technicality. According to Fletcher, Mia was still under the impression that Bliss got pregnant by stealing his semen from a used condom.

But it would've been easy enough for Mia to get copies of Girlie's summary judgment motion from the court records. And if she had, she would've learned precisely how Bliss conceived Harmony.

The fact that Mia was working behind the scenes to get Fletcher's own flesh and blood out of his life was the ultimate betrayal. Bliss' vengeful scheme and Fletcher's infidelity had ruined Mia's plans for an idyllic life of wealth and privilege.

And now, Mia was seeking her own brand of revenge. Not only had she killed Bliss, she was setting up Fletcher to take the fall.

CHAPTER 87

"It was worth a try," Thomas said, his voice full of resignation. "And it would've been more than a try if she hadn't lawyered up," Mankowski grumbled. "Lawyers screw up everything. I know I could've broken her down and gotten a confession."

"Well, we didn't get that opportunity, so where do we go from here?"

Mankowski pursed his lips. "Let's go check out her alibi."

The House of Carlton on Lincoln and Mindanao in Marina Del Rey was a pretty exclusive spot. The salon had no website or online listing. Decorated in cream and gold, even the styling chairs were a gold-colored faux leather. The place had so many standing appointments, it could take months to get in.

"I'm so glad I'm not a woman," Mankowski muttered.

"May I help you?" the receptionist asked.

Mankowski flashed his badge. "L.A.P.D. We'd like to speak to Carlton."

"Okay, I'll check to see if *Mr.* Carlton is available."

The girl scampered out of sight, but was back in a flash.

"Mr. Carlton would like to know what this is about."

"You tell *Carlton* it's going to be about his arrest, if he doesn't get his rear end out here."

The girl disappeared again, and this time, took longer to return.

"It'll be a minute. Mr. Carlton is just finishing up a service."

"We don't mind talking to him while he works."

"Oh no. We have a very exclusive clientele. Mr. Carlton works only in private." The girl leaned over the counter and lowered her voice. "Mr. Carlton's weaves are better than real hair. Our clients don't like people to know they have weaves. Which is why Mr. Carlton does all of his work in his private quarters."

The detectives took a seat. It was another twenty-three minutes before they were allowed an audience with the king of weaves. To their surprise, Mr. Carlton was at least six-foot-two with a linebacker's build and a deep baritone to match. His private quarters were more tastefully decorated than the rest of the shop, with muted blue walls and soothing lime furniture.

"How can I help you, gentlemen?"

"We understand that Mia Richardson is a client of yours."

"I'm sorry. I have a very elite clientele. I can't reveal that information without their permission."

"Ms. Richardson has given her permission, which is why we even knew to come here. We'd like to know if she had an appointment with you last Tuesday."

Carlton opened his leather appointment book. "Yes. That wasn't her regular day, but she asked me to squeeze her in for a weave tightening."

"What's a weave tightening?" Mankowski asked.

"I'll tell you later," Thomas said. "What time was her appointment?"

"Eight-thirty."

"Did she arrive on time?"

"On the nose."

"Did she seem upset or frazzled?"

"Nope. She's not exactly my friendliest client. She was reading some legal documents."

They asked a few more questions then left. They drove back to Bliss' neighborhood and parked near the intersection of Jefferson and Playa Vista Drive.

Mankowski pointed toward the intersection. "That traffic camera shows Mia driving eastbound on Jefferson, then turning right onto Playa Vista Drive at seven-fifty-five. Bliss' townhouse is about a minute away. That means she had thirty-five minutes to cap her ex-friend and make it over to The House of Carlton to get her weave tightened."

Thomas set his watch as Mankowski drove from Bliss' townhouse on Kiyot Way, through the intersection to the House of Carlton on Lincoln. There were six traffic lights between the two locations.

Mankowski pulled into a parking stall in front of the salon. "Okay, how long did it take?"

"Six minutes and thirty-five seconds. She even had enough time to catch a bite to eat."

Mankowski nodded. "Mia Richardson may've gotten her weave tightened last Tuesday evening, but she also took care of some other business while she was on this side of town. And we're going to prove it."

CHAPTER 88

Fletcher lay in bed spooning Mia's warm body, which was curled tight against his. They'd arrived home just after 2 a.m. and he still hadn't been able to fall asleep though it was just past six now.

This was all his fault. He was the one who'd driven Mia to do this. Although he'd threatened Bliss, he didn't have the balls to follow through on his threats. Mia had always been stronger than he was. He didn't blame her for doing what he didn't have the guts to do. And he planned to pull every string within his reach to make sure she got off.

Mia began to stir, then turned around to face him.

"I love you," Fletcher said.

"I love you too." Mia pressed her lips to his, morning breath and all.

He'd been anxiously waiting for Mia to talk to him. To tell him what she'd done. But she'd seemed almost catatonic when he picked her up from the police station. He was surprised that she had yet to ask him whether the police found anything when they searched the house. She had to be worried that they had discovered the gun she'd hidden in his closet.

Mia glanced around their bedroom, which was larger than most L.A. apartments.

"It looks better than I thought it would in here," she said, surprised. "When the police execute a search warrant on TV, they always leave the place in shambles. I expected to find all my clothes strewn around the room."

"It was a lot messier than this," Fletcher said with a half chuckle. "My mother and Carina straightened up a bit."

It had taken some doing, but Fletcher had convinced his mother to return home. He didn't know what was in store for Mia, and he didn't need his mother buzzing around adding more stress to his already full plate.

He'd asked Carina to take Harmony away for a few days and put them up in a suite at the Four Seasons. Carina was more than happy for the mini-vacation, even if it meant caring for a three month old. He was lucky that Carina seemed to truly love his daughter. The woman had turned out to be a Godsend.

"Mia, honey, is there anything we need to talk about?"

She moved closer, resting her head across his chest.

Mia inhaled. "I'm scared. They think I killed Bliss." She started to whimper.

Think? You did, didn't you?

"You have nothing to be worried about," Fletcher lied, moving a few strands of hair from her face.

"According to Vernetta, this attorney I hired to represent you is the best there is. He once got a guy acquitted for murder even though the cops had an eyewitness, the guy confessed and his fingerprints were on the murder weapon."

"I just feel so bad. I have...I have something I need to say."

Every muscle in Fletcher's body constricted. Mia was about to confess that she killed Bliss.

"I'm listening, honey."

"Vernetta was right. That stuff I said about innocent people not going to jail was stupid. I'm innocent and they're about to railroad me. I need to apologize to her. She's a really good attorney. You should've seen how she took on those arrogant cops. Frankly, I wish she was representing me. But I know she won't do it because of the way I treated her."

Mia's tears dampened Fletcher's chest.

It was beginning to bug him that Mia was keeping up this facade of innocence. Didn't she trust him?

"Honey, you know you can tell me anything, right?"

"Of course."

"So you don't have anything else to tell me?"

Mia took a long time to respond. She turned on the lamp and propped herself up on her forearms.

"Fletcher, what are you asking me?"

His eyes lasered into hers. "What do you think I'm asking you?"

"I'm not sure, but I hope it's not what I'm thinking."

Why are you putting on this show? Just tell me you did it!

"I'd never judge you." Fletcher massaged her back. "And I'll love you no matter what."

"What?" Mia sprang out of bed, her bare feet slapping hard against the bamboo floor. "You think I killed Bliss?"

Fletcher sprang up in bed. "Mia, please calm down."

"I will *not* calm down. I can't believe you think that! How could you?"

Mia ran into the bathroom and slammed the door. He could hear her frantic sobs but had no idea what to do.

Fletcher was totally confused. Was he dealing with a crazy woman who'd talked herself into believing she was innocent? And if that was the case, was his own safety in jeopardy?

As he fell back against his pillow, his stress level spiked a notch. Even in death, Bliss Fenton was still screwing up his life.

CHAPTER 89

"Hey, homie," Colin climbs into the front seat of my Landcruiser and hurls his overnight bag into the backseat.

I agreed to pick him up at LAX so I could give him a brief overview of the case before his first meeting with his new client. He is a tall, gregarious Jamaican who was raised in England.

"Good to know that the Calvary is in town," I joke as we pull off from the curb.

"Indeed. Thanks for showing a brother some love," he says in a sultry British accent. "I'm surprised that the media hasn't jumped on this case. I searched online during the flight and all I found was the initial story on the day of the shooting."

"Oh, it's coming. Take a look at this." I reach for the *Star* magazine from a compartment along the door and hand it to him. "Check out this headline."

CORPORATE ATTORNEY SUSPECTED
IN BABY MAMA DRAMA MURDER

Colin blows out a breath. "Blood sucking cretins."

Most attorneys love cases that allow them to get their mugs in front of a TV camera. Colin feels differently and gives very few interviews. If he had, he'd be filthy rich. With his skills and success rate, he'd be the clear heir apparent to Johnnie Cochran.

He turns to face me. "So give me the background."

"We have some housekeeping chores first," I begin. "Now, I know we're buds and all, but let me say for the record that I'm only going to share general background info and the procedural status. As you know, I still have to maintain Fletcher McClain's confidences. If he ends up getting charged and our love birds decide to turn on each other, I don't want to be accused of breaching any attorney-client confidences."

Colin smiles. "Sounds like you learned a thing or two since law school, homie. If I were in your shoes, I'd be giving you the same spiel. Okay, shoot."

I begin my recap by telling Colin about Bliss' paternity case, then move on to Fletcher's fraud suit. By the time I get to my defense of Mia at the police station last night, Colin looks flabbergasted.

"Dang. That's some baby mama drama for your ass." He brushes his palms back and forth in excitement. "I haven't had a case this challenging in a while."

I stop short, way short, of mentioning Fletcher's discovery of the gun. I'm curious about whether Mia will disclose that to him. Colin mentions a local attorney he thinks might be a good fit to represent Fletcher in the event he's pulled into this. I wonder if Fletcher will tell his new counsel about the gun.

When we arrive at my office, Special is there waiting for us. I want Colin to hear firsthand the information Special has uncovered about Mystery Baby Daddy. After that, Colin has a meeting scheduled with Mia. He's going to be using my office as his base of operations.

"So this is the mysterious Colin T. Bowman," Special gives him a hug as if she's known him all her life.

"Glad to be working with you, counselor. The jury's gonna love that accent of yours."

Colin grins. "Where's the bog around here?"

"What the hell is a bog?" Special asks.

"Sorry." Colin looks embarrassed. "Where can I find a restroom?"

I direct him down the hall.

"Girl! Why didn't you tell me about that tall, handsome drink of water?"

"Forget it. He's married with children."

"Shoot! I might have to adopt Bliss' theory on dating. At least she was getting paid. I still can't believe Darius' lying ass had the nerve to cheat on me."

"Special, we're not going there again. So move on."

When Colin returns, we gather around the table in my office. Special fills him in on her investigation and the video she saw of the man who had argued with Bliss at Salt Creek Grille.

"I really like the work you've done," Colin says. "At trial, it's always good when you can point a finger at somebody else. It's hard for a jury to find guilt beyond a reasonable doubt when there's another possible suspect the police failed to properly investigate. I've gotten more than a few hung juries on that basis."

Special frowns. "None of Eli's cop friends have been able to run the license plate. They track all that stuff now and they could get in trouble for running a plate without a legitimate reason."

"I have a contact who can run that plate for us." Colin says. His eyes narrow and he looks as if he's in deep thought. "But for now, I'd really like to get a picture of the guy."

"No can do," Special says. "The security company wouldn't give me a copy of the video without a subpoena."

"Can you throw the guy a few more bucks to see if he'll show you the video again and let you record it on your phone?"

Special slaps her forehead with her palm and shoots out of her chair. "Wow! You're good! Why didn't I think of that? I'm going back over there right now."

"You should also have him freeze the screen and take a few still shots of the guy," Colin advises.

"Will do." She opens her purse and counts the cash in her wallet.

As Special leaves the room, Colin checks his Rolex. "My new client should be arriving any minute now."

CHAPTER 90

Special was still kicking herself. Why hadn't she thought of something as simple as videotaping the video? Now the greedy guard Carlos wanted another two hundred bucks. This time, he refused to let her into the Security office. He'd made Special hand over her phone and wait in her car.

As it turned out, it was well worth the wait. Carlos not only provided the video, but some pretty good still shots of Mystery Baby Daddy too.

She'd taken one of the still shots and cropped it on her phone. The picture was almost as good as if the guy had posed for it.

"Mystery Baby Daddy," Special said to the picture, "I'm going to find your ass. You might be the key to saving Mia Richardson from a lethal injection."

Special was halfway back to Vernetta's office when another idea came to her. Now that she had the photograph, she could show it to Jessica Winthrop to see if she recognized the guy. Until they could run his license plates, that was her best bet at figuring out his identity. Making a U-turn, she headed toward Bel Air.

Special knew she had to come up with another approach to get Jessica to talk to her. She'd decided to tell the woman that Bliss had been seeing two men the police knew nothing about and Special wanted to see if she recognized their pictures. She didn't plan to bring up Jonas' father at all, since that seemed to set Jessica off. Special figured she wanted to raise the little boy herself. So having Mystery Baby Daddy surface could throw a wrench in that plan.

Special selected a picture of Mystery Baby Daddy and downloaded one of Martin Zinzer from his firm's website. After uploading both pictures to the Walgreen's website, she stopped by the closest store to pick up the printed photographs. She pasted them on a piece of construction paper and, abracadabra, she had her first official photographic lineup. Special felt a smug sense of satisfaction. She was good at this, even if she hadn't come up with taking a video of the video.

If Jessica claimed she didn't recognize either of them, Special should be able to tell from her body language whether the woman was telling the truth. She'd taken an online course on body language and had also been reading up on it.

Twenty minutes later, she was pulling up in front of Jessica's home. Before she could knock on the door, Jessica snatched it open. "Why are you back here again? I'm calling the police."

"Just hold on a minute," Special pleaded, her hands raised, palms out. "I'm not here about Jonas' father. I gave up on trying to find that guy," she lied. "You should hear me out, because it may help you get custody of Bliss' daughter."

She'd come up with that fabrication on the fly. The curious interest in Jessica's eyes was exactly what Special had hoped to incite.

"How?" Jessica asked.

"Did you know Fletcher's girlfriend Mia Richardson is the primary suspect in Bliss' murder? Whether Mia or Fletcher goes on trial for murder, no judge is going to return Harmony to that household. So, we need to rule out all other potential suspects."

"So what do you want with me?"

The woman obviously wasn't too sharp. On her last visit, Special had said she was an investigator working on behalf of Fletcher. So obviously Special wouldn't now be trying to rule *out* other suspects.

"I have a picture of two men. I just want you to take a look to see if you recognize them."

Jessica stuck out her hand. "Let me see them."

"I prefer not to do this standing on your porch. I promise I'll only be inside for a few minutes. Then I'll be out of your hair for good."

Unless we need you to testify at trial.

After a long pause, Jessica opened the door and allowed her in.

When Special stepped inside, she found the entire living room littered with toys, big and small. There was a six-foot-tall stuffed giraffe, Tonka trucks, building blocks, a miniature tent and tons more stuff that could've been stolen from Neverland Ranch.

"Excuse the mess," Jessica said. "I kind of went a little overboard on toys for Jonas."

And that's exactly why kids today ain't worth a damn.

"We'll need to be quiet. Jonas is sleeping. He's a very light sleeper."

"Shouldn't he be in pre-school or something?"

"He's too young for that. Anyway, I plan to homeschool him."

Yet another reason why we're producing a bunch of over-protected, knucklehead kids who can't function in the real world.

Special followed Jessica into a humongous kitchen that opened into a great room with the highest ceilings she'd ever seen in a home.

"Can I get you something to drink?" Jessica asked.

"No, thanks. I just want to show you the pictures. Then I'll be on my way."

Special placed the two photographs on the island's black granite countertop. "Do you recognize either of these men? I think both of them had a relationship with Bliss."

Jessica ignored the picture of Mystery Baby Daddy, keeping her eyes glued on Zinzer. "I'm not sure I recognize either of them, but I better get my glasses just to be sure."

Disappointment flooded Special's face as Jessica left the room. She'd banked everything on Jessica recognizing Mystery Baby Daddy. Oh well. They would just have to find a way to track him down via his license plate number.

Special used the opportunity to nose around. She looked out through French doors into the backyard, which had so many plush plants, bushes and flowers it looked like an arboretum. The great room was decorated in relaxing, homey furniture, floral curtains with lace and ruffles, the kind of *Home and Gardens* decor that Special hated. She meandered over to the fireplace and started browsing the family pictures on the wall. One in particular drew her closer. As she leaned in to get a better look, her adrenalin level charged into overdrive.

"Oh my God!" She dashed back over to the kitchen island and snatched her phone from her purse. Her hands were shaking so badly, she could barely hold the phone. She went to her *Favorites* and tapped Vernetta's name.

"Oh my God! Oh my God! Oh my God! Pick up! Please pick up!"

When Vernetta finally answered, Special's brain was working faster than her lips.

"You'll never believe this! Mia didn't kill Bliss. Mystery Baby Daddy killed Bliss. And I know who he is. He's Jessica Winthrop's husband!"

Special abruptly stopped talking as Jessica reentered the room and charged up to her.

"What did you just say?"

Special hesitated, then blurted it out. "Your husband killed Bliss."

Jessica's thin brows furrowed. "That's nonsense."

"I'm sorry to have to tell you this, but your husband is Jonas' father."

Special expected a stunned reaction, but Jessica's bland eyes didn't even blink.

Did she already know?

"Your husband killed Bliss," Special repeated, "because she threatened to tell you about Jonas if he didn't give her five hundred thousand dollars. I think—"

"I don't want to hear any more of your lies! Get out of my house!"

"Fine." Special clasped the cell phone in her hand, hoping Vernetta was listening to every word of their conversation. "But when I leave here, I'm going straight to the police."

"And we'll sue you for defamation. I won't let you ruin my husband's career."

"If it's the truth, there's nothing you can do about it."

"It's not the truth," Jessica insisted. "Just because Bliss tried to blackmail Paul wasn't a reason to shoot her five times. Now leave!"

Special was about to grab her purse when Jessica's words signaled something in her brain, causing her to freeze.

Five times?

"What did you just say?" Special's eyes narrowed in suspicion. "How did you know Bliss was shot five times? The police didn't release that information to the public." She pointed a finger in Jessica's face. "You already knew your husband killed Bliss because he told you he did it!"

For several long seconds, the two women defiantly stared each other down.

"Get the hell out of my house," Jessica screeched. "Now!"

CHAPTER 91

As Colin and I wait for Mia to arrive, we hear a commotion just outside my office door.

"You're nothing but a goddamn liar! So your apology means nothing to me!"

I open the door to find Mia repeatedly jabbing Fletcher in the chest with her finger. "I guess I didn't blow you as well as your baby's mama did!"

When they notice us standing there, they step away from each other and act as if we didn't see what we just saw. They both look like they could use some sleep and some grooming tips. Fletcher forgot to shave. Mia's face is bare of makeup and her blouse could use a good ironing.

"Do you guys need a few minutes?" I ask.

Fletcher smiles. "Naw. Just a little lover's spat."

He takes Mia's hand. Her pinched lips tell me Fletcher's touch is making her skin crawl.

When they finally walk into my office, they usher in such a chill, I swear I start to shiver. It's easy to figure out what their fight was about. Mia finally found out about Fletcher's backseat blow job.

After introducing them to Colin, I grab my purse from underneath my desk. "Fletcher, let's go get some breakfast while they talk."

"Vernetta?" Mia says my name in an ultra soft voice. "I know you're not my attorney now, but I'd feel much better if you stayed."

I look first at Fletcher, then at Colin, whose eyes are signaling, *No friggin' way*.

"I can't do that," I say. "I represented Fletcher, so it would be a conflict of interest for me to be involved in your representation. You're a lawyer, so I'm sure you understand."

"But Fletcher can waive the privilege, can't he?"

"He could. But I wouldn't advise him to do that. We don't know that the police won't ultimately come after him."

It crosses my mind that Mia might actually *want* to create a conflict. Since I still think it's possible she set Fletcher up, this could be all part of her plan. In the event I relented and later decided to represent Fletcher, being in this interview would get me kicked off his case.

"I'll waive the privilege," Fletcher says. "Mia needs you. Besides you made it clear that you weren't going to represent me if I do end up getting charged. So I don't see the problem."

Colin and I exchange looks. The conflict rules are way too complicated to explain in full.

"It's just not a good idea," Colin says. "We don't want to—"

"I don't care about the rules," Fletcher snaps. "If Mia's going to feel better with Vernetta here, then we want her here."

I swallow hard. There's no way I want to get pulled into this case or find myself facing an ethical violation. But I'm also dying to know whether Mia's going to admit to Colin that she planted that gun in Fletcher's closet.

"How about this for a compromise?" I say. "I'll sit in just for today for consultation purposes only. But if you begin to broach a topic that I shouldn't hear, I'm going to step outside."

Colin shoots me a look that says, *Are you friggin' nuts? Didn't you hear these two lovebirds going at each other a second ago?*

"That's fine," Mia says, still speaking in a whisper.

"I really don't think Vernetta should be here," Colin repeats. "But if you both insist on acting against our counsel, we'll need to have that in writing." Colin opens his laptop and starts typing our cover-your-ass document.

In just a few minutes, Colin emails me the document, which I print out and have Fletcher and Mia sign. After Fletcher leaves, I join Colin and Mia at the table in the corner of my office. Colin reviews his retainer agreement with her and discusses some administrative matters.

"Okay, then, let's get started," he says.

Colin positions a yellow legal pad on the table and takes a pen from his jacket pocket. "So tell me what happened?"

Mia looks confused. "What do you mean, *what happened?* Nothing happened. I didn't kill Bliss."

"Okay, then. Why do the police think you killed her?"

"Because they're stupid!"

Here we go. Snotty Mia is back in all her glory. Colin gives me a look that says, *Why didn't you tell me she was such a drama queen?*

"Let's start with the conflicting information you gave the police. You initially told them you were at home reading, but later said you were getting your hair done."

Mia's eyes start to water and she looks as if she's ready to crumble. "I lied because I didn't want the police to know I'd been in the area. I really did have a hair appointment that day. I don't know what made me drive by Bliss' place. I wasn't going to do anything. I was just so mad at her for all the trouble she caused."

"Ms. Richardson, I need you to remember that I'm on your side. I can't represent you to the best of my ability unless you're completely honest with me."

Mia bursts into tears. "Oh my God! You're doing it too. Fletcher thinks I'm guilty and so do you!" Tears are flowing as if they're gushing from a busted water main.

I go to my desk, grab a box of Kleenex and place it on the table in front of Mia. She snatches three sheets and dabs her eyes. "I didn't kill her. I swear I didn't!"

When I hear the faint ringing of my phone, I hurry back to my desk and dig it out of my purse. I glance at the screen and see that it's Special. "I better get this."

Special is talking so fast, her words are completely indecipherable. "You have to slow down," I say. "I can't understand what you're saying."

She still doesn't slow her pace. But I do understand her next few words, which almost knock me off my feet.

"You'll never believe this! Mia didn't kill Bliss. Mystery Baby Daddy killed Bliss. And I know who he is. He's Jessica Winthrop's husband!"

I hear a female voice I don't recognize. As I continue to listen, an ominous chill slices through me.

Colin and Mia both charge over to my desk. I turn on the speakerphone.

"What's going on?" Colin places a hand on my shoulder.

"It's Special," I say, my mind whirling with excitement for Mia. "I think she may've just solved Bliss' murder."

CHAPTER 92

S pecial planted a hand on her hip, ignoring Jessica's order to leave. She wasn't going anywhere until she got some answers.

"Your husband killed Bliss. Just admit it and I'll be on my way."

Without a word, Jessica lifted her blouse, snatched a gun from her waistband and pointed it directly at Special. "I'm not going to let you destroy my life!"

"Whoa, hold on now." Special took a step back. "What are you doing? Put that thing away!"

Jessica's eyes zeroed in on the phone in Special's hand.

"Give me that phone!" She held the gun with both hands now, like she was an expert marksman aiming at a target.

Special wanted to yell out for Vernetta, to run or duck or scream. But her lips wouldn't move.

"Give me that phone," Jessica demanded.

Instead of handing over the phone, Special tapped the screen and slid it facedown on the island countertop next to her purse.

"Please just put the gun away, okay? We can talk this thing out."

Jessica stood on one side of the island, with Special on the other. Special tried to review her options, but realized there were none. Ducking for cover behind the island would save her for all of two seconds. She had no place to run. At least not that offered protection from a bullet.

"You lied to me," Jessica shouted. "You said you weren't here to ask about Jonas' father."

"I didn't know he was your husband. I swear I didn't. I'm so sorry."

"You're not sorry! And neither was Bliss!"

Special was afraid to speak again for fear of enraging the woman even more.

"I can't believe how she betrayed Jessica. Everybody thinks Jessica's sooooooo naïve. Poor, nice little Jessica."

It was making Special even more scared that Jessica was referring to herself in the third person. Only crazy people did that. When she'd spotted Mystery Baby Daddy and Jessica in the portrait over the fireplace, Special had instantly put two and two together and figured out that Paul Winthrop was Bliss' killer. She had to make Jessica understand that she wasn't to blame for what her husband had done.

"This isn't your fault," she said softly. "You did nothing wrong." But Jessica didn't seem to hear her.

"Jessica was the only one in the world who befriended Bliss and she not only screwed Jessica's husband, she bore his son. She deserved every one of those bullets!"

Rage painted Jessica's face a fiery red and in that moment, Special knew.

"Oh my God!" Special covered her mouth with both hands. "It wasn't your husband. You did it. *You* killed Bliss!"

"You seem surprised." A sinister smile eased across Jessica's face as she stuck out her chest, peacock proud. "Nobody thinks Jessica knows how to stand up for herself. But she does. Jessica had everything under control. Then you came along and messed it all up."

The reality of this situation hit Special like a gut punch. This cuckoo clock was a stone cold killer. She had better bounce.

"Look, I can just leave and pretend none of this ever happened. I'll just be on my way. Mum's the word."

When Special made a move toward her purse, Jessica cocked the gun.

"Oh, Lord Jesus, help me!" Special extended both hands out in front of her as if to keep Jessica at bay.

"Please put that thing away. I promise I won't tell anybody about this. Your secret's safe with me."

356 Pamela Samuels Young

"You're a liar. Just like Bliss is a liar and Jessica's husband is a liar. Everybody's a liar. Everybody lies to Jessica."

Help me, Jesus! Help me, Jesus! Help me, Jesus!

As far as Special was concerned, prayer was her only viable option for survival. She also prayed that Vernetta was still on the line listening to every word and had called the cops. Before setting down the phone, Special had actually hit the speakerphone button. She was now grateful that Jessica had kept repeating her own name. The police should be here in no time.

"How did you find out Jonas was your stepson?" Maybe if she kept Jessica talking, she wouldn't be shooting.

"He's not my stepson!" she screamed. "He's my son! Bliss wasn't a mother. I was the only real mother her kids ever had."

"Okay, okay. So how did you find out?"

"I hacked into Paul's computer." She smiled, but a split second later, the fury returned. "I found a confidentiality agreement he made Bliss sign. She betrayed me, but she never betrayed him. Bliss never disclosed their little secret to anyone. He actually bought that bitch a townhouse and paid her a million dollars. He was so stupid! If he'd just come to me, we could've taken Jonas from her. She didn't deserve to be anybody's mother."

"Mommy?" Jonas padded into the room, rubbing his eyes with both fists. He seemed barely awake.

A stunned Jessica lowered the gun, hiding it behind her back. Special dashed for Jonas, just as Jessica rushed toward him too. But Special was faster and reached him first. She grabbed him by the arms, picked him up and cradled him close. The boy was kicking and screaming at the top of his lungs.

"I know you don't want to hurt your son," Special said, breathless. "So put that gun away. Please, put it away."

For a moment, Jessica looked lost, as if she didn't have a clue about what move to make next.

"I understand how you feel," Special continued. Jonas was trying his best to wrestle himself away from her and Special's arms were growing tired fast. He had to be over thirty pounds. But the kid was her only chance at survival. She knew with certainty that Jessica would never fire the gun in her direction if there were even a chance of hitting him. So there was no way Special was letting him go.

"Bliss did you wrong." Special tried to talk over the boy's cries. "Maybe she deserved to die. But your son doesn't. And neither do I. If you don't put the gun away, it could go off and hit Jonas."

Jessica looked down at the gun in her hand and seemed to be contemplating what to do.

Special didn't know how much longer she'd be able to hold onto the kicking kid. The knowledge that the minute she put him down, Jessica would put a bullet between her eyes, helped prolong her strength.

"Auntie Jessica!" Jonas called out, which seemed to rattle Jessica even more.

Special took a step toward the counter to the right of where Jessica was standing. She'd spotted a cutlery block with several knives in it. If she could grab one of them, at least she'd have some kind of weapon.

Jessica must've read her mind.

"Get away from those knives!"

Jessica grabbed the entire wood block and hurled it into the hallway.

The woman's agitation level had spiked tenfold.

"Jessica had everything all planned out, but you messed it all up! Jessica even planted the murder weapon in Fletcher's closet. But you had to go asking about Jonas' father."

Jessica raised the gun, aiming it at Special's head.

"No!" Special yelled as she struggled to restrain Jonas. Her arms felt like they were on fire. "You can't hurt Jonas!"

Jessica spoke calmly now, as she took a giant step toward her. "You messed everything up. So Jessica has no choice but to kill you too."

CHAPTER 93

As Colin and Mia continue to listen to the confrontation between Jessica and Special on my cell, I grab my landline and dial 911.

"There's a hostage situation going on at the home of Jessica Winthrop," I yell into the phone.

"What do you mean by a hostage situation, ma'am?"

"I mean a crazy woman is holding a gun on my best friend!"

"Do you have an address?"

"No, I don't. You should be able to look it up. Her name is Jessica Winthrop. She lives in Bel Air."

"What's the address please?"

"I don't know the address!"

"Ma'am, I'm going to need you to calm down."

Mia points at her phone. "I just texted Fletcher, I'm sure he knows it."

Just then, Fletcher charges into my office. "What's going on?"

My heart is pounding so hard I fear it might fly out of my chest. "Please tell me you know Jessica Winthrop's address," I say to Fletcher.

"Yeah, I do, but why—"

"I don't have time to explain. Just give it to me!"

Fletcher flinches, then starts scrolling through his phone. "It's in Bel Air near Sunset."

The 911 operator calls out to me. "Ma'am, are you still there? We can't dispatch a patrol car unless we have an address."

"Just a second!" I snap.

Fletcher finally gives me an address on Stone Canyon Road, which I repeat to the operator, who's now asking me other questions."

I pause to listen to what's going on at Jessica's house and my fear intensifies.

"Somebody give me another phone. That woman's crazy. She's going to shoot Special."

Fletcher hands me his phone, while I continue to ignore the 911 operator's questions. I dial police headquarters and after two transfers, Mankowski finally comes on the line.

"Jessica Winthrop killed Bliss! She's holding my friend Special at gunpoint at her house, you have to get somebody over there now!"

I tell Mankowski as much as I know, then grab my purse and start for the door.

Colin, Fletcher and Mia are still listening to what's going on at Jessica's house on my cell. "Where are you going?" they ask in unison.

"Where do you think? To Jessica's house to keep that woman from killing my best friend."

CHAPTER 94

The distant sound of a police siren brought everything to a standstill. Even Jonas quieted down and stopped squirming.

Thank God!

Special had never been so happy to hear the sound of the po-po in her life.

Jessica was walking around in a small circle like a dog chasing its tail. The louder the siren grew, the more frantic she became. One second her eyes were bouncing all around the room and the next she was muttering to herself. Jonas clutched Special around the neck and now looked as scared as his loony-toon stepmother.

"Jessica, the police are coming." Special spoke just above a whisper, hoping not to set her off again.

"Please put the gun down. It's over."

"It's not over until Jessica says it's over!" she hissed.

Jessica raised her hand, then lowered it, pointing the gun toward the floor. Special thought about charging her. Normally, she'd have no trouble tackling a puny little woman like Jessica. But her arms were so tired from wrestling with Jonas, Jessica might easily overpower her.

The police cars screeched to a stop just outside. Seconds later, the house phone on the kitchen counter rang.

"That's probably the police," Special said. "You should pick it up."

On the fourth ring, Jessica snatched the receiver.

Special wished she could hear what was being said on the other end. Jessica remained silent and her hollow expression gave nothing away.

Without warning, Jessica hurled the phone across the room.

"Everybody thinks Jessica's stupid!" she cried, as tears spilled down her cheeks. "But Jessica isn't stupid. Jessica is brilliant."

She raised the gun again and, this time, pressed it to her temple.

"Jessica, no!" Special yelled.

"Auntie Jessica!" Jonas called out to her.

"Jonas needs you, Jessica," Special said, as gently as she could manage. "You're the only mother he ever had. What is he going to do without you?"

Jessica's eyes met Special's and her expression grew even darker.

"You're right," Jessica sobbed. "I can't leave Jonas. He has to come to heaven with me."

Crazy fool. Your behind ain't going nowhere near heaven.

Jessica was now aiming the gun at Jonas' head.

"No, Jessica, you can't hurt Jonas! You love him!"

Special dropped the boy to his feet and shoved him behind her, using her body to shield his. She tried to move sideways, out of Jessica's line of fire. But Jessica mirrored each step she took, clearly aiming at the child.

Jessica darted forward at the same time a loud explosion rocked the room.

Special hurled a protective arm around Jonas as she collapsed to the cold kitchen floor, covering the boy's body with her own like a human tent.

Jesus, oh Jesus! Please help me, Jesus!

It wasn't until Special saw Jonas crawling away from her that she realized he hadn't been hit. Men in SWAT gear poured into the room through the now-shattered French doors. That was when she saw Jessica only inches away, moaning and writhing on the floor, clutching her bloody left shoulder. The cops had fired through the French doors, shooting Jessica before she could kill Jonas.

The boy had almost made it over to Jessica when one of the cops scooped him up and carried him away.

One of the SWAT officers looked down at Special. "Are you okay?" the man asked. "Are you injured?"

Special couldn't seem to find her voice. The only sound coming from her lips was a low whimper, the emotion of what she'd just experienced too overwhelming for words. She extended her hand and the officer pulled her up and helped her outside.

The second they made it to the front of the house, Vernetta charged over. "Oh my God! Are you okay?"

Special collapsed into Vernetta's arms, still unable to speak.

"You're not hurt, are you?"

Special shook her head as Mankowski and Thomas crowded around them.

"Thanks for getting the cops here so fast," Vernetta thanked them.

The sight of the two detectives seemed to awaken something in Special.

"I guess y'all had the wrong suspect again," she gloated in a hoarse, shaky voice. "Looks like I solved another one for you, huh?"

EPILOGUE

Eight Months Later

"Your boy certainly flipped the script," Jefferson says. "Never thought I'd see a scene like this."

We are in Fletcher's backyard at Harmony's first birthday party. His Beverly Hills mansion is crawling with toddlers and preschoolers. Fletcher must've invited everyone he knew with a kid under five.

"Yep," I agree. "He seems to be taking fatherhood quite seriously."

Fletcher waves at us from across the yard. He's dipping a giggling Harmony in and out of the pool, while a host of kids splash all around them. Jonas and Aiden are having the most fun jumping off the low diving board.

A lot has happened over the past eight months. Jessica was charged in Bliss' murder, but she's currently in a psychiatric hospital. According to the most recent news reports, she plans to plead temporary insanity when her case goes to trial. So far, her husband Paul has been standing by her, using his extensive wealth to get her the best medical and legal help money can buy.

Dr. Franco and Lena approached Paul about adopting Jonas. He readily agreed, saying it was in Jonas' best interests to grow up with his brother.

Fletcher walks over with the birthday girl. Harmony is a gorgeous kid, with rosy cheeks and curly blonde hair. She definitely inherited her mother's striking looks.

"Thanks for everything." Fletcher gives me a big hug.

"Fletcher, if you keep thanking me every time we see each other, it's going to go to my head," I say. "And anyway, I'm not sure I did all that much."

"Yes, you did. For one, you hired that crackerjack investigator of yours. If it hadn't been for Special, Mia or even I, might be behind bars right now."

Special sneaks up behind him and pulls out her iPhone. "Excuse me, but could you repeat what you just said. And this time, please speak directly into the microphone."

Fletcher laughs and hugs Special too. "Thanks again for all your hard work."

She glows from the compliment. "No problem at all. I'm just glad you're still talking to me after you got my bill."

"You were worth every penny."

Someone calls out to Fletcher. "Excuse me a minute. Carina needs me."

Special wrinkles her nose as he walks away. "That situation was as predictable as church on Sunday morning. Lucky heffa."

She's referring to Carina's redefined relationship with Fletcher. As might've been predicted, she's been upgraded from nanny to live-in girlfriend.

Mia forgave Fletcher for his little backseat indiscretion with Bliss and, at first, it looked as if they were going to work everything out. But three weeks after Jessica's arrest, the *L.A. Times* ran a lengthy investigative piece about the case. Fletcher was outraged when he'd learned that Mia had offered Girlie Cortez fifty grand to help Jessica win custody of Harmony. The music mogul had been willing to stick by his woman when he thought she'd committed murder. Betraying him, however, was a deal breaker.

Special holds up a picture on her phone. "Let me show you guys this cutie I met on Christian Mingle.com. He's a dead ringer for The Rock."

"His name's Dwayne Johnson now," I say.

"I'm not having that. He'll always be The Rock to me."

Jefferson has a mystified look on his face. "Can you go three seconds without thinking about a man?"

"I ain't getting no younger," Special replies with plenty of attitude. "I have to be proactive. The brothers on this site are Christians, so they're more trustworthy."

Jefferson shakes his head. "Please tell me you're kidding. Some of the so-called Christian brothers I know are running more women in the church than my boys who don't even know how to spell church."

"I'm not going to let you rain on my parade. I prayed on it and God told me my husband was waiting for me on Christian Mingle."

As Special wanders off, Jefferson laughs. "I'll never understand how women can be so smart when it comes to their professional lives, but total fruitcakes when it comes to men."

"One of the wonders of life," I say. "Just be thankful you have a woman who's smart in every aspect of her life. I'm so smart in fact that I planned a little party for you tonight."

"Really?" He seductively arches a brow. "What's the occasion?"

"Don't need one. I figured we'd have a private hot tub party. We don't use that thing nearly as much as we should."

"Baby, you're not smart, you're brilliant." He pecks me on the lips. "Let's go."

"Okay, but let me find Fletcher so I can tell him we're leaving."

Special reappears from nowhere. "Where y'all going? Y'all can't leave yet."

"Nowhere," Jefferson responds, before I do. "See that guy over there?" He points across the yard and Special follows his gaze to an average-looking guy in a linen suit. "He makes twice as much money as Fletcher and he's here by himself."

"Serious? He ain't a bad lookin' brother."

"Yep. You should go introduce yourself," Jefferson urges her.

Special smooths down her skirt. "I think I will."

As she hurries off, all I can do is laugh. "That was wrong, Jefferson. Did you make that up?"

"Kinda. I don't know how much the dude makes but he did come solo."

"Why'd you do that?"

"Because I want to make sure your nutty little friend is occupied for the evening. That's the only way I can guarantee that she won't be crashing my hot tub party again."

Jefferson slides an arm around my shoulder and starts escorting me toward the door. "Now let's go get that party started."

DISCUSSION QUESTIONS FOR
LAWFUL DECEPTION

1. Do you think men have a level playing field in the courts when it comes to parental rights?
2. Do you think it is fair that the law requires a father to pay child support for a child conceived in the manner in which Bliss conceived Harmony?
3. Do you think that by virtue of their gender, women are naturally better caregivers for children than men?
4. An increasing number of fathers are opting to be stay-at-home dads while their wives are the major breadwinners. What are your personal views on that?
5. Do you think Vernetta should have turned down Fletcher's case from the start?
6. What are your thoughts on the way Girlie Cortez handled the legal representation of Bliss Fenton?
7. Who was more like Bliss Fenton, Mia Richardson or Girlie Cortez?
8. Did Special's feelings about dating Darius raise biases that you may have about persons with disabilities?
9. Despite Darius' behavior, did *Lawful Deception* make you think differently about how you might view someone with a spinal cord injury in the future?
10. What were some of the things you liked/disliked about *Lawful Deception?*

If you enjoyed *Lawful Deception,*
turn the page for an excerpt of
Pamela Samuels Young's award-winning thriller

ANYBODY'S DAUGHTER

PROLOGUE

Brianna sat cross-legged in the middle of her bed, her thumbs rhythmically tapping the screen of her iPhone. She paused, then hit the *Send* button, firing off a text message.

ready?

Her soft hazel eyes lasered into the screen, anticipating—no craving—an instantaneous response. Jaden had told her to text him when she was about to leave the house. *So why didn't he respond?*

She hopped off the bed and cracked open the door. A gentle tinkle—probably a spoon clanking against the side of a stainless steel pot—signaled that her mother was busy in the kitchen preparing breakfast.

Easing the door shut, Brianna leaned against it and closed her eyes. To pull this off, Brianna couldn't just act calm, she had to *be* calm. Otherwise, her mother would surely notice. But at only thirteen, she'd become pretty good at finding ways around her mother's unreasonable rules.

She gently shook the phone as if that might make Jaden's response instantly appear. Brianna was both thrilled and nervous about finally meeting Jaden, her first real boyfriend—a boyfriend she wasn't supposed to have. Texts and emails had been racing back and forth between them ever since Jaden friended her on Facebook five weeks earlier.

It still bothered Brianna—but only a little—that Jaden had refused to hook up with her on Skype or FaceTime or even talk to her on the phone. Jaden had explained that he wanted to hear her voice and see her face for the first time in person. When she thought about it, that *was* kind of romantic.

If it hadn't been for her Uncle Dre, Brianna would never have been able to have a secret boyfriend. When her uncle presented her with an iPhone for her birthday two months ago, her mother immediately launched into a tirade about perverts and predators on the Internet. But Uncle Dre had teased her mother for being so uptight and successfully pleaded her case.

Thank God her mother was such a techno-square. Although she'd insisted that they share the same Gmail account and barred her from Facebook, Brianna simply used her iPhone to open a Facebook account using a Yahoo email address that her mother knew nothing about. As for her texts, she immediately erased them.

A quiet chime signaled the message Brianna had been waiting for. A ripple of excitement shot through her.

Jaden: hey B almst there cant wait 2 c u
Brianna: me 2
Jaden: cant wait 2 kss dem lips
Brianna: lol!
Jaden: luv u grl!
Brianna: luv u 2

Brianna tossed the phone onto the bed and covered her mouth with both hands.

OMG!

She was finally going to meet the love of her life. Jaden's older brother Clint was taking them to the Starbucks off Wilmington. Her mother kept such tight reins on her, this was the only time she could get away. Jaden had promised her that Clint would make sure she got to school on time.

Turning around to face the mirror on the back of the door, Brianna untied her bushy ponytail and let her hair fall across her shoulders. The yellow-and-purple Lakers tank top her Uncle Dre had given her fit snugly across her chest, but wasn't slutty-looking. Jaden was a Kobe

Bryant fanatic just like she was. He would be impressed when she showed up sporting No. 24.

Slinging her backpack over her shoulder, Brianna trudged down the hallway toward the kitchen.

"Hey, Mama. I have to be at school early for a Math Club meeting."

Donna Walker turned away from the stove. "I'm making pancakes. You don't have time for breakfast?"

Brianna felt a stab of guilt. Her mother was trying harder than ever to be a model parent. Brianna had spent much of the last year living with her grandmother after her mother's last breakdown.

"Sorry." She grabbed a cinnamon-raisin bagel from the breadbox on the counter. "Gotta go."

Donna wiped her hand on a dishtowel. "It's too early for you to be walking by yourself. I can drop you off."

Brianna kept her face neutral. "No need. I'm picking up Sydney. We're walking together."

Brianna saw the hesitation in her mother's overprotective eyes.

Taller and darker than her daughter, Donna wore her hair in short, natural curls. Her lips came together like two plump pillows and her eyes were a permanently sad shade of brown.

Donna had spent several years as a social worker, but now worked as an administrative assistant at St. Francis Hospital. Work, church and Brianna. That was her mother's entire life. No man, no girlfriends, no fun.

Brianna wasn't having any of that. She was *gonna* have a life, no matter how hard her mother tried to keep her on a short leash like a prized pet.

Donna finally walked over and gave her daughter a peck on the cheek, then repeated the same words she said every single morning.

"You be careful."

Brianna bolted through the front door and hurried down the street. As expected, no one was out yet. Her legs grew shaky as she scurried past Sydney's house. Brianna had wanted to tell her BFF about hooking up with Jaden today, but he made her promise not to. Anyway, Sydney had the biggest mouth in the whole seventh grade. Brianna couldn't afford to have her business in the street. She'd made Sydney swear on the Bible before even telling her she'd been talking to Jaden on Facebook.

As she neared the end of the block, she saw it. The burgundy Escalade with the tinted windows was parked behind Mario's Fish Market just like Jaden said it would be. Brianna was so excited her hands began to tremble. She was only a few feet away from the SUV when the driver's door opened and a man climbed out.

"Hey, Brianna. I'm Clint, Jaden's brother. He's in the backseat."

Brianna unconsciously took a step back. Jaden's brother didn't look anything like him. On his Facebook picture, Jaden had dark eyes, a narrow nose and could've passed for T.I.'s twin brother. This man was dark-skinned with a flat nose and crooked teeth. And there was no way he was nineteen. He had to be even older than her Uncle Dre, who was thirty-something.

Brianna bit her lip. An uneasy feeling tinkered in her gut, causing her senses to see-saw between fear and excitement. But it was love, her love for Jaden, that won out. It didn't matter what his brother looked like. They probably had different daddies.

As Clint opened the back door, Brianna handed him her backpack and stooped to peer inside the SUV.

At the same horrifying moment that Brianna realized that the man inside was not Jaden, Clint snatched her legs out from under her and shoved her into the Escalade.

The man in the backseat grabbed a handful of her hair and jerked her toward him. Brianna tumbled face-first into his lap, inhaling sweat and weed and piss.

"Owwwww! Get your hands offa me!" Brianna shrieked, her arms and legs thrashing about like a drowning swimmer. "Where's Jaden? Let me go!"

"Relax, baby." The stinky man's voice sounded old and husky. "Just calm down."

"Get offa me. Let me go!"

She tried to pull away, but Stinky Man palmed the back of her head like a basketball, easily holding her in place. Clint, who was now in the front seat, reached down and snatched her arms behind her back and bound them with rope.

When Brianna heard the quiet revving of the engine and the door locks click into place, panic exploded from her ears. She violently kicked her feet, hoping to break the window. But each kick landed with a sharp thud that launched needles of pain back up her legs.

"Let me goooooo!"

The stinky man thrust a calloused hand down the back of Brianna's pants as she fought to squirm free.

"Dang, girl," he cackled. "The brothers are gonna love you."

"Cut it out, Leon," Clint shouted, turning away to grab something from the front seat. "I've told you before. Don't mess with the merchandise."

"Don't touch me!" Brianna cried. "Get away from me!"

She managed to twist around so that her face was no longer buried in Stinky Man's lap. That was when she saw Clint coming toward her. He covered her mouth with a cloth that smelled like one of the chemicals from her science class.

Brianna coughed violently as a warm sensation filled her body. In seconds, her eyelids felt like two heavy windows being forced shut. She tried to scream, but the ringing in her ears drowned out all sound. When she blinked up at Stinky Man, he had two—no three—heads.

Brianna could feel the motion of the SUV pulling away from Mario's Fish Market. She needed to do something. But her body was growing heavy and her head ached. The thick haze that cluttered her mind allowed only one desperate thought to seep through.

Mommy! Uncle Dre! Please help me!

DAY ONE MISSING

"Sex traffickers often recruit children because not only are children more unsuspecting and vulnerable than adults, but there is also a high market demand for young victims. Traffickers target victims on the telephone, on the Internet, through friends, at the mall, and in after-school programs."

—Teen Girls' Stories of Sex Trafficking in the U.S.
ABC News/Primetime

CHAPTER 1

Day One: 8:00 a.m.

Angela Evans zigzagged her Saab in and around the slow-moving cars inching up Hill Street, ignoring the blaring horns directed at her.

"Shoot!" She pounded the steering wheel.

The lot where she normally parked for court appearances had a *Full* sign out front. It could take another twenty minutes to find a place to park. Twenty minutes she didn't have.

She spotted a two-hour parking meter a few feet ahead and swerved into it. Grabbing her purse from the front seat, she tumbled from the car, not bothering to put change in the meter. She'd just have to deal with the fifty-dollar ticket.

When she rounded the corner, the line of people waiting to enter the Clara Shortridge Foltz Criminal Justice Center was at least fifty deep. The line for attorneys and staff was half as long. She strolled up to a middle-aged white guy in an expensive suit near the front of the attorneys' line and flashed him a hopeful smile.

"Cuts? Pretty please?" she said, trying to catch her breath. "I'm way late."

The man grinned and allowed Angela to step in front of him. A few people behind them had started to grumble, but by that time she was already dropping her purse onto the conveyor belt and walking through the metal detectors.

She jogged down the hallway and squeezed into an elevator seconds before the doors closed. The car shot straight to the fourth floor. When she finally reached the courtroom, Angela frowned. Shenae was supposed to be waiting outside.

Inside the courtroom, Angela was glad to find that the judge hadn't taken the bench yet. She grew incensed, however, as she scanned the gallery. Her client was sitting off to the right, next to a man in a sports jacket and tie. Angela presumed he was the detective who had picked her up from the group home. On the opposite side of the courtroom, Angela counted four women and five men. The whole rowdy, tattooed group looked as if they'd just broken out of county jail. One of the men craned his neck in Shenae's direction and scowled, confirming exactly what Angela had assumed.

She marched into the well of the courtroom and straight up to the deputy district attorney.

"Why haven't you cleared the courtroom?" she demanded. "If you don't get them out of here, I'm advising my client to take the Fifth."

"Good morning to you, too, Counselor," Monty Wyman replied with a forced smile. "I was going to do it. We haven't started yet."

Wyman was in his late twenties, with sandy hair and black-rimmed glasses. His doughy midsection publicized that exercise wasn't high on his agenda.

"If you want my client to testify, do it now." Angela cocked her head and smiled. "Pretty please."

Wyman had spent the last six months of his young legal career in the sex crimes unit. He knew how traumatic it was for a twelve-year-old child to face her pimp in court. It irked Angela that the defendant's homies were even allowed to be in the same building as Shenae.

Angela walked over to Shenae, greeted her with a hug, then escorted her to a bench in the hallway.

"You okay? You still want to do this, right?"

Shenae's timid eyes fell to the floor. "Uh, yeah." The thin, gangly girl never made eye contact for more than a few seconds.

Six months earlier, Shenae had been arrested for solicitation to commit prostitution. She was one of a dozen under-aged girls forced into prostitution by a pimp named Melvin Clark. Yet the justice system treated *her* like the criminal.

Angela represented Shenae in juvenile court on the solicitation charge and had arranged for her to be sent to a group home. As part of a special program, if she did well in school and stayed out of trouble for at least a year, the charge would be dismissed.

Angela was in court today to lend moral support.

"If I tell 'em everything I did, are you sure they're not gonna arrest me?" Shenae asked.

"Yes, I'm sure." Angela placed a hand on her shoulder. "I've already negotiated that with the prosecutor. You have full immunity. That means nothing you say can be used against you. Ever."

Just then, the defendant's cohorts were ushered out of the courtroom by the bailiff. Angela pulled Shenae close, blocking her face from the glares of her would-be intimidators.

Wyman stuck his head into the hallway. "We're ready."

Shenae wrung her hands. Her khaki pants and black sweater seemed a size too big. Her hair was gathered into a small puff that sat atop of her head, drawing attention away from her sad, round face.

"I know it's scary," Angela said softly. "But you can do it. You did really good when we practiced last week. Candace will be here any minute."

Angela glanced down the hallway, praying that Candace Holmes would indeed appear. "Just keep your eyes on Candace or me. And whatever you do, don't look at Melvin."

As if conjured up by magic, Candace Holmes raced up to them. "Sorry," she panted. "I had another client on the fifth floor."

Candace, who was not much taller than Shenae, worked for Saving Innocence, a non-profit group that provided an array of support services to sexually trafficked children. She was here today to serve as Shenae's witness advocate.

Candace swept her reddish-brown bangs off her face and bent to look Shenae in the eyes. "I'm proud of you. I know you're going to do great."

Angela opened the door of the courtroom. "Let's go."

Shenae didn't move. She looked up at Angela. "I...I would feel better if I could take your purse up there with me."

Angela glanced down at her camel-colored Dolce Gabbana bag. "My purse? Why?"

"It's a nice purse," Shenae said, her lower lip quivering a bit. "If I had it with me on the witness stand, I would look important. Like you."

A pained look passed between Angela and Candace. Angela handed the bag to Shenae and led the way inside.

The judge, jury and defendant were all in place now. Melvin, dressed in a suit and tie, sat next to his lawyer, a veteran public defender who'd obviously pulled the short straw. A portly man with a hard face, Melvin looked much older than twenty-eight. He glanced back at Shenae, but turned around when his lawyer tapped him on the arm.

Judge Willis Romer, known for both his shoe-polish-black hair and for nodding off on the bench, peered through his thick lenses. "Call your first witness, Mr. Wyman."

"I call Shenae M to the witness stand."

Shenae slowly rose to her feet and marched down the aisle, followed by Candace. After taking the oath, Shenae propped Angela's purse on her lap and curved her small fingers around the pearl handle. She sat arrow straight, chin forward, her face blank of any emotion.

Candace was sitting in a folding chair just to the right of the jury box, facing Shenae.

"Ladies and gentlemen of the jury," the judge began, "Ms. Candace Holmes is a witness advocate. She is here for emotional support for the witness, who is a juvenile. You should give no weight, pro or con, to her presence."

Wyman rose from the prosecutor's table and smiled warmly at Shenae. "Can you tell us your name for the record?"

"Shenae Mar—"

Wyman held up both hands. "That's okay. Since you're a juvenile we don't need your last name. Is it okay if I call you Shenae."

The girl smiled. "Yes."

"And how old are you?"

"Twelve."

"Do you know the defendant, Melvin Clark?"

Shenae nodded.

The judge leaned toward Shenae and spoke in a fatherly voice. "Shenae, we'll need you to speak out loud. The court reporter can't take down a nod of your head."

"Oh, I'm sorry. Yeah, I know him."

As instructed, Shenae did not take her eyes off of Candace, not even to face the judge.

"And how do you know Mr. Clark?" the prosecutor asked.

Shenae swallowed. "He was my pimp."

Melvin shifted in his seat, then angled his head and stroked his stubbly chin.

"Where did you first meet Mr. Clark?"

"At the Kentucky Fried Chicken on Crenshaw and Imperial. He bought me some chicken and fries cuz I was hungry."

"How did Mr. Clark know you were hungry?"

Shenae's slender shoulders rose, then fell. "I guess cuz he saw me eat somebody's leftover food after they walked out."

For the next few minutes, Shenae stoically recapped her tragic young life. At ten, she'd been placed in a foster home after her mother's boyfriend molested her. In the foster home, she was physically and verbally abused and ultimately ran away. She was eleven when Melvin offered to let her stay at his apartment.

"At first, he was nice," Shenae explained. "He didn't even try to have sex with me or nothing. He took me shopping and let me buy whatever I wanted."

"Did that ever change?" the prosecutor asked.

Shenae lowered her eyes. "After about a month we started having sex. But by then, he was my boyfriend, so that was okay."

One of the jurors, an older black woman who'd been carrying a Bible, puckered her lips.

"And then what happened?"

"One day, he told me that cuz he spent a lot of money on me, I had to make some money for him."

For the first time, Shenae stole a quick glance at Melvin. She clasped the handles of the purse even tighter.

"How did he want you to make money for him?"

The courtroom grew quiet as Shenae's eyes watered. "He put me on the track."

Angela took in the jury. A few faces appeared shocked, others displayed confusion.

"Tell the jury what the track is?"

Shenae began to gently rock back and forth, still holding onto the purse. "Where johns go to pick up ho's for sex."

"What did you do on the track?"

Shenae did not answer for a few seconds. Wyman waited.

"At first I…I just sucked…I mean…I gave blow jobs. I got fifty dollars every time. I gave all the money to Melvin. But later on, he put me in a motel room so johns could come there to have sex with me."

"I see a tattoo on your neck," the prosecutor said. "M-M-M. What does that mean?"

Shenae's hand absently caressed her slender neck. "Uh, it means Melvin's moneymaker."

Two female jurors gasped.

"How many men did you have sex with on a single day?"

"A lot," Shenae sniveled and wiped away a tear. "Sometimes up to twenty."

Several jurors winced. The black woman cupped a hand to her mouth.

"Did you want to have sex with those men?"

"No."

"What would happen if you refused?"

Shenae was weeping softly now. "Melvin would beat me."

Judge Romer spoke with genuine sympathy in his voice. "Shenae, are you okay? Are you able to continue?"

Shenae finally let go of the purse. She pressed both hands to her face and sobbed.

"Your Honor," Wyman said quietly, "we'd like to take a short break."

CHAPTER 2

Day One: 8:05 a.m.

When Brianna's voicemail clicked on again, Dre cursed under his breath and hung up.

That was the second time this morning that he'd tried to call his niece. He didn't even know why he even bothered calling her. Anybody under twenty only used a smartphone for texting. Talking took time away from their texting.

He chuckled to himself, then pecked out a text.

call me

Dre and his buddy Gus were installing tile in the bathroom of the two-bedroom house he'd recently picked up at an auction. The two men had done time together at Corcoran State Prison. Gus was good with his hands and Dre was happy to have the help.

Dre reached for a towel and wiped sweat from his shaved head. He was surprised when he didn't receive an instantaneous response from his niece. The girl was usually glued to her phone.

Brianna had gotten a real kick out of the fact that *he* had called *her* to help him pick out a nice restaurant for his date tonight. His niece wasn't your average thirteen-year-old. She was smart as a whip and knew almost as much about sports as he did. The fact that she looked more like him than his own son was another reason he loved her to death.

Dre had asked Brianna to go on the Internet and find him a nice restaurant in Marina Del Rey. He wanted just the right place for his reunion with Angela. Not super casual, but not too highbrow either. Brianna had given him three great choices.

Dre wanted to let Brianna know which restaurant he had selected. But he hadn't told anybody that he was hooking up with Angela tonight.

"Hey, man, what's going on?" Gus asked. He was in his late forties, with a lean, muscular body, perfected during his time behind bars. "Why you smiling so much today?"

"Didn't know I was smiling." Dre stroked his goatee. He was close to six feet with the kind of body built for hard work.

"Yeah, you were. Smiling *and* whistling. So what's up?"

Dre grabbed another tile and carefully set it into place. He wasn't sure he wanted to spill the beans about his plans tonight. It was as if doing so might jinx something. But he was excited as hell, so he had to tell somebody something.

"I'm taking Angela out tonight," Dre said.

Gus nodded, but left it at that.

"You don't have nothin' to say?" Dre asked.

"Hey, bruh, who you go out with is your business."

"Sounds like you think it's a bad idea."

"Ain't for me to judge."

Dre was surprised at Gus' response. His buddy was never one to keep an opinion to himself.

"Well, I'm asking."

Gus set aside the tile he was holding and looked over at Dre.

"You put it all on the line for that female and she left you hangin'. So if you ask me, hookin' up with her again might not be the best decision you could make."

This was no doubt the same reaction Dre would receive when he told his sister and mother that he was seeing Angela again. Unfortunately, they'd never gotten a chance to meet her. If they had, they'd surely feel differently. The only thing they knew about her was what they'd seen in the news reports. And that was bunk.

When Dre first met Angela at the Spectrum Athletic Club, she was weeks away from marrying some control-freak judge. She eventually broke off the engagement and they'd hooked up. Angela's ex, however, had refused to accept the breakup and started stalking her.

In the midst of that drama and before Dre could tell her himself, Angela found out that he'd been in the business of dealing crack cocaine and had served time for possession with intent to sell. She then broke it off with him too.

Worried about her safety, Dre stayed close and had been there to intercede when Angela and her ex were wrestling over a gun. The judge took a bullet to the gut and Dre took the rap. The media immediately jumped on the story. A love triangle involving a federal prosecutor, a superior court judge and a drug dealer made salacious news. No charges were ever filed because the shooting had been ruled self-defense.

Dre had been both pissed off and hurt by Angela's decision to move on, but the girl *was* a lawyer. Part of him understood her reluctance about having a relationship with an ex-con. He still kicked himself for not having been up front with her about his situation from day one.

It still amazed him that a woman he'd only known for a few weeks could take hold of his heart the way Angela Evans had. As hard as he tried, he couldn't shake his feelings for her. It had been three months since he'd last seen her. Last week he'd gathered the nerve to ask her out to dinner and to his relief, she accepted.

Now that he was getting a second chance at being with her, Dre didn't care what anybody thought. He was taking it.

He checked his smartphone again. Brianna still hadn't texted him back. She was probably already in class by now. He called her again anyway. No answer.

Dre couldn't wait to tell her about his date. At least Brianna would be happy for him.

CHAPTER 3

Day One: 8:10 a.m.

Clint glanced in the rearview mirror. Brianna was stretched out across the backseat, still knocked out cold, her head resting in Leon's lap. Leon was alternately snoring and smacking his lips.

The grab had worked precisely according to plan. Clint just hoped it wouldn't take too long to break in Little Miss Brianna. The girl looked like she had a lot of fight in her.

He punched a button on his cell.

"We should have her on lockdown in a few," Clint said into the phone. "This one's real fresh, man. Got them light eyes. She's gonna bring in some long dough."

He barked several instructions, then hung up.

Clint was relieved that everything had gone so well. You never knew what could happen when you were snatching a girl in broad daylight. So far, the Facebook scam was working like a charm. His boss was a genius.

Clint smiled to himself. "Mo' money, mo' money, mo' money."

Leon yawned from the backseat. "How far away are we?"

"A long way," Clint said. "Just shut up."

Leon ran a hand over Brianna's rear end. "This girl is bangin'."

"Don't mess with the merchandise," Clint snapped, eyeing him in the rearview mirror.

"I'm just sayin'." He stroked Brianna's face.

A phone began to ring. Leon looked around, then realized the sound was coming from Brianna's backpack.

"Don't answer it!" Clint shouted. "Give it here."

Leon pulled the iPhone from an outside pocket on the backpack and tossed it to Clint. The caller ID read *Uncle Dre*. He turned it off, then placed it on the console between the seats.

"I'm hungry," Leon complained. "We need to hit a drive-thru."

"We ain't stoppin'. I ain't about to risk nobody seeing that girl tied up in the backseat."

Clint shook his head. His cousin was such a screw-up. But what did he expect from a crack head? His boss would have a big problem with Clint having brought someone into the operation without his personal approval. Hopefully, he would never find out. This was the second and last time he planned to use Leon. His regular cohort, Darnell, had to make a run to Oakland to pick up some new girls. Clint didn't want to reschedule "Jaden's" hookup with Brianna. Leon had worked out okay on a last-minute grab a couple of weeks ago in Inglewood. So Clint had called on him again.

It took close to an hour in rush-hour traffic before the SUV exited the Harbor Freeway at Gage. Clint drove a few more miles and slowed when he reached a yellow house that was little more than a shack. Except for a group of boys strolling along the sidewalk, the street was empty. Clint hit a button opening the electronic gates, then steered the Escalade down a short driveway and parked on the grass behind the house.

Leon hopped out first, followed by Clint. Leon bounced on his tip toes as Clint pulled a money clip from his front pocket and peeled off fifty bucks.

"You can go now." Clint shoved the money into Leon's hands.

"Thanks, cuz!" Leon gazed excitedly at the bills. "When you gonna need me again?"

Never. "I'll let you know. Just make sure you keep your big mouth shut."

Leon was already trotting back down the driveway. Clint knew exactly where he was headed. To get high at one of three neighborhood crack houses.

After first opening the back door to the house, Clint easily collected Brianna's limp body from the backseat and hurled her over his shoulder.

The house was stuffy and night-time dark, even though it was still morning. Every windowpane in the place had been painted black. He flicked on a light switch in the kitchen and marched down a narrow hallway. He stopped outside the second bedroom on the west side of the house. Using a single key, he unlocked the three deadbolts on the door.

Inside, a low-watt bulb hanging from the ceiling provided minimal light. A naked girl with wild blonde hair sat huddled in a corner hugging her knees to her chest. Her face was clear and smooth, but her chest, arms and legs bore red, black and blue markings that stood out against her white skin. The filthy mattress where she sat was the only piece of furniture in the room.

"I brought you some company," Clint announced. He dumped Brianna on the mattress next to the frail girl.

"If you're ready to act like you got some sense, I'll bring you something to eat."

The girl, who looked to be close to Brianna's age, didn't respond.

"Well?" Clint said.

"Yes," she mumbled. "I want something to eat."

"Okay then. You better get with the program. Next time, just do what I tell you or I'ma beat your ass again."

He pointed toward Brianna.

"When the new girl wakes up, you tell her the deal. Let her know that if she plays along, everything'll be fine. But if she plans on being hard headed like you, life is gonna be rough."

ACKNOWLEDGEMENTS

As always, I'd like to start by thanking my diehard friends and family members who critiqued *Lawful Deception* before it made its way into print: Jennifer Stone (a big shout out to Go On Girl! Book Club), Jerome Norris, Gloria Falls, Joyce Gaston, Molly Byock, Sheila Henderson, Albertha Vaultz, Ellen Farrell, Cynthia Hebron, and Kenneth Stokes. To Bookalicious Book Club members Judi Johnson, Kamillah Clayton, Lesleigh Kelly, Lee Kelly and Claudette Knight, thanks for reading the manuscript and providing your critiques on such short notice.

I am also grateful for the people whose expertise I relied upon to fill my knowledge gap in the areas discussed in *Lawful Deception*: Dr. Glenna Tolbert, a physiatrist specializing in helping patients recover functionality after experiencing traumas such as a stroke, brain injury or spinal cord injury; my goddaughter, Nicole Fuller, Doctor of Physical Therapy, specializing in neurological rehabilitation (I'm so proud of you!), LaTrice Allen, the Consultation Manager at a Los Angeles-area sperm bank (thanks for answering all of my questions about paternity testing and artificial insemination), Los Angeles-area divorce attorney Merissa V. Grayson (thanks for schooling me on the intricacies of divorce law and for coming to my aid at the eleventh hour; visit Merissa's website at www.yourfamilyslawyer.com), L.A. litigator Larry Lawrence (I really miss working with you!), and my law school homie and Oakland criminal defense attorney Colin T. Bowen. I hope you never need him, but if you do, visit Colin's website at www.cbowenlaw.com.

To my do-it-all assistant/life coach Lynel Washington, thanks for burning the late night oil with me on this one. Couldn't have done it without you. To my publicist extraordinaire Ella Curry of EDC Creations Media Group, LLC, you are my girl!

As always, thanks to my writing group members, who helped me shape this project from conception to birth, Arlene L. Walker, Adrienne Byers and Jane Howard-Martin.

And last but certainly not least, thank you Edwin Vaultz for getting me back on my writing journey after a long hiatus. You nudged me, encouraged me and supported me in amazing ways (like flying down to Palm Springs just so you could drive back to L.A. with me after my week of solitary writing). I truly appreciate you. Smooches!

To my fans, thanks for reading my books. Boy, do I have a lot more in store for you!

We hope you enjoyed *Lawful Deception*. All of Pamela's novels are available in print, e-book and audio book formats, everywhere books are sold.

To read an excerpt of all of Pamela's books, visit www.pamelasamuelsyoung.com.

Vernetta Henderson Series

Every Reasonable Doubt (1st in series)

In Firm Pursuit (2nd in series)

Murder on the Down Low (3rd in series)

Attorney-Client Privilege (4th in series)

Lawful Deception (5th in series)

Dre Thomas Series

Buying Time (1st in series)

Anybody's Daughter (2nd in series)

Short Stories

The Setup

Easy Money

Unlawful Greed

Non-Fiction

Kinky Coily: A Natural Hair Resource Guide

ABOUT THE AUTHOR

Pamela Samuels Young is a practicing attorney and bestselling author of several legal thrillers. A passionate advocate for sexually exploited children, Pamela speaks frequently on the topic of child sex trafficking and is the founder of BLAST (Book Lovers Against Sex Trafficking). Pamela is also a natural hair enthusiast and the author of *Kinky Coily: A Natural Hair Resource Guide.*

In addition to writing legal thrillers and working as an in-house employment attorney for a major corporation in Southern California, Pamela is a diehard member of Sisters in Crime-L.A., an organization dedicated to the advancement of women mystery writers. The former journalist and Compton native is a graduate of USC, Northwestern University and UC Berkeley's School of Law. She is married and lives in the Los Angeles area.

Pamela loves to hear from readers! There are a multitude of ways to connect with her.

Email: authorpamelasamuelsyoung@gmail.com

Website: www.pamelasamuelsyoung.com

BLAST: www.blastunited.com

Facebook: www.facebook.com/pamelasamuelsyoung and

              www.facebook.com/kinkycoilypamela

Twitter: www.twitter.com/pamsamuelsyoung

LinkedIn: www.linkedin.com/pamelasamuelsyoung

Pinterest: www.pinterest.com/kinkycoily

YouTube: www.youtube.com/kinkycoilypamela

MeetUp: www.meetup.com/natural-born-beauties

To schedule Pamela for a speaking engagement or book club meeting via speakerphone, Skype, FaceTime or in person, visit her website at www.pamelasamuelsyoung.com.

CPSIA information can be obtained at www.ICGtesting.com
Printed in the USA
LVOW11s1413010516

486173LV00002B/517/P